ONCE UPON A SPY
SECRETS AND SEDUCTION
BOOK III

SHERIDAN JEANE

OTHER BOOKS BY SHERIDAN JEANE

Gambling on a Scoundrel

Books in the Secrets and Seduction Series

Lady Cecilia Is Cordially Disinvited

For Christmas (a prequel)

It Takes a Spy …

Lady Catherine's Secret

Once Upon a Spy

My Lady, My Spy

Along Came a Spy

Once Upon a Spy
Sheridan Jeane
Copyright 2015 Sheridan Jeane

ISBN-13: 978-1-63303-007-7

Flowers and Fullerton, LLC

Cover Design by Earthly Charms

Flowers and Fullerton, LLC

❦ I ❧

Politics have no relation to morals.

— NICCOLO MACHIAVELLI

◈

London, January 6, 1854

The turning point in a man's life isn't always accompanied by a crash of thunder. Sometimes it's marked by something much more subtle. Much easier to miss. It could be something as simple as the flash of a silver gown or the rich hue of a twist of chestnut hair.

Robert, Earl of Wentworth, managed to dismiss his turning point almost entirely.

It came in the form of a petite woman he glimpsed at the Russian embassy's ball. A tremendously alluring woman— so much so that he found his feet moving him in her direction before he realized he'd changed course. Once he realized what he was doing, he came to a halt and forced himself to turn away from the power he felt pulling them together.

He shook his head. His odd behavior must have been nothing more than a reaction to her beauty.

A woman that could affect him in such a profound way as that represented a precipice. Danger. One he needed to avoid.

He decided to ignore the silver-gowned woman and her pull of destiny. Instead, he stepped out onto the patio to let the chill January air envelop him and drive away the oppressive heat of the ballroom.

"Robert, come join us," his brother called to him from the dimly lit patio. "Lord Percival is telling the most preposterous story."

Once his eyes adjusted to the soft glow of the flickering torches, he was able to identify Frederick sitting with a group of men at a stone table near the edge of the lawn.

As he strode across the paving stones, Robert considered how fundamentally wrong it was for the Russian Ambassador's winter solstice celebration to be held in a building so overheated the temperature drove the guests outdoors.

His brother shifted his chair to one side and made space for him to pull up a seat and join the group. The low oil lamps on the table illuminated the listeners' rapt faces as that buffoon, Lord Percival, recounted his latest yarn.

As usual, Lord Percival appeared well-groomed, with his neatly trimmed beard, white gloves, and perfectly tailored evening coat all speaking to the excellence of his valet. Looks could be deceiving.

Cigar smoke surrounded this particular group, but the odor of Percival's whiskey-laden breath managed to cut through the cloud. The evening was still fresh and young. Percival must have been drinking all afternoon to have such a strong stench of alcohol oozing from his pores.

"You'll love this part," Frederick murmured. The corners of his eyes crinkled as he smiled.

Lord Percival sucked on his cigar, pausing for effect as he

slowly exhaled, and said "...and I forcibly tossed him from the carriage. He landed directly in a steaming pile of manure!" Lord Percival slapped his hand down on the marble table to emphasize his words, but he accidentally managed to clip one of the oil lamps.

The container flipped over. Oil splashed on the table and Lord Percival's tightly clutched cigar, which immediately burst into flame.

Percival let it fall to the table and squealed in panic and pain. The cigar landed in the spreading puddle of oil and set the surface of the table on fire.

Everyone jumped back, knocking their chairs to the ground. In an instant, fire swept down the length of the stone tabletop.

Frederick jumped back too, but his thin evening gloves were already drenched in oil. With horror, Robert watched as his brother froze for an heartbeat and flames seemed to erupt from his hands.

The sickening image chilled him. If Frederick had been a performer on stage, the audience would have burst into applause, but this was no trick. No sleight of hand. It was real, and Frederick's hands were on fire.

Robert lurched forward to help just as Frederick stumbled back on the uneven lawn and shoved his hands under his arms, suffocating the flames.

As the spreading fire came in contact with puddles of ice on the table, they spluttered and sprayed scalding droplets, like water in a skillet. Two men batted at their clothing, putting out tiny fires from the flying drops of burning oil.

Fire swept up Lord Tamworth's entire sleeve. "Help!" he cried. "Someone help me!" He waved his arm, but that only served to make the fire burn more brightly. Then he started battling at it with his other hand.

One of the other men stripped out of his evening jacket and used it to smother Lord Tamworth's arm.

The entire fiasco was short-lived. Once the fire consumed all the oil, it quickly withered and died. Overturned chairs littered the area.

The door leading from the ballroom burst open, and a small army of footmen came rushing toward them. One of Lord Tamworth's friends lowered him into one of the few remaining upright chairs.

"Good god, Percival!" Robert shouted. "You're a threat to everyone, you bottle-head! You're drunk, and you're dangerous. Get yourself under control. It's a wonder you didn't ignite as well with so much alcohol in your veins."

Lord Percival lifted his hands in supplication. "It was an accident. Surely you don't think I'd intentionally--"

Robert grabbed him by his lapels. "You created this situation. Don't try to pretend you bear no responsibility for what happened. This is entirely your doing."

"Let him go, Robert," Frederick said from somewhere behind him. "Come here and help me."

Robert gave the other man a shove, spun on his heel, and stalked into the darkness, toward the sound of his brother's voice.

He found Frederick pacing in circles, tramping a path through the snow near the edge of the lawn and muttering curses under his breath. He still had one of his hands tucked under his arm.

"You should put ice on that to help numb the pain," Robert suggested. "The Russians must have ice here someplace." He locked eyes with an approaching footman who had obviously overheard him.

"I will bring some immediately, my lord," the footman said in heavily accented English.

"And some scotch," Frederick added.

The footman nodded, turned, and hurried into the embassy.

A flurry of activity surrounding Lord Tamworth caught Robert's attention. The man's face appeared pale and drawn in the flickering torchlight. The fabric of his clothing had been burned away, and Robert had a clear view of the sickeningly mottled arm and its black and red skin. Robert's stomach knotted as he turned to face his brother. Was Frederick's injury as bad as Lord Tamworth's?

"This is terrible," Frederick said.

Robert's stomach sank. He dreaded seeing the hand. "How bad is it?" he asked.

"Bad. Very bad." Frederick moved even farther away from the others and didn't stop until he reached the decorative railing.

"Does it hurt?" Robert followed his brother.

"What? My hand? Of course, it hurts." Frederick looked confused for a moment. "Oh, you thought I was talking about—that's not what I meant." Frederick glanced around and lowered his voice. "I'm here tonight on an assignment for the Foreign Office."

Robert rocked back on his heels. If Frederick was worried about his assignment, the burn couldn't be too severe, could it? "That explains why you wanted to attend the ball with me at the last minute. I was under the delusion that you wanted to spend time with your estimable older brother. Foolish of me."

"Indubitably. Quite foolish."

The footman returned, bearing a tray with two tumblers of scotch and a bundle of ice wrapped in a white cloth. "Can I bring you anything else?" he asked.

Frederick shook his head. "I'll be fine. Don't trouble yourself. Lord Tamworth is the one who needs your attention, not me. My injury is minor."

The footman bowed before hurrying toward the group gathered around Lord Tamworth.

"I can't risk letting anyone examine my hand," Frederick said. "Any undue notice regarding me or my movements tonight could jeopardize my ability to complete my assignment."

A gust of wind ruffled Robert's dark hair, and he shoved it out of his eyes as he glanced around. Few guests braved the frigid courtyard, so their section of the lawn accorded them the privacy they needed for their conversation. "Why are you telling me about your plans for tonight?"

The bundle of ice clattered as Frederick lifted it. Robert caught a glimpse of the scorched remnants of Frederick's cotton gloves and the large blisters on his fingertips before he pressed the bundle back down.

"With my hand like this, I won't be able to complete my assignment. I won't have the manual dexterity that's required. I'll need your help."

Robert held up his hands and stepped back. "No. Definitely not. Last year after I was nearly killed, you promised me you wouldn't involve me in another one of your schemes. I'm not cut from the same cloth as you-- I hate dealing in subterfuge."

"I know, I know, but this is different. The fate of the world is at stake. We're risking outright war."

"War?" Robert stood stunned for a moment.

"At this moment, there is a book, a church register, sitting in a diplomatic pouch locked in Ambassador Revnik's desk. I'm supposed to pick the locks and retrieve it. How will I manage if I can't manipulate tools with my fingers? I'll never be able to hold them. If you don't help, England and Russia will go to war."

Robert stared at his brother blankly. "I thought war with Russia was inevitable at this point. Hardly a day goes by without some newsboy chasing me down the street and trying to sell me a newspaper with a headline demanding that Britain respond to the Battle of Sinop."

"That was an atrocity," Frederick muttered.

"The British citizens want justice." Last November, Russian Admiral Nakhimov had discovered a Turkish naval squadron taking shelter in the port of Sinop during bad weather, and he had attacked them using Russia's new explosive shells. He'd easily won within two hours but, even with his victory in hand, he'd continued shelling, destroying all but one stranded ship. The massacre was unconscionable. The destruction, wanton. The suffering, immeasurable.

"The Queen plans to use the church register to demand justice," Frederick said. "It contains sensitive information she'll use to force the czar's hand, but the timing is critical. Everything hinges on what we do tonight."

More chess moves. Trust Frederick to consider every nuance of a plan.

Frederick winced as he gingerly pulled the remnants of his burned gloves from his hands and let them fall to the ground. He swallowed and took a shaky breath.

Frederick's single-minded focus on world affairs in the face of his injuries astounded Robert. Was he telling the truth? Could tonight's actions prevent a war? "Do you agree war with Russia is inevitable? If so, why should you and I put ourselves at risk and steal the book?"

"Inevitable? Perhaps-- perhaps not. Remember, the timing and circumstances of a declaration are for the Queen to decide, not the two of us. I have a mission to complete, and it isn't up for debate. We must retrieve the book before the courier arrives. He'll be here within the hour."

"How can the fate of the world rest on such a small thing?" Robert took a step backward and raked his fingers through his hair. Frederick must be exaggerating. How could something as commonplace as a church register be so important?

"In my experience, it's always the little things that cause the biggest problems. 'For want of a nail the shoe was lost.'" Frederick stared down at his blistered hands.

The corner of Robert's mouth twitched. He couldn't hold back the quip that sprang to his tongue. "Or in this case, for Percival's want of good sense..."

Frederick let out a snort of derision. "The use of my fingers was lost. Yes."

"Are they any better?" Robert asked. Even as he uttered the

words, he knew Frederick's burns hadn't miraculously healed in the past two minutes. But one could hope.

"The ice helps, but they still hurt like the blazes. Fortunately, the injury to my left hand is minor, so I'm not entirely incapacitated. I can get through this." He fixed his gaze on Robert. "With your help."

A heavy weight settled over Robert. He dreaded shouldering this yoke of responsibility yet again. It chafed. Unfortunately, he'd have to help. Brotherly duty demanded it, as did duty to his queen.

Frederick viewed life as nothing more than a chessboard. One in which he calculated every possible move in an instant, choosing the one best suited to his purposes while minimizing his risk. But in tonight's game, did he plan to use Robert as his knight, or his pawn?

Given the stakes, did it matter?

"Tell me what we need to do." Robert dragged his fingers through his hair again. "You know I detest doing this sort of thing-- becoming involved in someone else's lies and schemes. Ever since Father forced me to help hide his"-- he glanced over his shoulder, afraid of being overheard-- "his indiscretion."

Frederick snorted. "Indiscretion? That's a rather mild description. For me, the word 'treason' comes to mind." He shook his head. "I know you detest being dragged into other people's problems, and I can't say I blame you. What Father forced you to do was reprehensible, but this is entirely different. What he demanded of you was illegal and corrupt, whereas what I'm asking of you is entirely honorable."

"But still illegal."

"Honorable," Frederick insisted. "This is at the Queen's request."

Honor. Frederick was obsessed with it. Perhaps they both were.

Frederick pushed away from the balustrade and stiffened his

spine. "We need to do this now. I want to have the book in hand and be well clear of this place before that courier arrives." He strode toward the doors leading into the embassy.

Frederick moved gracefully. No one would guess he'd been injured if not for the damp cloth wrapped around his hand.

A footman opened the doors at their approach, and they reentered the glittering ballroom where the elite members of London society gathered for the culminating event of the Russian winter solstice celebration Koliada. They squeezed through the dense crowd as they made their way toward the main foyer. They hadn't gone far when Frederick stopped abruptly.

"What is it?" Razors of anxiety lanced through Robert. Had something gone wrong already? Had Frederick spotted the courier?

"Lady Harrington." Frederick licked his lips. "She saw me. I think she's headed this way."

Robert's tension disappeared with the speed of a bursting soap-bubble, leaving him feeling slightly giddy with relief. His brother was having trouble with his ladylove? He grinned. "I thought she was a 'dear friend' of yours. Why is having her see you a problem?" A sudden, sobering thought struck him. Unless... "Is she a spy too?" he asked in a near whisper.

Frederick shot him a scathing glance. "Of course not. It's nothing like that. I merely told her I wouldn't be here tonight."

That certainly wasn't the reply he'd expected, and it left him momentarily dumbfounded. "You mean you lied?" What an interesting turn of events.

The tips of Frederick's ears reddened. "She always arrives late for these things, and I planned to leave before she made an appearance."

"Are you saying you want to avoid her so much you lied to her?"

"Who says I want to avoid her?"

Robert assessed his brother's demeanor. "Something has

changed between the two of you." He leaned closer so he couldn't be overheard. "You've never mentioned what happened the night of your tryst," he murmured. "Did something go wrong?"

Frederick's face began to flush as well. "A gentleman doesn't speak of such things."

"Considering what's at stake, why don't you simply explain, so we can get on with it-- how much of a risk does she pose tonight?"

The tension stretched between them, as taut as an over-wound violin string. Finally, Frederick let out a sigh. "Things between us became a bit more complicated than I expected." He wouldn't meet Robert's eyes. "Quite frankly, I don't think it's wise to spend more time with her."

Robert raised an eyebrow. "Are you saying you have feelings for the woman?"

The tips of Frederick's ears turned a brighter shade of red. "Don't be ridiculous. We don't have time for this nonsense." He stared at something behind Robert. "Someone waylaid her. Let's go before she breaks free and tries to corner me."

As they entered the large foyer, Frederick pointed out a spot behind an enormous urn near the cloakroom. "We can temporarily hide the book there once we retrieve it."

Robert made a mental note of the location as he surveyed the room. Everyone seemed engrossed in conversation. Everyone except the woman in the silver gown he'd noticed earlier.

His attention-- his entire being-- was drawn to her yet again.

She stood still, her chestnut-brown hair pinned up with curling tendrils teasing the nape of her neck, gazing at the balcony above her. What was it about her that captivated him? Perhaps if he'd stopped to speak with her earlier, this entire night would have unfolded differently. Perhaps that explained his odd aware-ness of fate when he'd seen her. Perhaps by turning his back on her, he'd chosen this path-- one which excluded romantic entan-glements.

Frederick grabbed Robert by the arm and dragged him

through a door that dumped them into a silent hallway dotted with many closed doors. "This is where the embassy's offices are located." He led them to a servants' staircase, and they quickly made their way upstairs.

"While we're up here, we need to act like normal guests who accidentally wandered into a forbidden area while exploring the embassy. After all, the building's renovations were only completed a month ago. Our curiosity will hardly be commented upon."

Robert took a moment to count the number of doors dotting the hallway from the balcony to the hidden servants' staircase. When he'd been at Eton, his friend Daniel had been Robert's partner in crime and had taught him how to sneak around the grounds undetected. Counting doors had been one of Robert's assignments. Daniel had always stressed the importance of an escape route. They'd often slipped down to the school's pantry to pick locks and pilfer some food, or sneaked off school grounds to go into town. They'd been rarely seen, and thanks to careful planning, they'd never been caught.

Robert and Frederick came to a stop next to the balcony overlooking the grand foyer. The marble entryway below appeared deserted except for the footman standing at the base of the staircase with his back to them.

Frederick pulled him away from the railing. "I'd wager the footman is stationed down there to keep guests from venturing up those stairs," he murmured. "Stay out of sight." He edged over to the balcony, glanced down, and muttered a stifled curse before ducking back.

"What is it?"

"Lady Harrington. She's in the foyer below, and she caught a glimpse of me."

"Will that cause a problem?"

"Maybe. We should hurry."

At that moment, a young boy's sweet soprano tones rose above the other sounds, and the guests immediately grew silent.

After a moment, other children's voices joined in, and the sound evoked another memory of Eton. He'd loved being part of the choir there. He might have disappointed his teachers in other ways, but they'd always praised him for his voice.

"Damn," he muttered. "This was the main reason I wanted to come tonight-- to hear the choir."

"We can hear them perfectly from up here."

Robert shook his head. "It isn't the same. My attention is divided." When he focused on music, it transported him. Elevated him. He hated letting it become nothing but another background noise.

A strange pattering sound intruded. Was that rain?

Robert glanced down and spotted fat drops of water falling from his brother's ice-filled cloth onto the hardwood floor. He touched Frederick's sleeve and pointed down.

Frederick's gaze traveled along the corridor, taking in the trail of water on the gleaming surface. "Blast," he whispered. "I need to clean that up. It's as bad as leaving a trail of breadcrumbs."

As his brother lifted the edge of the cloth to glance at the burns, Robert caught a glimpse. The blisters had swollen and looked as though they might burst.

Frederick's determined gray eyes met his. "Let's get to the ambassador's rooms. You can pick the lock while I search for something to wipe up this water. It would be simpler if I had a key, but the locks were all replaced during the renovation and I couldn't get one."

Before asking his brother for the lock picks, Robert tested the porcelain doorknob. It was unlocked. He shot Frederick a relieved smile and pushed the door open. They both slipped inside.

It took Robert's eyes a moment to adjust to the dim glow from the fireplace's dying embers.

He surveyed the suite and spotted the ambassador's desk near a large window overlooking the courtyard below.

"Here," Frederick said, handing him a rolled length of leather. "You'll need these."

Robert recognized the bundle as he took it-- as familiar as an old friend. He liked the feel of it against his palm.

Frederick began prowling around the room and Robert turned to his own task. After all, this was why his brother needed him tonight-- for his nefarious skill.

In the dim light, he leaned over to examine the enormous pedestal desk. It had a lap drawer in the center with a set of drawers on either side. Only the lower ones looked large enough to contain a diplomatic pouch, but when he tugged on them, he discovered both were locked.

With a flick of his hand, Robert unfurled the rolled length of leather onto the desk with practiced ease. He folded back the top layer of leather, revealing an assortment of lock picks gleaming in the moonlight, each fitted snugly into its pocket. It looked surprisingly similar to his own set, and he realized Daniel must have given them identical gifts.

"I can use this to clean up that water," Frederick said, holding up a cloth as he approached Robert. "Find the book while I'm gone. It's easy to identify. It's battered-looking with a Russian Orthodox cross on the tooled-leather cover."

Robert's hand froze midway in pulling a lock pick from the roll, and he met Frederick's gaze as he licked his lips nervously. "I prefer you stay. This won't take long. What if someone comes in?"

"I'll be right outside. If anyone shows up, I'll draw them away, and I'll do it loudly enough that you'll hear me. Everyone is busy downstairs. It isn't likely we'll be discovered."

"You can't expect me to--"

"Yes, I can. You'll be fine." Frederick stared at him for a long moment, as though weighing his next words. "When we were children, you stole pastries from the cook when his back was turned. You rode the horse Father forbade you to ride. You convinced the coachman to teach you everything he knew about racing a phaeton. You even brought your new friend Daniel home from Eton for a visit. He turned out to be a wild boy who knew how to pick a pocket, fight with a knife, and open any lock. Admit it. You enjoy taking risks. That's why I want you to join me in working for the Foreign Office."

"I won't be dragged into some scandal again," Robert protested.

"You're simply afraid you'll be obliged to fix someone else's mistakes." He gave Robert an easy nod, as though he'd come to some realization that pleased him. "Helping me could be a way for you to finally break free of Father's influence over your life. After all, the man's been dead for years. The way I see it, you need to make a choice. Either immerse yourself in this role and become involved in the world around you, or continue to remain apart. Why not change the direction of not only your own future, but of England's as well? Do it! Commit to something. Be the man you want to be rather than the one Father forced you to become."

A smile tugged at the corner of Robert's mouth. "That's a rousing speech."

Frederick grinned back at him. "I'm practicing for Parliament. Do you think I have a future?"

"Undoubtedly. As long as they don't find out you used your untrained brother as a last-minute replacement on a critical assignment for the Queen. 'For want of a hand, the kingdom was lost.'"

Frederick scowled.

"Don't worry. Your secret's safe with me." Robert pushed down his feeling of trepidation and jutted his chin toward the door. "Go. Clean up your trail of water. I'll be your hands. I'll pick your locks. I'll steal the church register. But you owe me."

Frederick gave a wry smile and silently slipped from the room.

Robert knelt to examine the locks more closely and selected

two picks from the set. He started with the drawer on the right, since it was more readily accessible.

He still couldn't believe he was doing this. If he hadn't seen Frederick get burned with his own eyes, he'd suspect him of having planned this entire evening.

Chess moves. Perhaps he really was Frederick's pawn tonight.

The lock gave way. Robert slid open the drawer and reached into its depths, hoping to brush against the form of a diplomatic pouch.

Footsteps in the corridor. He froze.

Was that a woman's voice? A feminine trill of laughter? He kept listening.

Seconds ticked by. A log settled in the dying fire, sending off a burst of sparks, but no other noises intruded. Perhaps he'd been mistaken. The voice might have come from downstairs in the foyer.

He reached again into the drawer's depths, and his hand grazed an object that could be the diplomatic pouch. He held his breath as he extracted it and rose to his feet. When he set it on the desk, he let out a sigh of relief.

As he bent to examine it, he was surprised to discover the diplomatic pouch was unlocked. No seals had been affixed to it. He'd expected this step in tonight's thievery to be more difficult. Could the ambassador be unaware of the importance of the church register?

Robert opened it and withdrew a small leather-bound volume.

The book was exactly as Frederick had described, right down to the tooled-leather cover bearing the cross of the Russian Orthodox Church. It appeared to have been through a great deal of misuse over the years. Strange for an item that normally resided in a church.

As he thumbed through the book, it fell open to a particular page as though someone had frequently turned to it. In the dim light, he recognized the shapes of the Cyrillic letters. It had been too long since he'd studied Russian and full comprehension eluded him, but he found pages of names and dates, along with annotations regarding important events.

He flipped the book shut. Frederick had been gone too long.

He returned the diplomatic pouch to the drawer, relocked it, stowed the lock picks, unbuttoned his tailcoat, and tucked the battered church register down the back of his waistband. The corners of the little book would be discernible through the fabric of his form-fitting tailcoat, wouldn't they? Robert shrugged. This would do for now.

He slipped out into the silent, empty hallway.

Where in blazes was his brother?

Every fact is related on one side to sensation, and, on the other, to morals.
The game of thought is, on the appearance of one of these two sides, to find
the other: given the upper, to find the under side.

— RALPH WALDO EMERSON

obert stepped into the corridor and immediately reached two conclusions.

The first, Frederick was insane for wanting to be a spy.

The second, Frederick was no where in sight.

No water drops marred the pristine surface of the hallway. Apparently, Frederick had completed his task before managing to completely disappear.

Had he been spotted, or worse, apprehended?

A burst of applause rose from the ballroom. As it faded, the children's choir began a new song. Judging by its simple melody,

Robert took it for a Russian peasant song rather than a more formal piece. He probably only had a couple of minutes before it ended.

As Robert crept back down the hallway toward the concealed door, he glanced over the balcony to the open foyer below.

Empty.

Not even the footman guarding it remained.

The unprotected staircase tempted him to risk a quick escape. Should he take it or stay and search for Frederick?

He knew what his brother would say. The book must be his first priority. Frowning, Robert decided to stash the book near the cloakroom as they'd planned, and then return to search for his brother.

The staircase tempted him, and he edged closer.

To his surprise, a small brown-haired woman rounded the bend on the stairs, startling him as she rushed up the last few steps. He immediately recognized her.

The woman in silver.

Robert took a step back, struck by her intensity of purpose. She remained focused on the foyer below and didn't see him watching her.

She was young, probably twenty or so. Her youth and vibrancy made her attractive, but her delicately sculpted features made her beautiful. She seemed to have appeared straight out of his imagination as the embodiment of temptation. She wore an elaborate silvery-gray ball gown with a form-fitting bodice that revealed the curves of her breasts while concealing the rest of her beneath layers of delicate fabric.

She'd anchored her chestnut-brown hair in place with simple hairpins rather than ornate clips, but—where was her glittering jewelry?

More importantly, where was her chaperone?

He couldn't recall ever seeing her with anyone else tonight. Her lack of jewels suggested she possessed rank but no money.

Robert weighed that bit of information but set it aside. It had no bearing on the current situation.

He needed to take control.

"What are you doing up here?" he demanded. "This area is off-limits. Guests are to remain in the public areas." He stepped closer, forcing her to crane her neck back to look at him. His height could be intimidating. He'd learned to make it work to his advantage.

Startled, she met his gaze as she paused in mid-movement on the last step of the staircase. He caught a glimpse of irritation on her face, which surprised him. Bewilderment or embarrassment he would expect, but irritation?

Or had he been mistaken?

Now she appeared relieved to see him.

"I'm sorry," she said, her warm, copper-brown eyes making something deep within him tremble with fascination. "I-I needed to get away from all those people for a moment. I hope I'm not intruding."

Upon hearing her voice, a burst of awareness fizzed within Robert like a stream of champagne bubbles climbing up the side of a glass. She glowed with vitality. This was a woman who could shape a man's destiny. A fresh scent of orange blossoms enveloped her. She looked more like an illusion than a real flesh-and-blood woman.

And she was so small.

Pausing on the staircase one step down from him, she barely came up to his chest. Despite her size, he sensed strength in this woman.

Her unusually direct gaze gave her away.

Her silvery-gray dress now put him in mind of steel. She all but radiated determination.

An instant later, she lowered her lashes and clutched her hands together, transforming from a strong, proud woman into a fretful one. He found her sudden metamorphosis both startling and intriguing. Had his senses deceived him? Had he entirely misjudged her? She fumbled at the side of her ball gown and withdrew a small handkerchief from a pocket, delicately dabbing it under her eye as she stepped up onto the landing.

"I don't know what came over me," she said. She swayed slightly, and her lower lip trembled.

"Do you feel faint?" he asked, lurching forward to offer his arm. What if she tumbled down the stairs? When she willingly accepted it, his remaining misgivings evaporated, and when she met his eyes, her beseeching expression pierced him to his very soul.

"I'm a bit lightheaded." Her fingers curled tightly around his arm and she leaned on it momentarily for support.

"Perhaps it's the heat." Robert breathed deeply, allowing her fresh scent of orange blossoms to invade him. But with her nearness, a sudden realization came over him.

What about the book? Would she discern its sharp corners poking through his evening coat?

Where the devil was Frederick? Robert kept expecting him to burst from one of the rooms at any moment.

He could just imagine what Frederick would say if he caught Robert dallying with this woman he'd conjured from his dreams.

His charming, inconvenient companion leaned against him, causing a sharp corner of the church register to poke him in the back.

Robert cleared his throat. "Will you permit me to find your escort for you?"

"No." The single word was sharp and forceful, but then she smiled up at him in a way that soothed the bite of her perfunctory reply. "I'd prefer to avoid the press of the crowd. I'm certain I'll feel better in a moment. Perhaps if we walk, it will help me recover." She took a step down the hallway, back toward the ambassador's suite of rooms.

Blast.

His escape route was in the opposite direction.

"We should avoid the residential wing," he said, turning them around toward the servants' staircase and his escape.

"Oh, my. Are Ambassador Revnik's rooms back there? I hadn't realized." She widened her eyes, causing him to stare into them. Their not-quite-burnished color of a nearly new copper penny transfixed him.

It suddenly struck him that something about her seemed familiar. Despite his earlier flight of fancy, she hadn't stepped from his dreams. He'd certainly remember any visions she might grace.

"Have we met?" he asked. "Since we're alone, I'm afraid I'm obliged to introduce myself. I'm Robert—Robert Woolsy, Earl of Wentworth." Why on earth had he stumbled and offered her his given name? She'd think him a bumbling fool.

Her eyes widened. Did she recognize his name? A blush suffused her face, making her seem even more vulnerable. "My, but we are alone, aren't we? You've reminded me of how inappropriate it is for me to be here with you, let alone to speak to you without a chaperone. I'm not in the habit of offering my name to a man without a formal introduction." She pulled away from him, leaving his embrace empty of her.

Robert stiffened. Why had he behaved in such a forward manner? And toward such a gently bred young lady. He dropped his arm as if caught in an illicit act.

The copper-eyed young woman tensed, but after a moment, she inhaled shakily in an attempt to regain her composure. Taking another step down the hallway, Copper-Eyes kept reaching out and touching the wall as though she needed its solid reassurance to keep from falling.

Robert kept pace with her.

Eventually, she smiled up at him in a token of forgiveness.

His chest tightened.

She stumbled sideways into one of the shallow alcoves that held a door, and her hand gripped the knob as she steadied herself. Then she linked her free arm through his again, surprising him. As her eyes met his, her smile changed, somehow becoming more enticing—more inviting.

He smiled back, entranced by her. Had this surprising and intriguing woman forgiven him so quickly for his breach of etiquette?

Then her hand turned the white porcelain doorknob, startling him.

What was this?

She pushed open the door and plunged into the darkened room, dragging him with her.

In the light from the hallway he spotted a bed in the odd, windowless room. Her forwardness shocked him.

She rose on her tiptoes, her breath hot on his neck, her hands caressing his chest as they slipped beneath his jacket. She reached around his back and slid her palms up his shoulders as she pressed herself against him.

Robert was no novice in the ways of women, but this brazen behavior left him speechless and more aroused than he cared to admit.

She seemed about to kiss him, so he leaned into her.

An instant before his lips touched hers, Copper-Eyes shoved him hard in the chest with enough force to make him stumble back a step.

She spun around and ran from the room, slamming the door behind her and leaving him alone in the pitch-black room.

He heard a scrape of metal, and then she spoke through the door. "I'm sorry, my lord. Truly I am."

"Wait!" Robert jumped up and scrambled for the door. He located it in the pitch-black room and rattled the doorknob.

Locked.

Where had she found a key? Even Frederick hadn't been able to locate one.

"Open this door!" he shouted, and then paused to listen. He held his breath, but heard nothing.

Nothing at all.

❆ 3 ❆

Shallow men believe in luck. Strong men believe in cause and effect.

— RALPH WALDO EMERSON

Antonia Winter turned the key in the lock, trapping Lord Wentworth inside. She trembled, hardly daring to believe she'd stolen the book.

Thank the stars she hadn't lingered downstairs. If she'd arrived a moment later, he might have already disappeared with the prize. It would be even worse if she'd arrived one minute sooner to discover him in the ambassador's suite.

She closed her eyes for a moment as she pressed her palm against the locked door. Of all the men in the world, why did it have to be Lord Wentworth who'd stolen the book?

When he'd offered his name, he'd nearly startled her into abandoning her plan. She already owed him so much. Stealing from him must surely damn her for ingratitude. If she didn't have her sisters to worry about—

She tightened her grip on the innocent-looking book. She couldn't believe she held it at last. Her entire future depended on it—on what the Russian Orthodox priest had recorded on its pages.

Even so, she regretted deceiving Lord Wentworth. He'd been kind to her with no ulterior motive. She wasn't used to that sort of solicitude. At least, not since the abrupt change in her social status.

But, then again, he *had* stolen the church register. It saddened her to realize he must be yet another player in this elaborate game of nations.

His expression of confusion and betrayal just before she'd slammed the door would haunt her.

The odd bulge at the back of his coat had made her suspicious. At first, she could only guess at what lay hidden there. When her fingers grazed the tooled-leather cover, she'd immediately recognized the Russian Orthodox cross by touch, with its distinctive emblem of two parallel crossbeams and a third one at a slight downward angle.

With it back in her possession, she'd be much more careful about who she trusted with its safekeeping. She wouldn't let the Russians take it from her.

Not again.

"I'm sorry, my lord. Truly I am," she murmured to the closed door, knowing he couldn't hear her.

A thrill shot through her as she recalled pulling him close, his breath warm on her cheek, just as it had been in her dreams. She'd nearly given in to a sudden impulse to steal a kiss from him, but she'd resisted. The book was too important to let herself be distracted by a man. Even if the man was Lord Wentworth.

Antonia paused to lift the hem of her dress, exposing the large pocket she'd sewn into one of her many layers of petticoats. She quickly stashed the church register there along with the key she'd brought.

Although she owned one of the hoop skirts many of the ladies wore this season, she hadn't worn it tonight. With tonight's cold temperatures, her many petticoats with their stiffened layers of starched crinoline would keep her warm. They'd also do a much better job of concealing the book.

She brushed her skirts back in place. The smooth shape of her gown drooped slightly from the book's added weight, but she didn't think anyone would notice.

Wentworth banged against the door, startling Antonia. She took a quick step backward. What if he made enough noise to attract someone's attention? But he wouldn't, would he? After all, he couldn't afford to be discovered here any more than she could.

It struck Antonia that the children's choir had stopped singing. How long ago had that happened? The orchestra played now, and the notes of a waltz drifted up from the ballroom below.

She darted toward the main staircase, intent upon her escape.

Antonia's feet flew down the treads. As she turned the corner on the landing, she spied the liveried footman with his back to her, guarding the stairs against intruders.

❦ 4 ❧

Boldness be my friend.

— WILLIAM SHAKESPEARE

A sudden bolt of comprehension jolted Robert.

The church register. It wasn't digging into his back. In fact, it was no longer tucked in his waistband.

He patted the floor of the dark room, hoping to find the leather-bound book, but he already knew it was gone. He recalled the temptress's hands caressing his back and pulling him closer. The little thief had stolen the church register right out from under him. Or to be more specific, right out from under his waistband.

It couldn't be a coincidence they'd met. Copper-Eyes must have planned it. There was no other explanation. She'd even had a key. One she must have brought with her. Even Frederick, with all of his schemes and plans, hadn't been able to obtain one for the embassy's new door locks.

Robert was a fool—a complete and utter fool. She'd played him from the beginning. Recalling her sudden change in demeanor when he'd first seen her, he realized he should have recognized it for what it was.

Deceit.

That initial flash of emotion had been her only mistake, and he'd ignored it because he'd pitied her.

Robert shook his head, chiding himself. Honestly, it hadn't been pity that had moved him, but something much more primal. He'd been attracted to Copper-Eyes. He'd wanted to protect her, to win her.

She'd taken him in with her beauty and false frailty—more the fool him.

An explosive sigh burst from his lips. Had there ever been a bigger simpleton? He *knew* better.

Frederick would be furious, and rightly so.

And where, precisely, was Frederick?

Robert reached for his brother's lock pick set. This is what came of breaking one of his rules. "Don't involve yourself in other people's problems," he muttered. "It only leads to trouble. Will I ever learn?"

He focused entirely upon the door's lock. Since the tiny room had no windows to let in light, he closed his eyes and concentrated on his other senses.

He'd opened many locks in the dark. When he'd honed the skill at Eton, he'd believed he'd been rebelling against his father's ruthless manipulations; later, he'd begun to wonder if he wasn't simply following in the man's footsteps.

Robert's hand slipped and he let out a curse. He wiped his hand on his trousers and began again. After another moment, the lock gave way.

Relief surged in his chest.

Perhaps he had a future in house-breaking.

Now to find that thieving coquette.

As Robert cracked open the door to peer out, a man in a black evening coat walked directly in front of the opening.

Robert froze.

Then he pulled the door wide open and stepped out into the hall, directly behind the man.

"Frederick?" Robert took in his brother's disheveled hair and rumpled clothes. "Where have you been?"

Frederick whirled around to face him, his cheeks flushed with emotion. Had he escaped from attackers—or had a woman been running her fingers through his hair? One was infinitely preferable to the other.

Frederick peered into the darkened room from which Robert had just emerged. "I should ask you the same question. Why were you in there?"

"I'll explain on our way downstairs. We need to hurry."

Little Miss Copper-Eyes was probably escaping at that precise moment. Robert sped toward the door leading to the servants' staircase with Frederick right behind him.

As he reached it, he heard the rattle of a doorknob behind him. Someone else was up here. In one smooth movement, Robert opened the staircase door and slipped inside with Frederick at his heels. Robert gently closed the door and then raced down the staircase after his brother.

Frederick waited for him at the bottom of the stairs.

Robert peeked out to check the hallway.

Empty. Finally, something happened in his favor. Perhaps his luck was turning. Now he simply needed to catch the thief before she escaped.

Oh, and confess to his brother that he'd been duped.

❦   *5*   ❦

Wisely, and slow. They stumble that run fast.

— *WILLIAM SHAKESPEARE*

Antonia slowed to a more sedate pace on the staircase in the main foyer.

She needed to consider this to be nothing more than another excellent opportunity for her to employ her acting skills.

Letting out a soft yet dramatic moan, she pretended to slump against the banister, clinging to it for support.

The footman turned, startled by the sound, and immediately hurried up the staircase toward her, his face filled with concern.

The poor man.

He might be too gullible for his own good, but all the better for her.

"Help me?" she said, gazing up at him with a pleading expression. "I'm feeling so lightheaded I'm afraid I'll fall."

The man narrowed his eyes as he examined her face and then

frowned. "Why are you here?" he asked in a thick Russian accent. "Is off-limits to guests. I am posted here for warning people away."

The words "off-limits" and "posted" sounded rather military. Perhaps he was more than an ordinary footman. She would need to play him carefully.

"Off-limits?" Antonia said, widening her eyes. "I had no idea. I simply walked up here to escape the crowd. Why didn't you stop me?"

He looked stunned. Momentarily speechless at having her turn the blame back on him.

She scrutinized him. "Did something distract you—or perhaps some one ?" She smiled indulgently and patted his arm. "I promise I won't tell the ambassador. I'd hate for you to be disciplined on my account."

"That—that is kind of you."

"Don't worry. Your secret is safe with me." Antonia leaned to one side to look past him and into a room off the foyer, where she spied a rotund matron along the far wall. The woman would make the perfect stand-in as her mother.

Antonia pretended to be relieved as she gestured toward the woman. "I should return to my mother. I'm sure she's looking for me."

The footman stepped aside to let her pass.

As Antonia entered the opulent room, she took note of the other guests, but for the most part, everyone seemed oblivious to her.

One elderly man leered at her. Had he recognized her? She avoided his gaze and pointedly began examining the room's decor.

Many paintings graced the golden-yellow walls, but one in particular caught her eye—so close she could have reached out and touched it. A painting by Vladamir Nevsky.

Her grandfather.

Memories of happier days and a better life swept over her her as she gazed at the vibrant canvas. The outdoor scene depicted Russian foot travelers on a country road wearing brightly colored clothing. Her grandfather had loved color. She smiled as she recalled him saying the world needed more purple. Standing next to it must be a good omen.

She had no doubt that if he were still alive, he would have supported her decisions. He'd always been a practical man.

She glanced up to find the footman staring at her again. Apparently she hadn't completely allayed his suspicions.

Rather than lingering at the doorway, she moved purposefully toward the woman she'd identified as her mother. Now, however, the lady chatted with a young woman, presumably her real daughter.

"Excuse me," Antonia said as she joined the pair, "but can you direct me to the punch table? I find myself quite parched."

The matron's eyes widened in surprise at being addressed by a stranger. Antonia tried to appear forlorn in the hope of appealing to some motherly instinct.

It worked. The woman's expression softened. She gave Antonia a commiserating smile. "It is quite warm in here, yes?" she asked, her Russian accent thick. "Drinks are being served in next room, through door."

A wave of nostalgia swept over her. Mother's accent had been much more subtle than this woman's, but she'd never shaken the remnants of her Russian roots.

Suddenly, Antonia missed her desperately.

Antonia nodded and clasped the matron's soft upper arm in thanks. The touch might be overdoing things a bit, but that excessively observant footman might still be watching.

As she made her way toward the door to the adjoining room, she glanced back and found the footman's gaze tracking her progress, but he seemed uninterested, as though dismissing her as a threat.

He glanced back up the stairs to the second floor.

Had something caught his attention? Or someone? If the Russians caught Lord Wentworth escaping the room before she left, the footman might become suspicious of her again.

That would be disastrous. She needed to disappear.

Upon entering the adjoining room, she sidestepped the punch table and took a roundabout path to the cloakroom, avoiding the footman in the foyer. He might be distracted now, but she was certain his suspicions were on a low simmer. If he saw her leave, they'd boil over, landing her in trouble.

Someone sneezed from inside the cloakroom as Antonia approached the door. She entered the small room and spotted a young woman dabbing at her nose with a handkerchief. She wore a neat black dress with a starched white cap and apron, and she appeared to be suffering from a cold. Maybe that would make her less likely to question Antonia's early departure.

"Bless you," Antonia said.

The woman looked both surprised and embarrassed to see her, but she still offered a faint smile. "Thank you."

"I need to leave," Antonia said, handing over a numbered metal disk.

The cloakroom attendant turned to locate her garment, passing it to Antonia with hardly a glance.

Antonia counted herself fortunate the woman didn't question her for collecting her own cloak rather than having her escort do so. The other servants in this household had been much more observant and suspicious.

A moment later, Antonia stepped out the front door. She wasn't safe yet, but luck was again in her favor.

Instead of facing a gauntlet of servants, she discovered a group of young footmen standing huddled together against the cold January wind. One of them spotted her and broke away from the group to approach her. The others snapped to attention in a surprisingly military fashion. Or perhaps it wasn't so surprising, considering the military bearing of the footman she'd deceived.

"I need to hire a cab," she told him. He made a crisp turn and hurried to do her bidding. A moment later, a well-appointed carriage pulled up to the door. Its driver sat bundled against the cold and wore a muffler and ear-warmers.

"Where to, miss?" the footman asked as he stepped forward and opened the carriage door for her.

"Where?" Antonia froze for a moment and stared blankly into his hazel eyes.

She certainly didn't want to give her true destination. After all, the Russians were certain to discover the theft of the church register once the courier arrived. What if they decided to investigate any guests who departed early? The footmen would tell them there she'd asked to go, and someone would follow her there. Her true destination would be as good as a calling card.

Why hadn't she considered this sooner? She needed to think of someplace else. Fast.

The footman stared at her expectantly. She opened her mouth, hoping a lie would spring to her lips, but she could think of nothing.

He narrowed his eyes. "Is something wrong?"

$$\text{❧} \quad 6 \quad \text{❧}$$

A person who doubts himself is like a man who would enlist in the ranks of his enemies and bear arms against himself. He makes his failure certain by himself being the first person to be convinced of it.

— *ALEXANDRE DUMAS*

Robert and his brother strode down the empty corridor as they rushed past closed office doors.

"Aren't you going to ask where I was?" Frederick asked.

"What?" Robert was so focused on finding Copper-Eyes that it took him a moment to remember he'd been worried about his brother's disappearance.

With a quick glance, he again noted Frederick's mussed hair and rumpled clothing. He cocked one eyebrow. "Fine. I'll ask. You look a bit rough. Where were you?"

"In one of the vacant bedrooms. Lady Harrington followed us up there and waylaid me."

The blunt confession left Robert momentarily stunned. He paused, his gaze raking over his brother, seeing his dishabille in a different light and noting the way he cradled his newly re-bandaged hand.

"You entered a bedroom with her? Are you telling me that while you were off trysting with a beautiful young widow, you left me to—" he lowered his voice—"to recover that bloody book?"

Frederick's face reddened. "Don't be ridiculous. Trysting? I was *not* trysting. Lady Harrington was merely concerned about my injuries. Where *is* that bloody book?"

"Your unkempt hair makes me doubt you're telling me the whole truth, but to answer your question, the book is gone. Stolen right out from under me." He met his brother's gaze. "I'm sorry. I've failed you."

"What? You let someone take it? How could you be so careless?"

A surge of emotion ripped through Robert, and his anger and frustration caused him to snap. "If you'd been where you were supposed to be, it never would have happened. I might have been a fool for losing it, but you were completely irresponsible for disappearing. We both share the blame."

Robert tried to keep walking, but Frederick stepped in front of him, forcing him to halt.

"What happened? Who stole it?"

Robert took a deep breath. "A woman. She tricked me into believing—" He shook his head. "It doesn't matter. What does matter is that we find her before she leaves the embassy. We don't have time to argue."

He stepped around his brother and continued down the corridor.

Frederick remained where he was, clearly stunned by the news.

Guilt flooded Robert. If the only way to correct his error was to track down Copper-Eyes, then track her down he would. He might hate being pulled into someone else's problems, but he'd be damned if he'd fail at it once he'd made the commitment. Especially not when war was at stake.

Robert heard his brother hurrying to catch up with him as he shouldered his way through the door separating the office corridor from the Koliada Ball—and straight into the path of one of the last people he wanted to encounter—a footman wearing full livery.

Although being tall, young, and handsome were standard requirements for a footman, this particular man appeared to be quite a bit older than most, and he had a military bearing.

The man stepped away from Robert, lifted his chin, and widened his stance as though preparing for battle. Judging by his air of steely determination, he wouldn't be easily swayed.

The delicate situation called for guile, so Robert ignored his urge to punch the man. That would be tantamount to admitting guilt, and he couldn't afford to set off an international incident.

Robert considered his options. Perhaps he should take a page from the copper-eyed thief's book of tricks.

He stumbled to a stop, clutched the door frame in a white-knuckled grip, and swayed on his feet. "I'm not feeling well," he mumbled.

Frederick appeared in the doorway next to him, and Robert loosened his grip on the door frame to grab his brother's arm, squeezing it in a warning.

"Assist me," Robert demanded, glaring at the footman. Then he clamped his hand over his mouth. "I think I ate a bad shrimp."

The faux-footman's eyes widened, and he scooted back, apparently eager to remove himself from Robert's trajectory. He muttered something in Russian which Robert recognized as a curse. Russian curse words had been among his favorites to collect as a boy at Eton.

"Chamber closet is there," he said in a thick Russian accent, pointing toward a door, "or you can use privy outside."

"Privy. Please. Hurry. I don't want anyone to witness this."

The footman sped through the door from which Robert and Frederick had just emerged and nearly ran as he led them down the corridor to the rear of the embassy.

Once outside, the footman pointed wordlessly toward a privy near the stables. Frederick wrapped Robert's arm over his shoulders and helped him lurch toward the tiny outbuilding.

"You showed some quick thinking," Frederick murmured.

"Let's hope it works, and fast. We don't have time to waste." Robert stumbled inside and slammed the door, latching it behind him. When he peeked back outside through a gap near the hinge, he could view the footman standing at attention.

The man was most certainly a soldier.

Robert swore softly to himself.

"He needs more convincing," Frederick murmured through the door.

More convincing? How? "We're running out of time," Robert said." She could be escaping while we're stuck out here."

"And we could be detained if you don't convince that man you're really sick."

Robert considered his options. After a moment, he began making retching noises. Loud ones.

"That should do it," Frederick said. From his tone, he seemed to be enjoying himself far too much.

"You'd better not be smiling," Robert said. "You sound entirely too cheerful. You'll give us away."

"Not to worry. I'm pacing and looking distraught." More loudly he said, "Do—do you need assistance?" The hesitation in his tone made it clear he didn't want to make the offer but believed doing so was his brotherly duty.

Robert made more stentorian retching noises.

"He's leaving," Frederick said in a low voice. "And fast. Perhaps my pointed stare in his direction when I offered to find you some assistance drove him away. Either that or he decided to find someone to help."

"Let's go." Robert pushed on the door, but it wouldn't open. Through the cracks, he could see Frederick leaning against it.

"Wait a moment. I can still see him."

Robert stood in the fetid privy as seconds ticked past. Finally, the door inched open. His brother jutted his grinning face inside. "That was a fine hookem-snivey," he said.

"Pardon me? A hooking what?" Frederick grinned more broadly. "A hookem-snivey. What, you've never heard of it? A hookem-snivey is when someone pretends to have an ailment in order to beg alms. You'd excel at it. I'm certain you'd be successful if you ever needed to employ it for 'some of the ready.'"

Robert arched an eyebrow at his brother's use of cant. "Is this another skill you've developed? Speaking in slang?"

"It's like learning another language." Frederick grinned. "If our worrisome footman takes pity on you and offers up 'some blunt,' I'll split it with you."

"You're enjoying yourself entirely too much," Robert said, but as he glanced up, he saw his brother disappearing in the darkness in the direction of the house.

Did he plan to return to the ball?

"The girl must be gone by now," Robert said, pitching his voice so only his brother could hear him, even as he hurried to catch up. "Why don't we simply leave from here and try to find her?"

Frederick responded without slowing his pace. "There are a multitude of reasons, one being that our hats and cloaks are in there, and I would prefer not to lose them. There's also the fact that leaving them behind would strike our host as suspicious." They passed through a pool of light emanating from one of the windows, and Frederick glanced at him. "But paramount is the fact we must search the embassy for your thief. She might still be here."

As Frederick pushed the door open, he glanced back at Robert. "Remember to appear unwell."

"And remember you injured your hand," Robert replied.

"I'm not at risk of forgetting. It hurts like the blazes. Fortunately, the whiskey seems to be taking the edge off of the pain. Lady Harrington insisted I drink some as well—for medicinal purposes. You know I don't hold my liquor well."

Not hold it well? That was an understatement. Alcohol might relax Frederick at first, but it didn't take long for him to become irritable and antagonistic. The few times in their lives they'd ever come to blows had been after Frederick had had too much to drink. The man simply didn't have the temperament for the stuff.

Robert had the distinct impression that Frederick's relaxed phase was coming to an end. It wouldn't be long now before his darker side surfaced.

Once inside, the two men prowled through the public areas and scanned for the thief. As they entered a room with tables piled high with a tempting buffet, Frederick nudged him. "Is that her?"

Robert followed his gaze toward a solitary young woman perched on a chair. The padded bench next to her sat vacant, and as Robert watched, an older woman claimed it. "No. Our girl is smaller and prettier, with rather unusual chestnut-brown hair with some lighter bits—it put me in mind of a sunset on an overcast day."

Frederick froze and then slowly turned to peer at Robert, his eyes narrowing in a knowing way. "Lord. She seduced it away from you. It's obvious."

Robert could feel the heat rising in his face. "You're one to talk. Where were you again, while all this took place?"

Frederick's face reddened. "I don't like your implication. The lady was worried about my injury." He turned his back on Robert, leading them toward the only room they hadn't yet searched.

Robert followed him into the large Golden Hall. A beautiful

crystal chandelier illuminated the space with steady gas lit flames. The crystals sent glimmers of reflected light onto the butter-colored walls adorned with paintings by Russian artists.

As Robert and his brother weaved their way through the room, guests pressed against them from all sides. With his height, Robert found it relatively easy to identify most people, but he worried he might miss the small thief in the crowd. He scoured the room with the dwindling hope of spotting the woman who'd deceived him so thoroughly. He found no sign of her.

He'd failed. "She isn't here."

Frederick's shoulders slumped as though all his energy suddenly left him. They moved past the small grand piano and a blond woman in a blue dress spun around to face them. Robert immediately recognized her.

When she saw Frederick, she let out a small gasp of surprise, and her hand darted out to touch his arm, halting him.

"Josephine—I mean, Lady Harrington," Frederick said. His face reddened.

She yanked her hand away. "Lady Harrington? We're back to that?" she asked, her voice tinged with ice. "I'm surprised to discover you here— again. I thought you needed to leave most urgently. After the way you hurried me downstairs with claims of a dire emergency, I never would have dreamed you'd still be here." She glanced at Robert. "I can hardly fail to notice nothing dreadful befell your brother." She lifted her chin, her eyes cold with dignity and a deep-seated anger.

Josephine looked glorious. Her glossy blond hair had a lustrous glow as luminous as the strand of golden pearls draped around her neck—probably chosen for that very reason.

Despite Frederick's relationship with her, even Robert had to admit he found Lady Harrington both beautiful and beguiling—not that he'd ever act on it.

Clad in a distinctive shade of light-blue satin, her signature color, she stood in sharp contrast to Frederick's coal-black hair and black tailcoat. Where Frederick might intimidate people with his air of underlying intensity, Josephine drew them in with her goodness and light.

Frederick must be certifiably mad for avoiding her. By every appearance, they made a perfect couple—whether Frederick chose to acknowledge it or not.

Even Robert sensed the charged atmosphere surrounding them. They held themselves apart from the other guests, frozen in place by the powerful, intense emotions entangling them.

Robert averted his eyes from their intimacy and focused his attention on the pastoral scene of Russian peasants depicted in the nearest painting. He distracted himself by noting the artist's choice of subject matter offered a sharp counterpoint to the room's opulent decor, much as the dark and brooding counterpoint Frederick provided while standing next to Josephine.

Someone jostled Frederick while passing, and he let out a hiss of pain.

Josephine loosened her grip on Frederick's sleeve and glanced down at his burned right hand, wrapped in a dry white cloth. Her expression immediately softened, all anger swept away by her concern. "Are you in much pain?" she asked.

Frederick gave an unconcerned shrug. "The vodka helped."

Vodka?

When had Frederick drunk vodka? And what had possessed him to drink both whiskey and vodka?

Robert began growing impatient. They needed to continue their search, but he didn't know how to proceed if Copper-Eyes had already escaped. He needed to consult with his brother, but not while standing in the middle of the Golden Hall.

"He puts on a brave front," Robert said, "but I think we should leave and tend to his injury."

"I'll go with you," Josephine said. Her tone made it obvious she would brook no argument. "My housekeeper is quite skilled at concocting poultices. I'll send my carriage to bring her to your home." But then something changed in her face—a tensing of the jaw, a narrowing of the eyes. "That will give us a chance to have that conversation you've been avoiding."

Frederick sent Robert a pleading glance.

Poor man. Robert had seen that expression on a woman's face before, and woe to any man who tried to thwart her.

He hated interfering, but their urgent need to recover the book prompted him to intervene. "That isn't necessary. I don't want to inconvenience you. Our physician can care for him."

"Fiddlesticks," Lady Harrington said. "I couldn't possibly stay and enjoy myself knowing Fre—Mr. Woolsy is suffering." She pressed her lips in a thin line.

Frederick glanced at Robert and raised a not-so-subtle eyebrow, begging him to intervene further, but Robert only shrugged in reply. He'd already meddled more than he should. Frederick needed to solve his own dilemma. Besides, he could tell Frederick's ire was rising. Robert didn't want to become a convenient target.

He moved away from the couple and leaned against the inner curve of the grand piano. In a false show of indifference, he settled in for what he assumed would be a rather interesting exchange. He only hoped it would be brief as well.

Frederick shot him a disgusted scowl before returning his attention to Josephine. "I can assure you, Lady Harrington, there's no need for you to trouble yourself." Frederick's gaze darted around the room. "My brother is using my hand as an excuse for leaving when the true reason lies with him. Don't abandon the ball on my account."

Lady Harrington peered at him more closely. "I beg to disagree. I examined your hand earlier and am well aware of the severity of the burn. You're quite pale and there is a sheen about you I find most troubling. I believe your hand pains you much more than you're willing to admit." At that, Robert examined his brother more closely. Lady Harrington was right. Frederick did appear rather unwell.

"Perhaps we should accept the offer," Robert suggested.

"We? I was unaware you'd been burned as well." Frederick's ire flickered for a moment, but then it faded. Apparently, anything more than a brief flash of temper was beyond him at the moment.

That troubled Robert even more. "It's settled," Robert said, pushing himself away from the piano.

"No, it isn't," Frederick said too loudly, his anger taking hold.

This wasn't good. Frederick rarely lost control, but when he did, things rarely ended well.

They needed to leave.

A nearby couple glanced in their direction.

Robert stepped forward. "Not here. Not now. Don't compound tonight's mistakes by drawing attention to us."

"My biggest mistake is that I relied upon you," Frederick interrupted, glaring at him. "Tonight has been an unmitigated catastrophe."

"I already apologized for my error, and I'm trying to correct it, but I'm not the only one who made mistakes tonight."

"Fine," Frederick said too loudly, "have it your way. *Eto moya vina .*" *It's all my fault.*

Several people with furrowed brows and tense expressions turned to stare at them. Robert reddened. This was not the way to avoid notice.

He leaned toward Frederick and Lady Harrington. "Rather than staging a public scene, I suggest we send for our carriage."

"Fine, but I refuse to rely on you again. I'll send for the carriage myself." Frederick spun on his heel and stalked off, heading directly toward the cloakroom.

Lady Harrington's gaze sought Robert's and she raised one eyebrow in a question, but he simply shrugged.

"The injury's making him short-tempered."

She narrowed her eyes, and Robert could tell she thought he

might be hiding something from her, but rather than arguing with him, she nodded and followed Frederick.

Robert turned to follow them, but someone laid a heavy hand on his arm.

"Lord Wentworth," Ambassador Revnik said from directly behind him, "I'm so pleased you could join us tonight. Excuse me for asking, but what is your brother's fault?"

Robert tensed, but then forced himself to relax as he turned to face the ambassador. "Pardon me?"

"Your brother said '*Eto moya vina*,' did he not?" the ambassador asked, stroking his thumb and forefinger down his dark horse-shoe-shaped mustache to smooth it down the sides of his chin. "What is his fault?"

"I—I'm sorry. My brother and I argued. I apologize for being disruptive."

"Ah, yes. Brothers. They can anger us greatly, can they not? I didn't realize either of you spoke Russian."

"I don't speak it well. We both studied it years ago at Eton, but I was never a good student."

Revnik gave him a condescending smile. "You must visit us again so you can practice. It is a beautiful language. Such a shame to let your skills decline. Did you enjoy our children's choir?"

"Very much so," Robert said with more enthusiasm. "They were exceptional."

Revnik dipped his head slightly in thanks for the compliment, but he seemed wary. "I hoped to speak to your brother as well, but he rushed off too quickly. Will he return?" Judging by the twitch in Revnik's cheek and his narrowed eyes, there was more behind his question.

"No," Robert replied, wondering how long Revnik had been observing them. Had they been overheard? "He's sending for our carriage. The burns he received are troubling him."

Revnik narrowed his eyes and he stroked his mustache again.

"I also hoped to convince you to sing for us. Will I be disappointed in that as well?"

"Now?" Robert asked, startled. But he shouldn't have been. After all, he received these requests fairly often. He slid his hand along the ebony finish of the grand piano. "I'm not certain—that is, I don't think I'm up to it this evening." He searched for an excuse that would satisfy the ambassador, and chose the same one he'd used with the footman. "You see, I'm not quite feeling myself." It was as though he'd uttered the magic words Revnik had been anticipating.

"Ah, yes. Your 'bad shrimp'?"

"You heard about that?" Robert blurted in surprise.

Revnik's dark mustache partially obscured his smile. "My footmen always inform me of unusual incidents involving my guests." He peered into Robert's eyes more intently. "I don't recall that we served any shrimp this evening."

"I ate some at home before coming here. One didn't taste quite right." Robert swallowed hard, and the ambassador's gaze focused on his Adam's apple as it bobbed up and down. "I hoped to avoid mentioning such an unpleasant subject. Please forgive me."

Revnik nodded and peered at him more closely. "It appears both you and your brother are out of sorts this evening. Is that why you argued?" Robert smiled.

"How did you guess?" He swallowed again.

Revnik twitched one shoulder as though embarrassed. "I am a student of human nature. I must admit, his irritation with you perplexed me. I couldn't resist investigating. Please allow me to ensure your carriage arrives promptly." Revnik nodded at a footman lingering at his elbow. The man turned to fulfill the order with military precision.

Robert observed the man as he walked away. "Your footmen are a bit older than most."

"That's because they're soldiers, assigned to the embassy.

When I host events such as these, they double as footmen. But you already guessed as much, didn't you?" Revnik's stared at him again, more closely. "You're an observant man."

Robert swallowed yet again. Would Revnik take his frequent swallowing as an indication of nausea? "A habit, I'm sure. One which annoys my brother to no end. Perhaps that's why I developed it." Robert glanced up and saw Frederick beckoning him from across the room.

The ambassador glanced between the two brothers suspiciously.

Robert quickly covered his mouth and widened his eyes, as though suddenly overcome by his illness. "I believe our carriage is ready. And just in time, I fear."

"Make haste," Ambassador Revnik said, unable to hide his grimace of distaste. "I insist."

Robert nodded and hurried into the foyer to grab his cloak, hat, and cane from an attendant before following his companions toward the large double doors.

He glanced over his shoulder to the balcony above the foyer just in time to witness the ambassador's secretary barreling down the staircase with the diplomatic pouch in his hand.

※ 7 ※

I see you stand like greyhounds in the slips, Straining upon the start. The game's afoot.

— *WILLIAM SHAKESPEARE*

Antonia gathered her scattered thoughts. Where could she tell the driver to take her? Someplace on the far side of the palace grounds and Hyde Park. That would do. And then she'd find another carriage to take her the rest of the way.

Wait. Hadn't her friend Zelda mentioned something about a soirée tonight in—"Grosvenor Square," Antonia blurted, before her hesitation became too obvious.

"Yes, miss." The footman didn't bat an eye. "Grosvenor Square!" he called to the driver.

The carriage took off with a lurch, throwing Antonia back against the cushions. Could her escape be this easy? She held her breath as they passed through the gate and didn't exhale until her carriage was safely on the main road.

British soil.

She settled against the comfortable cushions and grinned. She'd done it. She'd retrieved the book.

She vowed this time would be different. This time she'd hide it someplace where no one would ever think to look for it. The Russians would *not* take it from her again.

How on earth had Lord Wentworth ended up with her church register? She'd been so startled at seeing him she'd come close to forgetting her goal. It had taken every ounce of willpower not to steal a kiss from him. But she couldn't. Not in good conscience. Stealing the book from him was already a terrible betrayal.

"Right, Antonia. Go ahead and lie to yourself," she mumbled. Conscience wasn't the real reason she hadn't kissed him. No, it was doubt about her own willpower that had checked her. If she'd kissed him, she might never have been able to stop. Not after fantasizing about him for the past five years.

Why did it have to have been Lord Wentworth? Why had she been forced to betray the one man to whom her family owed so much? She'd been dreaming of meeting him face-to-face for so long.

In her fantasies, she'd always behaved in a perfectly proper way. And he'd always found her fascinating. Never once had she imagined shoving him into a bedroom and betraying him.

She tried to imagine how he'd react to seeing her now—his pale-blue eyes hard with anger. That he'd be furious went without saying. He'd never forgive her for what she'd done.

She forcefully pushed all thoughts of Lord Wentworth from her mind. The night wasn't over yet.

Her anxiety began creeping back. How would she manage to arrive at her true destination on time with this added detour to Grosvenor Square?

Suddenly, the pleasant carriage felt like it was crawling along slower than an inchworm. She'd simply have to hail a different cab once she arrived.

As the carriage rattled along Park Lane, Antonia glanced out into the darkness of Hyde Park to her left. If only she could slip into that darkness. But no. Sneaking through a deserted park at night would be even more foolish for a solitary woman. There were predators out there—of the two-footed variety.

When the carriage finally dropped her off in front of a brightly lit residence in Grosvenor Square, a number of other guests were arriving as well. It only took a moment for Antonia to procure one of the vacant hansom cabs.

"Haymarket Theatre, please," she said. "Can you take me to the rear entrance?"

The driver mumbled his agreement and helped her into the open cab before climbing back up to the driver's seat behind her. It might be a chillier ride than the one provided by the more lavish carriage she'd just exited, but it was going in the right direction.

Antonia pulled her small watch from its little pocket at the waist of her dress and checked it in the dim light of a gas lantern along their path.

It was later than she'd thought. She hoped the stage manager wouldn't be furious with her. Claude was notoriously short-tempered. She imagined the stocky Frenchman's reaction to her tardiness. Claude would remind her that there was a line of women waiting to take her place. He would rail and panic. He would threaten and cajole.

And he'd be right.

She'd never have taken this risk under normal circumstances. She couldn't afford to lose this job.

Not now. Not yet.

She slid her hand over her skirt to feel the book tucked away in the secret pocket. It was the key to solving all her problems.

As the carriage approached Piccadilly Square, she checked her watch again. She'd arrive in time, but just barely.

The traffic became thick and impassable as they neared the theater. Antonia paid the driver and hurried ahead on foot. She absolutely could not be late.

She flew through the stage door, bringing a gust of frigid air inside with her. It swept away the odors of greasepaint, fresh lumber, and dust that normally greeted her.

"Antonia, you're here! *Merde*!" Claude's French accent was thick, a sure indication of his anger. He scrubbed his hands over his round belly before shaking a finger at her. "This is inexcusable. I had Pamela put on your costume. Hurry! Go change with her so everyone's in place before the curtain rises."

"Yes, sir." Out of the corner of her eye, Antonia caught the stricken expression of her understudy. Pamela's normally pale face was covered with face powder, and she wore her blond hair artfully arranged in a neat chignon, but her borrowed gown was too short since she was four inches taller than Antonia. Antonia noted the girl's irritated expression.

There was always someone waiting to take your place, hoping for their big chance at success. If things worked out the way Antonia hoped they would, Pamela might end up taking over her role on a permanent basis.

Claude braced his hands on his hips and spread his feet wide. He narrowed his eyes. "You know I don't tolerate lateness. I expect the cast to be here early every single night. No exceptions."

Antonia nodded, trying to look as contrite as she felt.

Claude continued to glower at her. "I'm sorry," she said. "I won't let it happen again."

His scowl seemed to follow her as she hurried off to the dressing area below stage. There was a similar room in the wings, but it was small and she only used it during scene changes. When changing in and out of her street clothes, she preferred to use the larger area below stairs.

The moment she stepped into the room, she stripped out of her cloak, dress, and petticoats. As she hung her garments on pegs, she kept the church register well hidden.

A moment later, her understudy handed her the costume and then slipped away. Antonia hurriedly donned the old-fashioned wide panniers and gown. After checking her reflection one last time, she hurried upstairs toward the stage.

When Claude caught sight of her in the wings, he turned and walked out onto the apron in front of the curtain. From her vantage point, she could see him raise his arms, and the crowd fell silent.

"Thank you for your patience," he boomed, causing the audience to fall silent. "It's my pleasure to inform you that contrary to what you may have been told when you arrived, Antonia Winter will be performing the title role in tonight's performance of Westland Marston's play, *Anne Blake*."

Enthusiastic applause greeted the announcement. Claude's stage smile still plastered his face as he brushed past Antonia, but then he paused to look at her, his face stern. "They might applaud you tonight, but in time they could come to love Pamela even more. Audiences are fickle."

Antonia nodded as her stomach clenched. She couldn't afford to lose this role. It paid her room and board, and kept her sisters clothed and fed.

$$\text{\ding{113} \quad 8 \quad \ding{113}}$$

Divide each difficulty into as many parts as is feasible and necessary to resolve it.

— *RENÉE DESCARTES*

J ust as the double doors of the embassy began to close behind Robert, pounding footsteps thundered toward the entrance.

A man shouted, "Shut the doors and keep them locked!"

The doors slammed as though someone had shoved them. Robert felt momentarily stunned.

If the man issuing orders had instead said, "Don't let anyone leave," they would have been dragged back inside and searched. The lock picks he carried would have damned him even without the church register.

Rather than pausing to wonder at his good fortune, Robert tucked his cane under his arm at a jaunty angle and glanced around in time to spot a departing carriage. Had someone else left the ball early?

His stomach tightened. Could it have been the thief?

He ignored the possibility for a moment. They weren't safe yet. That gate still separated the Russian embassy from Lyall Street and British soil.

Robert's carriage stood waiting, ready to whisk them away.

Frederick shot him a worried glance. He'd obviously heard the order to close the doors. It might be true they needed to leave quickly, but it couldn't appear as though they were rushing.

Robert leaned on his cane in a casual pose as Frederick insisted on helping Lady Harrington into the carriage using his better hand.

"Thank you, Frederick," she said softly.

Frederick's face turned red.

What was this? Robert narrowed his eyes as Frederick followed her inside.

"Why did you revert to calling me Lady Harrington?" she asked Frederick, her voice soft and beguiling. "I much prefer it when you call me Josephine."

"I'd thought to protect your reputation, but you seem firmly committed to tarnishing it. Nearly everyone at the ball must have seen you leave with me."

"Fiddlesticks. As I already explained, a widow has much more latitude than a debutante."

"Not *this* much."

"Your brother is with us, and neither of you is rumored to be a rake. My reputation is safe enough."

Robert listened with curiosity, beginning to suspect Frederick cared much more for Josephine than he'd admit even to himself.

As Robert settled on his seat, she glanced at him. "You should call me Josephine as well," she said in a more matter-of-fact tone.

"Thank you. You must call me Robert." He'd be seeing more of this woman—that much was obvious.

Through the window, Robert scanned the courtyard, noting two men opening the gates leading to the street. Robert slumped back in the seat opposite Josephine and Frederick.

"It's quite kind of you to offer your assistance, Josephine," Robert said.

"She didn't offer. She insisted," Frederick said, obviously displeased.

"Fiddlesticks. You know this will be more expedient. My carriage can pick up my housekeeper and bring her to you. You wouldn't have me wasting my time sitting outside in the cold, would you?"

Frederick's face softened. "Of course not."

One of the footmen stepped forward to close the carriage door and then slapped the side of the coach, signaling their coachman that he could leave.

Robert rested his hand on his cane, using it as a barrier between himself and his brother. He liked the smooth texture of the silver pistol-grip handle against his palm, but even more, he liked the security of knowing that it concealed a slim sword, or more precisely, an épée.

He stared out the window, too tense to speak until they'd left the embassy's grounds and were safely back on British soil. His eyes tracked the cast-iron streetlamps as they seemed to glide past the window. They burned with a steady glow, as if they were sentinels watching the night's events unfold. It was as though they had wills of their own and wanted to ensure that all was well and proper in England.

"Robert, what did the ambassador want?" Josephine asked, breaking the silence. "He seemed quite intent on speaking with you."

Robert glanced at Frederick, uncomfortable with her question. "Nothing in particular."

At his cryptic reply, she narrowed her eyes. "He seemed insistent."

"He witnessed our argument and came over to investigate."

"Were you able to explain everything to his satisfaction?" Frederick asked in a sharp tone.

"I mentioned I'd eaten a bad shrimp and had an urgent need to return home. It turned out he already knew about it, which I found peculiar. He assumed you were in a temper because of your burned hand."

"In a temper?" Josephine retorted. "Is that how he characterizes a man who is injured during his ball?" If she could sprout thorns, she'd pierce the ambassador with them.

"That's the proper term to use when anyone lets their anger take control of them in a public setting," Robert replied.

"You're one to talk," Frederick muttered. "I can't count the number of times I've seen you lose your temper."

Robert ignored the comment. "We need a plan."

Frederick glanced at Josephine and inhaled deeply, obviously trying to control himself. He held his breath for a moment and then exhaled slowly. "I assumed you'd prefer to be quit of me and tonight's entanglements. I know how much you dislike being involved in my work."

"Unfortunately, I happen to be responsible for—for what went wrong. I'm already involved, and I plan to rectify my error."

"Hmm," Frederick replied, sounding more annoyed than convinced. "In that case, it would be best for you to focus on recalling where you've seen the woman before. I think we should separate and pursue this problem from different angles. You go after the girl while I investigate the people I believe are behind the—" he glanced at Josephine "—the incident."

"You should be resting," she interjected.

Frederick let out a sigh. "Josephine, more is taking place tonight than is apparent. If you'll refrain from asking questions for the moment, I'll do my best to explain everything later."

"Of course 'more is taking place,'" she snapped. "I assume it has something to do with your work for the Foreign Office. Is that why you were at the embassy tonight? To spy on the Russians?"

When Frederick's jaw dropped, she let a slow smile spread across her face. "Don't worry, darling. I'll never repeat a word. I'm completely discreet."

"How—how long have you known?" Frederick asked.

"Oh, my. It's been quite some time now." She tapped her gloved index finger against her lower lip. "At least a year. Perhaps a bit more."

"And you never confronted me?"

"I didn't want to intrude," she said, holding up her hands as if absolving herself of involvement. "I assumed you'd tell me eventually, but since tonight's situation appears to be a pressing one, I decided to reveal what I know." She gave Robert a commiserating look. "I'm guessing the two of you were forced to improvise after Lord Percival's fire. That must have been a challenge."

Frederick let out a sigh of exasperation. "If you knew all of that, why did you follow me upstairs?"

"I *am* sorry about that. I didn't realize you must have been on an assignment until later. I'd make a terrible spy, wouldn't I? I never considered that I might one day stumble across you while you were on a *mission*. I always imagined those sorts of tasks taking place in dark, scurrilous places."

Frederick gestured for her to stop. "I really must speak candidly with my brother. I'd rather not involve you in this any further. It's safer for you if you don't know anything. We'll halt the carriage so he and I can walk for a moment."

"Fiddlesticks. I'm involved already. And you must know I'd never betray you. I never said a word about what happened last year with Lord and Lady Huntley, did I? And I never will. Nor will I repeat anything you say in front of me now. Pretend I'm not here."

Frederick remained silent.

"You already trust her," Robert said, noting the casual way

their shoulders brushed against each other, "otherwise she wouldn't be in the carriage with us. You'd never have permitted it."

Frederick met Josephine's gaze. "Trust isn't the issue," he said, stroking the back of his left hand against her cloak in an unconsciously possessive gesture. "I want to protect you from this part of my life, not drag you into it. But you're right. I've already involved you in this. Too many people saw us leave together."

"I can take care of myself," she insisted. "I've been doing so for the past two years."

Ever since she'd become a widow, Robert realized.

Frederick's jaw tensed, but after a long pause, he nodded. "Letting you listen won't put you at any greater risk." Frederick closed his eyes and pressed the heel of his hand to his forehead. A moment later, he blinked them open and focused his gaze on Robert. "I've been considering who might have taken the book. Obviously we didn't do it, nor did the Russians. The only logical alternative is the French. I considered the Ottomans, but I've ruled them out. Their involvement is highly unlikely."

"But aren't we allies with the French? Why would they steal it from me?"

"The situation is complex. With so many pieces in play on the board, it can be challenging to predict the next move." Frederick let out a deep sigh of frustration. "If I'm right and the French are behind the theft, I think I may know the identity of the man who orchestrated tonight's debacle. You mentioned she had a key. This man is one of the few people who would have been able to acquire one. By my calculations, he's the only other player with the skills and connections to have choreographed tonight's events. Your little thief will probably pass the church register to him as soon as possible. I know where he lives. If I can catch him at home, I can watch him until she shows herself. As soon as she makes contact, I'll grab the book."

Robert nodded. "It's a solid plan, as long as you're certain you know who her contact will be."

"That's the problem. This is my best guess, but since I'm missing key facts, I could be wrong. That's why I want you to try to locate the woman using your own methods. If we attack the problem from two different directions, we have a better chance of succeeding."

"I don't like this," Josephine interjected. "I know I promised you wouldn't know I was here, but I can't remain silent. You're injured, you're tired, and you've been drinking. You shouldn't go haring off alone in the dark after some thief."

"I have no choice. You don't understand the severity of the situation. It's imperative we recover that book. Everything depends upon it."

"Not without my help," she insisted. When Frederick opened his mouth to protest, she held up her hand to silence him and continued speaking. "I'll accompany you. Don't worry about my reputation. As I already pointed out, I'm a widow, so no one bothers about that sort of thing where I'm concerned. I refuse to allow you to do this alone. It's obvious you and your brother need to separate, so I'm the only person who can help you."

Robert pulled his gaze away from the dark shadows of Hyde Park and faced his brother. "I like the plan." He glanced at Josephine, and she shot him a look of gratitude. He dipped his head in acknowledgment. "The book is too important to allow anything to get in the way. Recovering it has to be our priority."

"I know this will come as a surprise to both of you, but I like the plan too," Frederick said. "Thank you for your generous offer, Josephine."

Her delighted smile lit her face.

Frederick's intense brown eyes bored into Robert's. "I can't tell you how pleased I am that you want to do this. I like seeing you commit to something."

Robert flexed his jaw and trained his gaze on the handle of his cane, rubbing his palm against it. "Don't worry. I'm sure it isn't a permanent change in my character. I'm firmly committed to remaining unencumbered by other people's problems."

"You're brilliant when you put your mind to a task, Robert. Stop trying to hide it from the world."

"And that whiskey has given you a soft head." Suddenly, Robert found the interior of the carriage to be stifling. He couldn't bear to sit there any longer. He needed to act. To move. To put the plan into action.

Just past Hyde Park, Robert banged his cane on the ceiling of the carriage to get the driver's attention.

"What are you doing?" Frederick asked.

"There's no need for me to return home with you. I need to remember where I saw that woman, and I'll think better if I'm walking."

The coachman pulled the horses to a halt at the street corner and Robert jumped out, snapping the door shut behind him.

The frigid night air hit his face and immediately soothed some of his tension.

"Take them home," Robert called up to Crupper, his driver, "and remain at their disposal for the evening."

Crupper urged the matched pair of bays into the night.

Robert glanced up and down the road and then strode toward a bustling cross street in the distance. He needed to be around people. Perhaps something would spur his memory and help him identify Copper-Eyes.

What chance did he really have, though?

His steps faltered for a moment, but then he forged onward. He'd walk all night if he had to. He had no other alternative. He must remember where he'd seen the woman.

Failure was too terrible to contemplate.

❦ 9 ❦

Our deeds disguise us. People need endless time to try on their deeds, until each knows the proper deeds for him to do. But every day, every hour, rushes by. There is no time.

— JOHN LOCKE

⚜

Robert concentrated on recalling every detail about the sweet-faced thief in the silvery-gray dress. Her gestures. Her words. Her figure and form. The sound of her voice. Even her gait.

He found her entrancing—and achingly familiar. He'd seen her before—but where? No matter how hard he tried, her identity eluded him.

As he replayed the evening's events, his anger grew, both with himself and with her.

He couldn't place the blame entirely on Copper-Eyes's shoulders—that book had been his responsibility. If he hadn't been so gullible, she never would have deceived him—betrayed him.

The footman hadn't been guarding the staircase and foyer when he'd first left the ambassador's suite. If he'd ignored her and simply walked down the stairs, he could have returned to the ball with the church register in his possession and no one would have been the wiser. They could have been delivering the book into the Queen's hands even now.

War. The word sent a cold chill down his spine. If Frederick was right, lives would now be lost because of that single moment of distraction.

She'd been devilishly distracting, too. Could anyone else have tempted him so?

He recalled holding Copper-Eyes in his arms—the pleasure of having her small, lithe body pressed against his. He shook his head, forcibly wrenching his thoughts away from the memory.

He couldn't think about her that way. Not when British lives were at stake.

He couldn't allow himself to dwell on thoughts of self-recrimination, either. They would get him nowhere. He needed to find her if he wanted to find a way out of this quagmire, and once he did, he'd know better than to trust her again. That is, if he ever remembered where he'd seen her.

As he came to each intersection in the streets of London, he chose the path more crowded with pedestrians. He needed to surround himself with faces and voices, because eventually, something he saw or heard would trigger his faint recollection of her identity.

Where had he seen her before? Where?

He noticed a crush of people just ahead, and glanced around for a landmark. Where was he?

He quickly realized he'd walked through Piccadilly Circus without taking note of his surroundings. He'd managed to wander all the way to the theater district and still hadn't remembered where he'd seen Copper-Eyes.

Posters, both old and new, dotted the sides of the buildings in the vicinity. Entertainments of every variety abounded. Operas, magicians, concerts, plays—even a circus. The bright splashes of color on the notices vied for his attention, but the overall effect was that of a cacophony for the eye.

Rather than trying to focus on a single element in the flurry of images, he simply accepted them as a whole. But from the midst of the riot of color, an old and tattered poster of the tragic clown from *Rigoletto* captured Robert's attention.

Why?

He stepped closer to it. Was it something within the image, or simply the movement of the ripped edge of the notice? He stared at it, searching for a clue. It niggled at his mind, as though the solution to his problem lay right there in front of him, but it refused to come into focus.

With a sigh, Robert moved on, gazing ahead at the throng of theatergoers arriving for their various shows.

He stopped.

Theater, not opera—that was it . He'd seen her, or someone just like her, on one of the theater notices. But which one? It came to him in a flash. He'd seen Copper-Eyes in a poster for the play *Anne Blake*. He was certain of it.

Had the image on the poster simply been a coincidence? What if the artist who created it had simply drawn the face of a woman who looked similar to Copper-Eyes? But it had looked too much like her. It had to be the same woman.

Robert pushed his way through the bustling crowd, making his way toward Haymarket Theatre. People were streaming inside, passing the six columns of its classical facade.

Robert stood in the queue at the ticket office to purchase a seat for the evening's performance and gazed at her poster, staring into those eyes that were now so familiar to him. He found her name in bold letters.

Antonia Winter.

The small, slim clerk manning the counter raked his gaze over

Robert's formal evening attire. "Sorry, sir, but we don't have any seats left in the upper circle. There are a few left down in the pit, but I doubt you'll want to sit there."

Robert placed some coins on the counter. "It doesn't matter. I'll take one."

The man shrugged and slid a single ticket to him. Robert nodded, picked it up, and turned away.

"Your change, sir?"

"Keep it," he said over his shoulder.

Ticket in hand, he hurried toward the doors. He stood out among the other theatergoers on this level, not only because of his formal attire, but also his height. Few people here wore the elaborate evening wear that was the norm upstairs in the private boxes.

He held out the ticket to the gray-haired ticket-taker and then paused. Did this even make sense? How could Copper-Eyes possibly have made the trip to the theater quickly enough to be on stage after stealing the book?

Robert pulled the ticket back and turned away. This had been a foolish mistake. His time would be better spent continuing his search for her. The elderly ticket-taker noticed his movement.

"Sir," he called out, "if you're concerned Miss Winter won't be performing tonight, you can put your mind at ease. She'll be on stage after all."

Robert spun around to face the man. "She's here? And she's late?"

"Yes, sir. She was delayed, but I just got word. She'll go on, right enough."

"Will she then?" Robert grinned as he handed the helpful man his ticket. "Thank you. I can't tell you how pleased I am to hear the news."

"Enjoy the show," the usher said, tucking the ticket stub inside a playbill and handing it to Robert.

As Robert moved down the crowded aisle, he searched for his

seat. He located it quickly enough. It wasn't a very good one, and his view was partially obstructed by a pillar, but he could still see most of the stage.

He raised his gaze higher to examine the upper circle of seats and recognized a few members of society relaxing in the balconies. When Robert's gaze landed on his friend Daniel, Marquess of Huntley, their eyes locked.

Robert had the impression his friend was relieved to have finally caught his attention. The intensity in Daniel's expression made Robert pause. Daniel must have been observing him for a while.

He motioned for Robert to join him in the balcony. Daniel leaned toward his wife, Catherine, and murmured something while gesturing toward Robert.

Catherine's worried expression deepened, and Robert's internal alarm bells started ringing.

Something was wrong, and whatever it was made Lord and Lady Huntley uneasy.

Robert left his seat and took the stairs two at a time to the upper balcony. He located their box and slipped through the door, closing it behind him. There were four chairs on the private balcony, but only Daniel and Catherine were there. Based on the way her dress now rounded over her belly, they'd be hosting a baptism celebration in a few months.

Robert scanned the other boxes and noticed that quite a few members of society watched him as he greeted his friends. This wasn't the place for a clandestine meeting if that's what Daniel had in mind. His presence here would probably be remarked upon tomorrow in any number of London's many newspapers.

"Wentworth. It's good to see you," Daniel said, clapping him on the back. His joviality seemed forced, but Robert knew how to play his part and responded with appropriate enthusiasm.

Robert greeted Lady Catherine. "You look more radiant every time I see you."

"I believe you can thank Daniel for that," she replied, casting her husband a playful look. "I'm simply trying to keep you happy and healthy."

He pulled her closer to his side and grinned at Robert. "We've been working on keeping up her exercise regimen, but she's had to modify it since—" Daniel broke off and cleared his throat.

Robert understood. Of course, Daniel meant that she'd curtailed her activities due to her pregnancy. Not that a gentlemen would speak of such things in mixed company. What a ridiculous notion, to dance around her pregnancy as though it didn't exist. Or even worse, to behave as though pregnancy was somehow an embarrassment rather than a cause for joy. It was even more ludicrous since the evidence was right there before their eyes. But that was the way of things.

"Whatever you're doing seems to be working," Robert said.

Catherine blushed at that, and Robert pretended not to notice.

"Sit," Daniel said. Once they were settled, he spoke in a lower voice. "You were at the Russian embassy tonight?"

Robert stiffened. "Yes. I attended the ball."

Daniel nodded. "Something was stolen. It's as though someone poked a Russian ant hill with a great big stick. I don't know what was taken, but the Russians are desperate to get it back. They have men crawling all over town and tracking down everyone who left before the theft was discovered."

"They're looking for me?"

"You seem to be at the top of their list."

"How do you know about this?"

"They came swarming through the Ambridge Club not long ago. I stopped by to collect something on the way here, otherwise I wouldn't have known. The Russians wanted to locate you in particular."

Robert jutted out his lower lip in a frown as he considered the information. "That's not good."

"But what I don't understand is why you've come to Haymarket."

"It was a last-minute decision," Robert mumbled, not wanting to draw Daniel into this fiasco.

"The Russians are hunting you, and you suddenly had the urge to see a play?"

"In a manner of speaking. Actually, I need to see an actress."

Daniel's gaze sharpened, like a hawk spying the movement of a mouse. "Why is she important?"

"There's something about her that I find particularly intriguing." Such as the book she stole. "More than that, I'm not at liberty to say."

Daniel narrowed his eyes. The theater lights dimmed, and they were forced to stop talking as everyone fell silent.

Robert watched the stage closely, waiting to catch his first glimpse of Antonia Winter. Much to his consternation, the character of Anne Blake didn't appear on stage in the first scene, or even the second for that matter.

Robert found himself being pulled into the story despite himself, and when Miss Winter finally walked on stage, the sight of her yanked him from his enjoyment of the show.

He reached out to the railing in front of him and wrapped his fingers tightly around it as he leaned forward in his seat.

It was her. Copper-Eyes. He'd know her anywhere.

On stage, she played the ingénue, the same role she'd used when she'd met him.

His stomach flipped at the sight of her. She was as breathtaking as he remembered. Her presence overshadowed the other actors. She seemed to vibrate with energy.

Robert narrowed his eyes, evaluating her. Assessing her. How had she drawn him in so quickly at the ball? So completely? Even now, he could feel the tug of his attraction to her. He tried to hold himself aloof from her, but when the wide panniers of her old-fashioned gown swayed and dipped enticingly as she crossed the stage, she unwittingly drew him back in again.

Warmth suffused him and he found himself wanting her. Desire flooded him. He recalled the feel of her body as she'd pressed it against him, and he had to stifle a groan.

It wasn't until the curtain fell for the intermission that he finally leaned back in his chair. He'd never before been so enthralled by a woman as he had by this one. It was his bad luck she was precisely the wrong woman at precisely the wrong time.

It took a few moments for the theater lights to brighten. Someone from another box beckoned for Catherine to join them, and with a murmur to her husband, she left.

Daniel didn't waste a moment. "What's happening here? I saw the way you watched that actress. I watched your face. Your interest in her isn't simple attraction. There's something more."

That surprised him. "She took something from me, and I want it back."

"Do you plan to take it by force?"

Robert jerked his head back. "Of course not."

"Then you need a plan, and I doubt you have one." Daniel gave him a stern look. "You tend to be too direct. Too impetuous. But I doubt a forthright approach will work in this situation. You'll need to use guile."

"Guile, eh?" he said, pinching his bottom lip with his thumb and forefinger.

"I'm not very good at deceit."

"Which is probably why we get along so well. But I'm learning more and more about it all the time," Daniel said, glancing at the door through which his wife had departed, clearly thinking about her.

"What would Catherine suggest?"

"Catherine?"

"Based on your comment, I gather she's the expert on guile."

Daniel frowned and glanced back at the door. "I think all

women need to know how to use it. After all, men have all the power in this world, so it only makes sense for a woman to wield her influence by using every ounce of cunning she possesses. The game is already weighed heavily against them. They should use whatever skills they have in order to improve their lot."

Robert held his hands up. "My comment wasn't meant as a criticism of your wife. I like her. She's good for you."

Daniel relaxed.

"But what do you think she'd suggest I do?"

The door opened and Catherine walked in.

"Speak of the devil. Here she is. Let's ask her," Daniel said as he gestured her over.

Catherine peered at Robert. "You need my advice? My guess is that it has something to do with that actress. Am I right?"

The two men exchanged startled glances, but she just chuckled and dismissed their surprise with a flick of her hand. "I heard part of what you said through the door. And thank you, Robert, for saying that you like me." She gave him a prim smile. "I like you too," she said sweetly. "I find you to be an acquired taste. But tell me about your problem."

"Robert needs to get an item back from the actress playing Anne Blake. She took it from him."

"After I took it from someone else," Robert admitted. "But mine were the most noble of reasons, so don't judge me harshly."

"Then perhaps her reasons are noble as well," Catherine said.

"I doubt that."

"Still, since your own reasons are admirable ones, perhaps you can play upon her sympathies. If that doesn't work, there's always your charm."

Daniel snorted.

She nudged him with her elbow. "Stop that. He really can be quite charming when he tries. It's just that he can sometimes be a bit too impulsive and forthright. He sometimes acts or speaks without first considering the ramifications."

Robert scowled.

"Well, you do," she said, scowling back at Robert in a mocking way. "Stop making faces at me. You can charm the birds from the trees, and when you sing, you can even charm the angels from the clouds."

"Stop complimenting the man. You're making me jealous," Daniel said, but the smile he gave his wife belied his words.

"I'm sorry," she said, and a slow smile spread across her face as she inched closer to her husband. "I'll have to make it up to you."

Robert glanced away, suddenly feeling very much in the way.

"Were you invited to Lady Wilmot's soirée tonight?" Catherine asked. "I believe Miss Winter will be performing there along with some other members of her acting troupe. Perhaps you should try to approach her there."

Robert's mood brightened. "That's an excellent idea." He began plotting how he'd approach her as he stared at the theater-goers taking their seats below.

Something caught his eye. A latecomer hurried toward his seat, taking one that had previously been empty.

Robert recognized the man. He was one of the footmen from the embassy.

Had they tracked him here? Or had they tracked Miss Winter?

❧　10　❧

Experience demands that man is the only animal which devours his own kind, for I can apply no milder term to the general prey of the rich on the poor.

— *THOMAS JEFFERSON*

The lights illuminating the stage left Antonia semi-blind as she turned her back to them and made her way into the darkened wings.

She vibrated with the exultant rush and thrill that accompanied a successful performance, but tonight that thrill was tempered with fear.

She'd seen Lord Wentworth up in one of the balcony boxes, she was certain of it. She'd know him anywhere. While onstage, she couldn't stare at him openly, but it had been him.

She headed toward the staircase leading to the dressing rooms. "Antonia, don't go that way," Claude said in a soft voice. She peered through the dim light and could barely make out the

Frenchman's barrel-shaped form. When she'd last seen him before the show, he'd been angry with her for being late, but now he seemed worried.

"What's wrong?" she asked.

"A man asked about you." He closed the distance between them. "About your late arrival. I do not like him. He is up to no good."

Antonia could see Claude's face clearly now. She almost reached out to pat his arm and soothe away his worries, but something in his expression made her pause. The normally unflappable man seemed genuinely shaken.

"Do you think he's dangerous?"

Claude gave a loose-limbed shrug, but the intensity in his gaze and the tightness in his jaw were at odds with his relaxed movements. "He is Russian. You know how I feel about those Cossacks."

Russian? Had one of them managed to follow her trail? She would have sworn it was impossible. The sharp teeth of fear bit into her. She licked her lips, but suddenly found her mouth quite dry. "And he already knew I was late?"

Claude gave a sharp nod. "He asked if I knew what had delayed you. I revealed nothing, but everyone knows you were late. We had only just announced you weren't performing tonight when you finally arrived. Someone is sure to have mentioned it to him."

An invisible hand tightened around her stomach. "I'd rather avoid him," Antonia said. She distractedly bit at her thumbnail, but when she noticed Claude watching her, she dropped her hand to her side. "I have to perform at that event at Lady Wilmot's tonight," she muttered. "Maybe I could lose him. But how will I leave the theater without him seeing me?"

Claude grinned. "I already have a plan to help you." He lifted his arm, and she noticed him holding one of the cloaks she recognized from the costume room. With a swift movement, he draped it around her shoulders.

Dust tickled Antonia's nose, and she let out three sneezes in quick succession. "A cloak?"

"A cloak of invisibility," he said, grinning his crooked-toothed grin. "He'll never be able to identify you if you wear it tonight."

Claude pulled the hood up and arranged it so it covered her hair and concealed most of her face. "Look around us. Poof. You're invisible."

Antonia glanced around and noticed that all the other actors going to Lady Wilmot's wore identical cloaks.

A slow grin spread across her face. Claude was right. She was invisible. Just one anonymous cloaked actor in a sea of them.

"Thank you," she said, throwing her arms around the big man. Claude stiffened.

"None of that. I see the man now. Go. And hurry. I'll distract him."

She slipped away, blending in with the others. She nibbled at the corner of her thumbnail again. How much of Claude's concern was for her, and how much of it was for the show? She knew the man. The show was his first priority. He'd count helping her sneak out as another black mark against her.

The question was, how many would he tolerate before he tossed her out?

Happiness in this world, when it comes, comes incidentally. Make it the object of pursuit, and it leads us a wild goose chase, and is never attained. Follow some other object, and very possibly we may find that we have caught happiness without dreaming of it.

— NATHANIEL HAWTHORNE

Robert spotted a surprising number of swains hurrying backstage. Most of them clutched bunches of flowers or boxes of chocolates. A few cast suspicious looks toward Robert, making him wonder if they felt possessive of the objects of their obsession.

Robert quickly realized the place was too much of a rabbit warren for him to locate Miss Winter on his own. He looked around for whoever seemed to be both the busiest and the most competent.

He spotted a round-bellied man sorting through the stage props and arranging them for the following night's show. He'd probably get a straight answer from him, if only because the man would be too swamped to reply in any other way.

"I'm looking for Miss Winter."

"Why should I care?" the man replied in a thick French accent without looking up.

"I need to speak with her. It's important."

"I say to you what I say to the others. Leave her alone. She isn't interested. She's a good girl and plans to stay that way."

"You mistake my intentions."

The man stopped working and looked directly at Robert, sweeping him with an assessing gaze. "I've seen many men sniffing around backstage," he said in a thick French accent, "but you are new. Maybe you are different. Maybe you are not. Who is to say?" He turned back to his work.

"Will you tell me where I can find her? This place is a maze."

"You are too late. She is gone. Search if you like, but you will not find her. She had an engagement."

"Lady Wilmot's soirée?"

The man narrowed his eyes. "I could not say."

"Thank you," Robert said as he turned and strode away.

"She is well away from here," the man called after him. "You will not overtake her."

Robert made his way outside, but fighting the after-theater crowd for an empty hansom cab proved more difficult than he'd anticipated. Now he regretted sending his brother and Lady Harrington off with his carriage.

A mass of people exiting the various theaters swarmed the available carriages. He spotted one in the distance, moving against the traffic.

Robert hurried forward, waving his arm.

He caught a sudden movement from the corner of his eye as a man came barreling toward him from the side.

Robert quickly leapt back, narrowly avoiding the mammoth who seemed intent on knocking him to the ground.

The big man had a small scar near the corner of his mouth. Robert recognized him. He was the footman who'd attended them when Frederick had been burned at Ambassador Revnik's ball. He'd brought the ice.

"Ambassador wants you. Come now," he said in a gruff Russian accent. He advanced with dogged steps that left no doubt of his intentions. It would appear he intended to collect his quarry, whether Robert went willingly or not.

Robert didn't have time for this. He needed to put an end to this encounter as quickly as possible or he'd lose Miss Winter.

As he took a couple of steps back and began to formulate a plan to avoid the behemoth, two more men joined the first one. Now all three advanced on Robert, surrounding him.

He recognized the footman who'd directed him to the privy. The set of his jaw and his narrowed eyes betrayed his grim determination. It would seem he resented being tricked with the story of a bad shrimp.

Robert didn't like his odds. He especially didn't like the men's grim expressions.

The door of a nearby carriage banged open, startling Robert. He glanced toward the commotion and widened his eyes in surprise as he recognized Daniel launching himself from the carriage's dark interior.

His mad friend charged into the fray with a wickedly delighted gleam in his eye.

Catherine stood framed in the open doorway as she watched. She wasn't alarmed. If Robert didn't know better, he'd have sworn she wore a look of exhilaration.

Daniel slammed his shoulder into one of the men and knocked him off his feet using one of the underhanded fighting techniques he'd picked up on the streets of Edinburgh as a boy. His method of attack might not have been elegant or gentlemanly, but it was decidedly effective.

Daniel always said a man should avoid fights whenever possible, but once one became inevitable, he should bring it to a swift conclusion using any means necessary.

The other two attackers stiffened momentarily, apparently torn between helping their compatriot and abducting Robert. They quickly made their decision and turned their backs on the fallen man. In unison, they barreled toward Robert.

Robert yanked the silver épée from his cane and raised the tip toward the nearest man.

He stopped in his tracks with his chest inches from the sharp point. He stared down at it. When Robert flicked the tip up just an inch, the man scampered back.

From the corner of his eye, Robert noticed a movement at the door of Daniel's carriage. He risked a brief glance at it before returning his attention to the two Russians.

What the—?

He almost glanced back, but the Russians were watching him too closely. He couldn't risk it. But—had he just seen Catherine holding a deadly looking knife?

The largest man climbed to his feet and turned to face Robert. He lowered his shoulders and began advancing.

Robert tried to keep all three men in sight, but he couldn't stop thinking about what he'd seen.

Where had Catherine learned to handle a weapon like that? From Daniel? And why would a marchioness want to learn such a skill?

Catherine rushed forward, moving with the grace and intensity of a cat pouncing on its prey. The man she bore down upon widened his eyes and stumbled back, raising his empty hands in surrender.

He and the other two attackers exchanged nervous glances. They probably thought it child's play to pluck a lone man from the crowd and toss him into one of the ubiquitous black carriages.

The odds had changed.

"*Poshli*," one of them said. Let's go.

Robert blinked as the three men silently melted back into the crowd. Even the huge man managed to disappear.

The theatergoers swirling past them hardly seemed aware of the fight. The few who had taken note had wisely kept a safe distance from the scuffle and hurried away. Riots were always a danger in the crowded streets of London, and most prudent people did their best to avoid being swept up in one. The people now flowing past them seemed oblivious to the fact that an attack had just taken place.

"Did they harm you?" Daniel's gaze swept up and down Robert, apparently checking for injuries.

"I'm fine. Thanks to you."

"It was sheer chance we saw them through the window of our carriage," Catherine said.

Robert's gaze flicked toward the knife she still held. "Did Daniel teach you how to use that?"

She smiled as she tossed it in the air with a proficient flip and then grabbed it so that the tip pointed upward. Then she concealed the blade between her wrist and her body, completely hiding it from sight. "He thought it wise."

Robert raised an eyebrow at her apparent comfort and expertise with the weapon. She and Daniel had been even busier than Robert had guessed. "Did you see the look on that man's face? I thought he'd soil himself when you pointed your knife at him—" He cut off his words. Had he actually used the words "soil himself" in front of Daniel's wife? "Pardon me, Catherine. I forgot myself. But thank you. You tipped the scales in our favor."

She waved his apology away.

Daniel kept scanning the crowd, wary of another attack. "It isn't safe here. We should leave." He glanced at Robert. "Come with us."

Robert shook his head. "I don't want to put the two of you in danger. Go home. There's something important I need to do."

Daniel frowned. "I'll join you."

"You need to escort Catherine home. What if they follow your carriage?"

Daniel appeared torn, but he finally nodded. "I'll send word to your brother about the attack."

With a nod, Robert left them.

❧ 12 ☙

Thus it is that in war the victorious strategist only seeks battle after the victory has been won, whereas he who is destined to defeat first fights and afterwards looks for victory.

— *SUN TZU*

R obert entered Lady Wilmot's ballroom and spied his hostess and her daughter, Lady Elizabeth, standing along the back wall. The dowager countess loved holding events in her home. She selected her guests with care, only sending invitations to those people she found interesting or entertaining. On Robert's first visit, he'd unknowingly earned a permanent spot by singing Santa Lucia .

Lady Wilmot dragged her attention away from the perfor-mance on the makeshift stage and furrowed her brow at him as he approached. As soon as she recognized him, her mildly annoyed expression disappeared, and she seemed delighted to see him.

"I didn't think I'd see you tonight," she murmured. "Welcome." She glanced at the stage. "They've only just begun. I've always admired this acting troupe." She motioned for him to take a vacant chair and then returned to her daughter's side.

Robert nodded to Lady Wilmot's daughter Lady Elizabeth as she removed one of her glittering earbobs. Elizabeth nodded a greeting before returning her attention to the stage, rubbing at her earlobe. Perhaps her earbob had been clipped on too tightly. Elizabeth tended to fidget, always adjusting her jewelry or twirling one of her locks of curly black hair.

Despite Elizabeth's close friendship with Catherine, the two women were quite different. Where Catherine was calm, Elizabeth was dramatic.

Except—Catherine had that surprising expertise with the knife. That was decidedly dramatic. Intriguing as well.

On stage, Miss Winter fluttered a fan and batted her eyes, and Robert heard a number of audience members chuckle in response. He might not be able to follow the plot, but clearly Miss Winter had captured everyone's attention.

It only took a moment for Robert to become engrossed in the performance. The timing was precise as the actors quickly entered and exited the stage. Everyone kept barely missing one another as they searched for the character Miss Winter played. She managed to hide in plain sight by changing into boy's clothes, and no one recognized her. She laughed with the audience as she sent each of the other actors off on a wild goose chase.

Once the scene ended, Lady Wilmot's guests burst into exuberant applause. Miss Winter and the other members of her troupe made their bows and disappeared behind the curtain.

A moment later, one of the other actors stepped in front of the curtain. "Thank you for your kind ovation. You nourish our spirits with such generous favor. Once we've changed out of our costumes, we'll join you in the refreshment area, where Lady Wilmot will provide nourishment for our bodies as well."

Robert exited through an ornate side door and followed his

nose until he found tables laden with a variety of delicious-smelling delicacies. A glowing ice sculpture of a phoenix rising from the flames perched in the center. It appeared to be illuminated from below with a reddish glow. A lamp of some sort? How had they managed to do that without melting the ice? Or setting the table on fire?

He suddenly realized he was famished. Based on the crush of people surrounding the tables, many guests felt similar hunger pangs. It only took a few moments to fill his plate with some choice morsels, including some rather appetizing-looking shrimp. He bit into one, mentally apologizing to it for having maligned one of its brethren earlier that evening.

He glanced up and noticed that most of the actors had arrived while he'd been preoccupied. Scanning the room, Robert searched for the diminutive Miss Winter. Movement near a door leading to the rear garden caught his attention and he recognized the little actress, now dressed in a pale-pink gown. A man wearing evening clothes disappeared through the doorway, and she followed him into the night.

Just that fast, they were both gone.

Blast it. How could he have let food distract him? He was terrible at being a spy. Frederick was much better at this sort of skullduggery.

Although Robert hadn't caught a glimpse of the man's face, something about him set off mental alarm bells. The assignation must be important, otherwise she'd never have left with him.

He thrust his plate into the hands of a passing footman and hurried after them.

His feet clattered on the cold paving stones as he stepped into the courtyard and peered into the darkness. A cluster of wrought-iron chairs and a low table were all that greeted him. Miss Winter and her companion were gone.

How could they disappear so quickly? After all, the moon

shined brightly tonight—Miss Winter's pale-pink gown should have been obvious.

Since he could rule out supernatural involvement, he made the logical conclusion that they'd slipped back inside the house through another door.

Robert crept closer to the next entrance, treading softly on the pavers so his leather-soled shoes didn't betray him. In the near silence, the only sound came from the rustle of his clothing and the chaffing of tree branches.

He stopped next to the door and pressed his body against the brick wall as he listened intently.

There it was—the low rumble of a man's voice followed by a woman's soft reply.

Robert leaned closer and risked glancing inside. The heavy curtains covering the door were open. However, a sheer fabric panel partially obscured his view. Even so, he spotted movement as an item passed from her hands to his.

It had to be the church register. He moved closer for a better view, and the couple sprang apart as though caught in some illicit act.

They'd spotted him.

The pair banged through the room, no longer attempting to remain silent as they rushed toward the interior door—their only escape.

"Damn." Robert yanked open the exterior door. The billowing fabric of the sheer curtain wafted outside, along with a gust of warm air. As he pushed his way through, the curtain wrapped around his sleeve. He came close to yanking the supporting rod from the wall as he untangled himself. By the time he broke free, he was alone.

He'd lost them.

Robert stumbled through the room. He needed to catch them. It had been Miss Winter. He was certain of it. He'd recognized her pale-pink dress and the way she moved, even if he hadn't seen her face. But who was the man?

By the time Robert reached the hallway, it was empty. He sprinted down the corridor and through the doorway at the end, only to find himself back in the refreshment area.

He quickly composed his features and raked his fingers through his hair. Not five feet in front of him stood Miss Winter, speaking with Lady Wilmot and Elizabeth. The book was nowhere in sight.

Robert took a quick side-step and ducked away before Miss Winter spotted him. He scanned the nearby guests, but couldn't identify the man she'd met. He sighed. Why couldn't things be easier? Who had the blasted book? Every man in the room was dressed nearly identically, and not one of them was brandishing a church register.

"Marvelous. Simply marvelous," Lady Wilmot said to Miss Winter. "I couldn't have been more pleased."

Elizabeth nodded her agreement, her ebony curls bouncing enthusiastically.

The pair turned their attention to the next guest, and Miss Winter took the opportunity to move toward the buffet table, seemingly oblivious to Robert's presence. He'd never locate that book without her help. He closed in behind her, intent on bringing down his prey. He only needed a few minutes alone with her—

She'd only taken a couple of steps when two young women moved to block her path. They were both taller than Miss Winter, and at first they pretended not to see her despite their obvious tactics to intercept her. One of the women wore a dismal-looking pale-pink gown. Its skirts had the smaller silhouette that had been in fashion two seasons ago. The other woman's pale-yellow gown made her resemble an anemic daffodil. The green ribbons trimming the dress only served to accentuate the effect.

Frustrated, Robert eased to one side so he could pounce the moment the pair moved on.

"All that running around on stage seemed quite foolish," Pinky said. She pitched her bored voice so everyone nearby could hear her. "I can't imagine why Mother insisted upon coming here tonight to see it."

"Perhaps she wanted us to see how far the mighty had fallen," Daffodil replied with a smirk as she raked her gaze over Miss Winter.

The actress couldn't fail to register their comments, but she proceeded to skirt past the pair as though oblivious to their presence.

"Oh my, speaking of whom," Pinky said, "here's the infamous Miss Winter." As she turned her narrowed gaze toward her target, the sharp edge of her smile could have drawn blood. "I didn't expect to find you here on display with the rest of the performers. I'd assumed you'd want to leave. It must be so difficult for you to perform at a function you formerly might have hoped to attend."

Robert tensed. What was this?

The line of Miss Winter's mouth tightened as she stopped to face the woman, but she gave no other sign that the barb had hit home. "Good evening, Miss Binford. What a surprise." Her gaze raked over the outdated gown. "I hadn't supposed I'd see you here this evening either."

Pinky—or rather, Miss Binford—gaped. "What?"

Daffodil stepped forward. "How dare you, of all people, suggest that my dear friend doesn't belong here? Her circumstances are not your concern. You overstep yourself."

Miss Winter looked confused, but when she replied, she addressed Miss Binford. "I'm sorry I offended you. It would be inexcusably rude of me to comment on your family's straits. Even obliquely. You can't imagine I'd stoop to such gauche behavior. It's just that you've frequently mentioned your distaste for the theater, so naturally one would assume—but forgive me."

He wanted to applaud her. Well done.

Miss Binford's face flushed a shade darker than her dress. "Your words suggest you believe you possess a certain intimacy with me which I find unacceptable. I never should have spoken to someone of your status, and rest assured, it won't happen again." She spun on her heel and hurried away, her daffodil-dressed friend following closely behind.

A titter of laughter erupted as a swirl of pale-green satin in the form of Lady Lydia swung to a stop in front of Miss Winter. Many people found Lydia's barbed comments entertaining, but Robert wasn't among them. Unfortunately, he doubted Miss Winter would either. Terrifying might be a more apt word from the victim's point of view, and he had no doubt that Miss Winter had become a tempting target. Lydia's nose for scandal frequently turned even the smallest infraction into a shocking scene.

Lydia tapped her fingers against the furled fan she held as she contemplated the actress. "That was quite the set-down." She flicked her fan open and examined it in a studied manner. "Am I to gather you're well acquainted with Miss Binford?"

Miss Winter swallowed. "As I'm sure you must have overheard, Miss Binford does not count me among her acquaintances."

Lady Lydia smiled in a crafty way as she met Miss Winter's eyes. "That's rather uncharitable of her. After all, you're from the same town, are you not? Maidenhead?"

Miss Winter didn't hide her stunned expression quickly enough. Robert felt stunned as well. He knew a Squire Winter in Maidenhead. Was it possible? Could she be—

"That's what I thought. And you used to be a gentleman's daughter, but now you're not. Is that right?"

"Used to be?" Miss Winter asked, uttering Robert's thoughts as she raised her chin. What did Lydia mean by that comment?

Robert held his breath. In the portentous pause, Lady Lydia appeared to savor the moment. He dreaded witnessing the sharp slice of her vicious tongue he knew was forthcoming. She wouldn't be able to resist attacking such a vulnerable target. It wasn't in her nature to be merciful. Despite his anger toward Miss Winter, listening to her being eviscerated by Lady Lydia would be a decidedly unpleasant experience. Should he intervene, or would that cause him to risk too much? Perhaps he should remain hidden and follow her.

But this was Lydia.

Damn. He had no real choice. He'd have to intervene.

He took two steps toward her, only to be shouldered to one side by a brusque young man.

"Miss Winter." The boorish man stopped directly in front of her, smiling broadly and wholly unaware he'd placed himself between the two sparring women.

Startled by the turn of events, Robert eased back, curious to see how events would now unfold.

Perhaps it was Robert's movement, perhaps something else, but Miss Winter glanced in his direction. Catching sight of him, her gaze first flickered with confusion and then recognition. As her eyes locked on his, she went pale.

He had to admire her aplomb when she turned away from him and smiled up at the brash young man.

13

The aim of art is to represent not the outward appearance of things, but their inward significance.

— ARISTOTLE

Antonia's mouth went dry at the sight of Lord Wentworth, but her head swirled as she felt his pull of attraction.

He must have been the man she thought she'd seen peering through the window. Did he know she'd passed along the book? Probably not, or he wouldn't be looking at her this way. He'd be cornering the man who had it and trying to take it by force.

She glanced up at the young man who'd stepped between her and Lady Lydia.

"Mister Yarrow," Lady Lydia said from behind him, "apparently this will come as a surprise to you, but you happen to make an abysmally poor window."

Antonia had to force herself not to smile at the look of astonishment on the young man's face as he spun to one side and blinked at Lady Lydia.

"I beg your pardon, but you must have me confused with someone else. I have never put my hand to the task of building a window." He glanced from Antonia to Lady Lydia and back again.

Antonia sifted through her options. What would Lord Wentworth do? Would he make a scene? Try to drag her away by force? Waylay her at the end of the evening?

Lady Lydia gave the young man a flat stare. "No, Mister Yarrow, I'm quite certain you haven't. Apparently I must speak more simply to you." She snapped her fan shut and then tapped it against the gloved palm of her hand. "I was referring to the fact that your figure is not made of a transparent substance such as a window pane. I assumed when you stood directly in front of me, you must have been under the impression that you were made of glass and thus would not interfere with my conversation with Miss Winter."

The young man's mouth opened, closed, and then opened again, but he didn't utter a word as his face turned a rather florid shade.

"It appears you've been struck dumb," Lady Lydia said as she flicked her fan back open. "Which I count as a distinct improvement."

"Ex-excuse me, Lady Lydia." Mister Yarrow fumbled as he reached for her hand in a clumsy attempt to apologize.

Lady Lydia furled her fan and rapped the back of his hand with it, causing him to yelp in pain.

Antonia's eyes went wide.

Lord Wentworth was stalking across the room directly toward her.

"Miss Winter," he said, taking her hand and lifting it to his lips.

He pressed a soft kiss against her skin, just above the spot where her glove ended. A shiver cascaded down her spine.

"I must compliment you on a superb performance," he murmured. "You were quite lovely when disguised as a young boy, and surprisingly believable. I would never have guessed you could fool me so easily."

She recalled her deception at the embassy and blushed.

Lady Lydia let out a snort of disdain. "She's fooled many over the years. Ask her about her parents." She turned on her heel and stalked away.

The sting of Lydia's sharp tongue left Antonia speechless for a moment. Even after a year, words could still wound her. She needed to pull herself together. She inhaled sharply and then gave Lord Wentworth one of her most brilliant smiles. "Thank you for your generous praise. I always enjoy that particular role. It isn't often I have the opportunity to dress as a boy."

"Your character in Anne Blake was such a sweet, innocent young girl. Quite different from this one."

Her smile faltered.

"I saw it tonight. I was relieved when I heard you'd be able to take the stage. Imagine my disappointment if I hadn't caught you tonight."

She opened her mouth and then closed it again. "How did you find me?"

He gave her a slow, easy smile. "When I saw the show poster with your image, I found I couldn't resist coming to see you."

"The posters." She closed her eyes and let out a soft sigh of frustration. "I'd forgotten about them."

"Miss Winter." Another young man stepped forward, intent on speaking with her. "You were charming tonight."

A crowd of waiting admirers surged forward. Lord Wentworth caught her eye as he leaned closer to her. Having him so close overwhelmed her senses. "We'll speak more later," he murmured into her ear before stepping away.

It took a moment for her to recognize the import of his words. He planned to follow her tonight when she left.

Not if she had anything to say about it.

14

Life seems but a quick succession of busy nothings.

— *JANE AUSTEN*

Now that he'd found her, he didn't plan to lose her.

"That was an entertaining moment," Lady Elizabeth said from right next to him.

Robert spun to face her and quickly reviewed every word he'd just spoken. He'd said nothing that would have given him away, he was certain of it, but even so, Elizabeth's eyes danced with suppressed laughter.

"I wondered if I might need to intervene on Miss Winter's behalf and protect her from Lady Lydia," she said, "but when first Mr. Yarrow and then you stepped in, I decided my efforts weren't necessary."

Robert relaxed. She'd been referring to the scene with Lady Lydia and Mr. Yarrow, not to his reaction to Miss Winter. "I believe poor Mr. Yarrow is the one most in need of your sympathy."

"It's no more that he deserved. The man simply must learn some manners." She tilted her head to one side as she tugged on her ear. "Lady Lydia gave him the dressing-down we've all wanted to since the start of the season."

"Are you saying she did something beneficial?"

Elizabeth grinned. "In a way. The others have been more subtle in their set downs, but perhaps her more direct method has its merits."

"You are perhaps the only woman I've heard who has had anything positive to say about Lady Lydia."

Lady Elizabeth glanced across the room, and Robert followed her gaze to Lady Lydia. "I think there's more to her than she reveals. Much more."

"Catherine claims you notice things others miss."

"That's kind of her. She's such a staunch-hearted friend." Her eyes glittered mischievously. "Would you like an example of my powers of observation?" She raised an eyebrow.

He nodded. "By all means."

"You've hardly taken your eyes off Miss Winter tonight. She disappeared shortly after entering the ballroom, as did you. Were you having an assignation?"

Robert found himself shaking his head even before he decided to reply. "I can assure you, we weren't together." He peered at Elizabeth with curiosity. "Apparently Catherine's right. You are unusually observant."

"That last part was simply a guess. I wanted to eliminate the possibility from my speculations. I doubt anyone else would have surmised the same thing," she said, giving his forearm a reassuring pat. "I must admit, however, you've piqued my curiosity. I do believe you find her attractive, but you appear to be analyzing her rather than simply admiring her. I wager your interest isn't purely romantic, is it?"

The woman was uncanny. "Perhaps," he said, hoping his enigmatic answer would keep her from asking more questions.

Her eyes glinted. He'd managed to intrigue her rather than put her off with his answer.

Perhaps he should be slightly more direct. "I hope you'll understand my discretion."

"Oh? I suppose discretion is an admirable quality," she said, her lower lip jutting out in a small pout. "Miss Winter has had a tragic year. I wouldn't dream of adding to her burdens."

That caught his attention. "What—"

"Good evening, Lord Wentworth," Lady Wilmot said. "I do hope you won't mind if I steal my daughter away from you for a moment. I so want to introduce her to Lord Cary."

Robert glanced around the room until he spotted the venerable gentleman. Surely Lady Wilmot couldn't be considering the man as a match for her daughter, could she? He must be fifty. As he glanced back down at Lady Wilmot, he noted a frisson of excitement emanating from her. Interesting. Of course, Lady Wilmot was probably only forty or so. Hardly elderly. Given that she'd been a widow for a few years now, perhaps her interest in the man was on her own behalf rather than her daughter's.

The pair swept away into the crowd, leaving Robert alone.

He checked on his quarry and quickly spotted Miss Winter. Her press of admirers made her easy to locate. He was surprised to find her staring at him.

Their gazes locked, and something passed between them. A realization stunned him. Miss Winter found him attractive.

She tensed and quickly glanced away, a faint blush rising in her cheeks. He stared at her for a moment longer, considering his effect on her, and then forced himself to look away. He wanted to go to her now—carry her away and kiss her—no! Question her! Although a kiss... well, it would be pleasant. Perhaps more than pleasant.

He reined in his errant thoughts. It wasn't as if he could throw her over his shoulder and haul her away, and he was certain she wouldn't willingly leave with him. No, he'd stay here, bide his time, chat with other guests, and pounce once she was alone.

A minute or two later, Monsieur LeCompte drifted his way. Robert became wary.

LeCompte could be extraordinarily entertaining and diverting as he shared the latest scandals, but he was the bane of anyone with a secret to keep. His direct questions were difficult to avoid, and his zeal in chasing down a morsel of gossip was akin to a ferret going down a rat hole. The man always seemed to know when someone had something to hide.

Robert forced himself not to glance at Miss Winter.

"*Bon soir.*" LeCompte's gaze swept him up and down, leaving him with the distinct impression that the man hadn't missed a single detail.

"*Bon soir,*" Robert replied with equal nonchalance.

"If you were trying to make a grand entrance this evening by arriving late, you missed your mark. Your audience had its attention focused on the stage."

Robert raised one eyebrow. "Except you, it would seem."

"You showed abysmally poor timing," LeCompte said flippantly. "How did you expect anyone to notice you once the actors took the stage? And why aren't you bothering to speak with any of the ladies in attendance? One might wonder why you decided to make an appearance at all."

"Might one?" Robert raised one eyebrow. "I hadn't thought anyone would take particular notice of me." He shifted to one side so he could watch Miss Winter over LeCompte's shoulder without the man being any the wiser.

"Me? Take notice of you? Perish the thought. Your comings and goings are less memorable to me than a good meal. Perhaps even less memorable than an average one. It's quite impossible for me to dwell upon anything of substance. I much prefer to speak of the inconsequential."

Robert couldn't help but smile at the Frenchman's inanities. An idea struck him. "I would have been here sooner," Robert said, "but a shrimp I ate wasn't willing to let me escape from its foul clutches unscathed." He glanced at Miss Winter. As she met his gaze, she glanced at LeCompte and tensed. Did she know about the man's penchant for gossip?

"Hmm." LeCompte peered at him intently. "Is that why you slipped out to the garden shortly after you entered the room? For some fresh air? You do look a bit pale this evening."

"Do I?" Robert asked, startled. It was a good thing he'd invented that shrimp tonight. It had helped him multiple times. Of course, his pale complexion could be explained by the fact that it was currently the dead of winter, but he wouldn't point that out to LeCompte. How was it that the Frenchman wasn't pale as well? "You're looking remarkably healthy."

He glanced over LeCompte's shoulder at Miss Winter and noticed her lips pressed in a thin line of worry.

Lady Wilmot paused to join them. "Good evening, gentlemen. I hope I'm not interrupting anything."

"You're interrupting nothing at all," Robert said, twitching one corner of his mouth. "Our conversation abounds with empty comments and observations."

"Of course we're discussing nothing," LeCompte said as though offended. "I quite excel at it. 'Nothing' is my *spécialité* ."

Robert chuckled. "My apologies. You transcend us with your abilities." He checked on Miss Winter again and noted her relaxed smile as she replied to one of her admirers. Whatever had troubled her must have resolved itself.

"You must allow me to contribute as well. Monsieur LeCompte," Lady Wilmot said, fixing her clear gaze on the man, "tell me about your trip to the southern coast of France. Was your sojourn there a pleasant one? Did you swim in the sea? Sail on one of those little boats?"

"*Mais oui*," LeCompte said. "I spent some time in Cannes, and then I visited my family in Paris for Christmas. My mother quite enjoyed my visit, as did I."

Hunger began gnawing at Robert, and he excused himself from the pair. He filled a plate from the buffet and found a place near the wall where he could eat. As he glanced back toward Miss Winter, he bit into a piece of bread. The crowd pressing around her had thinned slightly, and now he could see her profile quite clearly, as well as her small, shell-shaped ears. He'd never before thought of ears as being attractive, but the perfection of Miss Winter's drew his notice.

He finished his small meal more quickly than might be proper and set his empty plate on an abandoned table. He looked up just in time to see Miss Winter darting toward the door farthest from him.

She was trying to lose him.

Robert hurried to follow her, but a group of guests cut in front of him, blocking his path. He maneuvered his way through them, but by the time he could break free, Miss Winter had disappeared from view.

He rushed into the main foyer. A few guests were departing, but he couldn't see her anywhere.

Elizabeth strode toward him. "By any chance, are you searching for Miss Winter?"

Robert narrowed his eyes. "And if I am?"

She smiled conspiratorially. "She left in a hurry and used the servants' entrance. If you make haste, you should be able to catch her."

"Thank you," Robert said, and darted to the cloakroom to retrieve his cloak and cane. He trotted down the front steps and scanned the street.

Could that be her in the distance? On foot?

Blast. It *was* her.

Robert strode after the small woman as quickly as he dared. He didn't want to draw the attention of the other departing guests by breaking into a run. With his luck, LeCompte would be watching. He didn't want to become the butt of every joke for the next week because he'd been seen chasing after an actress.

His cane beat time with his footsteps as it clicked against the paving stones.

She wouldn't escape him. Not again.

15

Do not be too moral. You may cheat yourself out of much life so. Aim above morality. Be not simply good; be good for something.

— *HENRY DAVID THOREAU*

Thick fog swallowed Antonia's boots and the hem of her dress as she approached a cross street. Sound traveled unusually well, and from a half-block behind her came the echoes of the rhythmic click of a metal-tipped cane striking the paving stones.

She'd first become aware of the sound not long after she'd left Lady Wilmot's residence. It continued to pursue her with every turn she made. She'd glanced back and caught sight of a man wearing a black cloak, but his features were indistinguishable beneath his top hat.

Lord Wentworth must be following her. There was no other explanation.

She ducked down the next side street, hoping to lose him.

She tried to silence her footsteps as she strained her ears. She was about halfway down the narrower street when the sound of metal clicking against stone changed and became more resonant as it reverberated along the buildings. That could mean only one thing. Lord Wentworth had turned onto the narrow street as well.

She should have remained with her troupe, that much was obvious. At the very least, she should have asked a servant to secure a hackney. But when she'd seen her chance to escape, she'd grabbed it.

Of course, there was always the possibility that someone other than Lord Wentworth followed her. After all, her pursuer carried a cane. She certainly would have recalled seeing one in his lordship's hand. Did that mean he wasn't the man stalking her? But if not him, who could it be? Could it be someone from the Russian embassy? A random assailant?

Antonia's chest tightened as panic squeezed at her, and she tried to take a deep, calming breath to fend it off.

It didn't help.

Beating a hasty retreat from the soirée had been foolish, but now, as she began to take stock of her surroundings, she realized she'd made yet another terrible error.

She couldn't have chosen a worse place to walk alone.

Her gaze skittered across the damp brick walls. The tall buildings blocked any breeze that might ease the stench of rotting refuse in the narrow street. The heavy, stagnant fog hid many unpleasant things from sight. She heard skittering movements and tried not to imagine the size of the vermin concealed in the miasma.

She glanced up at the shuttered windows above her and then moved closer to the center of the street. Based on the smell, she suspected that a few of the residents might be illegally emptying chamber pots out the windows, and she didn't want to end up with something quite disgusting plummeting down upon her head.

A door opened ahead of her, and a burst of noise and conversation broke the quiet of the night. It was abruptly cut off as the door closed again, but gruff voices continued to echo off the tightly packed buildings.

Drunk and boisterous voices.

Judging by the sound, the men were heading in her direction. Her predicament was about to become much, much worse.

Antonia glanced around, but found no refuge. She could hear her pursuer's cane clicking steadily away at the cobblestones in time with his measured steps.

Antonia's stomach tensed. Which way should she go? Which threat presented the greatest danger? Should she fear the man steadily pursuing her, or the random group of drunken strangers?

She glanced forward again and saw the shapes of two men breaking through the fog. She'd waited too long to hide. If she could see them, surely they could see her as well.

Her only choice was to continue along the narrow street and exhibit confidence she didn't really possess. Fortunately, the men couldn't hear her heart thudding as though she'd been running down the street rather than walking. Only she knew of her growing terror.

Wait. She had her blade. How had she forgotten about it? Antonia leaned over to pluck it from her boot.

"What have we here?" one of the men called out. "Looking for someone to keep you warm tonight, are ye, love?"

The man's words caused Antonia to stumble as she stood back up clutching her knife. Her hand trembled, so she tightened her grip.

Antonia kept moving without offering a reply, hoping that he'd take her silence as a rejection of his advances. The sooner she made it to the end of this street, the better.

"Who are you talking to?" a second man shouted.

"This little doxy. She looks chilled to the bone to my eye."

Antonia felt bile rise in her throat when she realized he assumed her to be a prostitute.

The two men stopped as they watched her approach. Still, she kept marching forward, ignoring their comments.

"She ain't no doxy. Look at her. She's a lady."

"Of course she's a doxy. Why else would she be out here alone?" the first man said as she skirted around him, keeping him on her left side. His hand darted out and grabbed her upper arm, his fingers so tight they pinched deep into her muscle.

Antonia spun to face him, jerking her arm from his grasp while raising her knife for the men to see.

"Be careful, Timms," the second man said. "She has claws."

From behind her, Antonia heard the sound of someone running toward them, but she couldn't see him. It had to be her pursuer. The man with the cane.

"Your friend has the right idea," Lord Wentworth called out. "You don't want to go bothering the young lady."

Relief washed through her as she registered that it was Lord Wentworth. She recognized his voice even if she couldn't see him.

Her heart swelled. He wanted to defend her—even after she'd betrayed him. She'd always thought of him as the consummate gentleman. Generous, kindhearted, helpful—

Right up to the moment she'd turned on him.

The two men stood shoulder to shoulder as they turned toward the sound of his voice.

Antonia scooted closer to one of the alley walls, but the first man, Timms, saw her move and darted forward to grab her arm again, squeezing it even tighter this time.

"Where do you think yer goin'?" Timms asked as he leered down at her. The ale he'd been drinking made his breath sour as he exhaled into her face.

Antonia raised her knife and jabbed it toward him, hoping to force him to let her go. He made a grab at it and missed, and Antonia managed to slice open his finger.

Timms maintained his iron grip on her upper arm. Antonia knew his fingers were leaving a deep, painful bruise. One that would last for days.

If she lived that long.

Lord Wentworth's lean, black-clad figure broke through the fog, and his cloak billowed open. He seemed large and menacing as he came to a halt and took in the scene, narrowing his eyes as he lifted his cane horizontally across his body. He grabbed the shaft with his free hand and, with a twist, extracted a long sword from it. He dropped the now-empty sheath to the ground with a clatter.

Every inch of Lord Wentworth exuded danger. How could this be the same dashing man she'd dreamed about for years? If he'd appeared to her this way at the embassy, she never would have dared steal the book from him. Not even to save her life.

The drunkard pushed her away and Antonia lost her balance, stumbling back.

She righted herself and whirled to face her attacker, but he and his companion were focused entirely on Lord Wentworth. Their eyes were wide as they stepped back from him in unison.

"Sorry, sir. We didn't know she was yours," Timms said, holding his empty hands up as he eyed Wentworth. Blood trickled down his palm. "We was just tryin' ta be friendly."

"I take exception to every word you just uttered. The young lady is not mine. But neither is she yours. Nor am I the one to whom you owe an apology."

"No, sir. Sorry, sir," Timms stammered. But at seeing Lord Wentworth's thunderous expression, his face paled and he turned to glance at her. "I mean, sorry, miss."

Antonia waved her hand dismissively but edged a bit closer to Lord Wentworth.

"The two of you should leave," Lord Wentworth said, his gaze fixed on Timms.

The pair stayed frozen to the spot.

"Now!" He slashed his sword in an arc.

In a sudden flurry of movement, they scrambled backward, and both men turned and ran back the way they'd come, desperate to get as far as possible from the tip of Lord Wentworth's sword. They disappeared into the fog, but Antonia didn't move until the echoing sound of their running feet faded into the distance.

She listened so intently to the disappearing footfalls that the sound of metal sliding against metal from right next to her made her jump and turn in fright. Lord Wentworth stood inches away as he slid his sword the rest of the way into its sheath, transforming it back into a nondescript black cane.

"You saved me. Why did you do that?"

He seemed surprised by her question. He shook his head. "It's a mystery to me. I need the book." He held his hand out. "Give it to me."

She shook her head and stepped out of his reach, eying his false cane. "I can't."

"Of course you can. You just don't want to."

"No, really. I can't," she said, taking another step back. "I don't have it. I gave it to someone else for safekeeping."

He didn't look surprised. Instead, he looked determined as he took a step closer to her and dropped his hand to his side. "Then we'll go retrieve it."

"That's impossible."

Wentworth sighed and closed his eyes for a moment. When he opened them, he seemed calmer. He cast an assessing gaze along the dingy alleyway. "I don't want to stand here with you and argue. The stench is appalling. I'll escort you home and we can talk along the way. I'm sure we can find a hackney once we're on a main road again." He offered his arm, just as any gentleman would for any lady.

Just as he had in her many fantasies of him over the past five years.

She stared at his arm.

Something inside her heart broke at that simple gesture. Why, after such a horrible night, should that small sign of respect pierce her so?

Her hand trembled as she reached out to wrap it around his proffered arm. It was such an inconsequential, gentlemanly thing for him to do, but it symbolized everything she'd lost over the past year.

He must have noticed her hand shake, because his arm tensed and then he pulled her closer to him. "You're safe with me," he said in a gruff tone. "I won't harm you."

Antonia chided herself. This wasn't her fantasy. This was reality. And in this reality, Lord Wentworth expected fear from her. He wasn't her knight in shining armor. He was her adversary.

At least he hadn't guessed the real reason she trembled. Having him know the truth would be much, much worse. Because then he might pity her, and his pity had the power to wound her more deeply than his sword ever could.

As they moved down the alleyway, the warmth of Lord Wentworth's body began to seep into her. That felt wonderful. At least she didn't need to feel guilty about stealing his body heat. She wished she could turn her face into his shoulder to avoid the stench of the refuse, but he'd probably think her mad. What kind of woman sniffed a man?

As they exited the narrow alleyway and turned onto a much broader and cleaner street, Antonia realized she still clutched the knife in her hand. She tried to tuck it one-handed into the pocket of her cloak, but fumbled.

Lord Wentworth must have noticed the movement, because he stopped abruptly and glared at the weapon. "What is it with women and knives tonight?" He sounded exasperated.

"My lord?"

"Nothing," he said, shaking his head. "Just put it away."

She paused, wondering if he'd elaborate on his cryptic

comment. When he didn't, she tucked the knife into her pocket and then fell in step with him as he continued down the sidewalk.

There were streetlamps along this particular road, and as they passed beneath one, she glanced up at his profile. "I want to thank you."

He looked down at her and attempted to smile, but his lips only pressed into a thin line. "For which part of the night? Saving you from those two men? Intervening with Lady Lydia? Or perhaps you want to thank me for stealing the church register from the ambassador's desk so you could take it from me?"

She blushed at this and glanced away. "I'm aware my apology is no consolation, but I am sorry I locked you in that room."

"I should hold you accountable for that, but I'm feeling magnanimous. After all, I willingly Alli wed you to pull me in there. It's unfortunate what transpired next wasn't what I'd hoped." The smile that curved his lips sent tingles of awareness down her spine.

She stared at his mouth as heat rose in her face and her stomach fluttered. She recalled the strength and contours of his body as she'd pressed against him in that bedroom. Would his taste have been as delicious as his touch? She'd nearly known the answer to that. She'd barely resisted stealing a kiss from him along with the book. Perhaps she should have taken one as her prize. She licked her lips and couldn't drag her eyes away from him. "I'm sorry I tricked you, my lord."

"'My lord—' that seems so formal. You must call me Robert. After all, we thieves should be on a first-name basis, don't you agree?"

She arched her eyebrows. "You're stepping outside the boundaries of propriety with that request. I'm nothing but a lowly actress."

"There's nothing lowly about you," he said, his voice a deep rumble that made her toes curl. He leaned closer as he murmured in her ear, "You'll find I'm quite shocking at times. My family's grown to expect it."

His breath brushed against her neck, warming it in an intimate way. Lord, but this man overwhelmed her.

Antonia pulled away, not wanting him to see how much he affected her. She shouldn't let him move her so deeply. After all, they weren't even friends.

They were adversaries—a fact she needed to remember.

❧ 16 ❧

Let every eye negotiate for itself and trust no agent.

— WILLIAM SHAKESPEARE

◈

Robert glanced back at the sound of a carriage approaching behind them and spied a hackney. He hailed it, and soon he'd bundled her inside it and claimed the seat next to her.

"Where to?" the driver asked.

Robert shot her a questioning glance.

Antonia let out a heavy sigh, glared at Robert, and gave the man her address.

The hackney was a small one. The narrow seat gave him little room, and as the horse began moving, Antonia shifted sideways, her shoulder pressing against his.

"I need the book," he said.

"And I can't give it to you."

He let out a sigh of frustration. "Are we at an impasse so quickly?"

"What did you expect? Only one of us can have the thing we both want."

"I watched you all night. You passed it to someone immediately after the performance, didn't you?"

"That *was* you outside the window. I thought as much."

"If I thought you had it now, I'd take it from you."

"I know."

"At this point, I need you. You're the only person I can find who knows where it is."

She held her breath for a moment. "What do you plan to do about that?" she whispered.

"I'm hoping I can convince you to tell me who has it." In the darkness, her copper eyes were barely discernible, but he could still make them out as she returned his gaze. He tilted his head down, breathing in her scent. "What would it take for you to reveal his name?" He grazed his lips against hers in the promise of a kiss. The temptation of one.

She gasped, and her lips softened.

Then she pulled away.

"More than that, Lord Wentworth," she said, her voice tart.

He smiled as he leaned back. "You must call me Robert. Don't forget."

"Don't think you'll seduce that book out from under me. It won't work."

A slow, seductive smile spread across his face. "Won't it?"

"Absolutely not."

The carriage came to a stop, and Antonia glanced out the window. "We're here," she said pertly.

She moved toward the door, but couldn't move far. Robert realized he was sitting on her cloak. He'd need to get up to release her.

She glared at him. "After you."

He grinned, opened the door, exited the hackney, and then lifted her down to stand beside him.

He glanced up at her rooming house as they approached the door. "Is this where most of the actresses from Haymarket Theatre live?" He glanced up and down the foggy residential street, but could see very little.

She shook her head. "Most of the others either live with their families or share rooms. My sisters aren't in a position to have me live with them, but I still need a place where they can come visit me, so I chose to live here. Mrs. Hill runs a respectable boardinghouse."

"You have a family then?"

"Of course," she said, furrowing her brows as she shot him a frown. "Or did you think they grew actresses in a garden?"

"Touchy."

"Tired," she said with a sigh. She placed her hand on the doorknob. "There's nothing more we can do tonight. I'm too tired, and I can't conjure the book out of thin air." She sighed and rubbed her eyes with her thumb and forefinger. "You know where I live. Come speak to me tomorrow. We can go to the tea room down the street."

"How do I know you won't disappear—pardon the expression —like a thief in the night?"

"It crossed my mind, but I'm not willing to give up my role in Anne Blake , so at least until the show ends, it appears I won't be able to avoid you."

She turned back toward the door again, but he wrapped her hand in his, stopping her. She paused to look up at him. In the darkness, she couldn't see his face very well.

"Stay safe. Promise me you won't wander off alone again the way you did tonight." He let go of her hand and brushed his finger across her cheek, tucking a strand of hair behind her ear. "There are dangers lurking in the dark."

17

The only secrets are the secrets that keep themselves.

— GEORGE BERNARD SHAW

A ntonia's cheek tingled from Robert's touch as he turned and trotted down the steps, leaving her standing on the front stoop.

A sudden wave of loneliness nearly overwhelmed her as she slipped inside her boardinghouse and closed the door firmly behind her. She leaned her forehead against the solid wood for a moment, closing her eyes.

She was tired, and only now did she allow herself to notice the deep bruise where that drunkard had grabbed her. There were, indeed, dangers in the dark.

She moved to the small window next to the door, pressing her nose against the cool glass. She could barely make out Robert as he climbed into the hackney. A moment later, the carriage lurched away.

Perhaps meeting Lord Wentworth—Robert—had been fate.

She certainly hoped not. She straightened her spine and turned her back to the door.

Of late, fate hadn't been treating her kindly. If Robert was a part of some grand destiny, things couldn't possibly end well.

Antonia moved toward the stairs. The soothing tick-tock sounds from Mrs. Hill's longcase clock seemed to fill the small foyer. Mrs. Hill had mentioned that it had been a favorite of her late husband's, and although she claimed not to like it, she kept it wound and oiled.

Could it really be three in the morning? Weariness wrapped itself around her like a heavy blanket.

Next to the entrance, a collection of dry umbrellas sat neatly furled in the elephant-foot umbrella stand, and Antonia spotted a cane tucked in amongst them. Before tonight, she'd never realized a gentleman's cane might conceal something else. Could this one hold some secret compartment or weapon, just like Robert's? She picked it up and measured its weight in her hand. It seemed perfectly ordinary.

She twirled the cane as she let her thoughts drift. Robert was far from ordinary, especially when compared with most gentry she'd met.

That near-kiss had nearly undone her. Even now, the memory of it made her tremble. To almost kiss him twice in one night— after dreaming of it for so long—left her weak and confused.

She'd first seen him five years ago when he'd come to Father's rescue. At the time, she knew Father had been deeply worried about money he'd lost in a business venture. She'd overheard her parents discussing her dowry, and Father mentioned he was afraid his mistake would jeopardize her marriage prospects.

But everything changed after Lord Wentworth's visit. Antonia had been fifteen at the time. She'd been upstairs with her sisters, and when Mother came rushing in, shushing Evangeline, Antonia had been stunned to learn an earl was downstairs at that very moment, speaking with Father in his study. Despite Mother's sharp eye, Antonia had managed to slip away and spy on him as he was leaving.

She'd expected someone old and wizened, but the man she saw leaving Father's study was young, and handsome as sin. His broad shoulders, dark, wavy hair, and piercing blue eyes were all delicious attributes, but his air of sadness made her arms ache to comfort him.

She'd only glimpsed him and knew better than to let him discover her. The moment he was gone, she darted out of her hiding spot to press her nose against the window as he drove away in his sumptuous carriage.

Father came up behind her and put his hands on her shoulders. "There goes an impressive young man. He isn't at all what I would have expected. He's quite different from his—" He glanced down at Antonia's upturned face. "That young man just managed to save me from my own folly. I'll be forever in his debt."

"What did he do?"

Father smiled. "He restored your dowry. Yours and your sisters'. But he went to great lengths to pretend the money wasn't from him. He doesn't want any thanks."

Now, Antonia tightened her grip on the cane. If that dowry were still hers—but no. It was gone now.

With a sigh, she turned her attention back to the cane and grasped the pistol-grip handle to examine it. No catches. No release mechanisms. Just an ordinary cane. How perfectly boring.

She recalled the way Robert's icy blue eyes had swept over her when he'd first seen her at the ambassador's ball. He'd been interested. Attracted.

Just as she was attracted to him.

Antonia frowned, irritated with the direction of her thoughts. She needed to banish them, and quickly, before they took root and kept her awake all night.

Robert's kindness would evaporate once he discovered how society viewed her.

As nothing but a nameless bastard.

Antonia shoved the cane back into the umbrella stand and turned toward the staircase. She passed the sliding door leading to the dining room. It was the public space all the residents were welcome to use. As she glanced toward it, she noticed that the dark oak pocket doors weren't closed all the way. There was a gap of about an inch between them.

Something moved behind that gap, and Antonia froze. She held her breath to listen. Was someone watching her? She stared at the opening. Had she imagined it?

One of the double doors slid open with a rattle, causing Antonia to stumble back. She was startled, yes, but she wasn't at all surprised when her landlady, Mrs. Hill, revealed herself.

The older woman wore a dark-green robe over her white nightclothes, and her gray eyebrows were drawn together in a way that etched her frown even deeper her face. "What do you mean by bringing some man back here? You know the rules."

Antonia stiffened her back. "I didn't bring some man back, as you so uncharitably put it. A gentleman escorted me to the door to ensure my safety."

Mrs. Hill snorted. One of her graying curls escaped its hairpin and flopped over her eye, like a loose spring from a broken clock. "Some rich bloke, I'll wager. My sister might have vouched for you so I'd let you stay here, but don't think that grants you any special treatment. I know what your kind are like, coming home at such late hours. Actresses." She pursed her lips as though she were about to spit, but then thought better of it and resorted to glaring at Antonia. "I happen to know your play ended almost three hours ago. You were off trysting with that man. Don't try to deny it. I know your type. You're all born liars. That's what makes you perfect for the stage."

Antonia took a breath and counted to five before speaking,

but the technique did little to quell her anger. "I owe you no explanation, but I'll give it this one time. My troupe had an engagement to perform a scene at Lady Wilmot's residence this evening. I have no doubt that it will be mentioned in tomorrow's newspapers. If you don't believe me, you can read all about it in the morning. Even though I doubt I'll receive an apology from you, I hope you'll remember to hold your tongue in the future and not fling such baseless accusations."

Mrs. Hill pressed her lips into a thin line, causing her chin to pucker. "You've no right to speak to me that way."

"Nor do you. I pay for my room and board, and I follow your rules." Antonia glared at the woman for a moment, wanting to force her to—to what? Respect her? That didn't seem likely at this point. The woman's goodwill had always been tenuous at best, and of late it seemed to border on the nonexistent. If Antonia wanted to continue living here, she needed to remain on good terms with Mrs. Hill. After all, the landlady held all the power.

Antonia's temper immediately cooled. Reality tended to have that affect. If she wanted to live someplace where her sisters could visit without risking their reputations, then she needed to win over this narrow-minded dragon. Otherwise, she could end up searching for new accommodations.

She released a sigh of pent-up frustration. "I appreciate your kindness in renting a room to me. I truly do. But I wish you'd try to trust me. After all, your sister has known me for years and has vouched for me. I know right from wrong. She taught me well."

Mrs. Hill's frown deepened. "Why she wasted her life taking care of the likes of you, I'll never know. She should have stayed here, with her own family, and helped run this place." She glared at Antonia as though she were personally to blame for Miss Galloway's defection. "I'll be checking that newspaper in the morning, and if I find out you lied, you'll be out. Do you hear me? Out!" She spun on her heel and scuttled back into the dark dining room. She glared at Antonia as she slid the double doors closed with a bang, barely missing her own nose.

Antonia whirled away from the doors and glared at the contents of the elephant-foot umbrella stand as she tried to control her anger.

It was good, after all, that the cane didn't contain a sword.

As Antonia began to climb the three flights to her room, the stairs creaked their annoyance with her. There must be a root cause to her landlady's antagonism. She needed to identify it if she wanted to remain in this house. She focused on the essential question—what made Mrs. Hill behave as she did? As an actress, she'd learned the importance of understanding the character she played in order to make her come to life on stage. Perhaps applying the same methods of analyzing a character to Mrs. Hill would help her better understand the woman.

She paused as she reached the first landing and considered Mrs. Hill's comment about Miss Galloway wasting her life. Had it been a revealing jab? Perhaps it betrayed the true source of her animosity. Could it be that simple? Did she resent the Winter family for stealing her sister away from her?

As she continued her climb, Antonia imagined acting in the role of a betrayed and abandoned sister and then began nodding to herself in rhythm with the creak of the stairs. By the time she reached her bedroom door, she'd developed a much better understanding of Mrs. Hill.

Antonia opened the door to her tiny room and stepped inside. It provided barely enough space for a small bed, a plump chair, a wardrobe, and a dresser.

A sudden jerk of movement from the overstuffed chair near the fireplace caught her eye. The fire had burned to embers, but by the glow of the oil lamp she could still see young Priscilla, the upstairs maid. The girl blinked open her eyes as she stumbled to her feet.

"Good evening, Priscilla." Antonia slid her cloak from her

shoulders and began to examine it. She'd need to brush it off tonight so it would look decent in the daylight tomorrow.

"Evenin', miss," she said, rubbing the sleep from her eyes. "Your chair is so nice. I fell asleep while I waited for you. I'm sorry."

"I don't mind. Let's hurry through this and get you off to bed, shall we?" Most nights, Antonia changed out of her costume at the theater, where one of the dressers helped her. Then she'd don one of her simple gowns for her trip home—one that didn't require assistance from a dresser or a lady's maid. However, on nights when she had a special performance, like the soirée tonight, she arranged for Priscilla to help her undress when she returned to her rooms. Most of the women who lived here wore simpler garments and didn't need this type of help, or if they did, they relied upon one another for assistance. But given Antonia's late hours, she'd taken to hiring Priscilla to help her.

The girl made quick work of the tiny buttons down the back of her bodice and then untied the corset strings hidden beneath it. It felt marvelous to remove the constricting garment and finally take a deep breath.

"Would you like me to brush out your cloak?" Priscilla asked, examining a stain. "Mrs. Hill keeps some nice clothes brushes in the laundry area. I can take care of it first thing in the morning and leave it in the front hall for you."

"That would be wonderful. Thank you."

"Good night, miss," Priscilla said as she slipped out of the room, closing the door behind her.

Antonia locked the door. The small room felt a bit chilly, so she added more fuel to the fire. She hated waking up to a cold room, but it was one of the new realities of life for her. She'd learned, however, that if she stoked the fire just right, the embers would usually last until morning, which made it much easier to coax it back to life.

A thought struck her, sending a cold chill down her spine. If

Robert had tracked her movements, would the Russians be able to do so as well? Could she be in danger? She tried to calm her fears. Of course Robert had found her easily. He already knew she'd taken the book. She was simply being overly cautious. He was probably an overly zealous admirer. The Russians would have no way of linking her to the theft.

Would they?

She peered out the window, hardly noticing the small evergreen tree growing in the rain gutter as she tried to make out the street below. It was dark and dreary, especially with the thick layer of fog swathing everything in shapeless cotton fluff. Nothing moved down there, so she snapped shut the drab green curtains with a deft flick of her wrists. Not that curtains would keep the Russians out, but at least they would block some of the morning sunlight.

The chair creaked softly as Antonia sat down and let out a deep sigh. The dark green upholstered chair was her favorite thing about this room. The mattress was so lumpy that whenever she slept on it she ended up tossing and turning throughout the night. The chair was her salvation, and she preferred sleeping in it rather than the bed. She wondered if Mrs. Hill would take it away if she ever admitted how much she liked it. She should probably keep that bit of information to herself.

Antonia stared into the fire, but as she watched the flames dance, they began to reenact the moment when those two men had accosted her. She saw their leering grins. And that flicker of orange reminded her of the hard, hurtful hand that had grabbed her. She rubbed at the ache in her arm. Would she have been able to fight off two men with her knife? Her thoughts skittered away from the idea, not wanting to peek behind that particular curtain.

Antonia closed her eyes and concentrated on Robert.

Lord Wentworth.

Shakespeare had it right. *"Good Night, Good night! Parting is such sweet sorrow, that I shall say good night till it be morrow*." Her words seemed to echo in the empty room, mocking her.

A deep flush of shame swept over her. What was she thinking, quoting Juliet while sitting in this lonely room? She didn't love Robert. The thought was ludicrous. It was simply an infatuation she'd carried forward from childhood.

It wasn't the first time she'd used thoughts of Robert to help herself drift off to sleep. She'd fallen back into the habit without a conscious decision. He'd been so kind tonight. She wasn't used to kindness. She'd been on her own for months now, and all the young men who'd formerly trailed after her, declaring their undying love, had fallen away.

Nobody wanted someone like her.

Nobody wanted a woman with no name.

Antonia's eyes snapped open.

Apparently thoughts of Robert weren't going to work tonight. How would she ever get any sleep if she kept dwelling on her fears?

Antonia stood and lit a taper from the fire and set it to the lamp wick. She turned the knob to adjust the light to give her just enough light to read by and then tossed the taper into the fireplace. Reading a familiar book usually worked to drive away her errant thoughts on nights like this.

She looked at her small collection of novels. *A Christmas Carol* was one of her favorites, but she didn't think she could enjoy Mr. Scrooge and his three insomniac spirits tonight. Instead, she picked up a copy of *Oliver Twist* . Her own life held certain parallels to young Oliver's, but hers was unfolding in reverse when compared to his.

Oliver had been raised in a life of poverty, but had finally found his proper place in society when he'd been reunited with his family, whereas Antonia been born into wealth and privilege with loving parents. Then they'd been taken from her, and her uncle had cast her out into a life of poverty. She'd been left with nothing but the clothes on her back.

Her uncle had even wanted to take away her name. Winter. In a sense, he had done so simply by making his revelation. He'd later relented, saying they could continue using the surname, but his initial demand still stung like salt on an open wound.

Now, Antonia's entire future depended upon the book she'd stolen. The key to reclaiming her birthright.

She needed to focus on her goal. She'd come this close before, only to have the Russians steal the book and crush her dreams. She tightened her grip on *The Adventures of Oliver Twist* as her determination solidified. She refused to lose the church register again.

No one, not even Robert, Earl of Wentworth, would take it from her ever again.

❧ 18 ❧

A short time later, Robert jumped down from the hackney. The heavy London mist had seeped into his cloak, leaving it damp, and the ensuing chill sank into his bones. He missed having Antonia tucked next to him in the carriage. They'd kept each other warm.

As he shuffled forward, the overcast sky and the fog conspired to make locating the bottommost step to his home a greater challenge than usual.

The light from the streetlamps provided no help, since their glow couldn't reach the ground. Fortunately, he could make out his large, ornate front door, so he edged his foot forward until he bumped against the first step. The other steps rose up from the mist like a floating staircase.

Robert heard the sound of an approaching carriage. The thick fog didn't hinder him. He could identify that particular combination of rattles and hoofbeats anywhere. After all, it was his carriage.

Frederick must be returning home. He'd want to know if Robert had found the thief.

Antonia. His attraction to her couldn't be ignored. What was he to do with her? Certainly not what he wanted. He could imagine his brother's reaction if he brought Antonia home and into his bed. Frederick would be justified in ripping him to shreds.

The carriage drew closer. In a flash, Robert crept behind one of the boxwood topiaries in a planter at the foot of the steps and crouched down to conceal his six-foot-one frame.

Once Frederick had become an agent for the Queen, Robert had made it his mission to test him. Frederick needed to develop the habit of constant vigilance—or, at least, that was the excuse Robert gave. Frederick tended to lose himself in his thoughts, and that sort of carelessness could get him killed. It was Robert's duty to help him sharpen his skills, wasn't it?

The carriage rolled to a halt. Frederick kicked open the door and heaved himself out. He appeared to avoid grabbing the handhold—probably because of his burns—and stumbled as his foot hit the pavement hidden beneath the fog. "Blast."

Robert tensed, breathing shallowly so Frederick couldn't hear him.

Frederick elbowed the door of the carriage shut. He didn't immediately make his way toward the front door. Instead, he paused and glanced around. Frederick stood silent and still. The only sound came from the water dripping from the eaves.

Did Frederick sense his presence? The bandages on Frederick's hands seemed to glow in the dim streetlights. The carriage pulled away, resuming its loud rattle and clop as it headed toward the stables.

After a moment, Frederick took a step forward, and his gaze focused on the topiary behind which Robert hid. "I know you're there," Frederick said. "I heard your hackney leave, and I can see your top hat."

Robert stepped out to greet his brother, grinning. "Well done. You're getting much better at this."

"I've had to. You've left me with little choice."

Robert pushed open the door and Frederick followed him inside. A large round table sat in the center of the foyer and bore a single envelope addressed to Frederick. Robert recognized Daniel's handwriting. He'd been true to his word and sent Frederick news of the attack. Apparently, Frederick hadn't been home to read it.

Robert plucked it from the table. "This is for you, but I want to discuss it with you in person. Care to join me for a drink?"

Frederick glanced at the letter and then down at his bandaged hands. He gave a shrug and asked, "Do you mind if we use the drawing room? I could use some help changing these bandages, and the supplies are in there."

They left their coats and hats in the foyer, and Robert led the way to the drawing room. After his father's death, it had become his favorite room in Woolsy House, displacing his father's study in his affections. He'd left that haunted room abandoned for ages. Only in the past year or so had the wood-paneled study started tempting him to spend time there once again. He'd rearranged the furnishings and purchased some new items, making the room his own, but he still hadn't fully explored it. He wondered if he ever would.

Tonight, the study's lurking shadows might be difficult to ignore. Fortunately, the drawing room held no similar ghosts to distract him.

The drawing room fireplace still held embers buried in the ashes, so Robert carefully nursed the flames back to life. In the meantime, Frederick lit a taper and used it to light the lamps. As the room grew brighter, Robert spotted his sister Emily's sewing basket and her book sitting near her favorite chair. An unfamiliar sack sat on one of the end tables.

Frederick let out a sharp hiss of pain.

Still crouched in front of the fire, Robert swiveled to look at his brother.

Apparently Frederick had poured measures of Robert's favorite scotch whiskey into matching tumblers and then tried to pick up a glass in each hand.

"I'll get those," Robert said, springing forward and crossing the room to meet his brother.

Frederick took a quick swallow from one of the glasses, grimacing slightly as usual. His response to good whiskey always annoyed Robert, and tonight was no exception. Why contort one's face in response to something so sublime? Mark it as yet another way he and his brother differed.

"Maybe this will do the trick. My hand started throbbing about a half-hour ago. The effects of the poultice wore off." He let out a heavy sigh. "We've certainly had our share of bad luck. First my hand, then that thief absconding with the book. It's a wonder so many things went wrong and yet we still managed to escape."

"Fate?" Robert suggested.

"Perhaps." Frederick stared pensively toward the fireplace, but half his face remained in shadow.

Robert pulled Daniel's letter from his jacket pocket. "You should read this." He held it out to Frederick.

Frederick glanced at the letter and then down at his hands. "Open it, please. I don't think I can manage."

Robert tore open the envelope and extracted the folded sheet of paper.

Frederick took it and quickly scanned its contents. "How many men did Revnik send after you?"

"Three. All those years of fencing haven't gone to waste, but I must admit, if Daniel and his wife hadn't intervened, I might not be standing here."

"Lady Huntley?"

He grinned at Frederick's look of surprise. "She carries a knife."

"Are you telling me she knows how to use it?"

Robert nodded. "I'd never have guessed. Daniel's always been clever with a blade. He probably taught her. You should have seen those men's faces when they realized the lone, unarmed man they attacked had an épée and two knife-wielding friends."

Frederick didn't appear amused. "You're lucky they helped. I'm glad our evening's bad luck didn't catch up with you at that moment. Damn that woman."

"Lady Huntley?"

"Of course not." He tossed back the remaining contents of his glass with a grimace and let out a sigh of frustration. "I was referring to your little thief. If I ever find out who she is, I'm having her arrested and tried for treason."

Robert nearly choked on his whiskey. This definitely wasn't the time to mention he'd identified her. He'd wait until Frederick's temper cooled. The pain was making him angry.

"Is there any more ice?" Frederick tipped his head toward a silver ice bucket sitting next to the unfamiliar sack.

Robert lifted the container's lid and peered inside. "A bit, but it's mostly ice water."

"Hand it to me."

Robert passed him the bucket and set the lid on the table. "Did Lady Harrington's poultice help?" He crossed to the side table to collect the bottle of whiskey and then refilled both their glasses.

"As a matter of fact, yes. For a while, at least. From the moment she applied it, I felt immediate relief. That housekeeper of hers is amazing at mixing herbs," he said, impatiently unwrapping the bandages wound about his hand. "Unfortunately, the effects faded over time." He plunged his bare hand into the ice bucket. "Ah. Now that feels good."

It was a good thing the maids always rinsed out the ice bucket when they cleaned each morning. Discovering bits of dried poultice leaves floating in his drink would sour his disposition—not to mention ruining a fine glass of whiskey.

Some of the tension in Frederick's face eased, but he still appeared wan and overtired. Robert reached a decision. He could manage the situation without his brother's help—or his interference. After Robert met with Antonia tomorrow, he'd have something more solid to report. With some luck, he might even have the church register.

"You said you wanted me to rebandage your hands?"

Frederick didn't try to mask his relief. "Do you see the sack on the table? It contains Mrs. Drummer's poultice-making supplies. I'd planned to ask my valet to prepare it, but since you're here..."

"You know how to make a poultice?"

Frederick let out a snort of laughter. "Only this particular one. Mrs. Drummer explained each step and then had me recite it back to her. The real trick comes in choosing the right plants."

"Which ones did she use?" Robert asked. He pulled the bag open, releasing the sharp, green scent of cut leaves.

"Plantain leaves, comfrey leaves, and chickweed."

"Do I need to know which is which?" Robert asked, pulling out the leaves. On the bottom of the sack, he found a heavy stone bowl and—ah, yes. A pestle. She'd left them a mortar and pestle to use to smash the leaves.

"No. Just mash them together."

Robert examined them. Mother would have called them all weeds. The wide ones might be plantain leaves. He'd seen them often enough in her garden. She'd deal with them by plucking them from the ground, root and all.

He sorted through the leaves and noted some had a sandpapery texture, but he wasn't sure what they were. With a shrug, he tore them into pieces and began mashing them with the mortar and pestle. The scent filling his nostrils brought with it a promise of spring. "Tell me about your night. Were you able to locate the man you believed organized the theft?"

"When Turner and I first arrived to watch the man's house, we spotted him through the windows. He left about two hours later in his carriage." Frederick removed his less injured hand from the ice water, flicked off the water, and took a sip of straight whiskey from his glass, grimacing again. "We followed him, but he must have known we were watching him. He'd traded places with someone else."

"I thought you were taking Josephine."

"It's safer not to involve her. I sent her home and brought young Turner instead."

Robert did some quick mental calculations. If Frederick and Turner had watched the man's house for two hours before he went anywhere, he could easily be the same man Antonia had met at the soirée. "What's his name? What does he look like?"

Frederick glanced down at his bandaged hand. "I've been ordered not to reveal his identity to anyone, not even you. It could put his life in danger."

A bright spark of irritation shot through Robert, but he quashed it. After all, he shouldn't begrudge Frederick his secrets. Robert had his own to keep and didn't need the burden of anyone else's. "What can you tell me?"

"Almost nothing. You're quite good at piecing together random scraps of information and creating a coherent explanation. And too often, you're very close to the truth. I can't risk letting you guess who he is."

"What of Josephine? I'm surprised she let you put her off so easily. Did you lie to her to convince her to leave?"

Frederick gave a grimace of disgust with himself. "What else could I do? The woman is altogether too tenacious."

Robert cocked his eyebrow. "Interesting."

"What?"

"It would appear your relationship with Josephine is deeper than you led me to believe."

When Frederick's gaze met Robert's, he appeared confused. "What makes you say that?"

"You're protecting her rather than using her."

"I-I—"

Robert held up his hand, forestalling his brother's explanation. "It was an observation, nothing more."

"Hmm." Frederick's gaze seemed to turn inward.

"She's right for you. You must see that. You should marry her. Commit to her."

"And drag her into a life of espionage? A life where the revelation of Father's crimes might topple our family without warning? I think not." Frederick gestured toward the pestle. "You'll need to smear the goo on a bit of flannel."

Robert lifted the large piece of flannel from the pile of Mrs. Drummer's supplies. "This is too big."

"I suggest you cut it up."

Robert checked the sack. No scissors. He crossed to his sister's embroidery box and flipped it open.

"You're a great one to talk about commitment. You've avoided it for years," Frederick said, ignoring the interruption.

"What on earth are you on about? There's no woman in my life." Robert paused, thinking of a pair of copper eyes that had softened with desire just a short time ago, then shook himself. He refused to think of her right now.

Robert poked through the sewing box, shoving aside a lace-edged white handkerchief Emily had been embroidering. The strands of embroidery floss were in varying shades ranging from pale pink to fuchsia. Beneath it he found a variety of buttons and thimbles and—yes—scissors.

"I *meant* you need to commit in a broader way. Stop holding yourself aloof from entanglements. You can't continue to remain detached from life. 'No man is an island,' and all that."

"Don't quote John Donne to me." The sewing basket wouldn't close, and Robert gave the contents an exasperated shove. A sharp stab of pain pierced his fingertip, and he yanked it back to see a small pin dangling from the end. He plucked it out and dropped it back in the sewing basket. A tiny bead of blood welled up on his index finger, and he yanked it away from Emily's white handkerchief. She'd be furious if he left a stain.

"You act as though I do nothing but gad about all day, gambling and wasting my time." He pressed his fingertip against his palm. When he examined it, the blood had ceased to flow.

"That's not what I—"

"How dare you accuse me of lacking commitment? For years, I've worked to restore the money Father stole from the people he convinced to invest in his railroad scheme. With Daniel's help, I've saved many from financial ruin." Squire Winter among them. "I only wish I could move more swiftly, but earning money takes time, as does finding the best way to help."

Frederick's jaw dropped. "That's what you feel obliged to address? The money? What about Father's treason?"

"I think you and your conscience are already addressing that particular aspect."

"What do you mean by that?"

Robert stared at him stonily. "Don't be obtuse. You've dedicated your life to the Queen. You root out secrets and spies for her. Exactly the kind of secrets Father tried to hide. What do you call that if not self-sacrifice? You do it to atone for both yourself and our father. You might not admit it to me, but at least admit it to yourself."

Frederick shot him a look of cold fury. "This isn't atonement. Think, man. Not only am I well-suited to this role, I excel at it. I relish bringing men to justice."

"And what produced your drive and passion? A betrayal. Our father's betrayal. A betrayal so fundamental it formed the man you've become."

"What difference does it make? I am who I am, and my passions and desires drive my decisions, just as they drive yours. So what if you're right? So what if I serve the crown to soothe my conscience? At least I'm taking action. What of you?"

"Don't stand in judgment of me. I already told you I'm helping the people Father stole from."

"Ah, yes. You're paying them back. Does that soothe your conscience?"

Robert opened his mouth to retort but paused. Instead, he said, "I'm not trying to soothe my conscience. I'm trying to right a wrong. It's the honorable thing to do. I'm not looking for your approval. I should never have mentioned it." He smoothed out the piece of flannel on the table and used Emily's sewing scissors to cut a length from it.

As Frederick watched him, he sighed. "I don't want to fight. I'm exhausted and in pain. Let's set our argument aside. We can come back to it later."

"Don't we always?" The corner of Robert's mouth twitched up.

"It's like worrying at a sore tooth. It's always there, and it's always irritating—for both of us." Their gazes met and then slid away.

Robert pulled the bowl of mashed leaves closer to him.

"You'll need to add a bit of vinegar now. Mrs. Drummer said to use enough to moisten the leaves."

Robert glanced at the small stoppered bottle. A smooth layer of wax coated the neck, sealing it closed. He gave the cork a swift twist, breaking the wax. The sharp, vinegary smell burst forth, and he added a few drops to the mashed leaves. The scent bit his nostrils. He'd never much liked the odor of vinegar.

"It worries me that Revnik sent men to detain you," Frederick murmured. "He's a threat we can't ignore." Frederick's gaze became unfocused as he stared off into space.

"What do you suggest we do?"

"Confront Revnik," Frederick said after a moment. "Remaining silent would be tantamount to admitting guilt. Send him a letter first thing in the morning and insist we meet. Make sure the missive drips with all the affronted dignity you can muster. It should throw him off our scent."

"Good idea. You said 'our scent.' Will you be joining me?"

"Most assuredly. Revnik's already tried to kidnap you once. We can't simply deliver you to his doorstep. We need to arrive with a great deal of noise and commotion so he can't make you disappear and later pretend you were never there."

"I can arrange that. A bit of pomp and splendor should do the trick. I'll bring a dozen or so footmen along."

Frederick grinned. "They should provide an impressive entourage."

Robert spread the concoction onto the piece of flannel and then held out a cotton towel to Frederick. "Dry your hands. The poultice is ready."

Frederick took the towel gratefully. He gently pressed his fingertips against it and let the soft cloth absorb the water from his skin. Even though he handled it gingerly, he still winced.

"I'll try to be as gentle as possible, but I'm afraid this will hurt."

Frederick gave a terse nod, but he held his hand steady as Robert laid the bit of flannel over his burned flesh. After a moment, he seemed to relax slightly. "That helps."

Robert began wrapping the bandage around the poultice to hold it in place. The bindings needed to be wound firmly so the poultice wouldn't fall off, yet still remain loose enough so as not to add to Frederick's pain.

He paused. Perhaps he should use that same technique with Antonia. Use a guiding hand firm enough to keep her from bolting, yet light enough she wouldn't feel threatened by him.

Or perhaps he could simply kiss the information out of her.

Robert sighed his frustration as he tucked the end of the

bandage in place so it wouldn't unwind. He hated thinking about manipulating people. That was Frederick's area of expertise. Robert wished he could confide in him. He could use some advice.

"We need to compose that letter to the ambassador," Frederick said.

"If you're still alert enough to compose something, you can dictate it to me."

At Frederick's nod, Robert crossed to a small writing desk and sat down to ready his writing supplies. He dipped the end of his pen in India ink, drew a line on a scrap of paper, and when he was satisfied with the flow, wrote a salutation at the top of the letter.

"Say something along the lines of 'I insist we meet immediately to discuss the outrageous actions of your men outside the theater last night.' Keep it brief. Perhaps throw in a threat. Something like 'If I don't hear from you by noon today, I'll be forced to bring your actions to the attention of the Queen.' That should light a fire under him."

Robert nodded as he dipped his pen in the ink. He scribbled away, the silence broken only by the crackling of the fire and the scratching of the nib. He sat up straighter, rolled his shoulders, and handed the missive to his brother. As Frederick read it, Robert scribbled a brief note on a slip of paper.

Frederick handed it back to him. "Excellent." Robert waved the scrap of paper. "I'm leaving Landon instructions for it to be delivered first thing in the morning."

Frederick nodded. "I'll see you tomorrow."

As his brother left the room, Robert stared into the dying fire and pictured Antonia's beguiling copper eyes in the flames.

The book. It had to be his first priority.

He felt overwhelmed by a sudden need to have her without consequence. That near-kiss haunted him. He ached to press her against him. It was as if he'd been overtaken by some animal urge.

He had to stop this. She was a traitor.

He needed to think before he took the next step. Not that there would be one. Being attracted to her didn't mean he should do anything about it. His goal needed to be to get the book and move on.

But he wanted more from her.

He shook his head. He needed to end this strange attraction. He needed to eradicate it from himself.

Tomorrow. He'd see her tomorrow. He'd be able to put an end to this in the light of day. Night was the time for seduction. Day was for reality and responsibility.

Tomorrow morning he'd get the book and be done with her.

19

It is my feeling that Time ripens all things; with Time all things are revealed; Time is the father of truth.

— FRANCOIS RABELAIS

Robert's carriage arrived in front of Antonia's boardinghouse shortly past noon, and he glanced at the gray winter sky. So much for daylight bringing clarity. If the sky also had a silvery sheen to it, the color would have been nearly identical to the gown Antonia wore to last night's Koliada ball.

He calculated how much time he'd be able to spend here before he needed to leave to meet Revnik. The man had replied to his letter, begging his pardon, assuring him there must have been a misunderstanding, and inviting him to the embassy later in the afternoon.

Robert didn't like the delay. It smacked of deceit and provided ample time for Revnik to pursue his own agenda. But unless Robert wanted to involve the Queen, he'd have to agree to the timing of the meeting. So instead, he practiced caution. He'd entered his carriage while it was still at the stables rather than having it brought round to the front entrance. It seemed to have worked since no one had followed him, but if the Russians still intended to abduct him, that deception would only work once.

Robert stepped down from his carriage. He examined his surroundings and noted the well-maintained street. The residents obviously cared for their homes. Clusters of young mothers with children moved through the streets. For the most part, the women either pushed prams along the sidewalk or held the hands of youngsters. Their day dresses were well-made without being extravagant, and the children's clothing was clean and fit their growing bodies as though newly made for them.

Everyone seemed to be headed toward the nearby park. How pleasant to stumble upon such a charming scene in the heart of London.

Robert strode toward the front door of Antonia's boarding-house, but a boy darted down the street, forcing him to take a quick step to one side to avoid being bowled over. The child barreled past Robert and an annoyed-looking woman scurried after him.

"Sorry, sir," the youth called over his shoulder.

"Nathan. Stop this instant, young man," his mother demanded.

Either young Nathan had faulty hearing or he knew he wouldn't be punished, because he didn't slow his pace. A moment later, another boy, apparently spurred on by Nathan's success, escaped from his mother and clattered down the street as well.

The two mothers murmured words of apology as they hurried past Robert.

He grinned, remembering when he and Frederick had made similar dashes to freedom as children. Of course, they'd been with their nanny rather than their mother. He glanced around, noticing that there were no uniformed nannies in evidence.

Robert knocked on the front door of Antonia's boardinghouse and waited for someone to greet him.

He glanced at the carefully selected bouquet he carried. Every young woman of quality understood the secret language of flowers. Each blossom had its own meaning, and woe to the man who chose his bouquet carelessly, lest he offend. Choosing flowers in January made his task challenging but not impossible, thanks to the conservatory at Woolsy House. His gardeners kept the house supplied with greenery year-round. He'd finally settled on a few white carnations to signify endearment and some saffron-colored crocuses to signify mirth, but the most important flowers in the bouquet were the gardenias. Their hidden message would tell Antonia he found her lovely, but they'd also hint that he might hold a secret love for her.

An older, gray-haired woman opened the door. She clutched a newspaper in one hand and smiled brightly at first, but once her gaze focused on Robert and his bouquet, her smile transformed into a scowl.

The forbidding look reminded him of a former nanny for whom he and Frederick had developed a particularly intense dislike. One of her favorite punishments had been to send Robert to bed with no supper. Finally, when the odious woman paddled Frederick for sneaking Robert a thick slice of bread with butter, both boys had decided she'd gone too far and devised a plan to drive her away. Once they'd united their efforts, she hadn't lasted long. Nannies don't like live mice by the dozen—especially when they find them nesting in their beds.

"Good day, madam," Robert said as he tucked his cane under his arm and plucked a white carnation from the bouquet. "Is Miss Winter receiving callers?" He presented her the flower along with his most engaging smile. This was a technique guaranteed to melt even the frostiest of hearts.

But not hers. She was immune to him—or perhaps she simply had no heart.

"I doubt she's awake," the harridan said. "And she's not permitted to have callers in her room."

"Of course not," he said as he slid the rejected flower back in the bouquet. "But couldn't she greet me in your drawing room?" He drew a calling card from his pocket.

"I think not."

The woman baffled him. "Then how can she receive me?"

"She can't."

"Are you saying that you refuse to tell Miss Winter I'm here?" He raised his eyebrows.

The woman's lips thinned to the point of disappearing altogether. She glanced down at the folded newspaper she held and let out a deep sigh of annoyance. "Fine, then." She eyed the bouquet. "Those are for her?"

Robert nodded.

"Wait outside and I'll deliver your card." She held her hand out and Robert passed her his plain white calling card. She took it from his hand, grabbed the bouquet, and closed the front door in his face.

Robert Woolsy, Earl of Wentworth, stared at the door in amazement. He'd never before experienced having one shut in his face.

He didn't much like it.

Not only that, but that wretched woman had foiled his plan to watch Antonia's reaction when she first saw his bouquet.

He snatched his cane from under his arm, clutching it tightly in his fist. He paced in front of the boardinghouse for a while, earning a number of odd looks from the neighborhood matrons. The street didn't look pleasant and inviting anymore. Instead it looked rigid and unwelcoming. How would he seduce Antonia into helping him recover the book if her landlady refused to allow him to speak to her?

He tapped the end of his cane against one of the paving stones, hitting it harder and harder as he jabbed at its center, imagining piercing the target of a practice dummy with his fencing foil—a dummy that wore the face of that insufferable landlady. As he tried to decide whether he should leave or begin searching for another way inside, the front door finally burst open.

Antonia hurried out, scolding someone still inside while simultaneously tying her bonnet's pink ribbons under her chin. Her dark cloak hid most of her ivory dress, but he noticed the small pink flowers dotting the fabric that peeked out from beneath it. He also noticed the gardenia she'd pinned to her cloak.

His gardenia.

"You have the proof in your hand, Mrs. Hill," Antonia said. "Your insistence upon believing the worst about me is simply insupportable." She turned to face Robert and let out a huff of indignation. Without a backward glance at Mrs. Hill, she yanked the door closed and then tucked her hand in the crook of Robert's arm.

As he smiled down at her, he realized all his irritation had evaporated at seeing her. She looked lovely.

"Do you mind if we take a walk?" she asked without preamble. "Since I have no one to serve as chaperone, we can either stop at the tea room or stroll through the park. Those are both public places. I need a break from that house and that woman. If I stay any longer I'll end up saying something I'll regret."

Antonia didn't wait for his reply, but headed in the same direction young Nathan and his entourage had taken, and at only a slightly slower pace.

Hurrying along beside her, Robert remained silent as long as he was able, but finally his curiosity regarding her living situation won out. "Why do you remain there?"

"What, you thought I'd leave during the night? You'd only track me down again. As long as I'm performing in Anne Blake , I can't hide from you. And since I can't stop working if I want to keep eating, there's no sense in trying to avoid you."

"That's not what I meant," he said uncomfortably. "I was referring to your living situation and your landlady."

"Oh, that." Antonia shook her head, but slowed her steps to a more normal pace. "It's complicated. Suffice it to say she serves a purpose. One which I require. I'm fortunate she lets me live there at all. She's only doing it as a favor to—to a mutual friend." Antonia shook her head. "I must constantly remind myself of that so I don't lose my temper with her."

"I see she gave you my flowers," he said, awkwardly using his cane to indicate the gardenia. "I thought she might not."

Antonia touched the pale white blossom pinned to her cloak. "It's beautiful. How did you know gardenias were my favorite?"

Her favorite? His heart sank. Just his luck. She hadn't guessed he'd included it for its secret meaning. "I had no idea. It's just that they're so lovely, I thought they suited you."

Antonia's cheeks pinkened and she smiled up at him shyly. "You constantly surprise me, Lord Wentworth."

It worked. She *did* know its secret meaning—and it pleased her. He had to suppress his grin. "Call me Robert. Remember?"

She ducked her head. "Robert."

He needed to press her. Now. He glanced around, searching for potential eavesdroppers, but spied no one close enough to overhear. "I'm sorry to be blunt, but I need you to help me recover that church register. It's of vital importance."

Antonia stiffened and glanced up at him. The warmth disappeared from her eyes, and something tightened around Robert's heart. "I told you, I no longer have it. Why can't you people just leave me alone?"

That took him aback. "'You people'?" he repeated back to her. "What are you talking about?"

"You government people. Who do you work for anyway? The Russians? The French?"

"Queen Victoria," Robert said stiffly.

Antonia's mouth fell open and she raised her hand as though warding him off. "The Queen? The British government is involved too?"

Robert's stomach tightened. She had to be acting. Her surprise couldn't be genuine, could it? "This is England. Your theft took place on British soil, didn't it? Of course we're involved."

Antonia lifted her chin. "Technically, the embassy is on Russian soil."

"It still took place here in England," he said, rapping the tip of his cane on the sidewalk to emphasize his point, "right under the nose of your queen. Your actions last night could land you in prison for treason."

"Treason!" Antonia came to a halt and faced him, letting go of his arm. Her surprise was so complete that Robert couldn't believe she was pretending.

"What did you expect?" he asked, gripping the handle of his cane in frustration. He didn't know which he wanted to do more —throttle her or kiss her. "You've read the newspapers. We're on the brink of war with Russia. The Ottoman Empire is begging us for help. If we can't manage to negotiate a peace in the Crimean Peninsula, the only course left to us will be to declare war."

Antonia took a step back. "What are you talking about? It's only a church register! It lists births, deaths, and marriages. How can it start a war?"

Robert knew he needed to tread carefully. "Don't pretend you aren't aware of the book's importance. Why else would you have stolen it?"

"I need it." She crossed her arms in front of her chest. "My entire future depends on what's recorded in those pages."

Robert's patience snapped. "Don't be melodramatic about your self-interest," he retorted. "We're talking war. Men's lives depend on that book."

Antonia's eyes seemed to blaze at him. She took a step closer, clenching her fists at her sides. "You're only accusing me of being melodramatic because I'm an actress. You're the one being melodramatic. I refuse to believe a church register will bring about a war. Why is it so important?"

"I'm not at liberty to tell you." He pressed his lips together in a thin line. He hated trying to bluff when he didn't know what cards he held in his hand. It left him at a distinct disadvantage.

Antonia became alert. She narrowed her eyes as she scrutinized him. "You're lying. I can tell. You don't know why the register is important, do you?" She smirked at him. "And you accuse me of being melodramatic. At least I know what I'm talking about. I'm not the one flinging wild accusations."

Robert stiffened his spine as he fixed his gaze on her. All thoughts of seducing her disappeared under her reproachful gaze. He took her arm and tucked it through his arm in a perfunctory manner and then began to walk down the street again. "I might not know the details of the book's contents, but I'm confident it's vital to our current peace negotiations. You may have pushed us into war, Miss Winter. And war means death. Try to remember that when you're spending the illicit money you just earned."

Antonia stopped and stared at him, but she didn't pull away this time. "You're telling me the truth? The church register really could start a war?"

"Yes."

She tightened her grip on his arm. "I had no idea. I knew the Russians were desperate to recover it, but war? If I'd known, I never would have passed it on to—to my friend. I'm no traitor to England."

Robert scrutinized her. "I notice you didn't say you wouldn't have stolen it."

Antonia closed her eyes. "I had no choice. I've stolen that church register twice now, and I'll do it again if necessary. You can't understand how vital it is to me. To my future."

Something about her plea gave him pause. Why would she

risk everything, even prison, for the book? What drove her? Why was she so blasted determined to have it?

He tilted his head closer to her, speaking softly in her ear. "In that case, you need to help me understand. Tell me why that little book is so important to you. Please, Antonia. Tell me everything."

She wouldn't meet his gaze.

He touched her chin with his finger, urging her to look up at him.

She refused.

Robert sighed. "I don't want to be forced to turn you over to the authorities. But you aren't leaving me with an alternative."

❧ 20 ❧

Those things that nature denied to human sight, she revealed to the eyes of the soul.

— OVID

Antonia stopped breathing. He'd turn her in? A gust of frigid wind sent a chill down her spine. She couldn't go to prison! What would her sisters do without her support? Good lord—what if her sisters were arrested as well?

A lump of dread settled in her stomach. This meeting was not going well. Not at all.

She never should have trusted him. She should have disappeared into the cold night, leaving no trace. He'd never have found her.

She suddenly realized that wasn't true. If she managed to regain her place in society, it wouldn't be long before Robert tracked her down. Her fall might not have caught his attention, but once she scrabbled her way back up society's ladder, he'd notice, especially since her plan would create a scandal of its own.

She needed to tell him the truth. That much was obvious. Her story was so bizarre—could she convince him to believe it? It was the truth, yes, but would he think she was lying? She'd have to unwind her tale with great care if she wanted to avoid being thrown into prison.

The thought of failing sent a wave of nausea through her.

She swallowed.

She had to convince him. She had to.

She glanced at him. What would he think of her once she'd revealed everything to him? Once she'd bared all of her secrets? Would he react to her confession with scorn or pity? She'd experienced both responses too many times to count, but she still wasn't sure if one was worse than the other. Each offered its own unique sort of pain.

Even worse, she dreaded the way he'd withdraw from her.

Just like everyone else. He might have been willing to overlook her status as an actress—but this? No. Even he wasn't so noble.

But it didn't matter. She needed his cooperation, not his good opinion or his approval. She didn't care what he thought. She didn't care what any of them thought.

Not really.

She'd have to expose her family's most closely guarded secrets. She knew that with this man, only the truth would suffice.

Antonia glanced warily at the entrance to the tea room as they approached. The scent of the shop's signature clove biscuits wafted toward her on the winter air. Although she dearly loved those biscuits, today her stomach clenched at the smell. She couldn't bear the thought of food.

When Robert paused at the door, she tugged gently on his arm and tilted her head toward the entrance to the park. "I have some things I need to explain. Privacy is essential. I don't want some bored eavesdropper to spread my secrets throughout the neighborhood."

Robert seemed relieved as he fell in step beside her. With a pang of nostalgia, Antonia enjoyed the pleasant, everyday experience of walking arm in arm with a gentleman. She hadn't realized how much she missed this simple act. Her last such stroll had been a year ago.

A lifetime ago.

She was a different woman now.

They entered the park, a study of brown and white in the winter. The path was clear and dry. It wended its way around the outer edge of an open area covered in snow and continued between a few sparse trees in a large, meandering loop. The group of mothers from the neighborhood watched her and Robert. They'd become fodder for gossip simply by taking a circumspect walk.

She liked strolling with him—liked his choice of flowers for her bouquet. Especially the gardenias and their hidden message. Knowing he found her attractive sent a secret thrill through her.

Robert had featured as the central figure in her girlish fantasies ever since she'd seen him those many years ago. She'd imagined him noticing her one day when visiting her father and then immediately falling in love with her. In the past year, her foolish dreams had been dashed when confronted with the reality of her new circumstances. Even so, she found it difficult recasting Robert from the role of her hero to that of her adversary.

Antonia lifted her chin toward the nearest group of curious onlookers. "We have an audience."

"I noticed," he said, his gaze sliding over them.

"I suppose their presence will ensure we don't shout at one another."

She raised her eyebrows. "You believe you might shout at me? You don't strike me as the type."

Robert's mouth curled up at the corners in a most engaging

way and he gave his cane a twirl. "Don't I? My brother would disagree with you, but rest assured, I promise not to shout."

"Brothers," she said, watching his dexterous fingers spin the cane. "What can I say? It's the same with me and my sisters. We fly into fits of passion and say things to one another we'd never dream of saying to anyone else. Pointing out one another's failings is both the curse and the blessing of siblings. After all, who else loves you enough to tell you when you're behaving like a fool, if not a family member? I gave you every reason to scorn me last night, but you behaved as a complete gentleman."

"Not as a sibling?" The intensity of his gaze made her body pulse with heat, and her step faltered. "My feelings toward you are far from brotherly." He glanced away. The cane abruptly stopped spinning as he clenched it in his hand and lowered the tip to the ground. Their pace slowed, and he began to beat out a steady rhythm to accompany their walk.

Antonia's mouth suddenly felt dry as she felt her cheeks warm. She gnawed at her bottom lip as she watched a group of boys on the path ahead of them rolling hoops. "I need to thank you for your help. I never meant to create an international incident. Things have become so complicated."

"Explain everything to me. Help me understand." His tone was patient and soothing.

"I don't know where to begin."

"At the beginning."

Antonia sighed, breathing out a puff of white warmth into the frigid air. "It started a long time ago. With my parents. You see, my father was Squire Paul Winter of Maidenhead. Have you heard of him?"

"I know him."

She waited for him to continue, but he said nothing more.

"Perhaps you heard my parents died in a train accident a little over a year ago. Their deaths left me and my two younger sisters alone in the world."

His eyes flew to hers, full of compassion. "No. I hadn't heard. You have my heartfelt sympathy. To lose them both at once must have been a terrible blow. I'm sorry for your loss."

Tears pricked at her eyes, but she ignored them, only giving him a brief nod of acknowledgment. "In the days following the accident, we mourned them and dealt with their funerals, not knowing what would happen or what would become of us. But then my uncle, Walter Winter, appeared. Back from the dead, or so it seemed."

They approached one of the clusters of ladies along the path, and Antonia paused in her storytelling until the group was well out of earshot. The boys rolling their hoops pulled farther ahead along the path and ran alongside the rolling circles, laughing and shouting to one another.

Antonia glanced up at Robert. "At first we were overjoyed to discover we still had a living relative. Uncle Walter was my father's older brother, and everyone had believed him dead. He'd disappeared at a time when my grandparents were very angry with him. From what I could learn, he compromised a young woman of good family who lived nearby, and Grandfather insisted he marry her. Walter refused. He ran off, and the girl ended up dying. Some say she killed herself, others say she died of shame and a broken heart. No one heard from Uncle Walter again until he appeared after my parents died." Antonia paused for a moment, shaking her head. "It's a sordid tale. I hate dredging up my family secrets this way, but I don't know any other way to tell the story."

"I sympathize. I have family secrets as well, and the idea of revealing them to someone..." He grimaced as he shook his head. "I won't judge you based on a family member's actions. Perhaps you'll do me the same courtesy one day." Robert's sympathetic smile tugged at her, and she couldn't resist smiling back at him. Something warm fluttered in her stomach. This man's pale-blue eyes called to her like a clear winter sky. She could fall into them and soar away.

"Of course." She noted the breathless quality to her voice and the realization snapped her back to reality. She needed to stop staring dreamily into Robert's eyes like an infatuated schoolgirl and keep her head straight. She didn't want to end up in prison for treason.

Antonia swallowed. What had she been talking about? Ah, yes. "Uncle Walter claimed that because he was the eldest son, the land portion of Grandfather's inheritance had rightfully been his all along."

Robert's brow furrowed. "I'm not certain that's true. Did you speak with a solicitor?"

"Of course. But Uncle Walter wasn't specifically disinherited by my grandfather. He was simply presumed dead so that his share went to my father. He should have rightfully inherited our house and half of the remaining holdings."

"It must have been a blow to lose your home to someone you didn't even know was alive. But surely your father left you something more in his will."

Antonia's chest tightened. "It's more complicated." She forced herself to take a shaky breath. "When my parents first met, he was married to another woman. He'd met his first wife when he was young and reckless, and no one in Maidenhead knew anything about her. She was only interested in his income and the excitement they shared in the gambling halls, so when his father died and he decided to leave that sordid life behind, she became angry. She refused to live with him in Maidenhead and insisted upon remaining in the city. When it became obvious they'd never be happy together, Father offered her an allowance in exchange for leaving him alone, and she readily accepted. She said she loved gambling and the excitement of London. She'd never be content as the wife of a simple country squire."

Ahead of them, one of the smaller boys began running pell-mell along the path, and a moment later the hoops went crashing into one another. They clattered to the ground and a bigger boy began shouting at the smaller one who'd created the chaos. The younger one backed away, but the older one followed and wouldn't stop pestering him.

"Peter!" a woman called from behind them. "Come back here!"

The older boy's head snapped toward his mother's voice before turning back to the younger boy and saying something in a furious tone. Then he obediently collected his hoop and began trotting toward them. Antonia waited for Peter to pass before continuing her story.

"My father dedicated himself to managing the land he'd inherited. He said he saw it as a fresh start. When he met my mother, they immediately fell in love. He told her about his first wife, but Mother still wanted to marry him, even knowing the marriage wouldn't be legal."

"Why?" Robert asked. "If the secret got out, she'd be ruined. Any children they had would be considered illegitimate."

Everyone had asked that same question. Why? Blood rushed to her cheeks. "I've never understood it myself," she muttered, shaking her head.

Robert's face softened with sympathy. "You can live with someone your entire life and never understand them." When their eyes met, his seemed haunted by some well-remembered pain.

"My parents loved each other deeply. Even Grandfather Vladamir gave his permission for them to marry once he saw how much in love they were."

"Why would he give his permission?"

"Ah," she said with a smile. "That decision has its roots in another story from Grandfather's youth. It's a tragedy. Like Romeo and Juliet. He believed people in love shouldn't be kept apart. He'd been separated from his first love, and it had nearly destroyed him."

"You're full of stories," he said. His smile was tender as he gazed down at her.

"I'm sorry." She cast him a sidelong glance. She could swear he was still flirting with her, but how could that be? "I hope I'm not boring you." "

Not at all. You're a born storyteller."

The compliment sent blood rushing to her cheeks. "Father always said the same thing. My sisters and I loved to perform plays and pantomimes. I'm lucky I'm able to earn a living wage doing it now."

"Don't you have any other family who can help you?"

Antonia shook her head. "My only living relative is my uncle Walter. Mother is from Russia, and she had no siblings. She met Father on one of Grandfather's many trips to London."

"Do you speak Russian?"

"No. Mother never taught us." Antonia noticed that they were rounding the far end of the park and were about to begin heading back toward the entrance. "I need to continue my story or we'll have to take another turn around the park. I still have more to explain."

"By all means."

She took a breath. "Long ago, my grandfather loved the daughter of a wealthy man in his village in Russia. Her name was Tatianna, and Grandfather asked her father for her hand in marriage. Tatianna's father forbade it because Grandfather Vladamir was a mere artist. A painter. Not only did Tatianna's father reject Vladamir's proposal, but he also forced my great-grandfather to send Vladamir away to keep the young lovers apart. Tatianna's father promised that if Vladamir could return within two years and prove himself capable of supporting Tatianna, they could marry, but Vladamir had to promise not to contact her while he was gone.

"A little less than two years later, well within the allotted time, Grandfather Vladamir returned to the village. He'd earned a reputation as a talented artist, and he'd already accumulated enough wealth to prove himself worthy of Tatianna. Tragically, he discovered that while he was gone, Tatianna's father forced her into an unhappy marriage. She and her baby had both died in childbirth. Based on the date of Tatianna's death, Grandfather believed the infant must have been his child, not her husband's. He was devastated. Both his lover and his infant son had been dead for over a year, and he'd never even known."

She didn't want to see Robert's face. He must think she came from the most dreadful family. Illegitimate children, bigamous marriages, her own thievery—her family must sound appalling to him.

Then she felt him slide his hand over hers again and give it a gentle squeeze. It was a small gesture, but a comforting one. Antonia felt some of her confidence returning. After all, she hadn't caused any of this. She'd simply been the one left to deal with the consequences.

"Your grandfather's story is a tragic one," Robert murmured.

"Grandfather Vladamir vowed never to repeat those mistakes with his own children. He finally married, but they had only one child, my mother, and his wife died young. Mother said Grandfather always insisted she follow her heart when it came to love. The ironic part is that Grandfather Vladamir became such a successful artist that he died wealthy. Tatianna would have been better off with him than the man she was forced to marry."

Robert stumbled slightly as he shot her a look of surprise. "Your grandfather wouldn't happen to be Vladamir Nevsky, would he?"

Antonia didn't try to conceal her pride. "None other."

A surprised chortle burst from Robert's lips. "Now that's impressive. Didn't I see one of his paintings in the embassy last night?"

Antonia stood up straighter and nodded. "The outdoor scene. It's one of his earlier works. There's a girl along the side of the road, and he modeled her after Tatianna. Her image appears in many of his earlier works. Those paintings are referred to as his

Kozinski period—after Tatianna Kozinski. That's why I know so much about her. I was curious when I kept noticing her in Grandfather's paintings."

"But that makes you and your sisters, as his only surviving relatives, wealthy, doesn't it?"

"You'd think so, but not according to British law. You see, Grandfather died before my mother did, and he left her everything. But by British law, her inheritance went into my father's estate because a married woman has no rights to her own money. Not even the money she inherited from her family. It's absurd, but it's the law. So everything became Father's once they married."

"But I thought they weren't legally married. Wouldn't that inheritance have gone to you and your sisters when she died?" He absently slid his fingers over her gloved hand, as though stroking a cat, and the sensation sent a thrill through Antonia.

She sighed. "About a year after my parents married, Father's first wife died of some illness. Even though they were eager to legitimize their union, they wanted my grandfather to attend the wedding. Unfortunately, he was quite ill at the time and couldn't leave his village in Russia, so my parents visited him there. The local Russian Orthodox priest performed the ceremony legalizing their union, and Grandfather witnessed it."

"Wait, does that mean you and your sisters are legitimate after all?"

She sighed out another puff of whiteness that quickly dissipated in the winter air.

"It should, but my uncle claims the ceremony in Russia never took place. There's proof of the first marriage, but not the second one. The problem arises because Father's will states his children would inherit his estate upon his death, but the British court system says we aren't his legal children because we have no proof our parents were married in Russia before we were born. If we did, then Grandfather's estate would revert to me and my sisters, as would my father's estate. In order to prove we're legitimate, I need to prove the marriage took place in Russia."

"But if your parents weren't really married, then your Grandfather Vladamir's inheritance should rightfully go to you."

"That's where the last cruel twist of fate comes into play. Mother and Father were married in Gretna Green."

"A third time?"

She nodded. "They died when their train derailed as they were returning home. Their third marriage stole Grandfather's inheritance from us and left us penniless. The wedding took place the day before they both died, making their marriage legal, but leaving me and my sisters illegitimate. Mother's inheritance became Father's property once they were wed. When I went through Father's papers after his death, I discovered a letter from Uncle Walter that had arrived three days before they died. He claimed he'd investigated their marriage in Russia and believed it to be a lie. He said the church had burned down, destroying the church register. There was no proof their wedding ever took place. He threatened to expose Father as a bigamist."

"Walter Winter strikes again."

"He's at the root of it all."

Robert's pace slowed. "Is that why you need the church register? Is it from the church that burned down?"

Antonia nodded as she matched his stride. "My parents were married three times, yet my sisters and I are still considered illegitimate. The only wedding making us his heirs took place in my grandfather's village. Without that church register, we have no proof."

"The fire that destroyed it seems oddly convenient for your uncle." Robert frowned.

"Suspiciously so," Antonia agreed. "After he ejected us from our home, I wrote a letter to the Russian Orthodox priest who'd performed the wedding. His reply was so long in coming I began to believe I'd never hear from him, but Father Sergey finally contacted me. He'd fled Russia shortly after the fire and escaped to France. He's been hiding there for years. I'm lucky my letter finally made its way to him."

"He's helping you?" His genuine concern made her chest tighten.

"We're helping each other. Whoever burned down the church also stole the register. It wasn't destroyed as the government claims." She took a deep breath. "Arson wasn't the only crime committed that night. Father Sergey's wife was in the church, and the arsonist killed her as well."

"He's a murderer?" Robert stopped on the path and faced her, his shock evident.

"It almost destroyed Father Sergey."

"But wait. You said she was his wife, right? I thought Catholic priests couldn't marry."

"Russian Orthodox priests can. They follow different rules from those of the Roman Catholic priests. Father Sergey thinks his wife stumbled upon the arsonist. Apparently, someone hit her in the head and left her to die."

Robert looked stunned.

"Father Sergey says that on the day of the fire, a stranger with an English accent tried to bribe him to destroy the record of my parents' wedding. Father Sergey refused, of course, but the fire broke out that same night. A couple of days later, the same Englishman appeared in a nearby town with a serious burn on his arm."

"Strong evidence."

Antonia nodded. "But it's the next part of my story that doesn't make sense."

Robert raised his eyebrows. "It gets even more complicated?"

She mirrored his raised eyebrows and cocked her head slightly to one side. "Getting confused?"

"Not in the least. This is fascinating."

As he moved his hand, the tips of his fingers accidentally slid beneath the cuff of her dress and brushed her bare skin, making it difficult for her to concentrate.

"Are you cold, Antonia? You're trembling." A

ntonia felt her face heat with the intensity of her blush. "A bit," she lied. This man's touch affected her much too strongly.

He pulled her closer to his side and covered her forearm with his hand, sharing his body heat with her.

Antonia breathed in deeply and let out a slow, calming breath before continuing. "When Father Sergey reported that his church had burned down and his register had been stolen, Russian soldiers flooded the area, searching for the arsonist and the book. Can you imagine that? Soldiers searching for an arsonist?"

"That does seem strange," Robert said, slowing his steps. "Why would the military become involved in a case of arson?"

"Much of what transpired seems odd," she agreed. "Even with so many people searching for him, the man managed to escape with the register. According to Father Sergey, even the czar took an interest. For some reason, the official record states the church register was destroyed in the fire, but Father Sergey says the report is false."

Robert's hand tightened on her arm, and when she glanced up, she found him staring at her intently. "That's a strange thing to lie about. Why did Russian soldiers appear so quickly? Does Father Sergey think it had something to do with the arsonist, or with the church register itself?"

"He never offered his opinion. But it must be the register. Why else would the government lie and say it was destroyed? So many people keep stealing it—even Queen Victoria wants it now. Father Sergey probably knows why."

"I'll wager that's why he's hiding in France. If he's privy to a state secret, his life could be in danger."

"I've been thinking the same thing."

"You mentioned that you'd stolen the register twice. When did you take it the first time?"

"Father Sergey helped me—" she began.

"I thought he was in France."

"No, he came to London because he hoped to identify the man who murdered his wife."

"The arsonist is here? In England?" Robert asked, raising his eyebrows. "How can Father Sergey be sure? Has he seen the man?"

Antonia tightened her grip on his forearm and glanced away, not wanting to meet his gaze. "When Father Sergey arrived, I took him to the house where I grew up." Her throat felt tight. "Uncle Walter lives there now. It's his house." She paused for a moment until she knew she could speak without revealing the depth of her pain. She hated imagining Uncle Walter there, among her family's cherished possessions. Touching them, using them, discarding them. It turned her stomach. "We watched from the park across the street. As my uncle left, Father Sergey looked as though he'd seen a ghost."

Robert looked at her in silent shock.

"He's certain my uncle is the man who wanted him to destroy the proof of my parents' marriage."

"The same man who murdered his wife?"

Antonia nodded.

Robert let out a low whistle and then stopped walking to turn and stare at her.

Antonia didn't want to meet his gaze, but once she did, she saw more compassion than she'd dared hope for. More compassion than anyone else had shown her in months. He seemed to be peering into her very soul, and even though he knew her worst secrets, he didn't turn away.

"Life certainly has dealt you more than your share of woes. But you're a strong woman, Antonia Winter. Strong and resilient. I have the feeling you could take on the world if you needed to. And win."

Despite the winter chill, warmth suffused Antonia as she

stared back at this man. She lifted her chin, letting his words sink in. Was that what she was? Resilient? She would have said stubborn, but Robert's characterization had a much nicer sound to it. "Thank you."

"I'm simply stating the truth. No thanks are necessary." He twirled his cane once again and then began tapping on the ground in time with his steps. He seemed to carefully choose each spot where the tip landed. "Now that you know what your uncle is capable of, you'll need to be cautious. He's already killed once."

"I need the church register as evidence. Without it, all I have is one aging man's memories of a wedding that took place over twenty years ago."

"So you stole it."

"What else could I do?" She'd asked herself that same question so many times in the past week she'd lost track. But she'd had no good alternative. What if Uncle Walter found out? What if he destroyed the book? Taking it had been the safest alternative. "I made some educated guesses about where my uncle would hide the church register. After all, I grew up in that house. I know all the best hiding spots. It wasn't difficult to convince our old cook to let me inside."

"You found it?"

She nodded. "Uncle Walter kept the register in the library with all the other books, in plain sight." Antonia shook her head as she pressed her lips in a thin line. "I wish I'd been able to peek at the back of Grandfather's painting, but there simply wasn't enough time. But now I know I must."

"Why? What's so important about the painting?"

"It provides additional evidence that the wedding took place. If I could just check to make sure my uncle didn't damage it—" Antonia stopped mid-sentence at the sound of running footsteps fast approaching. She turned to look behind her barely in time to step aside as two young boys came tearing toward them in a footrace.

"Sorry," one of boys said as he darted past them.

"That would be Nathan," Robert commented. "He nearly bowled me over on the street earlier."

"He's a quick one. His mother must be exhausted after chasing after him all day."

They resumed their walk as they watched the boys dart off around the bend.

"You took the register that day?"

Antonia nodded. "I brought it with me when I joined Father Sergey in the park across the street. We hid it in his lodgings for safekeeping, but somehow the Russians discovered he had it. We never found out how. That same night, soldiers forced their way into his rooms and took it from him. He pleaded with them that I needed it, but they ignored him."

"So last night you stole it back from Ambassador Revnik?"

She nodded.

"But how did you know it was there?"

She could tell him part of it. Would that be enough? "Someone helped me. The man I passed it to at the soirée knew the ambassador's plan for sending it to Russia."

"Ah, yes. Your mysterious friend. I've been meaning to ask you about him."

This was it. The moment when she might lose all of Robert's goodwill. But what could she do? Betray one of her only allies? Turn on the man who had helped her recover the church register? No, that was something she wouldn't do. His identity wasn't her secret to reveal.

She leaned toward Robert. She wished she could draw out this moment of closeness a little longer. They'd forged a tenuous bond in the past half hour, and she hated the idea of breaking this fragile connection with him.

Antonia glanced at Robert, but kept her face still, trying not to let him read anything in it. "I hope you'll understand my need for secrecy. My friend also knows Father Sergey. He knew exactly where I could find the church register last night."

Robert gazed off into the trees for a moment. "You've mentioned France quite a few times. Is this man French?"

Antonia's jaw went slack before she snapped her mouth closed. Robert was much too clever. How had he guessed?

Robert nodded, apparently taking her surprise as confirmation. "So the French are helping Father Sergey, and they want to help you recover the church register, is that correct?"

She stared stonily ahead. How could she have been so careless? She was an actress, for heaven's sake. She should be able to keep her features composed. Unfortunately, she'd never been good at lying. "I won't discuss him with you. He helped me and I won't be responsible for leading you to him."

"Fair enough," Robert said. "Trust needs to be earned, after all, and you've already put a great deal of trust in me. I can't blame you for being cautious."

The wave of relief that swept through her was enough to make her stumble. She clutched at Robert's arm more tightly to regain her balance. "Do you believe I'm not working against the crown?"

"Oh, yes. I'm quite convinced."

She smiled with relief.

"But my brother won't be. He'll still want to have you arrested for treason. You'll need to help me recover that church register. Otherwise, Frederick won't stop until he puts you in prison."

❧ 21 ❧

Tricks and treachery are the practice of fools, that don't have brains enough to be honest.

— BENJAMIN FRANKLIN

Upon seeing Antonia's stricken expression, Robert's stomach sank to the path beneath his feet where her clever little booted heels could stomp on it. It was no more than he deserved.

He'd pushed too hard, that much was obvious.

Her gaze became unfocused. "You'll do what you must, as will I." Her words were soft, but they hit as hard as fists.

Why had he threatened her? She'd been entirely frank and open with him, and he'd repaid her with words as cruel as the blunt force of a truncheon. Could he fault her for being loyal? Of course not. Hadn't his own loyalty to his family driven him to lengths he never would have imagined?

Now she refused even to look at him. What other reaction

could he have expected? That she'd smile sweetly at the prospect of Frederick having her arrested her for treason?

He was much too blunt. Too direct. He also happened to be excellent at avoiding situations that might force him to become involved with other people's problems. It had been his chosen tactic over the years. Avoid and conquer. Or perhaps it was, avoid and avoid.

Since they'd met, he'd come to realize she saw him in a way that was much different from the way he saw himself. It was as though she viewed him as some sort of heroic figure.

Heroic.

Him.

He shook his head.

He knew instinctively that Antonia's story was true. Even so, he forced himself to examine it rationally, sifting through the details and searching for any contradictions or inconsistencies.

She'd endured an appalling year—one that might break a weaker woman. Her story might sound outlandish, but it provided a solid and logical explanation for why she'd stolen the book. All the particulars she'd provided seemed to hold together except for the part about Russian soldiers searching for the arsonist. But she'd admitted straightaway that their involvement seemed odd, so why would she have mentioned it if it hadn't been true?

"I'm sorry, Antonia, but I can't keep this from Frederick. I'd be committing treason," Robert said as the silence stretched between them.

She gave a sharp nod, but kept her lips pressed tightly together and fixed her stare at some point in the distance. She'd been so relaxed only a moment ago. How could he recover what they'd had together? Was it even possible?

His gaze fell to the gardenia pinned to her cloak, causing a flash of embarrassment to stab him at the reminder of his plan to manipulate her. Had he truly been attempting to deceive her, or had he merely been deceiving himself? Indecision tore at him.

How could he reconcile duty and loyalty to the crown with his need to do right by the woman standing before him?

For form's sake, he'd investigate her story. He was certain it would hold up to his scrutiny—but what if it unraveled? Would he be able to turn her over to Frederick?

Robert shook his head. It would never come to that. He already knew she was telling the truth. He almost laughed at himself. He believed her. Deep down, something about her resonated within him, and he had the sense that what they might create together could be sweet and harmonious.

As he watched Antonia, a realization swept over him. The silence between them pressed on him. "I just realized that isn't true," he said. "Treason be damned—I could never betray you to my brother. Not when it's so obvious you're telling me the truth."

She spun to face him, her face revealing her surprise and elation. She closed her eyes as a smile of relief spread across her face.

He wanted to pull her into his arms.

Antonia blinked her eyes open. "That means the world to me, but—your brother—treason—I can't let you put yourself at risk."

A connection tightened between them, its spun filaments strengthening as the seconds ticked by.

"I'll find a way. Your goals and Frederick's don't have to be mutually exclusive. First, we'll use the book to recover your inheritance, and then we'll hand it over to the Queen."

He just had to figure out how to make it happen. She squeezed his arm. "The measure of a man can't be taken by the beauty of his words, but by the path he chooses when faced with a difficult decision."

Self-confidence welled up within Robert. She inspired him. Made him want more—want to be more. He wanted to be the man she believed him to be.

She came to a stop, and he realized they'd reached the park entrance.

He wanted nothing more than to continue spending time with her—to learn more about her—explore what was growing between them. But he realized that not only were all the matrons in the park watching them, Antonia's cheeks and nose had turned pink with the cold. "I'll escort you back to your lodgings."

Antonia glanced at their audience. "That would be for the best. I need to write letters to my sisters and Miss Galloway before I leave for the theater."

"Are your sisters living with a relative?"

Antonia shook her head. "Miss Galloway is our former governess. She found a position teaching at Miss Hermitage's Collegiate School for Girls, and my sisters are permitted to share her living quarters. They don't attend classes or mix with the students. Miss Hermitage wouldn't allow it. But at least Stephanie and Eva are safe and living with someone who loves them as much as I do."

"Isn't that a burden for Miss Galloway?" He used his cane to snag a bit of soggy, crumpled newspaper that had blown across the sidewalk and was now stuck in a melting pile of snow. With a deft move, he lifted it and flung it into a nearby waste bin. It landed with a satisfyingly wet plop.

She smiled at his bit of showmanship. "I do what I can to lessen her load, but I don't know how I'd manage without her. I send her all the money I have left after paying my bills each week. Mrs. Hill is not only my landlady, but also my governess's sister. I know she seems gruff, but she's generous enough to rent me a room despite her intense dislike of theater people. Miss Galloway insists I live at a respectable address so she and my sisters can visit without risking a scandal."

Robert nodded slowly. Miss Galloway probably also wanted to ensure that Antonia lived someplace safe. It was unlikely that Miss Hermitage would allow an actress to cross her boarding school's threshold, even to visit her sisters. What if irate parents learned of her presence there and yanked their precious daughters from the school? It could drive Miss Hermitage to ruin.

Antonia was in a precarious situation.

Near the entrance to Mrs. Hill's boardinghouse, a cluster of three mothers stood watch over their little ones. The babies slept in their perambulators, and each mother held a parasol to shield her precious bundle from the weak winter sunlight.

As Robert glanced beyond the small group, a man emerged from the front door of Mrs. Hill's rooming house and quickly ducked into a waiting carriage. His face was partially obscured by the shadow his top hat cast across his eyes, but Robert found him strikingly familiar.

A tingle of foreboding swept over him. T

he man's carriage began moving toward them. In a moment, Robert would have a clear view of the passenger. Of course, that meant that the man would have a clear view of Robert as well.

"This way," Robert said, guiding Antonia around the cluster of parasols. He lifted his hand to acknowledge the women as they passed by and to block his face from view. He glanced at the man in the carriage.

"Is something wrong?" Antonia asked.

Robert instantly recognized him. He'd been among those who'd attacked him in front of the theater last night.

Had he followed Robert here? That seemed unlikely. His experience in front of the theater had left him cautious. Wary. He would have spotted anyone trailing him.

Then another thought gripped him. What if someone had seen Antonia at the ball and had tracked her here—was she in danger as well?

"I think we may have a problem."

Antonia peered up at him and her brows dipped into a V, like the dark, graceful wings of a bird. "What's wrong?"

Robert quickly told her of the attack from the previous night, and her eyes widened with horror.

"Are you certain he's one of your attackers?" she asked.

Robert gave a sharp nod. "Definitely."

She looked doubtful. "He must have followed you here. I don't think I could have been traced. I'm certain I didn't leave a trail anyone could follow. I even switched carriages after leaving the ball."

Doubt began to creep in. Had he been too careless? Had he been followed after all? "No," he finally said, "I'm certain I wasn't followed. There must be some other explanation."

"Let's speak to Mrs. Hill. She'll tell me if anything is amiss. I hope you're mistaken. I was extremely careful last night."

"I found you easily enough. You already stole the book once, and they know it. They'd suspect you whether they saw you at the ball or not. Have no doubt about that." Robert pushed open the door of the boardinghouse, standing to one side to allow Antonia to precede him.

❦ 2 2 ❦

I am no bird; and no net ensnares me; I am a free human being with an independent will.

— CHARLOTTE BRONTË

૭❧ゔ

ntonia hung her cloak on one of the hooks by the entrance, grateful to have Robert at her side.

The house was unusually quiet, and Antonia felt a chill of foreboding whisper down her neck. Had something happened to Mrs. Hill?

Her quick glance assured her that everything in the foyer was as she'd last seen it. Nothing was out of place. Her gaze caught on the cane in the umbrella stand that she'd inspected last night. Perhaps she could use it as a makeshift weapon. She avoided looking at Robert as she plucked the cane from the midst of the bouquet of umbrellas and then brandished it as she turned to face the drawing room doors.

Robert seemed at ease as he hung his hat on the rack next to her cloak, but she noticed he kept his cane firmly in his grasp. She ached for the comfort of his hand in hers, but ignored the urge. This past year of living on her own taught had her much, not the least of which was the saving grace of being free to move quickly when necessary. Holding his hand might slow her down.

She raised a shaking hand and knocked on one of the pocket doors.

There was no response.

"Mrs. Hill?" she called out. The double doors weren't closed all the way, and the opening between them was a scant inch wide. It didn't offer Antonia much of a view of the interior of the room. "I'd like to speak with you for a moment."

The woman didn't answer.

Robert moved to open the door, but she held up her hand to forestall him. "You might frighten her. Let me."

He paused, but then nodded. "Stay close."

Antonia knocked again. Her entire body was a tightly coiled spring, ready to explode with energy at the slightest touch. What if Robert had been right? What if the same man who'd attacked him outside the theater had tracked her here—and what if Mrs. Hill had fallen victim to him?

With the sound of her heart pounding in her ears, Antonia gingerly slid open the drawing room door, afraid of what she might find.

Her gaze skimmed the drawing room, but it was empty—or rather, empty of people, not of the clutter of objects.

The late Mr. Hill had filled every surface with items he'd collected during his travels, and now his widow lovingly preserved them. The hodgepodge of knickknacks nearly burst from the room—ivory carvings, Japanese swords, China dolls, blue and white plates of Delftware from the Netherlands, and a glass case on an ornate gold stand that contained a lush green fern.

What had Mrs. Hill said the container was called? A Wardian Case, named for the botanist who'd first invented it. Mother had owned one of those cases. It belonged to Uncle Walter now, just like everything else in her childhood home.

She saw no sign of Mrs. Hill. Not even this jumble could have concealed her.

"Mrs. Hill!" Antonia called out. She held her breath as she listened.

A clattering of china and a muffled outburst came from the adjoining room.

Antonia rushed toward the sound, her wide skirts brushing against the large pieces of furniture that attempted to slow her. She accidentally bumped an ivory figurine with the tip of the cane. It teetered precariously, but Robert reached out and snatched it before it could fall.

Before she could reach the door, Mrs. Hill stepped through it carrying a tea tray. Antonia stumbled to a halt, nearly colliding with her.

The woman's eyes widened in surprise. "What's all this cater-wauling? I know my sister taught you better. That's what comes from spending time with those theater people. They teach you to make your voice so loud it can be heard in the back row of the theater, don't they? Well, stop doing it inside my house." She continued on past them and set down the tea tray with a clatter on the small table in front of the sofa.

Antonia set the tip of the cane on the floor as she reached out with her other hand and gripped the back of a nearby chair for support. She mussed the frilly, white antimacassar as her fingers dug into the upholstery.

Robert stood close to her. He'd followed her headlong rush to rescue Mrs. Hill—from a teapot. As she released her grip and lowered her arm to her side, her shoulder brushed against his chest, causing her to become suddenly and intensely aware of him.

Mrs. Hill shot Antonia a sharp glance, and then turned to glare at Robert.

Antonia mastered herself. She glanced up at Robert. "I think I might have overreacted." She smoothed the antimacassar she'd mussed, arranging it so it matched the other squares of lace adorning the backs of Mrs. Hill's sofa and chairs.

"Understandably so," he replied, setting the small figurine he'd rescued on the nearest table.

Antonia glanced at the floral tea tray Mrs. Hill held. It bore two Delftware cups and a pot.

Two?

Mrs. Hill huffed. "What's all this about?"

"I thought I recognized a gentleman who just left your house," Robert said. "Did you have a visitor?"

Mrs. Hill glowered at him and then abruptly turned away and plopped onto the sofa. Was that a look of disappointment? As soon as Mrs. Hill realized Antonia was watching her, the expression disappeared.

Antonia crossed the room to get a better look at Mrs. Hill. Now she looked affronted. "Was he looking for me?" she asked.

"Who?" Mrs. Hill asked as she poured her tea.

"The man who just left," Antonia explained. "The one who rode away in the carriage."

"I have no idea what you're talking about," she said in tones that brought with it the chill of the London winter. "If someone came here asking for you, I'd tell you." She slipped her hand into the pocket of her dress as though reassuring herself of its contents. "If you did, indeed, see someone leave, perhaps he was visiting one of my other tenants. I do have other tenants, you know. And I don't keep track of everyone's comings and goings."

Antonia stared pointedly at the second teacup as she clenched the cane in her grip. "And for whom did you bring out that second teacup if not the visitor who just left?" Antonia asked, her voice oozing false sweetness.

"Miss Winter!" Mrs. Hill snapped. "There's no need for you to take that tone with me. I'm under no obligation to explain myself to the likes of you . If you don't like it here, you're free to move out. I'll even refund the rent you paid in advance."

Return the rent money? Mrs. Hill, the most tightfisted woman she'd ever met, offered to return the rent money? She'd never before mentioned the possibility. What if Mrs. Hill's next step would be to evict her?

Antonia couldn't let that happen. She simply couldn't.

"Well, Miss Winter? Would you like to leave?" The steely glint in Mrs. Hill's eyes underscored her ruthlessness.

Antonia shrank back. Leave? She couldn't leave. Where would she go? She couldn't afford to pay more than she already gave Mrs. Hill each week, and besides that, what respectable boardinghouse would permit an actress to live there? "I—I'm sorry I offended you," she said, the words tumbling out of her mouth in a rush. "I'm perfectly happy here. Content. I know you're doing your best to watch over me. I'd very much like to stay. I promise I'll be on my best behavior."

Mrs. Hill's angry gaze didn't waver.

Antonia took a hasty step back from the harridan and ran directly into Robert. She stumbled. He wrapped his arm around her waist, barely keeping her from falling.

"Humph." Mrs. Hill's upper lip curled as she glared at Robert's encircling arm. "You have an odd way of showing it. Have some decorum, young lady." "

Yes, Mrs. Hill." Antonia shrank away from Robert while keeping an eye on Mrs. Hill. She gave him a wide berth as she moved toward the door. She needed to make herself scarce before Mrs. Hill lost her temper entirely and evicted her. "If you'll excuse us, we'll leave you to your tea. Lord Wentworth was about to take his leave."

Mrs. Hill stared hard at her teapot, but Antonia could see her hand tremble as she reached for it.

As Antonia stepped out of the drawing room, she crushed her eyes shut, a chill wave of relief flooding her. That had been entirely too close. She'd nearly lost her room. And for what? Robert had had no more than a momentary glimpse of a man. A man who couldn't possibly have tracked her here. How could she have let herself be swayed so easily when logic told her he had to be mistaken?

Was she really so weak? So easily swayed by a few kind words? Was she that desperate to win his approval and give herself over to another person?

She didn't want to lose herself in another person. She already knew the devastation brought on when people left and everything changed.

She was better off alone. Safer.

It wasn't until Antonia slid the drawing room doors closed, creating a solid barrier between herself and Mrs. Hill, that she was able to breathe again.

Robert seized her hand and drew her closer, speaking in hushed, urgent tones. "You need to move out. It's the prudent thing to do."

Antonia's mouth dropped open, and she snatched her hand from his grasp. "You can't be serious. Do you have any idea how difficult it was to find a respectable establishment? One that would accept a single woman working as an actress? The only reason I'm here is because Mrs. Hill is my governess's sister. Leaving isn't an option." She thrust the ludicrous cane back into the umbrella stand with a loud thump.

"Your safety is of utmost importance." Robert seemed to radiate authority, and Antonia found his attitude immensely irritating. Who was he to make pronouncements and give orders?

"I'm entirely safe here," she said, using the icy tone she reserved for her most persistent and annoying admirers. How dare Robert march into her life and try to rule it? Did he think he owned her because he knew her secrets? Did he believe he now had power over her? "There's no need to be so heavy-handed with me. I've been taking care of myself for nearly a year now, and I'm managing quite well. You're overreacting, Lord Wentworth. You already admitted you might have been mistaken. If I found any proof supporting your claim that someone tracked me down, I wouldn't hesitate to leave, but that isn't the case, is it?"

Robert jerked his head back as though she'd sprouted thorns. The muscles along his jawline bulged. "My apologies, Miss Winter. I clearly overstepped."

"Clearly."

He snatched up his hat from a rack near the door. As he settled it in place, he glanced back at her. "I hope that despite my heavy-handedness, you'll not dismiss the possible threat to your safety. Please be careful."

He stared at her until she gave him a curt nod, and then he turned and let himself out.

Antonia froze in place, running through the scene back in the drawing room. Something still niggled at her. Some detail that seemed out of place.

The second teacup. Who had it been intended for? And Mrs. Hill had touched something in her pocket. A card? A memento? Had a visitor abandoned Mrs. Hill, or was she expecting a guest to arrive? Or perhaps it was something completely different. For all Antonia knew, Mrs. Hill was enacting some ritual of homage to her late husband in that mausoleum of a room. Perhaps she carried some memento of him—a lock of hair or a ring?

She glanced toward the closed doors. She was certain if she walked back through them right now, she'd be evicted.

Antonia turned toward the staircase, lifted the front hem of her skirt, and fled up the narrow stairs, hoping she hadn't just made one of the biggest mistakes of her life.

23

He *is the best man who, when making his plans, fears and reflects on everything that can happen to him, but in the moment of action is bold.*

— HERODOTUS

Less than forty-five minutes later, Robert faced his brother, who was leaning back against the carriage's cushions. Robert lifted his cane, closed one eye, and peered along its length. In contrast with his own duplicitous self, the gleaming black cane was perfectly straight and true.

Robert glanced at Frederick as he lowered the tip to the floor. His unrevealed knowledge of Antonia's identity rode with them in the carriage like an unwanted third passenger.

The moment he'd returned he'd sent a footman—young Turner—off on the train to Maidenhead to investigate her story. Turner was a clever one. He'd been grateful for his position in the household. He'd quickly made himself useful to Frederick by successfully completing a number of moderately clandestine tasks, and had shown great talent in carrying them out. Robert rarely made use of Turner's unusual skills, but he was confident in the footman's ability to ferret out information. If Antonia had fabricated her story, Turner would soon discover the truth.

But she'd been forthright. Robert was certain of it.

He paused—was he simply being diligent in sending Turner to investigate Antonia, or was his investigation a way to delay telling Frederick?

"Are you listening?" Frederick asked. "You need to focus."

"Of course," Robert lied. He closed his eyes as he tried to recall what his brother had just said. It was something about Revnik's state of mind, wasn't it? "Revnik made an enormous mistake in trying to kidnap me. Attempting to snatch a member of the peerage off the streets of London was an act of desperation. That single deed revealed the importance the church register holds for him. Now we know he's frantic to recover it, and it's driving him to make reckless decisions."

Frederick raised a single eyebrow. "It also reveals the lengths to which Ambassador Revnik is willing to go in order to reclaim it. You need to be careful. Don't do anything that could put you in danger."

"I don't normally travel with an entourage." He gestured toward one of the impromptu guards outside the window. "I'm not sure how much more careful I can be."

"Just don't disappear on us. I don't want his people to find you alone somewhere inside the embassy and decide to take advantage of the situation. That would be a foolish mistake."

The implied criticism rubbed like sandpaper against his frayed nerves. "I'm not a fool."

Frederick seemed oblivious that he'd given offense. "And make sure you follow the plan. I know how you like to improvise, but today isn't the day for that." He gingerly rested the heel of his hand on his knee, leaving his bandaged fingers dangling. He rolled his shoulders as though they were stiff, and they probably were.

Robert decided it was best not to reply—not if he couldn't remain civil.

It had been obvious this morning that Frederick's burns had given him a sleepless night. When Robert had entered the breakfast room a few hours go, he'd discovered his brother already seated there, looking pale and wan. He'd listlessly picked at his plate of food, gingerly holding his fork between the fingers of his left hand. His slumped shoulders and the dark circles under his eyes told Robert everything he needed to know about the pain he was enduring.

In an instant, he forgave his brother for being in one of his overly critical moods. Frederick's compulsion for perfection often overwhelmed him when he was exhausted. When he was like this, he would reexamine every minor detail of a plan ad nauseum. It was best to let him vent and not react. Offering a comment would only provide him with a target for his ire.

Robert's grand entourage entered the gates of the embassy twenty minutes late for his appointment, as planned. He sat patiently inside the carriage, not bothering to open the door. His performance as an "offended noble" began at this moment, and this would be his grand entrance. It wasn't until the footman opened the door that he finally descended with all the pomp and officiousness that the visit demanded. He knew from his previous night's foray into Revnik's study that the man had an excellent view of him right now, and he had no doubt he was being watched.

A servant ushered them upstairs to the ambassador's suite. They entered through a different door from the one Robert had used last night. This one led him into an outer waiting area rather than directly into the inner office.

Despite their late arrival, the ambassador's secretary kept the large group waiting. It was an obvious power play, and clumsily done. The ambassador wanted to demonstrate his control over them, but in doing so he revealed too much of himself and his plans. He'd made it obvious their meeting would be a contentious one.

Robert's footmen stood at attention, doing an admirable job of looking intimidating, and based on the secretary's frequent nervous glances, they were succeeding.

Although the leather chairs looked comfortable, they weren't. It was probably intentional. Welcome guests would be ushered into the inner office quickly, whereas unwelcome ones would be forced to endure the torturous chairs in silence.

Robert leafed through a London newspaper while Frederick perused a week-old Russian one. "You should brush up on your Russian," Frederick muttered. "You never know when it will come in handy."

Frederick had a point. It would have been nice to have been able to decipher a bit more of that book last night.

Robert picked up another of the week-old Cyrillic-print papers and glanced through it, but set it aside after a few moments. Reading it required more concentration than he could muster at the moment.

After five minutes of waiting, both Robert and Frederick stood on cue, as planned.

"Please give the ambassador our regrets. We have other pressing appointments and cannot linger," Robert said.

He and Frederick turned toward the exit.

Before Robert had taken more than two steps, the inner door leading to the ambassador's office flew open. Robert forced himself not to exchange glances with Frederick. So far, things were happening exactly as his brother had predicted.

More of Frederick's chess moves.

Had Ambassador Revnik been watching—or had the secretary signaled him in some way?

"Lord Wentworth, Mr. Woolsy, I'm so sorry to have kept you waiting."

"Ambassador Revnik," Robert replied in clipped tones. "We'd

abandoned all hope of meeting with you today. We were just leaving."

"Then I'm glad I caught you in time. Please, please, come in."

Robert paused long enough to see how Revnik would react if he thought Robert might leave. When the man stepped forward to usher him into the office, Robert relented.

Frederick followed them into the inner office, and the footmen waited in the receiving room.

"Please be seated," Revnik said, gesturing toward a pair of chairs. "Can I offer you some strong Russian tea?" Without waiting for them to respond, Revnik's secretary gave a nod and hurried off, presumably to prepare the beverage.

"I hope your health has fully recovered from last night's unfortunate episode," Revnik commented as he moved behind his desk.

"The shrimp?" Robert sat down alongside his brother in the pair of leather chairs facing the ambassador's wide desk. "Thank you, yes. And with no lasting effects, as you see."

"Yes." He pursed his lips as he examined Robert, apparently not liking what he saw. "A rather miraculous recovery, wouldn't you say?"

The secretary entered with a tea tray and bustled about serving everyone.

"Not necessarily. Once I purged it from my system, my recovery was swift. I was even able to attend the theater as a last-minute addition to Lord Huntley's box."

Revnik's lips pursed even more tightly, and Robert wondered absently if the ambassador's pucker might inadvertently swallow his entire face. "I heard as much, and it piqued my curiosity. You seemed so ill when last I spoke to you. The way you rushed from my ball, well, I must admit, I assumed you'd go directly home."

The secretary placed cups of tea on the small table between Robert and Frederick.

"Mr. Ambassador," Robert said, "this conversation is beginning to take on the tone of an interrogation."

The secretary's eyes grew wide and he scurried from the room.

"My apologies, my lord—"

Robert cut him off. "I came today to discuss something much more pressing than the state of my health. An appalling incident occurred last night as I exited the theater. Some of your men—footmen I recognized from your ball—tried to force me into a carriage. If not for the assistance of my friends, your men would have succeeded in kidnapping me off the streets of London. Considering the level of tension between our two countries, I'm astounded you would have resorted to such clumsy tactics."

Revnik didn't even blink. He simply stared at Robert as the seconds ticked by on the clock above his fireplace mantel.

Robert narrowed his eyes. "Don't you have anything to say? An apology perhaps? Or some excuse about a mistaken identity?"

"Would you believe either one?"

"Of course not."

"Then let's not bother. I prefer we have honesty between us."

"Honesty?" Robert almost snorted his contempt. "Please. Be honest. I'd love to hear what you have to say. After all, you tried to have me kidnapped."

"No—no. Not kidnapped. Never that. I simply wanted to ask you a few questions." The ambassador's thin smile was as false as his words. "You left quite suddenly last night, and it seemed unusual. I found it even more noteworthy when I discovered an item had gone missing."

Robert tightened his grip on the arms of his chair. "Are you accusing me of theft, ambassador? Do you believe I stole one of Russia's precious trinkets from your embassy? Did I walk out with a painting tucked under my arm? This is outrageous. You insult me, sir." Robert shoved himself to his feet, scraping his chair noisily against the floor as he did so.

"Calm yourself, my lord." Revnik made a soothing gesture as he rose to his feet as well.

"Calm myself? You attempt to kidnap me, question me regarding my brief indisposition last night, then accuse me of being a thief, and you expect me to react calmly? Does your czar know how you conduct yourself, sir? Our countries are on the brink of war. I doubt Czar Nicholas would approve of your methods."

Revnik let out an indignant huff of air and squared his shoulders. "You forget yourself, Lord Wentworth. You aren't on British soil right now. This embassy is Russia. I intend to do whatever it takes to recover what was stolen."

"This meeting is at an end, Revnik. And I assure you that Queen Victoria will hear of your abysmal behavior. I came here today because I hoped there was a simple misunderstanding that could be cleared up with a conversation, but now I see I was mistaken. Your actions have been reckless and reprehensible, and I refuse to tolerate your continued abuse. Good day."

As he turned his back, he saw Revnik's expression falter. Robert didn't hesitate, but flung open the door and strode through it with Frederick at his heels.

Robert turned to speak with Frederick and was gratified to see Revnik hurry around his desk. The man banged against something and let out a yelp of pain.

"Lord Wentworth. Please." Revnik hobbled forward, chasing Robert through his secretary's office. "My apologies, my lord. I believe you are right. There is a fundamental misunderstanding between us."

Robert paused and turned to face the ambassador. "Now you're telling me this is nothing more than a misunderstanding? Just a moment ago you didn't even believe an apology was in order."

"I was wrong. I'm sorry. For everything. Please. Come back into my office so we can talk. I—I need your help."

Robert and Frederick exchanged glances. Events were unfolding exactly as Frederick had predicted. No—planned. The man knew exactly how to manipulate people like pieces on a chess board.

Frederick finally spoke. "Perhaps, since Ambassador Revnik is willing to apologize, you should ask him to explain what drove him to act in such an injudicious manner before you decide whether or not to take this matter to the Queen."

Robert pretended to ponder his brother's advice, and then met Revnik's pleading gaze. "I have one condition. Before we continue, you must agree to stop playing these manipulative games. I have no more patience for them."

"Of course, Lord Wentworth." Revnik's tight smile revealed his anxiety. He stepped to one side and ushered them back into his inner office.

Once they'd returned to their seats, Revnik peered at Robert from across his desk. "Last night someone stole an item of importance right out of a diplomatic pouch. It's a severe breach of our embassy's security, and I've already taken measures to address the lapse. My first suspicions fell upon a certain young woman, but her involvement seemed unlikely since she wasn't on our restricted guest list. However, when I described her, one of my footmen recalled seeing her last night. I've been contacting all of my guests to learn if any of them might have seen her or spoken to her."

Robert arched one eyebrow. "And you decided to kidnap me to ask about her?"

Revnik's smile was as false as it was broad. "Kidnap! Never! As I said, I merely wished to speak with you. And since there was some urgency to the matter, I believed it was best to offer you an escort."

"Three armed escorts? Escorts who hardly spoke to me and tried to force me into a carriage?"

"That's outrageous!" Revnik's eyes widened to show, rather ostentatiously, that he was shocked. The man was a poor actor.

Antonia would have been much more convincing. "That can't be true. Can it?"

"Are you impugning my word?" Robert narrowed his eyes and let his anger build. Revnik eyed him nervously.

"But I know you wouldn't lie to me, Lord Wentworth. You're much too honorable a man. And noble. Yes, you're quite honorable and noble."

The man might not be able to act, but he had groveling down to an art form. A part of Robert took perverse pleasure in witnessing it. He almost felt guilty about it. Almost. "No," Robert said in tones that would freeze songbirds out of trees. "I would not."

Revnik paled. "Did—did you happen to see a small young woman with brown hair? According to some reports, she may have been wearing a silver dress."

Antonia? It had to be. But he'd seen Revnik's man at her boardinghouse less than an hour ago, so why was Revnik still looking for her? Either the man hadn't reported back that he'd found her, or he'd been mistaken, just as Antonia had claimed.

Robert skewered Revnik with a scathing look. "This is the urgent question you wanted to put to me last night? Did I see a woman in a silver dress?"

"Yes. I've been trying to track her movements, but she's been elusive. It seems unlikely that she could have stolen the—the item and have still made it to the theater in time for the performance."

"Wait." Robert frowned. "I thought you were asking if I'd seen her at the ball. But you want to know if I saw her at the theater last night?"

"No, no. I already know she performed. I simply need to know if you might have seen her at the embassy. After all, you were not with the other guests due to your—your indisposition. My footman mentioned he'd seen you exiting one of the unused hallways last night. Do you recall seeing her in some unlikely spot?"

"Unlikely spot?" Robert repeated, shooting Revnik a look of

extreme irritation. "I can assure you that I did not encounter a woman while I was on my way to or from the privy. Is that what you wanted to ask me?"

Frederick shifted in his chair. "What's so important about this woman? Why accost my brother on the street? Wouldn't it make more sense to ask her since you already know she performed? She's an actress, am I correct?"

Revnik froze at the suggestion. "I couldn't possibly—she's much too important—" He blanched. "My English fails me. I mean un important, of course."

Robert noticed the corner of Frederick's mouth twitch. So, Revnik believed Antonia was important, did he? But why? Was it because of her grandfather? He pinned Revnik with a stern look. "And you believed that kidnapping and questioning a member of the peerage was a wiser course of action than questioning an un important woman?"

The ambassador pressed his lips together. "I apologize for the behavior of my men. I assure you, they will be dealt with." He stood. "I regret you were inconvenienced. Please be assured that nothing like this will ever happen again." Robert glared at him for a moment, and then relented. He stood and smiled at the ambassador, doing his best to appear genial. Revnik held out his hand. Robert barely paused before shaking it. "Your sincere apology was all I needed. Good day to you." Robert collected his numerous footmen and they exited the building together. A cold gust of wind smacked him in the face as he walked out the front door, and he pulled up his collar against the chill. He and Frederick didn't exchange words until they were back inside the waiting carriage. "So, your little thief is too important to kidnap? Stranger and stranger," Frederick muttered.

"What do you make of it?"

"I have no idea," Frederick said, "but I plan to get to the bottom of this. If the Russians think she's important, then so do

I. We need to find her before they do, and now we know where to begin."

24

All the world's a stage, and all the men and women merely players; they have their exits and their entrances; and one man in his time plays many parts, his acts being seven ages.

— WILLIAM SHAKESPEARE

T he temperature dropped precipitously that afternoon, and by evening the frigid London streets were covered in a faint dusting of snow. Footprints and dark puddles broke the pristine white surface.

Antonia left early so she could save cab fare and walk to the theater, but the sidewalks were slick. If she stepped too close to one of the frozen puddles, she slipped as ice crunched under her shoe, so she did her best to skirt around them.

At first, she welcomed the fact that she needed to concentrate on where she should place her feet to keep from falling, because it temporarily distracted her from the thoughts that had been plaguing her all afternoon.

It didn't last. Her mind continued to work away at the knot in her life named Robert.

Was she foolish to have shared so much information with him? Had she been swayed by her growing attraction to him? She pushed the questions from her mind. It was done. In the past. It was impossible to undo what was done. She needed to move forward.

Why was she more nervous tonight than last night when she prepared to sneak into the embassy? The book was hers now. She should feel relieved, but when she remembered the way Robert had looked at her—the way he'd understood her when everyone else turned their backs on her—that might be what troubled her the most. It was as though he could see into her heart—or her very soul.

As she entered the stage door, Antonia shook her head, banishing all thoughts that didn't concern tonight's performance. At this moment, the cause of her tension didn't really matter. She needed to insulate herself from her worries so they didn't interfere with the show.

"You're nearly late."

Antonia spun around to face Claude. She shot a quick glance at the clock on the wall above his head. "I still have five minutes to spare. The roads were slick and delayed me." She removed her fur-lined hat and patted her hair to ensure her hairpins were still in place.

"After last night's near-disaster, you should have been here an hour early," he said, his French accent thick with annoyance. "I meant it when I said I'd replace you. You might be good, but you aren't great."

"I understand." Antonia pressed her lips together as she hurried down the staircase to the women's dressing room.

The other actresses in the play were in various stages of preparation for tonight's performance. They greeted Antonia cheerfully as she entered the dressing room and hung her coat on a peg. She made her way toward her dressing table and smiled as her good friend Zelda broke away from the others to join her.

"I could hear Claude scold you from all the way down here," Zelda said.

Antonia shot her a look of mock-suspicion. "You have unusually good hearing. The dressing room door usually blocks out every sound."

"You found me out," she said, grinning sheepishly. "I was standing at the bottom of the stairs, eavesdropping. Don't worry about Claude. He'll get over his anger with you soon."

"Only if I don't cause him any more trouble."

"Well, yes," Zelda agreed. "But you've never been late before. I'm sure you won't let it happen again." She glanced back, and Antonia followed her gaze. The other two actresses were examining the hem of one of the Lady Toppington costumes. Zelda turned her gaze back to Antonia. "I'm worried about you." Her honey-blond eyebrows drew closer together as she frowned. "You were late for last night's show and then you disappeared immediately after the soirée. Is anything wrong? Are you in some sort of trouble? You know you can always come to me."

Those compassionate words pierced Antonia's heart. Zelda had been kind to her ever since the first day of rehearsals. While most of the cast members had been welcoming, Zelda had gone out of her way to befriend Antonia. Even though this had been Antonia's first leading role on a London stage, Zelda hadn't begrudged her the part. Instead, she'd praised Antonia for her excellent audition and helped her learn her lines by running through them with her over and over.

She wanted to tell Zelda everything. About stealing the book, about meeting Robert, about the men who might be searching for her. But instead, she shook her head. "It's nothing."

"Let me know if you change your mind. I'd be happy to help if I can." She grinned. "After all, that's what the best-friend character in a play is for, right?"

Antonia laughed. "Right. Does that mean I can convince you to help me into my costume?"

"But of course," Zelda said, pulling Antonia to her feet as she gave her a grin. "I'm at your service, my lady." She bobbed a curtsy.

It didn't take long to put on the 1770's-style high-waisted riding costume, especially with Zelda's help. Later in the play, Antonia would change into the wire-frame panniers and stomacher that had been fashionable back then. Panniers were similar to the hoop skirts women wore today, but they only supported and extended the skirts at the sides while leaving the front and back of the dress flat. It was rather like wearing a large wire basket on each hip. A basket that could be collapsed up and tucked under the arms, but when lowered would support her skirts in the desired shape. Since her character was an orphaned, penniless relative, her skirts were only about three feet wide once she donned them over the panniers, but Lady Toppington's more elaborate gowns spanned a width of five feet.

As Antonia stood in the wings, waiting for her entrance, she concentrated on her upcoming scene. As she stepped on stage, her heartbeat thudded as her anxiety crescendoed. She channeled it so that its only outlet was to bring the character of Anne Blake to life. She spoke the lines she'd memorized. Those words of heartfelt loss. Her own despair and fear poured into her performance, bringing it to life.

The audience devoured it. Antonia sensed their growing excitement. At each appropriate moment, they either laughed or gasped or applauded with delight. Their enthusiasm filled her, and she in turn sent it back out to them.

At the scene change, Antonia took a deep breath as she stepped off stage and into the wings. Her body vibrated with intensity as she waited for her next cue. Claude moved to stand next to her in the near darkness, and she could just make out his crooked-toothed grin.

"They love you tonight," he murmured. "You took my scolding to heart, eh? Now you're trying to make yourself indispensable. Tu es magnifique ."

Antonia widened her eyes at his comment. Claude thought she was magnificent?

She shook her head in bemusement. She turned slightly as she prepared to enter the door on stage so her wide panniers could fit through it. The pain of her parents' deaths was still so fresh that when she drew upon it for this moment on stage, she was nearly overwhelmed. That was another thing she and her character had in common. Their status as orphans.

The next hour passed in a blur. When the curtain closed on the final scene, the audience paused only a moment before they rose to their feet with thunderous applause. The people on the ground floor of the theater shouted and stomped as they waited for another curtain call. When the red velvet drapes opened again, Antonia glanced higher up at the boxes surrounding the stage and saw that even the jaded members of the peerage were on their feet and applauding enthusiastically.

Antonia swirled back onto the stage and grinned as she made her curtsy hand in hand with Danny, the actor playing her love interest, Edward Thorold. As she stepped forward for her curtsy, the applause surged and the patrons shouted out their love and praise for her in waves of sound. It crashed over her, wrapping her in their approbation.

Antonia kissed her fingertips and then stretched her hands out to the audience, causing the crowd to cheer even louder.

Finally, the curtains closed for the last time, and the troupe made its way offstage. Danny raised both arms into the air in victory. He cut a fine figure in the old-fashioned eighteenth-century stockings and breeches. He was always a favorite of the ladies in the audience. When his gaze latched onto hers, he grinned and darted toward her, wrapping her in a bear hug.

Antonia laughed as she hugged him back. What a stupendous evening.

She spun away from him, laughing. She glanced up at the large man in the wings. The man who stared directly at her.

Antonia's heart thudded in her chest as she came to an abrupt halt.

The Russians. They'd tracked her down.

❧ 25 ❧

Love will find a way through paths where wolves fear to prey.

— *LORD BYRON*

⌘

The man stepped forward into the light, and Antonia's relief left her knees weak.

Robert.

Her thrill at seeing him quickly surpassed her previous burst of fear.

"You're here! But how? Claude never lets guests backstage during a performance." Antonia glanced around for the stage manager, but couldn't see him. "If he did, he must like you. He's very strict."

"That's possible," Robert said. He smiled at her, his eyes mischievous. "It might also be because of the small bribe I gave him."

She laughed. "That sounds much more likely."

"You were wonderful tonight. I couldn't take my eyes off you."

She hadn't thought the night could get any better, but his words made her heart soar to new heights. "Did you see the entire performance?"

He nodded. "I came backstage to watch the last act from the wings."

She slid her arm through his, and a thrill washed through her at the feel of him. "I need to change out of my costume. Come downstairs. You can wait for me outside the dressing room."

As they reached the top of the staircase, she noticed how tight her muscles had become. She rubbed her hand along the back of her neck, kneading at the stiffness. Channeling her anxiety may have carried her through the performance, but now the exhaustion from last night's activities was beginning to catch up with her. Using so much emotion drained her of every last drop of energy, leaving her feeling like a wrung-out washrag.

It suddenly dawned on her that her earlier anxiety had vanished. She felt safe. She glanced at Robert. It must be because he was here.

As she descended the stairs, he trailed after her like a guardian angel. With so many people descending the narrow staircase simultaneously, their footsteps echoed like rolling thunder. Once they reached the floor below, she swept past various large set pieces leaning against the walls and crowding the space. Ornate false doors leading nowhere sat next to windows made of nothing more than painted wood.

The hallway had been turned into "temporary" overflow storage for the pieces that wouldn't fit into the labyrinth of rooms beneath the stage. Those were crammed beyond capacity with sets, props, and costumes from previous theatrical productions. Of course, ever since Antonia had begun working at the theater, she'd never seen one of the large pieces move from its temporary spot.

As Antonia brushed past a curlicued length of fence leaning

against the wall, the wide skirts of her costume caught on something. She pulled up short, and Robert nearly stumbled into her.

"My dress. It's snagged on something," she said.

He stepped back and glanced down at her skirt. "It's caught on a sharp bit of metal. If you'll allow me, I can set you free."

They moved to one side and allowed the other cast members to squeeze past. She heard Robert's cane clatter to the floor as he knelt to examine whatever had ensnared her. Her head seemed to buzz and vibrate as everyone congratulated one another. She was exhausted. Unfortunately, this brief pause gave her exhaustion an opportunity to sink its claws deeper into her, digging into every joint and sinew. She positively ached with it.

Two men, apparently theatergoers, stepped forward from where they'd been waiting near the dressing rooms. They grinned, clutching their hats to their chests. They'd made their way backstage quickly. Antonia usually made it all the way to the dressing room before any outsiders appeared downstairs. This pair must be particularly eager.

"I almost have it," Robert muttered. "This bit of lace is badly tangled."

"Take your time." She glanced over her shoulder as she tried to see what he was doing, but the wide panniers blocked her view. "I'd hate for it to tear."

As Antonia faced forward, she smiled warmly at the two men. The last thing she needed was to develop a reputation for being rude or dismissive of patrons. They were her livelihood. Those wonderful fees she and the members of her troupe received for performing at soirées were too valuable to risk losing due to some careless word, so she always went out of her way to be gracious.

Nearly all the other cast members had already disappeared. Only Zelda lingered at the doorway for a moment. She shot Antonia a glance of sympathy at being cornered by the pair. Antonia waved her on. There was no reason for her to linger as well. Zelda fluttered her fingers as she stepped into the dressing room, closing the door behind her.

Then the two men moved forward in the hallway, effectively blocking the only path to the dressing rooms.

Something about one of the men caught Antonia's attention. He seemed familiar to her.

"Robert," she said.

"I almost have it," he said.

She stared at the familiar-looking man. Where did she know him from? Suddenly she knew. He was the footman she'd spoken with last night at the embassy ball. The one who'd been guarding the stairs.

Antonia froze.

"Done," Robert said. "You're free."

Robert had been right all along. The Russians really had tracked her down.

"Robert," she murmured so that only he could hear her, "Revnik's men are here."

The Russians' faces seemed to transform before her eyes. They dropped their friendly masks and an air of grim determination swept over them. They knew she'd recognized them. She could read it in their expressions.

Robert rose to his feet and stepped in front of her, shielding her with his body. She wrapped an arm around his waist from behind, standing as close to him as possible as she peeked around his shoulder.

The footman from last night stepped forward and locked gazes with her. "You recognize me. That will make things easier." Although he spoke with a Russian accent, it was faint.

"I-I don't know what you mean." Antonia matched his forward march with a back-step of her own and tugged Robert with her. He resisted only for a moment and then gave way to her gentle pressure.

The Russian footman let out a sharp laugh. "It will be easier if you don't pretend. We know you slipped into the ambassador's ball. I spoke to you myself." "What do you want?" she asked.

"I am Sergeant Davydov. My friend and I work for the ambassador. He wants to ask you a few questions. Nothing more. If you would come with us—" He stepped forward again and reached for her arm.

"Don't touch her," Robert said as he sidestepped to block the man's hand.

Both Russians stiffened. They glanced at one another, and then in unison they shifted their hands, revealing the knives they'd been concealing. They appeared particularly menacing as they glared at Robert.

Antonia felt lightheaded as she backed away again, tugging Robert along with her. She glanced down the deserted hallway beyond the pair, hoping to see her dressing room door open. Couldn't anyone hear them talking? Probably not. Those doors were nearly soundproof.

"Do not think you can keep her from us," Davydov's partner said in heavily accented English. "It will not go well for you."

She could feel Robert's muscles tense as he prepared to meet their attack. She couldn't let him fight them. What if they stabbed him? What if they killed him? Her knees felt weak for a moment and she staggered back, pulling Robert back another step before she managed to right herself.

She glanced down and noticed Robert's cane on the floor, lying useless in the abyss between them and Revnik's men. It might as well have been in his carriage for all the good it would do them right now.

They needed to escape. To hide.

But where?

Their options were limited. She glanced around, quickly discarding each idea that occurred to her. Could they run back up the stairs? Robert would expect her to go first, and she'd be so slow in these skirts that he'd feel obliged to protect her back—without his weapon.

Wait. What about the storage rooms beneath the stage?

Antonia glanced down the hallway beyond the two men again. The dressing room doors remained closed, but the Russians had no way of knowing that. Not unless they turned around and looked. It was time to use her acting skills. She plastered a bright smile on her face, focused on a spot behind them, and raised her hand in a greeting.

With alarmed expressions, the Russians whipped around to discover who was approaching.

Antonia seized her opportunity and dragged Robert down the hallway, away from the two men. She didn't pause to glance over her shoulder to see if they'd noticed. A moment later the sound of their scuffling feet told her they'd turned to give chase. "Stop," one of them called. "Miss Winter. Stop. You're in no danger from us."

Oh, really? Their knives told a different story.

She heard a loud crash from behind her and risked glancing back. One of the set pieces that had been propped against the wall had come crashing down, temporarily blocking their pursuers. Robert must have pushed it over as they passed it.

It wouldn't slow them for long. They were already shoving it out of their path, but the delay bought Antonia and Robert a few precious seconds.

With Robert in tow, she ran toward the staircase but she bypassed it and pulled him toward a well-concealed door beyond it. "This way," she said as she felt his grip on her hand loosen. She refused to let him stand his ground and fight those men.

If she and Robert could escape beneath the stage, they could disappear into the dark recesses of the storage rooms. She only hoped she remembered enough about the labyrinth to lose their pursuers. If she could lead them away from the doorway and then circle behind them, she and Robert could escape.

She made a desperate grab at the doorknob and twisted it as she threw her shoulder against the door, not wanting to waste even a fraction of a second slowing down. It banged open and they rushed through. Robert slammed it shut behind them, but it bounced open again. She dragged him forward, not letting him pause to close it again and waste precious time. Instead, they sped into the darkness under the stage.

Antonia was confronted by a maze of fake stone walls and painted trees. But it was a familiar maze. They moved far beneath the stage, and her eyes quickly adjusted to the low light. When silhouettes appeared in the doorway, Antonia slowed their headlong dash and ducked through the nearest opening, pulling Robert in with her.

"We need to keep quiet," she whispered into his ear.

He gave her a silent nod.

The space was much smaller than she'd expected. It was more of a cubbyhole. Her back pressed against a rough wall that felt a bit like brick, but she knew it wasn't. The texture and temperature weren't quite right. Perhaps it was a piece of a set that had been built to simulate stone.

She could hear the two men moving farther beneath the stage. Were she and Robert hidden well enough? She wrapped her arms around his waist, pulling him deeper into their niche. She could barely make out the glint of his eyes as he glanced back over his shoulder. She felt him move and then realized he was raising his coat collar. He folded his lapels over his white shirt so that it was concealed by the darker fabric of his formal jacket. That was quite clever of him. Now he blended more completely with the darkness.

Robert wrapped his arm around her waist and moved even closer to her, causing her to let out a soft gasp of surprise. A shudder of awareness coursed through her. His cologne and the scent of his freshly starched shirt filled her senses, and she closed her eyes as she breathed him in. The man overwhelmed her, pushing every other thought from her mind.

As Robert let out an unsteady breath, Antonia realized their close quarters must be affecting him as well.

He leaned down and his smooth cheek brushed against hers. She could feel the warmth of his breath next to her ear. "Was that the only door?" he asked so quietly it was almost as though he'd breathed the words.

She licked her lips and swallowed. "Yes." She closed her eyes to try to block him from her senses, but that only made her more aware of him. She opened them again to find him gazing at her. He made it so difficult to think clearly. "There are some trap doors leading up to the stage, but I don't think they'll be of any help. I can't climb through one wearing this costume."

"Miss Winter," Davydov called, "please be reasonable. We need to know what you may have seen at the ambassador's ball last night. Nothing more."

Judging by the location of their voices, they'd moved farther away from the door than she'd realized. Soon, she and Robert would be able to circle behind them.

His breath warmed her ear and sent a tingle through her body. "We'll wait here a bit longer and then sneak out the same way we came in," he said.

She nodded and turned, meaning to whisper something back, but instead her lips grazed his cheek.

They both froze. Her mouth was inches from his. She only needed to move slightly and—she closed the distance.

His lips were soft and warm against hers. They parted slightly as she kissed him, and she felt his tongue touch her lower lip, exploring and tasting her.

Antonia's knees gave way beneath her, and she leaned into him for support. He tightened his arms, pulling her firmly against him. She'd kissed a man before, but never like this. Never with so much passion—so much abandon. This moment blazed with intensity. She lifted her arms, wrapping one around his neck as she dug her fingers into his hair. She suddenly realized how much she'd been wanting to touch his hair. Perhaps ever since she'd seen him five years ago. It was as soft and silky as she'd imagined.

She'd worn hoop skirts for most of her adult life, and the way this particular costume, with its wide hips and flat skirt-front, allowed their bodies to brush against each other was a novel experience. She could feel the heat of his thighs through her skirts. As she shifted her weight to move closer, her leg bumped against his. Robert let out a stifled moan that he cut off almost immediately. He lowered one of his hands to her bottom and pressed her hips against his. He deepened his kiss, and she tightened her hold around his neck, clinging to him. The rest of the world disappeared. There was only him.

She could live inside this kiss. Inside this moment. For a brief instant in time, nothing else mattered, and her world became bliss.

A loud crash followed by a string of angry Russian words erupted from somewhere in the darkness, and the reality of her situation came rushing back. Antonia jerked away from the kiss, turning toward the sound. For a moment, confusion ruled her, and then she grasped the significance of what she'd heard.

"This is our chance," she whispered, regretting the need to say the words and break the spell. Her voice was breathless, as though even her lungs resented the need to exhale and leave the blissful moment behind. "They're far away from the door. We can slip out."

Robert didn't answer at first. His arms were still wrapped around her, and she could hear him breathing in the darkness. After a moment, he eased his hold on her, but he took her by the hand and squeezed it reassuringly. "Can you lead us out?"

"Yes, but we need to be very quiet." She couldn't risk knocking into something and giving them away. She let go of Robert's hand and adjusted her dress, lifting the stiff panniers up and tucking them under her arms so that her silhouette became much narrower. She held the panniers in place with her elbows as she eased past Robert. "Keep close," she murmured.

What had she done? What had possessed her to kiss him?

The narrow passageways were made up of stacks of boxes and crates. Her skirts barely rustled as she moved. She rested her palm on one of the beams supporting the stage as she circled around it. It felt grimy, and she snatched her hand back to wipe it against her skirt. The dust would wash away with a bit of clean water. But what about that kiss? It wouldn't be erased so easily.

"Miss Winter," Davydov called out from somewhere behind them, "we know who you are. You're Vladamir Nevsky's grand-daughter. You don't need to run from us. Don't you know we'd never harm you? We simply wanted to offer you whatever assistance the embassy might be able to provide."

She froze and glanced back at Robert. She could barely make him out in the darkness, but she moved closer to him and leaned in to whisper a question. "How do they know my parentage? No one recognized me at the ball yesterday. Did you mention my name to anyone?"

He shook his head vehemently. "Of course not, but Revnik asked me about you this afternoon. He already knows you were at the ball. He asked me about a woman in a silver gown."

"Does he know I have the book?" That would be a logical assumption.

"He suspects."

She certainly didn't believe Davydov's reassurances. He and his knife wouldn't hurt her? Bah! His promises were as false as he was. If those two men were footmen, she was the Princess of Patagonia.

She wouldn't let them catch her.

Faint light seeped through the needle-thin seams of the various trapdoors. If she hadn't already been familiar with the path between the support beams, she would have become lost.

There were only a couple of paths back to the entrance. The other areas were being used to store items or were blocked by crossbeams. She'd never be able to crawl under the beams wearing her dress.

She listened for their pursuers. It was obvious that they'd given up cajoling her into giving away her hiding place, because now they were trying to move silently. A moment later she heard a loud crack followed by a muffled curse. One of the men must have hit his head against a low ceiling beam. She grinned. At least she was short enough that she didn't have that problem.

Suddenly, she wasn't quite as scared as she had been only a moment ago. She had the advantage of knowing her way through this maze.

She inched forward in the darkness, reassured by Robert's presence. As she rounded a support beam, she glimpsed the still-open door leading back toward the dressing rooms.

She held her breath for a moment and listened.

A footstep. Far behind them, and nowhere near the doorway.

She listened for another moment, but heard no other noises.

This was it. She had to make her move now.

She squeezed Robert's hand and then darted for the door, pulling him with her. They burst through the door at the same moment that she heard one of the men shout an alarm. Without pausing to look back, she bolted around the corner at the bottom of the staircase and careened directly into a large, immovable man.

❦ 26 ❧

It's not the size of the dog in the fight, it's the size of the fight in the dog.

— *MARK TWAIN*

Robert barreled through the door after Antonia just in time to see her slam into a large man.

"Claude!" Antonia grabbed the man's arms to keep from falling. "Two men are chasing us. Outsiders," she emphasized. "They have knives."

Claude's face hardened. He moved around Antonia to stand next to Robert. The large man moved gracefully, like a cat. He clearly knew how to fight. Robert's confidence crept up a notch.

As Antonia turned to face the door beneath the stage as well, Robert caught her eye and shook his head. "It's you they want. Go in the dressing room and stay there until I come for you," Robert said. "We'll deal with these two. "

Without pausing, Antonia turned to do as he asked. She put

her hand on the dressing room door and then hesitated, looking as though she was about to argue with him.

"Antonia, go!" Robert roared. "Get out of sight!"

She jumped, pushed open the door, and stepped through it.

Davydov burst through the under-stage door next to the staircase. Then he caught sight of Claude and hesitated. The other man came storming through directly behind him. They paused a moment before surging forward in unison.

Robert braced himself for their attack as Claude moved to stand next to him.

Davydov and his partner abruptly swerved and bolted up the staircase. Robert didn't waste time staring after them in surprise. He snatched his cane from the floor where he'd dropped it earlier and swiftly pulled free the épée. He launched himself after them. They might have knives, but his reach would even the balance.

Robert's strides ate up the distance, and he tore up the stairs two at a time with Claude at his heels.

The Russians were fast. Before Robert reached the floor above, he could hear them thundering toward the stage door.

At the top of the stairs, Robert grabbed the handrail and used it to swing himself toward the stage entrance without slowing his headlong charge. Claude kept pace with him. The door leading out onto the street banged shut as he rushed toward it.

With his slim blade raised, he charged into the street. Two carriages stood there—his own and another blocking its path.

Claude darted past him and ran toward the horses of the first coach, stretching his arm out to reach for their harnesses.

"Go! Go!" Davydov shouted. He and his companion were scrambling inside their carriage. The coachman didn't wait for the door to latch before urging his horses forward.

Claude's hand missed the harness by inches, and he scrambled to one side to avoid being struck by the coach's wheels.

Robert charged ahead as the carriage door slammed shut. He continued a dozen or so yards before stopping. The carriage careened away, quickly outdistancing him. As it burst out of the alleyway and onto the street, it narrowly missed a pedestrian before disappearing around the corner.

"Bah!" Claude shouted, shaking his fist toward the end of the alley. "Criminals! They'd better not come back here."

An ice-cold fury hardened within Robert. Revnik was behind this. Apparently he no longer believed Antonia was "too important" to be bothered by his men.

This changed everything.

Antonia needed help. *His* help.

What was it she'd said to him earlier that afternoon? Something about the measure of a man being taken by the path he chooses when faced with a difficult situation.

But he found he'd already made his decision.

He'd chosen Antonia.

"Let's go back inside," he said to Claude.

Claude narrowed his eyes. "This trouble has something to do with you."

Robert shook his head. "I was worried something like this might happen, but I didn't bring this trouble to your door. Antonia's in danger."

He wanted her to be safe, and he wanted her to keep believing in him. When she looked at him, she saw the man he knew he could be rather than the man he'd let himself become. And he much preferred Antonia's vision of him.

Now all he needed to do was make it become his reality.

"She brought this trouble here? To my theater?" Claude's jaw clenched. "I need to speak to her. Now."

Love all, trust a few, do wrong to none.

— WILLIAM SHAKESPEARE

A ntonia peeked into the hallway and found it deserted. She darted out and grabbed the discarded shaft of Robert's cane. It felt slightly different from the way a normal cane would. The weight was off.

As she carried it back into the dressing room, she shut the door behind her and then laid the cane on her dressing table. She quickly began removing her costume.

"What happened?" Zelda asked.

"Those men—they had knives. I don't know what I would have done if not for—" She shook her head. What of Robert? She'd hated leaving him to face her attackers. Would he be safe? She touched her lips, thankful she'd finally kissed him.

Good lord. She became as still as a statue. Why had that thought crept into her mind? What was wrong with her? Did she believe she was going to lose him? Maybe she should help him. She glanced at the door.

"If not for what?" Zelda said. "What happened?"

"Claude and my friend chased them away."

"What if they come back?"

Antonia shivered. "I need to get out of here."

She let her gown and panniers fall to the floor and stepped out of the puddle of fabric. She stooped to pick it up, but Zelda stopped her.

"Don't worry about your costume. I'll put it away."

"Thank you." Antonia grabbed her corset from the peg and flipped it around her waist. She began fastening the front row of hooks with practiced speed. With Zelda's help, it didn't take her long to dress.

She hesitated, taking hold of Zelda's hand. "I wish I could explain it all to you."

"There will be time for that later. For now, you should hurry."

Antonia nodded and then snatched her cloak from the coat rack and flung it over her shoulders. She turned back to her dressing table and grabbed the shaft of Robert's cane, tucking it under her arm.

She stepped toward the door just as Robert and Claude burst through it, startling her into stumbling backward. Relief swept through her. He was safe.

Robert grabbed her upper arms and steadied her. The pressure of his hands was reassuring. They were so large they should have felt heavy, but instead they soothed her. He felt good—solid and reassuring. S

tanding this close to Robert, she caught another whiff of his starched shirt and the spicy, woody scent of bay rum. The man even smelled reassuring. She wanted nothing more than to step into his arms and have him hold her close. She wanted to float away in the blueness of his eyes.

But that could only happen in a dream. He was a lofty earl,

and she was nothing but a nameless bastard. If she wanted any sort of future with him she'd have to face the reality of her situation. She could steal kisses from him in the dark, underneath the stage, hidden from public scrutiny, but he could never be hers. Not really. Anything they might share together would be overshadowed by the situation of her birth.

Suddenly, gazing up at him was more than she could bear. She stepped back, breaking free of his embrace.

As she tried to look anywhere other than at Robert, she was startled to find Claude glaring at her.

"Explain yourself," Claude demanded. "Why were those men here?"

She paled. "I—I'm sorry. They said they wanted to talk to me, but they threatened me with knives, so I ran."

His eyes narrowed. "They wanted you? No one else?"

He glanced at Robert. "Are you sure they weren't after *him* ?" He said the word with a sneer.

"They said they wanted to ask me some questions," she said, shaking her head. "Lord Wentworth was swept up in their attack on me. They weren't after him."

"Are you telling me they would have attacked anyone who happened to be with you?"

She nodded. "I—"

"You've brought trouble to my theater. I will not have it." Claude's face contorted with anger. "The livelihood of everyone here depends on our ability to deliver a performance every night. You have put that at risk."

"I'm sorry."

"So am I." His face shifted slightly as his anger dimmed, softening his expression. "You've left me no choice. I'm replacing you."

Antonia stared at him, stunned by his words, and then she reached for his arm. "You can't. I need this job."

"I can." He shrugged away from of her hold. "Everyone else

here needs a job, too, and you're endangering that. Your understudy will be happy to take over."

He turned on his heel and left the room.

She felt Robert's warm hand clasp her upper arm and lifted her face to look at him. "What will I do?" she whispered.

"The same as you've always done," he replied, his tone gentle. "Persevere and find a solution."

She closed her eyes, trying to ease the tightness in her chest. How would she pay Mrs. Hill? How would she support her sisters? How would she eat?

She couldn't answer those questions. Not right now. But Robert was right. She would persevere. What was done was done, and there was no use in fretting about it. She needed to formulate a new plan, and she needed to do it quickly.

She glanced around the dressing room, but only Zelda seemed to have noticed the scene with Claude. Antonia couldn't meet her friend's sympathetic gaze as she bid her a hasty goodbye. She fled into the corridor and Robert followed her, closing the door behind them.

She peered up at him. "Tell me what happened. Did they escape?" She cleared her mind and focused on the problem at hand. The men. The chase. She took a small step back so she could look at him, but she couldn't force herself to release his wrist. She'd prefer to throw her arms around him, but this small contact—this small indiscretion—it would have to suffice. She needed to touch him, needed to know he was safe. "You're not injured, are you?"

He shook his head. "I never even caught up to them. They escaped before I could stop them."

"Perhaps that was for the best. What would you have done if you'd caught them?"

Robert smiled wryly. "I suppose I looked like my neighbor's dog when he goes tearing off after every passing carriage. I often wonder what he plans to do if he ever manages to catch one."

Antonia imagined Robert dropping to his hands and knees and sinking his teeth into the leg of one of their attackers, and she smiled.

"I hate to think what might have happened if I hadn't been here tonight," Robert said.

She nodded stiffly. Her hand began to ache from her deathlike grip on Robert's cane. She forced her fingers to uncurl. "Here," she said, handing it to him. "You should put your sword away."

She made the mistake of looking into those pale-blue eyes before releasing the cane, and she ended up holding onto it for a heartbeat too long, staring into them. His gaze transfixed her. How had she ever thought of his eyes as being icy? They were pale, yes, but they held none of the coldness of ice. As she gazed into them, they warmed her to the tips of her toes.

Antonia swallowed and glanced away, trying to think of something she might say to fill the silence stretching between them. "I can't thank you enough for being here tonight. I was surprised to find you backstage."

Metal rang against metal as he slid his sword back into its sheath. "I was worried I was right and the man I'd seen really was from the embassy. I'd rather have been wrong."

"I should have believed you."

He placed his hand at the small of her back as he escorted her toward the stairs leading to the main floor of the theater. "I came tonight to escort you safely back to your rooms."

"Rooms?" Antonia almost snorted, his choice of words momentarily distracting her from the way his hand, low on her waist, seemed to burn through her clothes and scorch her flesh. "You wouldn't call the pitiful six-foot by eight-foot space where I sleep 'rooms' if you saw it." She missed his hand the moment he dropped it from her back as she mounted the stairs.

The idea that another person would worry about her enough to watch over her overwhelmed her. She could hardly believe it, but Robert's presence was proof of his words. He valued her.

As they reached the top of the stairs, she glanced at him. It was dim here, but she could still make out his features. His strength and confidence reassured her. It would be so easy to let him into her life.

He held out his arm, and she automatically slid her gloved fingers under his elbow to rest against his forearm. Taking a gentleman's arm was feeling more natural again.

The jaded part of herself pointed out he might only be protecting her because he wanted the church register.

She didn't want to think that way. Not tonight. She gripped his arm a bit tighter as she pushed the thought aside. For now, she wanted to allow herself to believe that he wanted her purely for herself. It was nice to have a protector, and Robert made her feel safe. Perhaps she could relax her defenses around him.

Just for tonight.

There'd be plenty of time to keep him at a distance tomorrow.

"My carriage awaits," he said with a sweeping gesture toward the stage door.

"Riding in your carriage would be infinitely preferable to hiring a hansom cab. But can you forgo interrogating me tonight? I'm exhausted."

Robert chuckled, and she could feel the low rumble against the back of her hand where he held it tucked to his side. "I think I can refrain. As long as it's only for tonight."

Only for tonight. The words echoed between them.

Antonia stepped through the stage door into the narrow, icy alley, finding Robert's sumptuous carriage waiting for them. He reached out to pull open the door. "Your chariot, my lady."

How perfect. It was too bad she couldn't afford to have a carriage waiting for her every night. She ducked into its safety and settled into a dark corner.

Robert took the seat across from her. Small lanterns were affixed above each of the two doors of the carriage, and she could see him quite clearly in their low light.

She sighed and leaned back against the comfortable cushions. It had been a year since she'd enjoyed this kind of luxury. Father had been fairly well off, and he'd always kept a fine carriage. She hadn't realized how coddled her life had been until she'd had it ripped away. Robert's carriage even smelled pleasant—of lemon and sage. The coachman obviously worked diligently to maintain the interior as well as the exterior.

Antonia closed her eyes and breathed deeply. She felt safe with Robert. The carriage rocked gently on its springs in a soothing motion, and her tension ebbed. His caution allowed her to lower her guard for the moment. She hadn't realized how hypervigilant she'd been until she finally relaxed.

She let herself drift into a memory of the way things used to be. The way they should be still. Her life had been perfect, and she'd never even recognized it as such until it had been stolen from her. They'd all lived in modest luxury in their childhood home.

At the touch of a hand on her shoulders, Antonia's eyes flew open. Momentarily disoriented, she could barely make out the interior of the carriage. Robert must have dimmed the interior lanterns. A moment later, she realized the horses had come to a halt. "Did I fall asleep?"

"Rather abruptly," Robert murmured. He was close. Closer than she'd realized. "We're home now."

The carriage door opened, and the coachman stepped away from the doorway. He offered his hand as she negotiated the narrow treads of the unfamiliar conveyance. He released her as soon as her feet hit the pavement. Robert was next to her—how had he exited the carriage so quickly? She slipped her hand around his proffered arm.

She was exhausted. The day had been draining. He began guiding her forward. She looked up blearily, but when she focused on the building before her, she stopped short. "Where are we?" she asked, unable to conceal her shock upon seeing the building's cream-colored limestone facade. This was not Mrs. Hill's townhouse.

"I brought you home. My home."

The chill running through her had nothing to do with the frigid winter breeze tugging at her cloak. "I don't understand." She pulled away from him. "Why am I here?" Please, please, don't let him believe he could ignore propriety with her. She couldn't bear it if he treated her cheaply. Not tonight. Not from him.

His brows drew together and he met her gaze, his expression solemn and sincere, drawing her in.

She looked deeply into his eyes, the mirrors of his soul, trying to read the intent of this man who had come to her rescue so many times. Try as she might, she detected no glimmer of deceit in him. She breathed deeply to release some of her tension.

"You know you can't go home," he said softly. "They know where you live. You have no place else to go." He lifted his hand and brushed back the strand of hair that had swept across her face, tucking it behind her ear. "You'll be safe here. I promise you. Even from me, if that's what you want."

There is nothing like staying at home for real comfort.

— *JANE AUSTEN*

"Why bring me here?" Antonia searched his eyes for any telltale emotions. Despite his apparent sincerity, she couldn't rid herself of the nagging fear that her status as an actress had played a role in his decision. She'd been spurned too many times in the past year, and she'd come to expect it.

Perhaps sensing her tension, he stepped back. "This is my home. Woolsy House. I promise, you'll be perfectly safe. I could think of nowhere else to take you."

"There's my home, of course, or an inn." Antonia watched him suspiciously. A frigid gust caught her cloak and winter's cold fingers slid up her skirts, chilling her. She felt the absence of him next to her more deeply than she would have expected. Did this have anything to do with those theoretical gravitational forces

Father used to talk about? Could it be that those forces applied to people as well as planets? Because it seemed that as Robert stepped away from her, she missed his presence—more than she should have.

With him standing at a distance, the dark night seemed to press in on her. The world she lived in was harsh and lonely, and few people bolstered her confidence the way Robert did. That wasn't something to ignore. She believed in herself when she was with him. Was this false confidence? Or was it something she could trust? Was Robert some*one* she could trust?

"I can't take you back to Mrs. Hill's. Those men already know where you live. Please, Antonia. It's not as though I can abandon you at an inn with nothing but the clothes you're wearing. Certainly not at this hour. It isn't safe, especially with Revnik's men searching for you."

"What about my governess, Miss Galloway? I could stay with her at Miss Hermitage's Collegiate School for a few days."

"It's the middle of the night. If we went there now we'd risk waking everyone, and that might cost your friend her position."

Antonia's chest tightened and she forced out a sigh. "Sneaking in isn't an option either. There's a wall surrounding the entire school."

"Which leaves us only one logical solution."

"This?" She gestured toward his front door. "It simply won't do. It isn't proper. I already combat too many assumptions people have regarding actresses. I don't want to give them further reason to question my morals."

"Can you suggest another option?"

She glanced down, fixing her gaze on the worn, damp hem of her cloak. There were no other options. At least, none better than this one. "I can't, and I find that immensely frustrating." She squared her shoulders and raised her chin, looking him in the eyes. "You're right, of course. Your offer is more than generous." She paused and took a deep breath. "At the risk of offending you,

I must ask—what will we do if someone discovers I'm here? If people know I'm staying in your home without a chaperone, what's left of my reputation would be ruined."

He moved a step closer to her, and she found herself drawn toward him again. "I've given that consideration," he said in soothing tones. "My brother and sister live here as well, so I'll have Emily's lady's maid stand in as your chaperone until we find someone else."

Antonia's mouth went dry. "Your brother? Frederick? He wants me arrested for treason!"

Robert reached out and placed a hand on her arm. "I won't let him do anything to harm you. I promise."

When she let out a frustrated sigh, the tiny cloud her warm breath created hovered between them for an instant before it dissipated. "I wish I could think of a better alternative, but I can't. I'll stay here, but only until I can find more suitable accommodations." She slid her gloved fingers over his hand where it rested on her arm. "And thank you," she said, meeting his gaze.

He nodded and then tucked her hand through the crook of his arm and led her toward his home.

As she approached the gleaming white door, she eyed it with trepidation, but when Robert pushed it open, she didn't falter as they passed through it together.

She tried to conceal how much the grand foyer intimidated her. "Why is it called Woolsy House and not Wentworth House?"

"Woolsy is my family name. Wentworth is my title."

The round foyer was enormous, and its grand marble staircase rose up before her, seeming to beckon her to the balcony above.

A small, dapper man wearing a black suit entered from a door to the right. He must be the butler, looking crisp and neat even at this indecent hour of the morning."

"Landon. Is Frederick home?" Robert asked.

"No, m'lord. He's out for the evening and said he'd return home quite late."

Robert glanced at her and then back to Landon. "This is Miss Winter. She had a harrowing experience this evening, and as a consequence, she'll be obliged to stay here for a few days. Can you prepare a room for her?"

"The blue room is ready to accommodate a guest," Landon replied. "Does that meet with your approval?"

Robert gave a nod. "In the morning, please inform Tuttle I require her to stand in as Miss Winter's chaperone until I can find someone else. You can retire for the evening."

"Yes, m'lord."

Robert faced her, the warm lamplight making his eyes difficult to read. "I plan to have a whiskey before I turn in for the night. Can I offer you something as well?"

She considered his offer. She'd been desperately weary just a few minutes ago, but now energy seemed to hum through her body. Perhaps some whiskey would help soothe her nerves. She nodded. "Yes, thank you."

When Robert turned and headed down a hallway, she followed him. He pushed open a door and paused, fumbling with something just inside the entrance. A moment later, light blossomed from an oil lamp and the sharp scent of sulfur bit at her nostrils. Robert lit a long taper and tossed the blackened, smoking match into a small ceramic bowl on the table. He moved swiftly through the room, touching the flame to the lamps until their soft amber glow filled the room, and then tossed the taper into the fireplace.

A few framed architectural drawings dotted the burled oak walls of the masculine space, and a low table with a chess set sat before a reddish-brown leather sofa. Behind it sat two massive bookcases filled with leather volumes that her fingers itched to touch and explore. The power and nobility of the room drew her to it. She noticed a marble bust on a pedestal, but couldn't identify the face of the man it depicted. Could it have been of some ancient Roman? She didn't like his stern expression.

Near the large desk sat a smaller table, neatly arranged with a variety of bottles, decanters, and glassware. Robert made his way toward it as he waved his hand in the direction of the sofa. "Please be seated."

She tugged her gloves from her hands as she sat. When she placed her hand on the sofa's arm, she couldn't resist sliding her fingers across the buttery leather.

The room was full of texture and complexity, just like this man. The more he revealed about himself, the more intrigued she became. But she sensed there were facets of himself he hid from everyone. What would it be like to have this man lay himself bare to her? And what would it take to convince him to do so? She glanced at the array of bottles and glasses on the table. Perhaps after a drink or two—

"Would you like some sherry?" he asked, turning to glance at her.

She slid her hand off the soft leather and interlaced her fingers on her lap. "No, thank you. I prefer whiskey with a little water. Ice, too, if it isn't too much trouble." Robert raised his eyebrows.

"Whiskey? Not many ladies drink that."

"Well, I'm not breaking tradition, since I'm no longer considered a lady." There. She'd said it. She'd shone a light directly upon the difference in their social status. She felt herself relaxing. She liked this room. It soothed her.

To her surprise, Robert's only reaction was to chuckle wryly and open a large stoneware ice bucket to peer inside. "There's still a bit of ice in here. Landon must have brought some in for my brother. That's odd, since Frederick usually prefers to use the drawing room." He raised a slender ice pick and plunged it into the container with a loud crunch. He grabbed a pair of tongs and dropped a few pieces into a pair of glasses before adding a measure of whiskey to each. He added water to one and then crossed the room to hand it to her. She curled her hand around the glass, taking care not to touch him.

He took a step back and observed her as he tapped his fingers against the side of his glass. When she didn't move, he glanced at her drink as though urging her to sip it. From his intense interest, she suddenly realized he wanted to see her reaction to the whiskey.

Antonia breathed in the aroma of the liquid, letting its smoky scent fill her senses. She detected a faintly sweet note as well, but the liquid fire she knew she would find remained hidden—until she raised the glass to her lips.

The ice bumped against her mouth as she allowed the liquid to slide down her throat. The heat didn't hit her until the whiskey splashed against the back of her throat. She enjoyed the contradictory sensations of heat and ice as the liquid blazed its frigid fingers down her throat and hit her stomach. The very tip of her tongue tingled, and she flicked it across her lips to trap the bead of whiskey that lingered, savoring the droplet of smoky flavor.

Curling her fingers more firmly around the glass, Antonia glanced up at Robert and found him staring at her mouth as though mesmerized. When he noticed her regard, he shifted his attention to her eyes. His own darkened and seemed to devour her.

She stopped breathing. The man had wicked eyes. Eyes that could make her forget what was important.

She glanced away and took another sip of the whiskey, this time letting a piece of the ice slide into her mouth as she steadied her breathing. She crunched at it as she tried to evade Robert's steady gaze.

"Are you nervous?"

"What makes you think that?"

"The ice. The way you're clutching your glass."

To hide her surprise, she downed the rest of her whiskey. She fumbled as she set her glass on the table, trying to hide her disquiet by placing it squarely in the center of a small tray. "I'm tense. Who wouldn't be? I lost my only means of employment.

You must admit that it isn't every night that one escapes would-be kidnappers."

"Of course it is. It happened to me just yesterday."

She let out a laugh. "I suppose it did. It would seem that you're the exception to the rule. Perhaps I should distance myself from you and your life of danger and intrigue."

Robert stepped closer. "Just last night you risked everything to steal that church register. You don't strike me as someone who quakes at a challenge."

"I don't know about that. I won't shirk from tasks that must be done, but neither do I seek out excitement for its own sake. Stealing the book was different. I was taking action—taking control of my destiny. But tonight? Tonight those men tracked me down and chased us through the storage room. It was terrifying." The tension she thought she'd dispelled crept its way back into her body. "I feel like I'm some animal being stalked by a hunter." She shuddered and then rolled her shoulders. "I suppose it's the difference between being the predator and the prey."

"But we eluded them."

"I'm glad you were with me." She couldn't sit still any longer and rose to her feet. At the same time, Robert took another step forward, and she abruptly found herself standing with her face only inches from his chest. His warm, broad chest.

"My, but you're large," she said, tilting her head back to glance up at him. "I can see why those men ran from you."

"I've found my size to be an asset when it comes to physical intimidation," he murmured as he inched closer to her. "In fact, I tried to use it to manipulate you when we first met at the embassy. I did my damnedest to make you feel small, but you were undaunted. I must admit, I found that most intriguing."

Despite the thrill that shot through her at this admission, she rolled one shoulder in a dismissive gesture. "I never noticed," she lied. "I'm used to being the smallest person in the room. Everyone towers over me. I can't let my lack of physical stature unnerve me, or I'd never have any confidence at all. And anyway, I've found that if I look at a man in just the right way, I rattle him more than he could ever rattle me. It seemed to work to my benefit the night we met."

His eyes narrowed very slightly, and she tilted her head to the side to look at him coyly.

"Are you surprised to hear that?" she asked.

"It's a quite a claim. Are all men susceptible? Even those who are forewarned?"

"Perhaps you'd like to judge for yourself." She tilted her chin down slightly so she gazed up at him through her widened eyes and fixed him with a heated stare. After the kiss they'd already shared, she knew she was playing with fire, but she couldn't stop herself.

Robert met her gaze. His eyes narrowed slightly, but he didn't glance away. Instead, he kept his stare even, returning her fire and heat with his cool determination.

Rather than flustering him, the reverse was true. She found herself trapped in his gaze. His eyes were most fascinating. Although they were pale blue, the centers had shafts of a slightly darker hue radiating outward, like a frost-bound starburst. As she stared into their depths, heat wrapped around her throat and washed down her shoulders, as though she were wearing a fur wrap in an overheated room.

She knew she should end this stare-down, but she couldn't. Instead, she rose up on her tiptoes and leaned closer, inhaling the faint whiskey scent of him as she kept her gaze fixed on those two frozen starbursts.

Suddenly the pair of frozen, blue embers began to warm. She was transfixed as Robert leaned closer to her, wrapping his arms around her, engulfing her in his masculine heat and strength. He lowered his mouth to hers, and as their lips touched, she was surprised by his tenderness. She'd expected him to devour her, but he kept himself in check.

She should pull away, but she couldn't. Instead, she let out a soft sigh of contentment and opened her mouth under the pressure of his lips. They darted their tongues against each other, touching, tasting, and withdrawing, only to begin again more insistently.

She leaned into him. She wanted his support. His strength. She lifted her hands and allowed them to drift up his arms, sliding them over his shoulders until her fingers found their way back to the hair at the nape of his neck.

Robert moaned softly and pulled her closer. He ran one hand up and down her back. The heat of his palm radiated through her gown, intensifying the growing warmth within her.

That same feeling of safety and security engulfed her again. It would be such a simple matter to give herself over to him entirely.

Robert wrapped his arms more tightly around her waist and lifted her, pulling her firmly against his body as he moved them both closer to the sofa. She clung to him, her arms wrapped firmly around his shoulders, as he lowered them both to the soft, cool embrace of the leather. He pressed her back and began kissing her just beneath her ear. He trailed his lips down her neck, kissing every inch of skin along his path toward the top of her bodice.

Antonia raked her fingers through his hair, savoring the touch and feel of this man. She knew she should make him stop, but she couldn't force herself to say the words or to push him away. She wanted him, and she could hardly believe that he wanted her as well. A nobody. A nothing. A woman without a name.

But names were meaningless at a moment like this. Only the emotions and sensations coursing through her mattered.

Robert cupped her breast, and when he slid his thumb back and forth over the tip, she arched her back, yearning for more.

He paused and plunged his fingers into her hair, cupping her head and pulling her into him as he kissed her deeply. His hand fell to her front and he began working at the buttons that closed her bodice. It didn't take long before it was open and he was pushing it from her shoulders, revealing her corset and chemise.

She slid her hands inside his evening jacket and pushed it from his shoulders. He shrugged out of it, throwing it across the room and then pressing her to his chest. The heat of his skin through his linen shirt seared her, and she began to tug at his neckcloth.

"I want to see you," she murmured.

His eyes blazed with an icy fire as he quickly accommodated her, shedding his neckcloth and linen shirt in an instant.

The lamplight flickered, casting a warm glow over his lean, muscular chest and accentuating its hollows and ripples. She reached out, tracing them with her fingers, and Robert let out a ragged sigh of pleasure.

"Do you know what you're doing to me?" His voice wavered, as though he might be on the edge of losing control.

"I think it's the same thing you're doing to me."

He leaned forward, as though about to kiss her again, but then he stopped. "We can't do this," he said, pulling away from her.

For an instant, she nearly ignored his words. Her heart wanted her to close the distance between them. To take what she wanted and ignore the consequences.

But that was just it. There were consequences. She knew if she pressed her bared flesh against his, they'd both be swept along by their passion. Even now the current tugged at her, nearly impossible to resist. But she couldn't make this decision lightly. What of the future she wanted for herself? For her sisters?

She leaned back, just an inch, but that small movement was enough to divert the current. It no longer threatened to overpower her.

This was good. This was for the best. So why did her heart suddenly hurt so much?

"I'm sorry, Antonia. I should have been able to control myself. I never should have treated you so carelessly. You deserve better."

Antonia stopped breathing at his words. Those weren't the

things a man would say to someone of her station. He spoke as though he considered her to be a lady. "I don't—I don't understand. You know what I am. You know I have no name. No one would fault you if you decided to—" She couldn't bring herself to say it. "You speak as though I'm your equal."

Robert seemed momentarily astonished by her words. "Of course you're my equal. Why would I think otherwise? You should expect nothing less from me."

Hot tears sprang to Antonia's eyes and rolled down her cheeks. Who was this man? This noble and honorable man. Had he sprung from some dream? Some childish fantasy where a hero swept in and saved her from an awful fate? It was a foolish thought. This was real life, not some children's tale.

"Shhh." Robert pulled her into his arms. He brushed his thumb across her cheek, wiping her tears away. "These past two days have been strenuous." He tilted his head down and pressed his lips to her brow. "You're safe here."

Safe? No, she was far from safe right now. Somehow, the center of her being was no longer secure. The hardened shell that protected her essence from harm was melting away under the pressure of his affection. Its loss might very well destroy her. Her heart had never truly been in jeopardy until she'd met this man. He could easily become a necessity for her continued existence. A fundamental need. She could already feel the way it pulled on her. Like water or air or food. If this need continued to consume her, what would she be willing to sacrifice simply to be with him? How much of herself would she lose?

She closed her eyes, pressing her damp cheek against the fine hair on his chest that tapered down beneath the belt of his trousers.

They had now. This moment in each other's arms.

And for tonight, it was enough. His warmth and comfort soothed her, and she fell asleep.

❧ 29 ☙

— WILLIAM SHAKESPEARE

Robert cradled the back of Antonia's head in his palm as he pressed a tender kiss to her forehead. So sweet. So desirable. So much more vulnerable than she wanted to be.

Her breathing became even and deep as her exhaustion overtook her. This moment of tenderness, with her perfect trust in him, almost took his breath away.

Did he deserve her faith? Not yet. Not after what he'd almost stolen from her just moments ago. The strength of his remorse hit him so hard he had to force himself not to tense and accidentally awaken her. He never should have behaved so dishonorably. She deserved better. He wanted more from her than this one night. Much more.

He gazed down at their bared arms, hers so pale against his. Halting their lovemaking had required tremendous force of will. He'd had no right to take her, despite the fact that she'd freely offered herself. As a gentleman, he knew better. He knew the limits that restricted them both.

He'd wronged her. He'd never before spilled a virgin's blood. Doing so would have gone against everything he'd been taught. Taking it from Antonia tonight when she was exhausted and in need of his protection would have been tantamount to stealing it from her.

He closed his eyes and leaned his head back, shoving a cushion beneath it. Tonight wouldn't have been the first time this room had witnessed blood and dishonor. The thought made his stomach tighten reflexively, and he recalled the phantom tang of iron in the air. Suddenly his nostrils seemed to fill with it. Fifteen years ago, the scent had saturated the room.

Memories came flooding back in an instant. The blood, his mother's screams, the smell of gunpowder. The spreading pool of red under Father's head as it seeped across the desk. The sealed letter sitting neatly and squarely in front of Father, a faint misting of crimson splattered across it and Robert's own name written across it in his father's bold hand. Father's life's blood inching toward it, threatening to consume it.

Some instinct had made him snatch up the envelope, barely rescuing it from the vital fluid. The side of his finger accidentally brushed the warm liquid, and he had to take care not to mar his white shirt as he tucked the paper into his pocket.

Now, the hand he held against Antonia's head twitched as he remembered finally wiping the blood, the evidence of his actions, onto his dark trousers. His body remembered the moment well, even as he tried to push the memory from his mind. He didn't want to be reminded of his father's death. Not now. Not with this woman in his arms.

But those memories weren't so easily banished.

Perhaps they plagued him now for a reason. Perhaps there was some deeper connection to the present, and one part of his mind recognized a resonance of which he wasn't yet consciously aware.

The more he considered this possibility, the more he became convinced of it.

Assured of his decision, he allowed those long-suppressed memories to rise up—allowed himself to remember an afternoon he'd spent years trying to forget.

⁂

"No!" his mother cried out as she rushed into the room only a moment behind Robert. "No— no— no!"

She'd flown around the desk and grabbed Father by the shoulders, frantically shaking him as though he were asleep. In her bewilderment, she'd only managed to push the wheeled chair he was sitting on back far enough so that Father's body slid from it and toppled to the floor.

"No!" she screamed, falling to her knees next to him as the first of the servants came charging into the room.

As each new person entered the study, they came to a halt at the grisly sight that confronted them.

Their butler Landon arrived, forcing his way past the footmen and housemaids who were blocking his path. He quickly took in the scene— Mother draped over Father's body on the floor, the blood on the desk, and what Robert knew must have been his own stunned, pale expression.

Landon's face blanched momentarily and his jaw dropped, but then he lifted his chin and composed himself. With a deep inhale of breath, he took charge.

"Clear the room," he barked to one of the footmen. "Fetch the authorities," he commanded another. Then his gaze caught that of their housekeeper. "Send for the doctor." He glanced significantly at Robert's mother. "The living have need of him."

He spared Robert a glance, but then turned to advance on Lady Wentworth's sobbing form. Robert took a few tentative steps to follow him, rounding the corner of the desk.

Landon dropped to one knee and pulled gently at Mother's shoulders. "Shh, my lady. His physical form is beyond any help you might provide." He was able to pull her back a few inches. Landon plucked a white handkerchief from his pocket and began wiping the blood from Mother's hands. The red streaks were garish against the white cloth.

Robert looked away, but his gaze landed on the top of the desk. The gore he saw there was much more distressing, so he closed his eyes for a moment to suppress his rising nausea.

It helped only slightly. A loud ringing filled his ears, obliterating everything around him. He focused on that sound, letting it consume him.

"Robert," Landon said sharply.

The ringing sound ceased, and Robert's eyes flew open. He saw Landon staring at him questioningly and realized he must have spoken.

"Can you escort your mother upstairs and stay with her until the doctor arrives?" Landon repeated.

Robert felt numb. Could he even move? Could he control his own body? He tried, and managed to force out a stiff nod.

Landon rose to his feet and then helped Mother stand.

She slid her hand around Robert's slim arm, her grip tightening so that she was clinging to him as though she was afraid he'd disappear from her life as well. Her touch served to bring Robert back to himself. She needed him, and he'd be there for her no matter what.

Her stunned gaze locked on Robert. "What will we do? What will we say?"

Before Robert could reply, Landon said, "We'll tell them the truth. Lord Wentworth suffered a tragic accident while cleaning his gun." Then Landon crossed the room toward a bookcase, plucked a wooden box from the shelf that contained supplies for cleaning handguns, set it on the desk, and opened it.

Robert's free hand crept into his pocket and he touched the envelope concealed there. He kept one hand on it as he escorted his mother up the stairs and into her bedroom.

He sat on the chair at her dressing table while she paced. He watched her as he rubbed his thumb against the envelope's sharp corner, trying to make his scattered thoughts obey his will so he could think logically. Rationally. Then he pulled out the letter and began to read.

His father's death may have changed his world, but the contents of his note utterly destroyed it.

Just as Robert finished the last line of the letter, Dr. Samuels arrived. He looked grim, his lips pressed thin and his shoulders sagging under the weight of his role in this tragedy's aftermath. In one hand he held a satchel, and in the other he gripped an envelope.

Mother approached him, but the doctor cleared his throat and glanced away. "I found this letter in Lord Wentworth's coat pocket and thought it best to bring it to you, my lady." The man's Scottish lilt immediately calmed Robert, as it had throughout the years during which Dr. Samuels had cared for them all.

Mother held out her hand, silently entreating him to pass it to her. She must have assumed it was a suicide note. But since Robert was already privy to the contents of the other letter, he knew this to be the decoy Father had written to him about. He stayed silent, watching as the scene Father had set in motion began to unfold.

Dr. Samuels cleared his throat again and tightened his grip on the envelope. "It's sealed, and I'm afraid it's addressed to a Mrs. Eastland." The corners of his mouth turned down severely, and Robert knew the inarticulate look of censure was meant for his father, not his mother. "I haven't mentioned it to anyone."

Mother's hand dropped to her side like a dead thing, but then she lifted her chin and reached for the envelope again. "Thank you, Dr. Samuels."

Robert rose to his feet, his attention on the letter his mother now held. Its contents would devastate her, and Robert already knew the words it contained weren't true. As he approached her, the doctor intervened, placing a restraining hand on Robert's shoulder. "You must allow your mother to read the letter." The doctor's tone was well meaning, but chiding. "Stand here with me for a moment, son. I'm afraid she'll be needing your help and support."

She moved woodenly toward a small table and chair sitting in front of her bedroom window. When she sat down, she stared at the handwriting on the envelope for a long moment before finally flipping it over and tearing the seal. As her eyes darted back and forth, racing to read the words on the page, the doctor eased his grip enough that Robert was able to break free and hurry to stand next to her. When she finished the letter, her hand dropped to her lap and she let the sheets flutter to the floor, like dead autumn leaves. She was so pale. It was as though the life had bled from her as well.

Robert thrust the other letter into her limp hand. "Read this," he said.

She didn't respond. Didn't take the letter from him.

"Mother, you must read this. It explains everything. All is not as it appears."

He didn't know if it was because of his words, or the calm intensity of his voice, but she lifted her head to gaze at him, and then she tightened her grip on the new letter and began to read. The look of dread on her face caused a sharp pain to rip at Robert's heart.

Tears rolled down her cheeks and she suddenly grabbed Robert's hand in a fierce grip as she continued reading. When she finished it, she pulled Robert closer.

He leaned down to accept her desperate embrace.

"Thank god for your quick thinking," she murmured into his ear. "What's in this letter must remain between us and no one else." She turned and gave him a tear-dampened kiss on his cheek and released him. Then she folded the secret letter and tucked it into her bodice.

As Robert stepped away, Mother scooped up the first letter from the floor. Robert noticed that he'd accidentally trod upon one of the pages and marred it with his footprint.

Mother brushed it off, folded it, and handed it back to Dr. Samuels. "Although I shouldn't have read this, I believe it offers an explanation as to why my husband suffered such an unfortunate— accident. When the constable arrives, can you please ensure this is delivered to him? I trust he'll bring it to Mrs. Eastland's attention."

Grim-faced, Dr. Samuels accepted the letter and tucked it in his pocket. "Lady Wentworth, if you'll permit me, I'd like to offer you something for the shock."

She hesitated for a moment, then nodded. She didn't seem to notice Dr. Samuels shooing Robert from the room.

Robert was at a loss as to what to do, so he went to his bedroom. What should he say to his brother and sister? Neither the truth nor the lie that Father had fabricated were suitable for their ears. They were much too young. Perhaps it would be best to feign ignorance.

He closed his bedroom door firmly behind him and crossed to the fireplace, where he began the slow work of reviving the nearly dead fire. It was a task that had always soothed him, and he would grasp at anything at this moment to center his mind and calm his raging thoughts.

At least he and his mother knew the truth regarding Father's death. But that was small comfort. In fact, he wondered if he would have been better off not knowing. Not only had he lost his father today, he'd also lost his idealized image of the man. He wasn't certain which blow was more crushing. The longer Robert pondered this unwanted knowledge, the more certain he became that no one else should ever learn the truth behind what his father had done. It would be best to allow London to gossip about Father's letter to Mrs. Eastland and speculate about their relationship. Father believed that the lie about an affair was better than the truth they might otherwise discover.

The truth that Father had committed treason.

Robert fervently thanked whatever instinct had caused him to slip that letter into his pocket. The one addressed to Mrs. Eastland was bad enough, with its story of unrequited love and despair. But that part of the story was all a fabrication.

The truth was that Father's vast fortune had been built on lies and treachery. For a man whose public persona had become the embodiment of truth, integrity, and public service, this revelation was catastrophic.

Now Robert and his mother were the keepers of Father's secrets. Whether they wanted to be or not.

Father had avoided paying for his crimes by escaping into death. He'd run from his problems rather than face them.

Antonia sighed in her sleep and slid her arm across his chest, pulling him back to the present. He stroked her hair.

He refused to follow his father's path. He'd stand up for what he believed was right, and helping Antonia was the right thing to do. If Frederick and the Foreign Office didn't agree with him, then to hell with them. He'd face those consequences. But he wouldn't take a coward's path and simply ignore this situation. He'd spent his life avoiding this sort of entanglement because he was afraid that he'd someday collapse under the weight of the lie, just like his father had.

But he wasn't his father. He was better than that.

Frederick would rail against his decision once he learned of it — and Robert had no doubt he'd soon know. There was no question about it. Frederick could never let go of a problem once he got hold of it. He was like a terrier with a rat. There was no backing down or giving up once he set his teeth into a problem.

The best Robert could do on that front would be to postpone having his brother find out. He needed time to help Antonia, and he needed to know more.

He pressed a kiss to the top of Antonia's head. She was his now. She might not know it yet, but they were bound to one another. The rightness of them as a pair centered him. Helped him stay focused on the path he'd chosen.

He'd do what was right and what was best for Antonia, and then he'd see what he could do to save England.

❧ 30 ☙

There is frequently more to be learned from the unexpected questions of a child than the discourses of men.

— *JOHN LOCKE*

Robert gently disentangled himself from Antonia, taking care not to wake her. She stirred as he slid away, but then nestled back onto the sofa, never quite waking from her deep sleep. She had to be exhausted. Her skin seemed to glow in the gaslight, but its valleys and secrets remained hidden in shadow.

He turned away and strode over to a nearby chest to pull a blanket from it. Not only would the throw keep her warm, it also would hide her tempting curves from his gaze. Even now, he wanted to waken her with kisses and continue what he'd stopped.

He tugged open the drawer and extracted the soft-brown throw, and the clean scent of lavender came with it. Many a night he'd fallen asleep on that sofa, and one of his servants—probably Landon—had draped this throw over him.

As he placed it over her slumbering form, his hand brushed her upper arm and he noticed it was cool to his touch. He pulled the blanket up to cover it.

He intentionally turned his back to her as he crossed the room and gazed down at the pile of garments he'd tossed there. They told a story of reckless abandon, with recklessness being key to what had transpired between them. His shirt clung suggestively to her discarded bodice, reminding him of their entwined bodies, and he forced himself not to glance back at her.

Clear-headed reason was called for now. His earlier deplorable lack of self-control must have been triggered by the stress of the past two days. He might sometimes be short-tempered and mercurial, but never before had he flagrantly ignored the rules of propriety and come so close to deflowering a virgin.

He sorted through the pile of clothing, folding hers neatly and donning his own. He couldn't help but note the frayed edges on the cuffs of her sleeves. Her items were well made and well cared for, but worn.

He wondered if, in righting his father's wrong, he could have unintentionally set her current situation into motion. A few years ago, he'd helped Squire Winter recover his losses. The squire had been ecstatic when the investments Robert suggested had proven to be lucrative. He'd been able to generously fund all three of his daughter's dowries, make overdue repairs to his house, and make general improvements to his other holdings. Had that sudden influx of money drawn the attention of his brother?

Robert let out a heavy sigh. That sort of thinking could drive a man mad and freeze him in a state of inaction. A man had to make the best decision possible given the information before him. That was the only way to make a difference and do some good in this world.

Since meeting Antonia, his life had changed. With the flash of her copper eyes, she'd cut him free from his narrowly defined world and woven him into this new one. In this new reality, he willingly reached out and helped someone in need, not simply because he felt duty-bound to do so, but because he genuinely wanted to help. He liked this change—this new pattern of existence. He liked being someone who took a chance on trusting another person and willingly keeping her secrets.

He'd never felt more alive. More vital.

This had nothing to do with danger or excitement, and everything to do with the way Antonia looked at him—not simply her seductive gaze that had almost undone him—no—it was her perception of him. In her eyes, he could see the man he'd once believed he'd become. The revelation of his father's dark secrets had barricaded that path for him, preventing Robert from evolving into that particular version of himself. But now that he was with Antonia, he'd simply become that man. Not merely in her perception of him, but by his deeds as well.

He needed to protect her from any consequences that might arise from their reckless behavior tonight. No one would criticize him—he lived a life of privilege reserved to men of rank and fortune. But the same rules didn't apply to Antonia.

If anyone found her here, she'd be ruined.

He stuffed his neckcloth into his jacket pocket and then strode back to where Antonia lay sleeping. She had shifted since he'd left her, and now she lay sprawled across the sofa in an attitude of wild abandon—her arm flung above her head, one nearly bare breast peeking out from beneath the blanket, and a soft, delighted smile on her lips. It was as though she had frozen in mid-motion while dancing a tarantella.

He lifted her into his arms, tucking the blanket around her. She was so small that holding her took hardly any effort. A whiff of the lavender-scented throw filled his senses, bringing with it a rush of warmth and security.

At first she snuggled against him, leaving him wondering if she'd been in the habit of falling asleep on the sofa as a child and having her father cart her off to bed. But then she went rigid in his arms.

"What are you doing?" she asked in a tone that matched the tension in her body.

"I'm carrying you to your bed." He kept his voice soft and soothing, and he felt her relax slightly. "The house is silent. Now is the perfect time."

The clock struck three.

"My bodice," she said.

"I have it," he said, lifting the neatly folded item he held so she could catch a glimpse of it. "I hoped I could carry you up to your room without waking you."

She snuggled deeper into his arms. "That sounds heavenly."

As she relaxed, her body melted into his in a way that took his breath away. It took all of his self-control not to kiss her again right then and there. But if he kissed her now, he wouldn't be able to stop.

He glanced away from her.

If he kissed her now, he'd be lost.

With an almost herculean force of will, he hurried into the dark hallway and headed toward the staircase. It was nothing for him to navigate the house in the dark, and less than a minute later, he pushed his way into the bedchamber Landon had said was available.

In the moonlight, he was able to see the bed and deposit her on it. He fumbled for the matches he knew were in the drawer of the bedside table and then lit the small lamp.

He continued to avert his gaze, but she reached out and took his hand. "Robert." Her voice was soft, and he immediately glanced at her.

He sucked in his breath.

Her hair spilled down around her shoulders, and her lips looked tender and slightly swollen from his kisses. She looked like a woman who'd just been made love to. It was even more dangerous to realize that he wanted nothing more than to finish what they'd started.

He closed his eyes, if only to save his own sanity. "Tomorrow I'll make sure you have something proper to sleep in."

She was silent. When he glanced at her, she appeared confused. A look of hurt began to cloud her eyes.

"Not that I don't enjoy seeing you this way. You're breathtakingly stunning."

She blushed.

He couldn't manage to utter another word. Anything of significance would prolong their time together, and he didn't think his self-control could withstand further temptation. Nor could he bear to say something banal.

Silence was the best alternative.

He turned and walked from her room.

⚜

AFTER A FEW SCANT HOURS OF RESTLESS SLEEP, ROBERT ROSE early. He had a great deal to do today, so he'd best get started.

At the front door, Landon handed Robert his hat and gloves. "Will there be anything else, sir?"

"Please inform the others we have a house guest," Robert said. "If anyone asks about me, tell them I plan to be home before eleven."

"Very good, sir."

The front door burst open and Frederick rushed inside.

Robert gaped at him. It was obvious from his attire that he'd been out all night. "I don't think I've ever seen you come in at this hour before."

Frederick scowled at him. "What concern is it of yours?" He continued forward, knocking his shoulder against Robert's as he brushed past.

A knowing smile curved Robert's lips. "I'll wager this has something to do with Josephine."

Frederick spun on him. "Have a care, brother. You should know better than to sully Lady Harrington's name that way. I'm in a hurry right now, or I'd teach you some manners. Where are you going at such an early hour?"

Robert opened his mouth as he tried to invent a lie, but Frederick interrupted him.

"It doesn't matter." Frederick slashed the air between them with his hand. "I don't have time to question you. I have a meeting at the Foreign Office, and I'll be pressed to arrive on time."

Robert swept his cane toward his brother's attire. "Your evening clothes are likely to raise a few eyebrows."

"That's why I'm here. To change." He turned on his heel and hurried up the staircase. "I'll barely make it on time as it is."

Robert knew it was unlikely Antonia would awaken this early, but he decided to err on the side of caution. It would be just his luck if she and Frederick bumped into each other and he wasn't here to intervene.

He took his time adjusting his hat and donning his gloves. Frederick must have left his bedroom door open. Robert could hear his curses of frustration as he struggled to quickly change his clothes.

The moment Robert heard his brother's heavy footsteps rushing down the upstairs hallway, he stepped through the front door. He didn't want to be caught lingering. That was a sure way to raise Frederick's suspicions.

Robert hurried into his carriage. Overnight, he'd devised a plan for Antonia, and now he was impatient to set it in motion.

She must stay in his house. Try as he might, he could think of no safer alternative.

As he latched the door of his carriage, Frederick came darting outside. The hackney he'd arrived in was still waiting for him, and he sprinted toward it, oblivious to Robert's presence.

Robert leaned against the seat back as he heard Frederick's carriage rattle away, relieved he'd avoided the confrontation for now.

He considered his upcoming meeting with Lady Catherine—or rather Lady Huntley now. He grinned as he imagined the stunned amazement his request would elicit. The woman was much too composed. He hadn't managed to astound her in the past year, despite his many attempts, but with this particular request he might finally manage it.

It didn't take long for his coachman, Crupper, to drive to Daniel's new estate on the outskirts of London. The rounded, graceful lines of the newly renovated entrance were a vast improvement over the building's former bland exterior.

As Robert stepped from the carriage, he recalled how just a year ago he and his friend had walked through this estate together. Daniel hadn't been able to stop talking about his plans for the place. This new facade had been the first major change. A bowed entrance with two-story windows transformed the alabaster-colored building, giving it a fresh, new aspect. Robert particularly enjoyed its beauty at night. When crystal chandeliers were ablaze throughout the house, the building glittered with light.

As he strolled toward the entrance, he heard shuffling from behind the large boxwood shrubs to his left. He glanced over and locked gazes with a boy. The scamp's eyes widened and then he ducked down out of sight.

It was fairly obvious he wanted to remain hidden.

Had it only been early yesterday morning when he, too, had hidden by his front entrance to surprise Frederick? That bit of kinship tugged at him. The child's clothes looked warm enough, but filthy, as though he'd been on the streets for a while. Was he a thief? An orphan? Robert tugged at his bottom lip as he considered what to do.

Driven by a lingering sense of kinship with the boy, Robert stepped back to where Crupper sat perched behind the horses, murmured some instructions, and passed him some coins. As Robert returned to the entrance, Crupper drove away.

Robert studiously ignored the quaking boxwood as he rang the bell. When Daniel's butler Patterson opened the door, he didn't appear surprised to see Robert standing on the front step, despite the early hour.

"Is Huntley awake?"

"He's out riding," Patterson said, "but Lady Huntley is in the breakfast room."

"Splendid. She's just the person I hoped to see."

As Robert entered the breakfast room, he wasn't surprised when he found not only Catherine, but also Lady Elizabeth seated at the table. The two women were close friends and could often be found together.

Catherine sat in front of a nearly empty plate, sipping at a cup of tea, and Elizabeth sat before an unused plate to the left. Catherine's gently rounded belly pressed against the edge of the table, and her hand rested on it in a protective gesture.

"Robert," Catherine said, smiling warmly, "what a pleasant surprise. Have you eaten? Please join us. Daniel should be home soon."

"Thank you, but I'm not very hungry this morning," Robert said, taking the chair to her right.

"We have bacon."

That caught Robert's attention. "Well—perhaps just a bit. And toast."

"With raspberry jam," Catherine said, and glanced at one of

the footmen. He gave a polite acknowledgment and left the room, presumably to arrange for Robert's breakfast.

"You know me too well. I have a ridiculous weakness for bacon."

Catherine smiled indulgently as she stroked her belly in an unconscious gesture. "I'm happy to see you made it home safely after our run-in with those kidnappers."

Robert suppressed the flash of surprise that she'd mention the attack, and then glanced at Elizabeth. She smiled back at him knowingly. Of course she knew. Whatever one woman knew, the other one would learn soon thereafter. There were no secrets between them. "Only due to your efforts. Thank you."

"It was nothing."

He glanced around, remembering the room as being rather dark and unfriendly, but the transformation wrought on the space was nothing less than startling. Now it was cheerful and welcoming. The light from the overhead gas chandelier made the room brighter than it had been a year ago. He looked down at his place setting and noticed the way the light glinted off the blade of the knife. Ah, yes. Catherine's knife. He'd been wondering about that. "I didn't know Daniel had taught you to use a knife."

Catherine's entire body tensed at is words. "Should you have?" she asked tartly. "I imagine you're unaware of a number of things Daniel has taught me."

Her spark of annoyance startled him, but then he noticed Elizabeth's sharp interest. Perhaps Catherine did keep a few secrets. Robert cleared his throat. "Undoubtedly."

"A knife?" Elizabeth was animated as she turned to face her friend. "Catherine, is he saying you can wield a knife as a weapon? That's it, isn't it? Why didn't you ever tell me?"

Robert wished he could reel back the words. He'd never intended to divulge a secret.

"I—I suppose I was a bit embarrassed," she said, glancing down at her teacup and rubbing her thumb across the handle.

"Daniel insisted I needed to learn so I could protect myself. The knife was my engagement gift." Her cheeks turned a brighter shade of pink. "So many things happened during that time last year, between my wedding and adjusting to married life—"

"And the kidnapping," Elizabeth added. "You forgot to mention the kidnapping."

"I didn't forget. I just don't like to dwell on it. Speaking of it makes me feel as though someone is walking over my grave." She gave a small shudder. "When I imagine what might have happened, it terrifies me."

"She's quite good," Robert added. "With a knife, I mean. I ran into some would-be assailants outside the theater a couple of nights ago, and she and Daniel helped drive them away."

Catherine smiled. "And we quite enjoyed it, I assure you. People like that tend to run off when the odds aren't in their favor."

"'Outside the theater,' you said," Elizabeth interjected, her gaze resting on Robert in a pondering way. "Was this the same night you came late to our soirée?" She cocked her head to one side and glanced at Catherine. "If I remember correctly, you couldn't come because you had a box at the theater."

"I—uh—" Robert sputtered.

"Robert—I nearly forgot to ask!" Catherine snatched his wrist with her hand and squeezed it. "Did you manage to convince that actress to return whatever it was you wanted from her?"

"What actress?" Elizabeth asked. Her eyes narrowed. "Antonia Winter?"

He glanced from one woman to the other, not sure which question to answer. "No to your question, Catherine. She wouldn't give it to me." He glanced at Elizabeth. "And yes to yours. I was indeed looking for Antonia Winter."

"Robert joined us in our box," Catherine explained. "He was quite interested in Miss Winter."

"This sounds intriguing," Elizabeth said, scooting forward to sit on the front edge of her chair. "You followed her from the theater to the soirée? How romantic. Tell me everything." Her bright-green eyes seemed to glow with excitement. "I love a good story."

Tell her a story? Was she toying with him? He couldn't possibly. He felt the tips of his ears grow warm. Did his ears turn red when he was embarrassed, just like Frederick's? He opened his mouth and then closed it. Then he opened it again and glanced at Catherine. "Are you aware there is a boy lurking in your boxwoods?"

"I beg your pardon." Catherine arched her eyebrows and grained at him. "Is that some new bit of slang? If so, you'll have to explain it to me."

"Not slang," he said, the warmth spreading across his neck. "I was being literal. As I approached your front door, I happened to see him lurking there."

"Lurking?"

"Undeniably so. He looked rather forlorn. I sent my coachman to buy him a meat pasty." He still wasn't sure why he'd done that. "He looked a bit hungry."

"The poor thing. I'll have Patterson bring him in and tend to him." She glanced at one of the footmen, who nodded briefly and left the room.

"That's thoughtful of you, but after coming to know you so well over the past year, I should have expected nothing less. You're most considerate of those in need."

"You're too kind."

"In fact, it's your generous nature that inspired me to come here today. I need to beg a favor of you."

That evoked a look of mild surprise. "Why, Robert," she said, "I've known you for over a year now, and you've never asked anything of me. You know I'm happy to be of assistance. What can I do to help?"

"I need you to act as a chaperone for Antonia Winter while she resides at my home for a time. I believe her life is in danger."

And there it was. The look of complete amazement he'd been waiting for.

Robert grinned in satisfaction. He'd finally managed to shock Lady Huntley.

It had taken him less than a year to do so.

"One of the secrets of life is that all that is really worth doing is what we do for others."

— *LEWIS CARROLL*

"Stop being melodramatic," Elizabeth said, her voice harsh with what sounded like disappointment. "I'd wager you're the biggest danger poor Miss Winter is facing. You just admitted you attended her performance at the theater two nights ago and then again at my home only an hour later. You even followed her when she tried to slip away from you. I can't believe I helped you!"

"Elizabeth," Catherine interrupted. "That was unkind. Robert might be dramatic at times, but I'd never accuse him of being melo dramatic. You know he's always been a gentleman. He'd never harm Miss Winter."

Elizabeth managed to convey her skepticism with the curve of one eyebrow. "That may be true, but one never knows what lies in a man's heart."

Robert felt his cheeks redden.

"Robert isn't some ruffian off the street," Catherine said. "You've know him a long time, and there's never been a rumor or even a whisper to suggest he'd treat a lady badly." She reached out and took Elizabeth's hand. "Don't let other things cloud your judgment." She gave her friend a significant look that Robert couldn't decipher.

Robert held up his hands in surrender. "Perhaps you should hear what I have to say before you rush to judge me."

Elizabeth pressed her lips together as though suppressing a comment. After a moment, she nodded and gestured for him to continue.

Robert focused on Catherine. "Yesterday, I spotted one of my attempted kidnappers leaving Miss Winter's residence. I tried to warn her that she wasn't safe, but she didn't believe me. I'm afraid I didn't handle it well. She resented my interference."

"Of course she did. Really, Robert," Catherine said, using the scolding tones of a mother, "you must learn how to be more diplomatic. You have the tendency to sound quite angry when your emotions run high."

Robert thought back, recalling what he'd said in the foyer with Antonia. Could Catherine be right? Could he have been too forceful? Too dictatorial? Is that why Antonia had refused to leave?

From somewhere in the house, Robert heard a door slam shut. He glanced at Catherine, but she seemed just as surprised by the noise as he was. Perhaps Daniel had returned. But the man didn't usually slam doors. Shouting was more his style.

The loud noises stopped. After a moment, Robert continued. "Since I was worried for Miss Winter's safety, I went to the theater last night to escort her home, and thank god I did." His thoughts brought him up short. What would have happened if he hadn't decided to err on the side of caution and escort her home? If those men had taken her, no one would have known where she'd gone. A cold fist gripped his heart. "I walked with her to her dressing room after the show. As the cast members filed past, two Russian men managed to isolate us. They were frighteningly efficient."

Catherine and Elizabeth exchanged uneasy glances.

"That must have been terrifying for Miss Winter," Elizabeth said. "Was she frightened?"

"She must have been, but she refused to let those men see it."

Elizabeth nervously adjusted the collar of her dress, and Robert noted a glint of silver at her throat. A necklace? It was gone in an instant, so he couldn't be sure. "Did you take her to an inn for the night?" Elizabeth asked. "How can you be certain those men didn't follow you there?"

He waved away her question. "I was worried about the same thing, so I brought her to Woolsy House. She'll be safe there."

Catherine's back stiffened. "And she has no chaperone?"

Robert met her gaze evenly. "Emily's lady's maid is serving as chaperone for the moment, but I'd prefer someone with a bit more credibility. People might assume that a servant's discretion can be bought, although in my experience I've found them to be rather loose-tongued. I need your help. No one would doubt your word as her chaperone."

"I hadn't realized she'd already taken residence in your home. Of course we'll be there. And if Daniel balks, I'll remind him he owes you a debt," Catherine said. Robert raised his brows.

"He does?"

Catherine let out a huff of irritation. "Don't tell me you've forgotten about my kidnapping. You took a blow to the head that day. Did it make you forget everything that transpired?"

"Don't you remember?" Elizabeth asked, her voice edged with sarcasm. "The man so strangely obsessed with Catherine? The attack?" Her glower made him wonder if she suspected him of the same sort of obsessiveness toward Antonia. That might explain her attitude.

"Of course I remember," he said, rubbing at the spot hidden by his hair. He could trace the thicker line of his scar with his fingertips. "I'd always counted that debt against Alexander Gray rather than your husband," he said as he rolled the tension from his shoulders, "but it's one on which I doubt I'll ever collect. Gray disappeared shortly after that scrape. No one's seen him in London in nearly a year."

Catherine flushed and glanced away as though embarrassed, which seemed strange. After a moment, she met his gaze. "If not for your help, my husband would have walked into a trap. He owes you. We both owe you. I fully intend to remind him of that fact should he balk at helping you."

Robert grinned. "I won't say no to your twisting his arm. Is that how things are between you? You can bend him to your will? He certainly seems happy. And to think he came to London searching for a meek, mild-mannered bride."

"What he thought he wanted and what he needed were two entirely different things." Catherine folded her napkin and placed it on the table next to her teacup. "Bear that in mind if you ever go in search of a bride." She gave him a curious look. "Or perhaps you've already discovered that."

Robert frowned at her. "What—"

He was interrupted by a yell of "No!" emanating from behind the door leading toward the kitchen.

Catherine's eyes widened. She glanced at a footman and gestured for him to investigate. He hurried from the room.

A moment later the gray-haired housekeeper came in through the same door. "I beg your pardon, m'lady."

"What's the cause of all the commotion, Mrs. Henworth?"

"It's that boy," she said, glancing over her shoulder at the closed door. "He up and started yelling and caterwauling. I don't know what—"

The door banged open, and the boy Robert had seen lurking behind the shrubbery burst through. He was wide-eyed with fear, but when he caught sight of Robert and Catherine, he skidded to a stop.

"What's this?" Robert asked, rising to his feet.

Tears streamed down the boy's cheeks, and he panted in short, fast breaths. He seemed to suddenly take in his surroundings. He drew himself up straight and wiped away his tears with a sleeve, leaving a streak of clean skin behind. It only served to make him look more grubby and forlorn.

The tears seemed out of character. Not that Robert knew the boy, but there were certain characteristics he'd come to associate with children who looked as this one did—children who lived on the streets and survived by their wits. Without fail, they all had a brittle hardness about them. A weary resignation that suggested they'd seen too much of this world in their short years, and none of it good. Despite this boy's unkempt appearance and long, tangled hair, he had a peculiar air of fragility about him. Perhaps he was new to the streets. That might explain it.

"Come here, boy," Catherine said. "I expect you to be on your best behavior while you are in my house. Your yelling interrupted our meal."

The boy moved to stand in front of her. "Begging your pardon, m'lady." The look he gave her was full of hope. "Might you be Lady Huntley?"

"I am."

"I'm sorry for my rudeness." The boy glanced over his shoulder at Mrs. Henworth. "That one said she wanted to scrub me down right there in the kitchen. She was having people bring in water. I won't do that. It'd be indecent!" He poked his chin out mulishly.

"I can certainly see why you would feel that way. I can promise you that no one will force you to bathe if it isn't your wish, but why wouldn't you want to be clean? Wouldn't you like to have a nice, hot bath and wash away some of that grime? You look as though you're covered in coal dust."

The boy grimaced and glanced down at his clothes. "I slept in a coal bin two nights ago. I had no idea I'd get so filthy."

"Then we're in agreement. I'll have Mrs. Henworth set up a bath tub in one of the bedrooms and she can scrub—"

"No!" The boy backed away, his eyes wide with fear. "I don't want her to see me like that. She can't come in. I can do it myself."

Catherine seemed taken aback by the boy's vehemence. Then an expression crossed her face that Robert couldn't identify. She narrowed her eyes and peered at the boy more closely. "You already knew my name when you came into this room. I think it's time you told me who you are and why you're here."

The boy shot Robert a wary glance, and then focused his attention on Catherine. He opened his mouth and then closed it again. When he finally spoke, his words were barely audible. "I want to learn to fence."

"Oh, my," Catherine said, and her face blanched. She glanced at Mrs. Henworth. "Can you please find the—the boy something clean to wear? A bath can wait until he—"

"What's your name?" Robert demanded. Something strange was going on here.

The boy crimsoned. "I—I'm nobody, my lord."

"Surely you're somebody. You're hardly a figment of my imagination. Out with it. What's your name?"

"My name's Tidmore, Lord Huntley. Imogen Tidmore."

Imogen? He was—a she? Robert glanced at Catherine to see if she was as startled by the girl's revelation as he was. Her perfectly still expression told him everything he needed to know. Catherine wasn't at all surprised. In fact, she looked quite nervous.

"I—I've come to ask you to teach me to fence. Father approves, but Mother—well, Mother says it's unseemly. She says she doesn't care if a marchioness does it. Only the Queen herself could convince her that it's proper. Father says if a marquess can let his wife fence, then surely a judge can permit his daughter to do so." She beamed at Robert.

He suddenly realized that Imogen must think he was Lord Huntley. "We seemed to have skipped the necessary introductions earlier," Robert said. "I'm the Earl of Wentworth, a friend of Lord and Lady Huntley's."

The boy—girl looked dumbstruck. She opened her mouth, closed it, and opened it again. "Then where's Lord Huntley?" she asked.

"I'm right here," Daniel said as he entered the room. "And can someone tell me what's happening?"

"I'm glad you're here," Robert said. He tossed the napkin he'd been holding onto the table and strode across the room to confront his friend.

Daniel scowled at him. "Are you the cause of all this commotion?"

"No. But I'm about to add to it." He stepped in a bit closer, crowding Daniel. "It would seem that I have finally discovered what happened to that scamp, Alexander Gray. After he disappeared a year ago, I worried he'd met with some terrible end. Imagine my surprise to discover he's your wife ."

Daniel's eyes widened and his mouth fell open as he took a step back.

Robert glanced at Catherine, taking in her deep blush of embarrassment. "I'm not bothered that you're Gray. I'm offended that the two of you kept the secret from me."

She looked positively shocked. Twice in one day. "I—I—"

"You're Gray?" Elizabeth said, pushing away from the table and lurching to her feet. "Catherine! That's marvelous!"

As he took in Catherine's embarrassment and Elizabeth's excitement, Robert shook his head in bemusement and started chuckling. Quietly at first. Then louder. Then he let out a full-throated laugh, letting it fill him. Once he started, he found he couldn't make himself stop. In fact, he didn't want to make himself stop. He laughed so hard tears started streaming down his cheeks.

"It appears that I came to the right person to ask for help," he finally managed to say. "Once again, the mysterious Alexander Gray saves the day."

"Pull yourself together, Wentworth," Daniel said, placing an arm around his shoulders and guiding him back to his chair at the breakfast table. "You're laughing at my wife's expense." He settled into the seat next to Robert.

"I do apologize. I'm not laughing at her, but at myself. I should have seen it sooner."

Elizabeth leaned forward in her chair. "You're Alexander Gray?" she asked again. "Why didn't you tell me?"

"It seemed safest," Catherine mumbled. "The fewer people who knew—"

"Apparently your secret isn't very well-guarded if young Imogen knows about it," Robert commented.

All eyes turned toward the girl standing alone.

"I'm sorry, Lady Huntley," Imogen said. "I didn't mean to give you away." Her pained expression convinced Robert she was telling the truth.

"How did you find out?" Daniel asked. "Not many people know."

"I overheard my parents talking about it. Father wanted Mother to bring me here to meet Lady Huntley and perhaps take lessons, but Mother refused."

"Your name is Tidmore?" Robert knew that name. "Is your father Absolom Tidmore? Lord Tidmore? The judge ?"

Imogen's face fell. "Do you know him, sir?"

"Not well. Mostly by reputation." Robert peered more closely at Imogen, noting the family resemblance. It was in her eyes and the shape of her jaw. "He was one of the head boys at Eton when I first arrived." Robert had done his best to stay out of young

Absolom's sight. But even though he'd been stern and demanding, he'd also been fair.

Daniel leaned in. "Tidmore the Tyrant? He's your father? I remember him. Absolom had the uncanny ability to sniff out the culprit of every minor misdeed. On days when I'd misbehaved, I kept my distance."

"It would appear he's still good at ferreting out secrets. After all, he discovered yours," Robert said. "He's a judge now. I can't think of a man better suited for the role." Nor could he think of a man better positioned to help Antonia.

"Perhaps." Daniel raked his fingers through his hair.

"It's a pleasure to make your acquaintance, Miss Tidmore," Robert said. "Today has been a fortuitous day. Most fortuitous indeed."

❧ 32 ☙

He is happiest, be he king or peasant, who finds peace in his home.

— *JOHANN WOLFGANG VON GOETHE*

R obert returned home as the large clock in the foyer chimed eleven o'clock. He closed the large double doors leading to the street and was pleasantly surprised by the agreeable scent pervading the room. There, on the round table in the center of the foyer, sat an artful arrangement of flowers next to a letter addressed to him. He picked up the letter and opened it as he examined them.

The blooms must have come from his own greenhouse. Mother had frequently made similar elaborate arrangements, but that simple expression of everyday beauty had vanished from his life since her death. None of the servants had proven adept at the skill, and he hadn't placed enough importance on the task to bother filling the void. But now he wondered why he hadn't taken the time.

He scanned the brief letter and then tucked it into his breast pocket before turning his attention back to the centerpiece.

Fortunately, the fragrant blossoms overpowered the faintly unpleasant odor of the London streets that had swirled inside with him. His neighbor had chosen today to have workers dig out his privy, and because of that, it was not a good day to venture outdoors. Once the workmen spread lime, the odor would diminish. At least his neighbor was having the job done in the winter rather than in the heat of summer, thereby minimizing the noxious fumes.

Robert stepped closer to examine the arrangement. It could only be Antonia's handiwork. No one else had attempted to create anything this elaborate in years. She must have found Mother's flower-arranging supplies. He could detect bits of floral wire holding certain blooms in place.

As he peered at the creation, he was surprised to note that some of the items she'd used weren't flowers at all. She'd used dried seedpods and some unusual twigs. He didn't recall his mother ever using twigs in her arrangements. It was strange to see such common objects mixed with the extravagant flowers, but he liked the effect.

Robert took a step back to admire it. Antonia seemed quite adept at this particular skill. Apparently she was a woman of many hidden talents. Flower arranging, acting, knife fighting, thieving, kissing...

He dragged his index finger along his lower lip. Last night, when she'd stared at him in that seductive way, he'd been unable to back away from the challenge. Ever since meeting her at the embassy, he'd wanted her to gaze at him with exactly that expression in her eyes. That passion. Even though he'd known she was toying with him when she'd gazed at him that way— that she'd merely been trying to prove a point—he'd lost all control.

Now he breathed in deeply as he recalled the softness of her lips. At first they'd been slightly chilled from the ice in her whiskey, but they'd warmed quickly enough once he'd kissed her.

He wanted her. Of that he was certain.

With that thought in the forefront of his mind, he wasn't at all surprised to see Antonia breeze into the foyer. He could almost believe he'd summoned her to him with his thoughts, if not for the fact that she didn't seem to notice him.

She carried a small, round vase of pink rosebuds and she headed toward the main staircase with it cradled in her hands.

She looked deliciously tempting.

"I see you've been hard at work."

The vase bobbled in her hands, but Antonia managed to keep it from falling. "I didn't see you there." Her cheeks flushed, as though they'd stolen a bit of the color from the rosebuds she held.

Was she embarrassed? How could he put her at ease? Robert moved closer to her and indicated the pink roses arranged in a dense ball of color. "You seemed rather intent on your bouquet. Is it for your room?"

She shook her head, averting her gaze. She licked her lips nervously. "Your sister told me she loves pink roses, so I made this for her. Emily introduced herself to me this morning and showed me around. Your greenhouse is amazing." She glanced at him tentatively. "It's been a long time since I've had the luxury of indulging myself this way."

At the mention of Emily, Robert squared his shoulders. He wasn't alone in the house with Antonia. Others were nearby. He needed to remember that.

With the grace of a dancer, Antonia balanced the small vase in one hand as she gathered her skirts to walk up the stairs.

"Let me help you with that." Robert hurried over to her and took the vase as he accompanied her up the grand staircase. "Did you and my sister meet at breakfast?"

Antonia shied away from him. She nodded as she tugged off her gardening gloves and tucked them under her apron ties. "I'm afraid I startled her when I entered the breakfast room." She kept a bit more distance between them than he would have liked as they climbed the stairs.

The paintings of Robert's ancestors adorning the walls of the staircase seemed to watch him. Most of them cast him grim looks, but his great-grandmother's gaze held a hint of mischief, as always. His mother's portrait seemed different today. It held an uncharacteristic hint of disapproval. She'd always been a stickler for propriety, and she would have taken his behavior last night as a personal affront. He glanced guiltily away from her censure. She was right. He'd taken advantage of the situation.

And even worse, he wanted to do it again, at the earliest opportunity.

He cleared his throat. "I'm sorry I abandoned you this morning. I assumed you'd sleep late and then take breakfast in your room. I should have been here to make introductions."

"It's of no matter. Once I explained the circumstances, Emily was most understanding. I'm afraid, however, that she may have the impression that having you save me from kidnappers was an exciting adventure." She paused outside Emily's bedroom door and knocked briefly, but there was no response.

"My sister loves stories filled with intrigue and excitement. Mother was forever at her wits' end trying to make her behave as a proper lady should. But there's no stopping her." Robert handed her the flowers, and his hand grazed her bare one.

An awareness of their pent-up sexual energy sizzled between them, and Antonia snatched her hand back from his touch as though she'd felt an electric shock. Apparently, she was as acutely attuned to him as he was to her.

She looked at him warily and reached out once again to take the vase, this time being careful not to brush against his bare hand.

Fighting the urge to reach out and touch her, he took a step back. "I'll wait in the hallway while you put those in her room."

Antonia gave him a wary glance before she nodded and then opened Emily's bedroom door. The room seemed more youthful than Robert remembered. Or perhaps he simply hadn't looked through the door in a very long time. It was decorated in pale shades of pink and cream, with accents of soft green. The arrangement of bright pink roses Antonia had selected provided a punch of color in the faded room. She crossed the pale rug toward Emily's bedside table.

Robert took in his sister's domain. Mother had decorated it for Emily many years ago, but he doubted it still suited his vibrant sister, if it ever had. Perhaps he should ask her if she'd like to make any changes to it. She might prefer bolder colors to suit her personality. After all, she was a young woman now, just entering society.

As a child, she'd been entranced by the guest bedroom Antonia was using. Of course, that had more to do with the hidden staircase. Mother had had a terrible time keeping Emily out of it. Not long before Father had died, she'd rearranged the furniture so that the bed blocked access to the staircase. No one had used it in years. He had no doubt that if he let Emily take over the room, she'd shift the bed to one side and immediately put that staircase back into use.

He'd need to consider this a bit longer.

Antonia took a step back from the bedside table and then leaned forward to reposition the vase an inch to the left. With a nod, she glanced across the room at Robert and smiled.

She looked so natural and at ease in the room that Robert could only stare in wonder at her. She was beautiful—the perfect picture of a lady.

He liked seeing her this way. He liked seeing her in his home.

After a moment, he noticed her dress. It wasn't the same one she'd been wearing last night. An apron protected her pale-pink gown, and both articles of clothing looked as though they might have come from his sister's wardrobe. In fact, upon closer examination, he was certain of it. The attire suited Antonia, but it also made her appear much younger than he'd believed her to be.

"How old are you, Antonia?"

She was walking toward him to join him in the hallway, but at his question she paused, apparently startled. Her eyebrows rose, and her face became a shade pinker.

"Forgive me." Robert waved his hand, wishing he hadn't blurted out the question. "Sometimes I forget myself. It was rude of me to ask."

"After saving my life last night, I think you've earned a bit of candor." She shook her head as she stepped forward and rested her hand on Emily's doorknob, maintaining a discreet distance from him on the other side of the threshold. "I'm twenty-one."

So young. "It's no wonder you and Emily struck up a friendship so quickly. She's not much younger than you."

"It probably has more to do with the fact that I have two younger sisters."

"Ah, that reminds me—I was able to address the problem you raised last night."

A quick grin flitted across her lips, and she began fidgeting with the finger of one of the gloves she'd tucked into her waistband. "Which problem might that be? I have so many of them these days, it's becoming difficult to keep them straight."

Robert swallowed as he watched her play with the glove. Her movements might be innocent, but in his current state of mind, he found the way she stroked her fingers along the glove's digit to be highly suggestive and erotic. When she flicked a bit of dirt off the end of the index finger, he flinched. "That of having an appropriate chaperone," he said, tearing his gaze away. "I prefer you stay here where we can ensure your safety until you're no longer at risk of being kidnapped. I've arranged for Lady Huntley and her husband to join us for a few days. She can serve as your chaperone."

Antonia's posture suddenly relaxed. He hadn't been aware of

how stiffly she'd been holding herself until she stopped. "Thank you," she said.

"I also sent a letter to Miss Galloway." He handed her the reply. "She and your sisters will visit you here later this afternoon. I hope you find that acceptable."

"Miss Galloway is coming here?" Antonia's eyes widened, and she let the glove fall loose at her waist. Thank god that small torment was at an end. She continued to stare at him.

He couldn't read her expression. Was she annoyed with him? "This seemed like the perfect solution. I thought you'd be pleased."

"Pleased?" She paused. "You simply surprised me. When did you arrange everything?"

"This morning. You mentioned Miss Galloway's place of employment, so I wrote to her at Miss Hermitage's Collegiate School for Girls this morning. I also contacted Miss Hermitage and was able to arrange for a brief visit. Miss Hermitage was quite understanding once she learned of the situation." The cash donation he'd made to Miss Hermitage's school had also helped. Money had a way of smoothing away all sorts of obstacles. "She and your sisters should arrive this afternoon."

At his words, the internal battle Antonia seemed to be waging tipped in his favor. If her broad grin hadn't been enough to tell him of her pleasure, the way she began bouncing on her toes did. She rushed through Emily's doorway and grabbed his hands.

A jolt of desire swept through him at the feel of her bare skin. She squeezed his hands more firmly, but then abruptly released them.

"You're being much too kind to me," she said sternly as she stiffened her spine. "This can't continue."

He smiled at her jest, but she didn't respond with a smile of her own. Perhaps it wasn't a jest after all. "Why?"

"We live in different worlds, and I could never find a place in yours. Not one that would satisfy me. I'm no longer considered a lady, and I refuse to become some man's mistress. I'm afraid if I let myself fall in love with you, I'll lose who I am. A part of me will die."

Love? His throat tightened. It was too soon for talk of love, he knew, but somehow it seemed right. "Isn't that what love is? Giving up a part of yourself to become something more? Something new?" He reached out and took her hands in his again.

She shook her head. "I don't know. I've lost so much over the past year. I'm not prepared to give up anything more. Not right now." Her eyes glittered with unshed tears.

"Then let's not talk of it." He squeezed her fingers. "Let's focus on our immediate goals. Once we've achieved them, we can..."

"Talk of the future?" she murmured, staring down at their intertwined hands.

"Yes. It can wait." For now.

"Maybe I'll recover my birthright."

His heart beat faster than it should. Her hands were loose now, no longer clinging tightly to his. They were warm and soft. He ran his thumb across the backs of her knuckles and then pressed her hands together while bringing them closer to his chest.

"I'm certain you will," he murmured. She smelled of flowers and dirt, and a bit of dried leaf was caught in her hair near her left ear. He reached up to brush it away. "I have more good news. I may have found a judge who—"

"Well, isn't this a pretty scene?" Frederick interrupted.

Robert dropped Antonia's hands and spun around to see Frederick staring at him. At first glance, Frederick appeared to be relaxed, but Robert could see tension in his body.

Thank god Frederick hadn't stumbled across them just a moment earlier. What would he have said if he'd overheard their discussion of love? The idea that his brother had nearly witnessed that vulnerable moment was intolerable.

But perhaps even worse was the knowledge that he'd inadvertently sparked his brother's curiosity. That was precisely what he'd hoped to avoid.

"Frederick." Robert tried to regain some control of the situation as he stepped toward his brother. Perhaps he could still allay his suspicions. "It's good to see you. I hope your meeting went well." He tilted his head to Antonia. She was already the focus of his brother's inquisitive gaze. "This is our guest, Miss Antonia Winter. Miss Winter, I'd like you to meet my brother, Mr. Woolsy."

She gave a small curtsy.

"She'll be staying with us for a few days, along with Lord and Lady Huntley. Lady Huntley has kindly consented to serve as chaperone."

"Miss Winter? Now, where have I heard that name before?" Frederick's eyes narrowed as he glanced from Robert to Antonia and back again.

Robert froze. How could he have forgotten? Ambassador Revnik had mentioned Antonia's name.

"Ah, yes. Now I remember," Frederick said. "You're the actress I've heard so much about."

"Am I? I hope it was nothing bad."

"Not at all. I heard you gave a stunning performance in *Anne Blake* last night. You plan to stay here for a few days?"

Robert held his breath for a fraction of a second, but then reminded himself to breathe. Frederick would notice his tension and know he was hiding something.

But he underestimated his brother's cunning. Rather than behaving as though he was suspicious, Frederick suddenly unleashed his most devastating smile upon Antonia. Robert almost groaned with frustration at witnessing it. He'd frequently watched Frederick use that very same charm to convince someone that he or she was the most intriguing person in all of

England. It usually had the recipient melting under the warmth of his attention.

"This is a surprise," Frederick said in a soft, enthralling tone. "A most pleasant one."

Robert didn't like Antonia's answering smile, but at least she wasn't simpering. That was better than most women managed once Frederick targeted them with his charm.

"Do we have you to thank for that stunning floral arrangement in the foyer?" Frederick asked. That was part of his skill. He noticed things. He knew precisely how to elicit the response he desired, no matter the circumstances.

The only person immune to his manipulation was Robert.

"It was a simple matter since I had such a wide variety of flowers to choose from," Antonia said, glancing back into Emily's bedroom at the arrangement of pink roses. She smiled with satisfaction at her creation as she turned her gaze back to Frederick. "Your gardeners are quite talented to be able to coax such beautiful blooms during the winter."

"They're devoted to the task," Robert said in a tone that was much terser than he'd intended. He pressed his lips together, irritated with himself for revealing his tension to Frederick.

Frederick raised his eyebrows in victory, and Robert could have sworn his brother smirked. The man could catch the faintest whiff of deceit, just like a bloodhound searching for a fox's trail.

Robert cleared his throat. "Perhaps we should retire to the morning room. I only just arrived home, and I still need to speak to Landon to ensure rooms will be ready for our guests."

Frederick stepped forward, cutting between Robert and Antonia, and offered her his arm. "Take your time. I'll keep Miss Winter occupied while you sort out the details."

Robert glared at his brother, but Frederick only grinned more deeply. The man was insufferable. It was obvious that he wanted to separate them so he could question her.

Blast.

Antonia looked at Robert, furrowing her brows slightly as though trying to understand the undercurrents swirling between the two men.

Frederick watched them closely. Robert wished he could explain his complicated relationship with his brother. Lord. He wished he could explain it to *himself*. All he could do was give her a reassuring nod, like some idiot.

"I'll join you in the morning room in a few minutes."

Frederick held out his arm to Antonia. "I hope you don't mind me saying so, but your hair is a most unusual shade. It reminds me of a sunset on an overcast day." He glanced at Robert and smirked.

Frederick knew. He knew she was the thief, but he was biding his time.

Antonia cocked an eyebrow at Robert before gingerly accepting Frederick's arm. Robert felt a surge of pleasure when he realized she'd seen through his brother's artifice. Frederick had underestimated her, and now she'd be on guard.

Robert turned his back on the pair so Frederick wouldn't see his satisfaction. He couldn't resist glancing over his shoulder for one last glimpse of Antonia. She paused at the top of the staircase to look back at him. Her slight smirk as she flicked her eyes toward Frederick told Robert he had no need to worry.

Antonia could manage his brother.

Frederick may have finally met his match in her.

The thought gave him pause. He'd need to be careful once he joined them in the morning room. These two would be playing a game of wits. Navigating a safe course through a conversational maze with them would be more difficult than picking one of those new locks James Sargent seemed to be continually inventing.

In the dark.

Wearing gloves.

Perhaps he simply wouldn't speak. That would probably be for the best.

33

What is there more kindly than the feeling between host and guest?

— AESCHYLUS

F rederick was pleasant enough, but Antonia knew he was playing an elaborate game of cat and mouse with her. Whatever was happening, he seemed content to draw it out, and for now, that included chatting with her until Robert joined them.

"...and then Lord Percival knocked over the oil lamp and set the entire table on fire," Frederick said.

"That's how you burned your hand?" Antonia asked, glancing at his bandaged hand.

Frederick nodded. "The oil drenched both gloves. I'm not sure if they protected my hands or made the burns worse. My right hand suffered the most damage."

Warmth crept up the back of Antonia's neck and she glanced toward the door of the drawing room. Robert entered, keeping his gaze pinned on her. He warmed her to her toes, and it took a healthy measure of steely resolve to turn her attention back to Frederick.

"I got off lightly," Frederick continued, seeming unaware that he'd lost her attention for an instant. "Poor Lord Tamworth's entire arm was set on fire."

"Lord Percival is a drunken sot," Robert interjected, drawing his brother's gaze. "His antics will be the death of someone someday."

Frederick frowned. "You have the right of it. They very nearly were for Tamworth. He hasn't left his sickbed."

Robert crossed the room, heading toward the empty chair to her right. "A room is being prepared for Lord and Lady Huntley as we speak," he said as he sidestepped between her and Frederick.

For a moment, Robert blocked his brother's view of them both, and the warmth in Robert's eyes sent a thrill through her that she struggled to conceal. She glanced down at the garnet-colored sofa while she composed her features, taking care not to fidget or show any other sign of stress.

She watched Robert lower himself into the chair facing the door. "When do you expect them to arrive?" she asked.

"I don't have a definite time. Certainly within the hour. Perhaps within minutes."

Frederick scowled at Robert. "That isn't long. You'll need to hurry to fill me in regarding Miss Winter's presence in our household. She is the thief we've been searching for, isn't she?"

Antonia stopped breathing. She blinked in surprise. What would Robert say?

"Of course."

Antonia froze. That was it? That was Robert's plan to protect her identity?

Robert glanced her way and shrugged. "There's no use saying anything else. He already knows."

She gaped at him, her gaze bouncing back and forth between the two men.

Robert rubbed his hands together. "The room's a bit chilly," he said as he rose to his feet and moved toward the fireplace. He crouched down and used a poker from the stand on the hearth to prod the dying embers until they flickered to life. Then he grabbed some fuel from a nearby bin and added it to the flames.

Antonia relaxed in the continuing silence. He seemed so casual. Perhaps informing Frederick of her identity wasn't as dangerous as Robert had led her to believe.

"I went to the theater last night to speak with Miss Winter," Robert finally said, keeping his back to them. "My timing proved fortuitous. Two men from the Russian embassy slipped backstage and attempted to kidnap her."

When Frederick glanced at her for confirmation, she did her best to look appropriately worried. It wasn't difficult.

Frederick's brow furrowed. "That's a sudden change on Revnik's part. I thought she was too important."

"Too important?" Antonia asked. What on earth could he mean?

Frederick's eyes narrowed. "Didn't Robert tell you?" he asked. He glared at the back of Robert's head. "Can you please face me?" He let out an irritated sigh. "Why do you insist on tending the fire? It's annoying."

"I find it calming. You should try it sometime."

"Perhaps once my burns have healed. By all means, continue," Frederick snapped. "I'd hate for you not to be calm. Did you tell Miss Winter about our meeting with the ambassador?"

Robert rose to his feet, and Antonia noticed that he'd managed to coax some flames to life. "Not in detail," he said. "Last night's events proved distracting. The theater manager fired her because of the attack. Such a charitable man. I couldn't let Miss Winter return home while those men were searching for her, so I brought her here to keep her safe."

Antonia glanced from one brother to the other and finally stared at Frederick. "You mentioned something about the ambassador. You said he was looking for me. Did he tell you anything else?"

Frederick's gaze was cold and direct. "He told us that one of his footmen reported seeing Miss Winter at the ball wearing a silver dress. The woman who stole the church register from my brother happened to be wearing a silver dress as well, so I made the simple deduction that you are the mysterious woman who stole the book from my brother. You can imagine my surprise to find you here in our home as his guest."

"I-I—" What should she say? And why had Robert brought her here? Would Frederick have her arrested for treason? She glanced at the door, wondering if Frederick's burns would slow him if she decided to run.

Probably not.

"Can you explain why Ambassador Revnik believes you are 'too important' to question directly? Although, considering that he tried to have you kidnapped last night, perhaps he now thinks differently."

"'Too important'?" Antonia said. What on earth could Frederick be talking about? "That's ridiculous."

"Those were his words."

Antonia glanced at Robert for confirmation. He nodded. "Revnik tried to cover up his mistake, but I think he was being genuine when he claimed you were too important to question."

"But that makes no sense. I'm nobody. Less than nobody."

Frederick's cool gaze assessed her. "You honestly believe that. Interesting." "

But it's true."

"Clearly, Revnik or one of his superiors doesn't agree with you," Frederick said.

"Perhaps it has something to do with your grandfather,"

Robert suggested hesitantly, sounding as though he doubted his own words. "Who might that be?"

"The artist Vladamir Nevsky."

"But he's dead, isn't he?" Frederick glanced at her for confirmation, and she nodded. "Then it's unlikely that he's a factor. No one worries about offending a dead man. Any other important family members?"

She gave a wry smile. "My only surviving family members are my two younger sisters and an uncle who has disowned us. I can assure you, we wield no influence. None at all."

Movement at the doorway caught her attention.

"Antonia. There you are," Emily said as she swept into the drawing room. She made her way directly across the room and sat next to Antonia on the sofa. "I found your lovely roses on my nightstand." She took both of Antonia's hands in her own. "That was so kind of you. They're beautiful."

Antonia gave a warm squeeze to the younger woman's hands. "I'm glad you like them."

Emily's brows furrowed as she took in her surroundings. "What are the three of you doing in here? You rarely use this room."

"Lord and Lady Huntley will be arriving shortly, and we're waiting here to greet them," Robert said. "They'll stay with us for a few days."

A broad smile broke across Emily's face. "But that's marvelous."

"Miss Winter is looking for new accommodations, and Lady Huntley has agreed to act as chaperone in the meantime. She and her husband will remain our guests while Miss Winter searches to finds something appropriate," Robert said.

"Oh, I do hope it takes a while." Emily's eyes grew even wider, and she covered her mouth with her hand. "I didn't mean that the way it sounded," she said, turning to Antonia. "It's simply that I hope you can stay for at least a few days. It's wonderful to have some female companionship."

"I understand completely. I miss my sisters every day we're apart. Life isn't nearly as entertaining without them around."

Antonia glanced out the window. Her sofa was perpendicular to the tall windows that overlooked the street. Chocolate-brown velvet curtains with a garnet fringe stretched from the high ceiling to the floor, reminding her of the chocolate-covered cherries Mother had sometimes brought home as a treat. The curtains were drawn wide and allowed the weak midday sunlight into the room.

"Have you met Lady Huntley?" Emily asked. When Antonia shook her head, Emily said, "You'll adore her. She's quite clever, and very kind."

"I'm certain I'll enjoy her company."

"Miss Winter's sisters plan to visit her this afternoon as well," Robert said.

"How splendid," Emily said. "How many sisters do you have?"

"Two. I'm the eldest of the three, and then comes Evalina. Stephanie is the youngest, but she's also the tallest. She takes after our father. Other than height, we're all fairly similar in appearance. Brown hair, brown eyes."

"Brown hardly begins to describe the color of your hair," Emily said. "It has glimmers of a warm, coppery hue. It's quite lovely."

Antonia felt herself blushing. "How very kind of you to say so."

"And your complexion is so pale and smooth. It's like porcelain. But you're blushing. Am I embarrassing you?"

Robert snorted. "Of course you're embarrassing her. How else would she react?"

"Please forgive me. That wasn't my intent." Emily seemed flustered. "I suppose I'm overly excited at the prospect of having guests and I was trying too hard to make you like me. You do like me, don't you?"

Antonia stifled a bubble of laughter and instead squeezed the younger woman's hand. "Of course I like you," she said with a grin. "And wait until you meet my sisters. I'm certain one of them will say something quite mortifying within five minutes of entering the house."

"Oh! Then we'll get along splendidly," Emily said. She gave a sharp nod of affirmation. "I do that all the time."

Robert's butler arrived at the entrance.

"Yes, Landon?" Robert said.

"Lord and Lady Huntley have arrived."

"Show them in," Robert said.

The gentlemen rose to their feet as Lady Huntley swept into the room followed by her husband. He was tall and imposing, but Lady Huntley's warm smile immediately put Antonia at ease.

Robert quickly made introductions.

"Thank you for agreeing to serve as my chaperone, Lady Huntley. It was very generous of you."

"You must call me Catherine. I insist."

"Then you shall call me Antonia."

"What a lovely name," Catherine said, sitting on the sofa between Antonia and Emily. "One doesn't hear it very often."

Antonia smiled. "My mother chose names that reflected her Russian heritage. My name is an anglicized version of Antonina. My sisters are Evalina and Stephanie, which are also variants of Russian names."

Robert returned to the fireplace and gently placed a log on the smoldering embers. Lord Huntley crossed the room to join him there.

"Those are beautiful names. Daniel and I have been discussing names as well. For our baby. I've been suggesting family names, but Daniel thinks we should start with a clean slate so that our child doesn't feel weighed down by expectations."

Her husband raised one eyebrow. "You're being diplomatic. I believe I said I'd never saddle my child with my father's name. That had more to do with my dislike for the man than weighty expectations."

"You're right," Catherine said. "I was trying to be diplomatic. Much good it did. Now Antonia knows that you bear animosity toward your late father."

"Everyone knows I dislike my father. It's a well-known fact. There's no reason she shouldn't know it too."

Robert and Lord Huntley exchanged grins.

"I thought you were trying to distance yourself from your past and from him," Catherine said. "If you keep mentioning your animosity, it stays fresh in people's minds so they can't forget about it."

Daniel swayed his head from side to side. "Touché. I concede your point."

Catherine gave him a serene smile. "Thank you."

"But I still refuse to saddle my son with his name."

"As do I," she said agreeably.

"Then why in blazes are we discussing it again?"

"Daniel, I never said I wanted to name our son, should we have a son, after your father. Surely there are other names from your family or my family you might consider."

"Ah. Perhaps Solomon."

"Hmm," she said, tapping her chin.

"I was thinking of something more along the lines of Henry. Or perhaps Richard."

"Richard. I like Richard. It's settled."

Catherine raised her eyebrows. "Like that? No further discussion?"

"Or we could discuss it further," he agreed cautiously, obviously confused by her reaction.

Catherine grinned at Antonia. "He's great fun to tease," she murmured. "And he takes it so well."

"Miss Winter," Lord Huntley said, clearly trying to change the subject. "Robert filled us in regarding the attack last night. Please let me know if there's anything I can do to help. I detest kidnappers."

Catherine tensed. "Yes," she said. "We've had our own bad experiences along those lines and wouldn't wish them upon anyone."

Frederick rose to his feet. "You're both quite kind to offer your support to her, but I'm not certain it will be necessary." He locked gazes with Robert as he stalked across the room. "Because if I don't hear a reasonable explanation for why you're harboring a criminal within the next five minutes, I'm having Miss Winter arrested for treason."

Robert's jaw tightened. He pulled back his arm and launched his fist directly at Frederick's face.

34

Compromise is the best and cheapest lawyer.

— *ROBERT LOUIS STEVENSON*

Frederick stumbled back, narrowly avoiding the punch.

Robert closed the distance between them—furious. "How dare you threaten her?"

Frederick's eyes widened in shock. He opened and closed his mouth in surprise.

Daniel lurched forward, grabbed Robert by the shoulder, and pulled him away. "Step back," Daniel ordered.

When Robert moved around Daniel to glare at his brother, Antonia moved directly in his path. She flattened her palm against his chest.

"Don't hit him. He's your brother."

It took a moment for Robert to process her words, and then he simply gaped at her. "You'd defend him? After what he just said?"

"You're brothers. You can resolve this amicably. I'm certain of it. Talk to him."

Robert's anger still raged, but he pushed it down, suppressing it as he had so many other times in the past. The heat of Antonia's palm against his chest helped him focus. He looked down into her eyes—into their tranquil depths. Her serenity was like a lifeline in a storm.

"I know you and your brother respect one another. From what you've told me, he's a fair and reasonable man. I'm sure you can reach an agreement. I have confidence in both of you."

At her words, a sense of calm descended on him. He could do this. He could make his brother see reason. He closed his hand over Antonia's on his chest and nodded.

Her slow, soft smile warmed him. She slid her hand away and stepped aside.

Frederick had heard everything, but as he gazed at Antonia, he looked confused.

Robert moved closer to his brother. "I'm sorry, but what you said about Antonia—I lost my temper. Helping her is the right thing to do. If you understood why she needs the book, you'd support me in this." He took a deep breath. "But I understand your point of view. The circumstances make this look bad. Very bad."

"Then give me an explanation," Frederick pleaded, revealing a crack in his resolve as he glanced first at Robert and then at Antonia. "Tell me what's convinced you to champion her interests."

He explained Antonia's situation, but Frederick's frown persisted.

"I commend you for wanting to help someone in such a dire situation," Frederick said, "but the Queen needs that church register too. That book isn't some insignificant item. Something on those pages can incite a war. Surely that trumps Miss Winter's claim. She needs to turn it over for the greater good."

Antonia stepped forward, shaking her head as though

stunned. "I love my country, but you're asking me to make an enormous sacrifice. I need to prove my parents were legally married and that my sisters and I are their legitimate children. I shouldn't be sent to prison for that. Are you saying you're willing to turn me in for treason for the sake of the greater good? Would you be so willing to sacrifice yourself if the situation were reversed?"

Frederick couldn't have looked more stunned if she'd slapped him.

Robert narrowed his eyes. "Her words have more bite to them than she can possibly guess. Our family has secrets as well. You and I are simply fortunate we don't have a greedy relative who is willing to sacrifice us for his own gain."

"Turning over the church register to the Queen would be for the greater good," Frederick said, but his voice lacked conviction.

"What is this 'greater good'?" Robert asked, frustrated. "You've never been willing to tell me why Queen Victoria wants the book. How can you expect me to make this decision if you aren't willing to explain things to me?"

"It's not your choice to make," Frederick insisted.

"Don't be naive. I know you said the request came from the Queen, but unless you've been hiding something from me, you know nothing more about the significance of this book than I do."

Frederick glanced away and remained silent for a heartbeat too long.

Robert's jaw tightened. "You don't know, do you?"

"I follow orders, which is more than I can say for you."

"You blindly follow orders, you mean," Robert spat back.

"That's insulting."

"It was meant to be."

"You're intentionally goading me when I'm trying to help you? Why?"

"Because someone stole that seemingly insignificant book

from a Russian Orthodox Church, burned down the building, and murdered a woman to hide the crime. It appears to have been stolen to conceal Antonia's parents' marriage, but both the British and Russian governments want it as well. What is so blasted important about a list of weddings?"

Frederick sighed. "It contains information about births and deaths as well."

Robert narrowed his eyes upon hearing the cryptic reply. "Are you saying this book is important because it records someone's birth or death?"

Frederick hesitated and then nodded. "Actually, it records both a birth and a death. And that information is enough to topple a government, or at the very least, to start a civil war within Russia."

"Go on."

"I wish I could, but that's all I know. The book's secret is too big to entrust to me."

"But all of those births and deaths took place in a minor Russian town—hardly more than a village," Antonia insisted, tightening her grip on Robert's arm. "How could one insignificant person's birth or death affect an entire government?"

Robert scrubbed his face with his hands. "This makes me even more concerned about Antonia's safety. Based on what you're saying, the Russians would be willing to kill to keep it hidden."

"If it's wielded properly, our government might be able to convince the czar to pull his troops from the Crimean Peninsula and stop threatening the Eastern regions."

"So it's back to the Eastern Question again?" Daniel blurted out. "Every problem around the world seems to have its root in the fall of the Ottoman Empire."

"The Ottomans provided stability," Frederick said in a tone that made it sound as though he'd made the same statement many times before. "With them gone, other governments are moving in to fill the void."

"They're all scrambling for power," Antonia said.

Frederick gave her a suspicious look. "You're well-informed."

She shrugged. "It's all I ever see in the newspapers these days."

Frederick let out a heavy sigh and dropped back into the chair where he'd been sitting earlier. "If England can't convince the czar to withdraw from the peninsula, the Queen will ally with France and declare war on Russia."

Robert nearly sighed with relief at seeing his brother relax, and he eased into the seat next to Antonia. "That's because if Russia controls that waterway, it will give them power over the trade route." How many other people were currently repeating this same debate all over England? "We can't let that happen. We all understand what's at stake."

"In that case, you must realize why we need to turn over the book," Frederick said. His expression was stark. Pained. He understood the price Antonia would have to pay, but it was obvious he believed his logic was sound. Irrefutable.

"Wait. Hear me out," Robert said. "The register contains the proof Antonia's parents were married, and she must have it to claim her inheritance."

"All I need to do is show it to a judge," Antonia said. "Once he's seen it, I'll be able to recover everything my uncle stole from us."

"A judge?" Catherine asked.

"But why can't you turn it over to the crown first?" Robert asked. "If Miss Winter's claim is as valid as you say, our government could still allow her to use the book to support her case."

Robert raised one eyebrow. "Can you guarantee that? The Russians already stole it from her once. I stole it from the Russians. And the original thief not only stole it from a church but also committed both murder and arson to obtain it—too many people are after it."

"Did you say you need to show it to a judge?" Catherine asked.

"Which proves how important it is," Frederick said, ignoring Catherine. "Letting you keep the book is simply too risky." He turned to face Antonia. "You need to turn it over to me for safekeeping."

Antonia shook her head. "I can't. I don't have it anymore."

"What?" Frederick lifted his head, genuinely astounded.

"She turned it over to someone else for safekeeping just hours after she took it from me," Robert said. "It was gone by the time I tracked her down."

Frederick widened his eyes in dismay. "Who has it?"

Antonia glanced at Robert. "I'd rather not tell you who he is. He put himself at risk simply by helping me, but I promise, it's safe with him."

Robert took her hand in his and gave it a reassuring squeeze. "I don't know the man's name," he said to Frederick, "but he helped her locate the book in both instances. She trusts him to keep it for her until she presents it to a judge."

"A judge. Exactly my point," Catherine said. "Now—"

"I assume you believe she's in danger because of the kidnapping attempt," Frederick said.

Robert nodded.

"Then the Russians know Antonia has it?"

That was the question, wasn't it? Robert pondered it for a moment. "I don't know, but I think they must. Why else would they try to abduct her?"

Antonia seemed to stiffen. "When those men were chasing me, one of them kept trying to reassure me that they only wanted to talk to me. I didn't believe him."

What if he hadn't been there? Would the Russians have taken her?

Antonia met his gaze as she caught her lower lip between her teeth. "If I stay here, won't that arouse their suspicions regarding your involvement?"

"It's possible."

"We need to make sure no one knows she's here." Frederick rubbed his chin. "We can't afford to have her taken."

Robert felt a flicker of hope. Frederick said "we," not "you." That was a good sign. "We weren't followed last night. I'm certain of that."

"You're committed to protecting her. I can see that." Frederick's unfocused gaze stared at nothing while he pinched his lower lip between his thumb and forefinger. "What if Antonia asks her accomplice to give us the book?"

"Why would she do that?" Robert asked.

Frederick's eyes darted from side to side as though envisioning all of the steps needed to put his plan into action. "You can tell your friend you were attacked and ask him to give you the book so you can trade it for the protection of the British government."

"Protection? You mean, to protect me from the Russians?" Antonia asked.

"It would make Antonia the Queen's ally and eliminate the risk of having her charged with treason," Robert said.

Antonia shook her head. "That won't work. I need the book to prove my parents were legally married. I can't simply hand it over to the Queen."

"Excuse me," Catherine said. She had crossed the room and now pushed forward, forcing the others to look at her.

"Is something wrong?" Frederick asked.

"There certainly is. I've been trying to point out a perfectly obvious solution for the past two minutes but none of you will listen to me."

They all remained silent, waiting for her to speak.

"That's better." She met Robert's gaze. "I'm certain you remember meeting young Imogen this morning."

Daniel's eyes widened and he smacked his palm against his forehead. "Lord Tidmore. Of course."

"Tidmore the Tyrant?" Frederick asked.

"You know him?" Catherine asked.

"Everyone knows him," Frederick replied. "He keeps his court running efficiently and won't brook any disrespect."

"He speaks and reads Russian. Fluently." Daniel added.

"He may be harsh at times, but I always found him to be fair," Robert said.

"Harsh? Are you suggesting I go before a harsh judge?" Antonia asked, her face pale.

"You're in the right," Robert replied. "You aren't asking for something that isn't yours. You have a solid case and you have the proof your father's inheritance should have gone to you and your sisters."

Daniel nodded. "He'd be an excellent choice. He's known for dealing with tricky problems expeditiously. Given the situation, I'm certain he can be relied upon for both discretion and a speedy decision."

"But how will you convince him to hear my case?" Antonia asked. "You can't expect him to simply push another case aside to take up this one."

"He'll be grateful because of our help in locating Imogen. That should work in our favor," Catherine said.

"Does that mean you sent her home?" Robert asked.

"Not yet. I intended to escort her there later this afternoon after I'd established my presence here." Catherine glanced at Antonia. "We can change those plans. I think it would be better if you and Robert visit Lord Tidmore and bring him to my house to collect Imogen. I must admit, I was worried the child might bolt if she knew what I'd planned. If you and Robert are involved in returning her to her family, it will be much easier for you to ask his help."

Antonia nodded, but then narrowed her eyes and looked at Frederick. "Do I have your word that you won't arrest me for treason as soon as I recover the book, and that you'll let me use it as evidence in court?"

"You do. Since Robert trusts you, so do I."

Robert met his brother's eyes, and the look of confidence in them threatened to overwhelm him. It shouldn't have surprised him. After all, they'd been helping each other for years. What had made him believe that would suddenly change? He should have had more faith.

Antonia glanced at them and then gave a decisive nod. "Then I'll place my faith in Tidmore the Tyrant. And in you." She took a deep breath and then met Frederick's gaze. "I gave the book to Monsieur LeCompte. Do you know him?"

"LeCompte? That's ridiculous. The man's nothing more than a feckless dandy."

Frederick let out a heavy sigh. "Or a French spy. He's the very man I tried to follow the night of the Koliada ball."

35

Make a habit of two things: to help; or at least to do no harm.

— HIPPOCRATES

Although Antonia was happy to see her sisters and Miss Galloway when they arrived a short time later, she was worried as well. What if their presence here made them targets? The Russians might be watching the house even now.

For their part, Stephanie and Evalina were thrilled to be guests at Woolsy House.

"Lord Wentworth," Antonia said, "I'd like to introduce my sisters, Evalina and Stephanie Winter."

The two girls curtsied and dipped their heads. Miss Galloway smiled at their show of good manners.

"And this is Miss Galloway," she said, reaching out to grasp the dear woman's hand in hers. "She's so much more than a governess. She's more like a beloved aunt."

As Miss Galloway curtsied, her corset strings creaked ever so slightly.

Robert greeted them and then turned his attention on Miss Galloway. "I can't thank you enough for agreeing to bring Miss Winter's sisters."

Miss Galloway smiled, but Antonia knew it wasn't an expression that had crossed her face often in recent months. The crinkling of lines at the corners of her eyes gave evidence of the many years she'd spent smiling, but there was a new groove of worry between her brows that was so deeply etched that it didn't fade as she tilted her head back to gaze at Robert. "I'd never hesitate to come to Antonia's aid. She's always been a delight. I don't know what her sisters and I would do without the assistance she provides us."

"From what Miss Winter tells me, she couldn't have a better friend."

Antonia withdrew her arm from Stephanie's waist and reached out to squeeze Miss Galloway's arm. "You mean the world to us. I'm thrilled you were able to come to visit me."

Some of the worries weighing Miss Galloway down seemed to lift as she returned Antonia's smile. "That will be nice, won't it? I'll enjoy a bit of reminiscing. You have a talent for making everything so much more delightful."

"Can we perform a pantomime?" Stephanie's expressive face did nothing to conceal her excitement.

Antonia glanced at the others. "I'm sorry to say that I have an urgent errand to run and I'll have to leave you here with Emily for a couple of hours. But perhaps the three of you can prepare the pantomime while I'm gone."

Stephanie's face fell. "You're leaving us?"

"Not for long."

Emily stepped forward, smiling broadly at the two sisters. "I'd be happy to take you to the playroom. We have many costumes to choose from. I rarely have the opportunity to stage a pantomime. Mother and I used to love them so."

Evalina grinned at her, but then composed her face into a more prim expression. "Thank you, Lady Emily. You're most generous."

Stephanie's face went slack. "You're a—a lady?"

Antonia squeezed her hand reassuringly. "She's Lord Wentworth's sister."

"But you must call me Emily. I insist. It will become quite tedious otherwise. Would you like to come to the playroom with me? We can sort through the costumes."

The two sisters exchanged glances and then grinned broadly, nodding in unison.

A moment later, the girls fled the drawing room, and Miss Galloway moved to follow them.

"Miss Galloway, could you stay? We have a favor to ask," Robert said.

She straightened her shoulders. "Of course, my lord. I'd be happy to be of whatever use I can. You came to my Antonia's aid when she was in danger. I'll be forever grateful."

Robert cocked an eyebrow and gave her a conspiratorial grin. "Here's your chance to help her, too, if you don't mind running a small errand."

Miss Galloway assessed him and then gave an approving nod. "That I can manage, my lord."

LESS THAN AN HOUR LATER, ANTONIA WAITED FOR CATHERINE and Miss Galloway to join her in Robert's foyer.

Miss Galloway's eyes widened at the sight of her. "If I didn't know you, I never would have recognized you."

Antonia had been leaning against the wall and now she stood up straight, adjusting her to top hat and brushing a bit of nonexistent lint from the lapel of her gentleman's morning coat. She gave Miss Galloway a small bow.

"Oh, bravo," Miss Galloway said, clapping her hands in delight. "I'd never guess you were really a woman."

Despite her seemingly casual attitude, Antonia was nervous about the upcoming outing. Miss Galloway's comment might have eased some of her tension, but it wasn't until Robert came to stand next to her that the knot that had been forming in her stomach finally eased.

He positioned himself behind her, like a guardian, and his presence provided a sense of security that wrapped around her in an embrace. It seemed strange to have come to rely on him so quickly and so instinctively.

This past year had been full of turmoil, but Robert seemed to be the one solid thing in her life she could rely upon. She might not have a place in his life, but maybe—maybe allowing herself to care for him wouldn't be her undoing. Just a taste—

"I'm nervous," Miss Galloway said.

Antonia's attention snapped back to her friend. "You have nothing to worry about," she said, taking a steadying breath. "You'll be fine. All you need to do is walk to that cab stand on the corner and hire a hackney."

"That's not it. I'm not worried about me. I'm worried about you ." Miss Galloway's eyes widened, and she clutched Antonia's forearm. "What if those men come after you again?"

"That's exactly why I asked for your help. You'll put them off my trail. And don't forget, Lord Wentworth will be with me. Did you know he carries a sword hidden in that cane?" She nudged him with her elbow.

Robert shot Miss Galloway a wicked grin as he lifted his cane, released a small catch at the top, and partially extracted his blade.

"Oh, my," Miss Galloway said, stepping back and raising her hand to her chest in surprise.

Antonia gazed reassuringly at her friend. "You can do this.

You've procured a cab hundreds of times in your life. This time is no different."

Miss Galloway straightened her shoulders and gave a terse nod. "You're right. This is such a little thing you're asking of me. I'll be back in a trice."

Miss Galloway adjusted her head scarf and stepped outside into the cold afternoon sun light. Through the window, Antonia could see her striding down the street as she headed toward the cab stand around the corner. Robert moved closer and placed a hand on Antonia's shoulder in a reassuring gesture, and she instinctively leaned into its strength and comfort.

A few minutes later, Antonia watched through the window as a hansom cab drew to a stop in front of the house. The coachman jumped down and then assisted Miss Galloway as she stepped out of it. She spoke to the man and then hurried up the stairs and back into Woolsy House.

Antonia gave Miss Galloway's hand a quick squeeze. "That was perfect. Were there any problems?"

"None at all." Miss Galloway's smile was thin and tight.

Antonia ushered her friend into the adjoining drawing room and then paused at the doorway to glance back at Robert. When their gazes met, the corner of his mouth tipped up. A great deal could be communicated with a single look, and this one spoke volumes.

He radiated confidence in her, a confidence that seemed imbued with a fundamental belief in her abilities. But beyond that, there seemed to be something more in his expression. Something deeper and more carnal. Something that made her stomach flutter and sent a wave of heat sliding through her body.

The depth and intensity of his gaze nearly overwhelmed her. She found herself wanting to melt into him. She knew immediately that if they were alone together, he'd pull her into his arms and devour her.

She also knew she'd let him.

Despite the sensations growing within her, she forced herself to turn away. Whatever this was that was developing between them, it would have to wait.

But—not for long. Please let it be not for too long.

She held that thought close as she stepped through the doorway and into the drawing room. Once inside, she set her top hat on a side table and faced the others.

Catherine and her lady's maid were already there, waiting for Antonia and Miss Galloway's arrival. They had drawn the curtains closed so no one could see inside, and gas lamps helped brighten the gloomy space.

"This is so exciting," Catherine said. "I do hope our plan works. Where are your sisters?"

"They're with Emily. I expect we'll be treated to a pantomime following dinner."

Catherine grinned. "We'll all be playing dress-up today." Her smile slid away. "I only hope we'll have cause to celebrate when we return. What if something goes wrong?"

Miss Galloway draped her head scarf over the back of one of the chairs and tossed her cloak over it. "Nothing to worry about. I'm sure everything will go smoothly." Apparently now that her part of their plan was over, she was feeling much more confident.

Catherine began undoing the buttons down the side of her bodice, and her lady's maid stepped forward to pull at the ties holding her skirts in place. Across from them, Antonia assisted Miss Galloway in removing her dress.

Once their gowns were off, Miss Galloway handed hers to Antonia. Catherine's rounded belly from her pregnancy wasn't large yet, and as Antonia passed her Mrs. Galloway's more generously cut gown, she felt certain that it would fit. Catherine made quick work of donning the costume. It suited her so well that no one would ever guess that it had been made for someone else.

Once she was done, Antonia stepped back and scrutinized Catherine's attire. "Perfect. You look exactly like a governess."

Catherine shot her a nervous smile as she swirled Miss Galloway's cloak over her shoulders.

This was it. They were ready.

Miss Galloway touched Antonia's forearm. "You'll be careful, Miss Antonia, won't you?" The pink dress Miss Galloway now wore gave her an incongruously youthful appearance, especially when combined with her shy smile.

"I promise."

As they stepped out into the hallway, Daniel inspected his wife. "You may have swapped dresses, but you still don't look like a governess. Do you have anything you can use to cover your hair? That might help. It might also conceal part of your face."

"The head scarf!" Catherine cried. "Where did I leave it?"

Miss Galloway hurried inside the drawing room and returned carrying her black wool scarf along with Antonia's top hat.

"I'd forgotten that," Antonia said, as Miss Galloway handed the hat to her.

"We're all a bit nervous," Miss Galloway said, as she draped the scarf over Catherine's head and knotted it securely under her chin. "Remember to behave as a servant," she said, meeting the marchioness's gaze, "not as a lady. Keep your eyes downcast. Look as though you're trying not to offend anyone."

Catherine nodded and gave Miss Galloway's hand a squeeze. "Thank you. That's excellent advice." She glanced down and managed to abruptly transform into a humble governess.

Frederick's critical gaze swept over Catherine from head to foot before he nodded approvingly. "You're even wearing sensible shoes. That's what often gives people away. Footwear. Even the best of agents sometimes forget about them and wear expensive boots when trying to pose as a poor rag picker."

Antonia examined her as well and gave her a nod. "You look perfect."

Robert moved closer to Antonia. "Watch for me," he

murmured to her. "I should already be outside his house when you arrive, but I won't approach it until I see you."

Antonia nodded.

Mimicking Miss Galloway's perfect posture, Catherine pulled her shoulders back so far that it looked painful.

As Antonia turned and began to don her top hat, she fumbled her grip and it toppled to the floor. She leaned over and swept it up, checking it carefully for any damage. Fortunately it wasn't marred. She smiled at Robert for her own clumsiness and noticed a stunned expression on his face. It took her a moment to realize that he'd been staring at her bottom.

Antonia grinned.

"Trousers suit you," he said. Catherine and Daniel both chuckled.

"Women in trousers can be quite deadly," he said.

Catherine nudged him with her elbow. "Keep your eyes to yourself, husband."

"You know there's only one woman in trousers I'd ever—"

"Shh!" Catherine hissed, her cheeks turning pink.

Antonia shot Robert a questioning look, but he only shrugged. "Married people," he said. "They're forever speaking in code. Their conversation is much too esoteric for the likes of us."

"Perhaps a bit on the obscure side?" Antonia said.

"I was trying to be enigmatic," Catherine said, shooting Daniel a wifely glare. He merely grinned back at her.

Antonia realized she liked these people. She liked them very much. It was hard to believe they'd help her so readily. Their chatter helped distract her from what they were about to do and made it a bit easier to ignore the butterflies slamming into her stomach.

Catherine clutched the scarf under her chin and pulled open the front door, allowing Antonia to step through it first before she followed close behind.

A sharp gust of cold air hit both women, causing Antonia's

trousers to flap against her legs. She missed her layers of petticoats as she hurried toward the hansom cab. The sooner they were inside it, the safer they'd be.

The driver of the cab perked up as they approached, and he hurried to open the door. He seemed oblivious to the complete transformation of the woman who'd hired him. Once he had them inside, he tucked a traveling blanket over their laps and shut the cab doors, effectively trapping them inside until he released them at their destination.

Trying not to turn her head, Antonia glanced around to see if anyone was observing them. There were two men standing near a cart selling roasted chestnuts who might have been watching them as they drove away. She watched them surreptitiously and thought she recognized them from the embassy. Unfortunately, their tall hats partially obscured their faces, so she might be mistaken.

As the carriage turned at the next street, Catherine glanced past Antonia toward where the two men were standing, but she didn't train her gaze on them. Instead she focused on Antonia and smiled. "Our charade seems to be working. Those men have been watching the house since Daniel and I arrived an hour ago. It would seem you and I aren't worthy of their notice."

"Do you mean the ones standing near the chestnut stand?"

Catherine looked surprised. "You noticed them too?"

Antonia nodded. "They looked familiar, but I didn't want to stare.'

"Well done," Catherine said, smiling her approval. "We need to stop at a shop and pick up a package so we have something to carry inside with us when we return from visiting your friend. If anyone is watching the house, they'll assume we went shopping."

"I know just the place. There's a shop near LeCompte's house that sells tea. We can stop there."

"Perfect," Catherine said, in a satisfied tone. "It's so nice to spend time with a clever woman such as yourself."

A clatter of hooves against paving stones interrupted them as a man on horseback trotted past. Antonia knew it was Robert, but she also knew better than to look at him.

The two men near the chestnut cart scurried off toward a pair of waiting horses, but by the time they rode past Antonia and Catherine, Robert was nowhere in sight. Antonia tensed.

Catherine glanced at her and then grabbed her hand under the blanket. "He'll be fine," she said, squeezing her fingers in a comforting gesture. "He'll lead them on a merry chase in the wrong direction and still arrive before we will."

Antonia nodded, thankful for the physical connection. She hated Robert risking himself for her sake. What if those men set a trap for him? What if they kidnapped him? "I'm worried something terrible might happen."

"He's a capable man." Catherine grimaced and shot Antonia a sharp glance. "Just don't tell him I said that or I'll never hear the end of it. Despite our differences, he's grown on me over the past year."

❧ 36 ☙

There are no secrets that time does not reveal.

— *JEAN RACINE*

◌

When they turned onto LeCompte's street thirty minutes later, Antonia's nose was numb from the cold. Her ears were better off, protected as they were by her top hat. But she barely registered her discomfort.

She tried to inspect the street surreptitiously, but the farther along it the carriage moved, the tighter the ball of tension knotted in her chest.

Robert was nowhere in sight.

As their carriage pulled to a stop in front of a brick townhouse with a bright blue door, Antonia tried to convince herself he was simply being cautious by remaining out of sight. Surely he'd appear now.

The coachman slowly clambered down from his perch behind

them, unfastened their door latch, and helped them out of the cab.

"Wait for us," Antonia said. Her voice was gruff and her breath emerged in little bursts of white mist. "We'll be here about twenty minutes and then you'll need to drive us home."

"Yes, sir," the coachman mumbled as he turned to his horse. He seemed oblivious to the cold as he leaned over, pushed his shoulder against the animal's side, and then lifted the hoof. With a grunt of disapproval, he reached into his pocket and extracted a hoof pick, slid it against the inner part of the horse's hoof, and knocked a stone loose so that it clattered to the ground.

Antonia surveyed the street once more as she murmured to Catherine, "Why isn't Robert here? He said he'd arrive before we did."

Catherine pursed her lips. "Perhaps it proved more difficult to lose those men than he anticipated."

Antonia peered down the street, hoping to see him rounding the corner. When he didn't appear, she forced herself to approach the bright blue door and twist the bell.

The servant who opened it couldn't hide his surprise at seeing them there. His eyes widened even more as Antonia sensed movement behind them. She spun around to see what it was, and saw a man rushing toward them.

She opened her mouth to shout a warning. But even before the man managed to tug down his scarf and reveal his face, she recognized him. She'd recognize Robert anywhere.

The butler looked at them sternly. Robert's sudden appearance must have startled him as well.

The butler's sense of propriety overcame his momentary lapse of decorum and he ushered everyone inside.

He accepted Robert, Antonia, and Catherine's calling cards without bothering to glance at them and left the trio standing in the entryway while he disappeared into the back of the townhouse.

"You made it." Antonia grinned at Robert in relief.

"Did you think I wouldn't?"

"I was worried when I didn't see you waiting outside." His cheeks were ruddy from the cold winter's day and she almost reached up to touch his face. Her fingers twitched in response to the half-formed thought.

"At least the butler didn't make us stand in the street," Catherine muttered. "For a moment, he had me worried."

"I imagine that leaving the three of us waiting outside on such a cold day would draw a fair amount of speculation from the neighbors," Antonia said. "Monsieur LeCompte is the sort who hates gossip—when it concerns him ."

Catherine grinned. "I see you know him well. I've never come across a better informed man when it comes to the latest scandal."

"It's difficult to think of LeCompte as a French agent," Robert commented. "I've always found him to be a man of shallow interests."

"I suppose that shows how good he is at hiding in plain sight," Catherine said. "It would be counterproductive for him to appear overly competent. People would be less likely to let their secrets slip."

A moment later, the butler returned looking much more welcoming. "This way, please," he said, and then ushered them into the drawing room.

Monsieur LeCompte stood near the fireplace, his slim, lean form silhouetted by the flames.

"Lord Wentworth," LeCompte said, bowing gracefully.

Robert dipped his head.

"And Mademoiselle Winter," he said, turning to her with a delighted smile as he took in her appearance. "This is quite a surprise. Just look at you," he stepped forward and lifted her hands, holding them outstretched. "Why are you dressed in such a fashion? I heard you were no longer playing the leading role in

Anne Blake. Is it because you've found a new role where you must dress as a man?"

His reminder that she'd lost her position in the show left her speechless for an instant, but she quickly recovered. "Do I look the part?" Antonia performed a pirouette. "I borrowed these clothes to avoid being followed." She paused and then approached LeCompte. "You won't believe what's been happening. Ambassador Revnik seems to have lost all caution. First he tried to have Lord Wentworth kidnapped off the street, and then last night he sent his men to the theater to abduct me. If Lord Wentworth hadn't been there, I might not have escaped them."

"*Merde.* That *is* bad." LeCompte's face appeared blank of expression for a moment, and then he narrowed his eyes. "Is that why you're no longer in the show? Because of the kidnappers?"

He seemed to take her silence as agreement. "How is it that the three of you have come to know one another?" LeCompte's tone sounded casual, but his eyes were sharp as he watched them.

Antonia tensed. Despite knowing LeCompte wasn't the gossip monger he pretended to be and was instead a shrewd and intelligent man, she still treated him with a great deal of caution—or perhaps it was because she knew there was far more to this man than there appeared to be.

She'd seen him eviscerate men and women alike with his sharp tongue, but he'd never turned it on her. Looking at him now, she had a feeling that was about to change. She'd seen that expression before. LeCompte was about to maneuver them into an embarrassing situation.

She wouldn't make it easy for him.

Antonia decided to explain as succinctly as possible. "The night I took the church register from Lord Wentworth, he'd been helping his brother. They were stealing it at Queen Victoria's request. Since then, they've been desperate to recover it. They're afraid it could fall into the wrong hands, and the information it contains could push England and Russia into an immediate declaration of war."

She paused to let LeCompte respond, but he said nothing. Why didn't he react to her announcement? "Now that I'm aware of the British government's involvement, I feel obliged to alter my plans. I'm arranging matters so my personal needs can align with those of my country. Lord Wentworth and Lady Huntley offered to help me. They accompanied me here today so I could retrieve the book from you."

Monsieur LeCompte stared first at Robert and then at Catherine. He tugged at his ear and peered down at the rug beneath his feet as though it might hold the answers he needed.

He raised his eyes to peer at Antonia. "Are you certain that's wise?" he finally asked. His gaze seemed to pierce her. "Based on last night's events, it seems obvious the Russians already believe you have the book. What's to prevent them from stealing it from you?"

"I won't be alone. I'll have Robert's help."

LeCompte narrowed his eyes and glanced at Robert, who shifted his feet. Then he glanced back at Antonia with a scowl. "And what are you offering Robert in exchange for this—*help* ?" His gaze swept over her again, and his scorn almost scalded her. "I saw the way he watched you at the soirée. I imagine he could be quite convincing to one such as yourself. So desperate. So innocent. So unprotected."

Heat swept up the back of Antonia's neck and across her face and scalp. How could she have been so careless as to use Robert's given name? Even so, LeCompte's accusations infuriated her. How dare he make such lewd allegations?

Fury wrapped its fingers around her, tightening its grip until she knew she couldn't break away from it. Not only had LeCompte disparaged her, he'd also maligned Robert.

Robert, who'd been nothing but kind to her ever since they'd met.

Robert, who'd saved her twice, who'd given her a place to stay. Robert, who'd kissed her....

Antonia pulled her arm back and lurched forward, unleashing a powerful slap across LeCompte's cheek. The sting of her palm felt good. Felt right. Felt cleansing.

Catherine darted forward. "Stop."

LeCompte stepped back and lifted his palms in a quelling gesture one might use with a skittish horse. "*Non*," he said. "*C'est de ma faute.*" *It's my fault.* "I should never have suggested such a thing."

"You certainly shouldn't have. I'll thank you to keep your insinuations to yourself, Monsieur. I refuse to become another morsel of gossip for you to feed upon."

LeCompte pressed his palm against his cheek. "I apologize. I spend so much of my life playing the troublemaker that I sometimes forget when to stop, even when I no longer need to pretend."

The original insinuation still stung, but Antonia decided to give him a nod of tacit forgiveness. "Then you'll return the book to me?"

"*Oui.* If you'll excuse me for a moment, I'll fetch it." He waited until she nodded, and then slipped out the door, closing it behind him.

Antonia felt Robert step up behind her, and then he placed his hands on her shoulders. He leaned down so his lips were next to her ear. "Thank you for defending my honor," he murmured.

Blood rushed to Antonia's face. She glanced at him over her shoulder and gave him a chagrined smile. "I know that was foolish, but I couldn't let him think—that you—that I—"

Robert gave her shoulders a squeeze and then released her. She immediately missed his touch.

"You were brilliant," he murmured. "I think your reaction is what swayed him."

"I was afraid he'd refuse to give it to you," Catherine said.

"Why?" Antonia asked.

"Why not?" Catherine replied. "It sounds as though the church register is valuable. Why simply hand it over to you?"

"You don't understand. He's been helping me all along. If not for him, I never would have been able to recover it at all."

The door opened and LeCompte came back into the room with the book in his hand. It was such a small thing to have caused so much trouble. Its stained and tattered cover made it appear worthless.

LeCompte held it out to her.

"Do you know why it's so important?" Antonia asked, as she reached out to accept it.

LeCompte pulled the book back, just out of her grasp. He scrutinized her. "Are you telling me you don't know?"

"I know why *I* want it. I already told you. It proves that my parents were married in Russia."

"Is that all you know?"

Antonia tilted her head to one side. "Apparently there's something more in there. Much more. Whatever it is, it's something both Queen Victoria and Czar Nicholas care about."

LeCompte nodded slowly and stepped to a side table, where he laid down the book. "I believe I need to tell you why it is so important. You see, it has something to do with you. And with your grandfather."

Startled, Antonia stepped closer to him. "How could my family be involved? Why would a queen and a czar care about us?"

"You have more in common with at least one of them than you could ever imagine."

Robert moved forward to stand next to Antonia. She sidled closer to him, thankful to no longer be facing LeCompte alone.

"And what would that be?" Antonia asked, in a voice barely above that of a whisper.

"Why, your grandfather, of course." LeCompte seemed to enjoy his cryptic answers.

Antonia shook her head. "I don't understand."

"Did you know that your grandmother wasn't his first love?"

The irrelevancy of the question threw Antonia off balance. "Of course I know. When he was a young man, he fell in love with Tatianna Kozinski. She appears in so many of his paintings that I would have to have been blind not to notice her. Mother told me all about her."

"And do you know how she died?"

"In childbirth. She and her baby were buried together. Grandfather didn't find out about it until months later."

LeCompte shook his head. "That's only partially correct."

Antonia's brows drew together. "Of course it's correct."

"No. The baby. He didn't die. He lived."

"He did? But how can you know that?"

"Because everything is in that book," LeCompte said, gesturing toward the tattered volume. "The baby's birth. The mother's death. Even the new family who adopted the infant as their own."

"He lived? Why would that be a secret? Why would everyone say the baby was dead?" She pressed her fingers to her temples. This made no sense.

"Because that's what the czar wanted them to believe."

"That's ridiculous. Why should the czar care about some illegitimate orphan?" No one cared about bastards. She and her sisters were proof of that.

"Did you know that your grandfather's village was along a travel route?"

She dropped her hands to her sides and let out a sharp sigh, thrown off by his abrupt change in topic. "I suppose so. There was an inn there, and grandfather often painted travelers. But why—?"

"Did you know the former czar and his family stopped in your grandfather's village many times during their travels?"

Antonia furrowed her brow. "That would have been Czar Paul, right? Catherine the Great's son?"

"*Exactement.* The village inn used to be a regular resting place for his entourage when they traveled through that region, but the last time they were there, they were obliged to stay for a month because Czaritsa Maria and her infant son Nicholas became very sick."

"Mother never mentioned that. I wonder if she knew?"

LeCompte ignored her comment. "Czaritsa Maria was quite ill. So ill, in fact, that many believed she would die. Fortunately, she survived, but her baby was not so lucky. The illness carried him away during a time when Czaritsa Maria was unconscious and close to death."

"That's so sad. How terrible for them. But wait—you said her baby's name was Nicholas— " Antonia stared at him, her eyes growing wide. LeCompte couldn't be suggesting—it wasn't possible—

LeCompte stared into her eyes. "Czaritsa Maria's baby died shortly after Tatianna Kozinski did."

A cold chill ran up Antonia's back and over her shoulders, leaving ice in its wake. "What are you saying?" Antonia's breath came shorter. "Are you saying that the baby—that my grandfather's baby—that he became the—" She couldn't bring herself to finish the sentence.

LeCompte nodded. "That baby—your mother's half-brother— replaced the child Czaritsa Maria lost. She was so sick that Czar Paul refused to tell her. He was convinced the shock would kill her." He shook his head. "I know it sounds unlikely, but you need to understand that up until the day she died, Catherine the Great remained Czaritsa of Russia. She controlled everything, and she used her power to manipulate every aspect of her son's life. She and Paul hated one another."

Antonia nodded blankly, trying to make sense of everything LeCompte was telling her.

"Catherine had whisked away Maria's two older sons not long after their births so she could raise them herself. Maria rarely saw her own children. For some reason, Catherine allowed Maria to keep Nicholas. Perhaps it was because he had two older brothers. Perhaps for some other reason, but Nicholas was the first son Maria and Paul were permitted to keep and raise. Paul believed that losing this child would have crushed Maria, perhaps even have killed her."

"So they replaced her dead baby with Tatianna's motherless one," Antonia said through numb lips.

"*Oui. Exactement.*"

"So, my illegitimate uncle is the Czar of Russia."

"*Oui.*"

"*Merde.*"

"*Oui.*"

❈ 37 ❈

R obert was astounded by the revelation. He watched Antonia as her emotions flitted across her face. Stunned disbelief. Shock. Dismay. But he also identified the moment she moved beyond them and began analyzing the situation. She seemed to process LeCompte's revelation with startling speed, but then again, she'd made an astonishing number of adjustments over the past year. He'd never met a more resilient woman.

"What, precisely, is recorded in the church register?" Antonia asked the Frenchman.

"Father Sergey was conscientious in recording information regarding the people and events in his village," LeCompte replied.

"Every birth, marriage, and death is there. He also listed every child fostered with another family and every child who was adopted. Your uncle's adoption was no exception."

"And Nicholas's father, Czar Paul, was the only person in the family who knew what the book contained," she stated flatly. "That's why he sent soldiers to find it when he believed it was stolen."

"I suspect that when Father Sergey informed him the register was missing, he also told him of its contents. If the czar had known what it revealed, he never would have left it unguarded. Father Sergey fled Russia after it disappeared—he was afraid someone would attempt to suppress the information by eliminating him."

Antonia's face went white. "Murder a priest?"

LeCompte looked grim. "Whether it would be on the czar's order or at the hand of a zealot trying to curry favor, I couldn't hazard a guess. But dead is dead."

"I don't agree," Robert interjected. The others turned to stare at him. "Based on what Ambassador Revnik said, I believe Antonia has the czar's protection."

LeCompte raised one eyebrow. "What makes you think that?"

"I confronted Revnik about his attempt to kidnap me off the street. He said he meant me no harm, but merely wanted to ask me about a woman in a silver dress who'd attended the ball. He seemed quite concerned about her safety."

"Someone must have recognized me."

"Remember, Revnik said you were too important."

"Do you think that means Ambassador Revnik knows I'm related to Czar Nicholas?"

Robert shook his head. "Probably not. It's more likely that he assumes the czar is interested in your well-being because your grandfather was a respected artist. I doubt Revnik would have been so careless with the diplomatic pouch if he'd realized what it contained." He glanced at the innocuous-looking book that had caused him so much trouble. "It's highly unlikely the ambassador would direct his men to cause you any real harm, but given how urgently the Russian government wants to recover that book, Revnik might resort to more desperate measures to take it from you. I don't believe your life is in danger, but still, you need to be cautious."

LeCompte lifted his hand. "Don't forget that when the first thief stole the book from the church, he killed Father Sergey's wife."

"Father Sergey identified my uncle as the man who tried to bribe him to destroy the record of my parents' wedding. I'm certain he's the one who murdered Father Sergey's wife and set fire to the church."

"Could he have sent men to kidnap you?" LeCompte asked. "Perhaps he hoped to use you to blackmail the czar."

"My uncle is an opportunistic man. If he knew the czar's secret, I'm certain he would have resorted to blackmail by now. No," she said, shaking her head, "if he'd known what that book contained, he never would have left it sitting on a shelf in his library."

"I doubt your uncle has much interest in you at this point," Catherine said. "After all, he believes he's already vanquished you and stolen your inheritance. It would appear that the czar doesn't want you harmed either, so that leaves Revnik as your biggest threat." She looked at the other two men. "What do you think? Is there anything we can do to convince the ambassador to leave her alone?"

"I don't think he'll stop until he has the church register," Robert said. "For all we know, there could be other people searching for it as well." The thought of more people targeting Antonia chilled him.

Catherine frowned. "The simplest way to keep Antonia safe is to show Revnik we've handed over the book to the crown."

"No," Antonia said with a swipe of her hand. "This is my decision, and I refuse to relinquish it until I've used it to prove my parents were legally married." The stern look she shot Catherine should have made her wilt, but she merely smiled.

"Hear me out. I wasn't suggesting we should actually turn it over, but what if we convince the Russians that we've done so?" Catherine raised one eyebrow. "Wouldn't that fool them into leaving you alone?"

Antonia's raised her chin and cocked her head to one side. "You know, I think that might just work." She gave Catherine an appraising gaze. "My, but you have a devious mind."

"You don't know the half of it," Robert said, thinking of the way she'd duped him about her dual identity.

Catherine shot him a quelling look.

LeCompte's knowing smile left Robert wondering if he might already have discovered Catherine's alter ego as Alexander Gray.

Robert glanced at Antonia, and her expression momentarily transfixed him. She looked strong—resolute. He could only stare at her. It was obvious from the determined set of her jaw and the fire in her eyes that she'd stop at nothing to succeed.

She was beautiful like this—like Athena, goddess of wisdom and warfare. He briefly imagined her wearing a Grecian gown with her hair streaming down her back as she raised her sword of justice to smite her oppressors. And an instant later he imagined her naked in his bed, with the fire in her eyes turning to passion as she focused all her energy on him.

Robert inhaled sharply and closed his eyes to banish the image. He needed to concentrate. He needed to come up with a speedy path through this maze—a way to recover Antonia's inheritance while still keeping her safe.

With a start, he realized that this was new territory for him. He cared what would happen to her. Antonia was changing him. Was it her passion to seek justice and her conviction that she would succeed? All Robert knew was that he wanted to help her in any way he could.

❧ 38 ☙

One who deceives will always find those who allow themselves to be deceived.

— *NICCOLO MACHIAVELLI*

On the ride back to Woolsy House, Antonia caught glimpses of Robert riding escort. Sometimes his horse walked alongside their carriage, but when the streets became narrow, he was forced to fall behind them, out of sight.

Since no one had identified her in her disguise as a man when they'd left on their outing, her masquerade should continue to work.

Even so, she wouldn't risk letting anyone steal the book.

That was why Catherine now carried it.

Catherine clutched her reticule as though her life depended upon it, but it was Antonia's future she clung to. Having Catherine take possession of the tome might well have been the wisest decision in their current situation, but that didn't make the choice any easier for Antonia. Not only did she regret the need to put the other woman at risk, she also hated relinquishing control to anyone. She'd learned that if she wanted something done right, she needed to do it herself, but this situation was different.

If she wanted the book to be safe, she'd need to rely on others.

Antonia remained tense during the entire journey. It was only after they stepped over the threshold and Robert quickly closed the door to block the cold wind that she finally relaxed.

Frederick must have been listening for them because he came hurrying down the staircase. "Did you get the book?" he asked before he'd even reached the bottom step.

"We did," Antonia said, as Catherine pulled it from her reticule.

"You'll be astounded when you learn why the Russians want it," Robert added.

"You read it?" Frederick asked.

"LeCompte filled us in," Antonia said.

"My grasp of the Russian language was sufficient for me to verify his story when I read the pertinent sections of the church register," Robert said.

Catherine glanced at Antonia for permission before handing the book to Frederick.

She nodded.

He took it and then led the group into the nearby drawing room. Frederick claimed a spot on the sofa next to Antonia, and Catherine sat in a nearby chair. Robert circled behind the sofa and peered at the book over Frederick's shoulder.

Robert directed his brother to the pertinent pages as he explained Antonia's relationship to the current Czar of Russia.

Frederick's eyes widened with shock, but as he examined the church register, his expression turned to one of bemusement.

"No wonder the Queen wants this," he said.

"It's dangerous information." Robert strode across the room as he gestured toward a landmass depicted on a map on the wall.

"It would provide the Queen with the leverage she needs to force Czar Nicholas to pull his troops from the Crimean Peninsula." He stood examining the map.

"I imagine that's her intent," Frederick said, "but there's more at risk here. The czar won't readily bow to Queen Victoria's manipulations. He's determined to take Crimea. This tale of a supplanted monarch is an outlandish one—but it has the ring of truth." He tugged at his earlobe. "Some will be convinced the British fabricated the entire story. If Queen Victoria decides to use this information to her advantage, she'll have to be careful. If we accidentally trigger a Russian civil war, the resulting chaos could be even worse for Britain and the rest of the world than a war over the Crimean Peninsula." He closed the small book and gripped it with both hands as he stared at it pensively. Finally he met Antonia's stare. "Does this change anything for you?"

She shook her head. "I mean to follow through with our original plan," she said. "First we need to enlist Lord Tidmore's help. If he agrees, I'm hopeful he'll be able to resolve everything within a few days."

Frederick nodded. "While you were out, I sent a man to locate him and schedule a meeting. Unfortunately, he wasn't in court or at the courthouse. He's dealing with an emergency at home. No one knows when he plans to return."

Catherine's face turned pale. "Oh, my. It must be due to Imogen's disappearance."

"Yes. That must be it," Robert said.

"We need to contact him immediately." Catherine rose to her feet and began pacing the room, so Frederick stood to join the other gentlemen where they'd gathered in front of the map. He handed the book to Antonia as he passed her.

"He's probably at home," Antonia said.

"Or out searching for Imogene," Catherine added.

"We should go there straightaway," Robert said, leaving the others and moving to join Antonia. "You and I should go together.

You'll need to change. It would be best for you to look a bit more—"

She glanced down at her trousers and then grinned. "Like a woman?" Antonia raised one eyebrow. "I can be ready to leave in fifteen minutes."

39

Children begin by loving their parents; after a time they judge them; rarely, if ever, do they forgive them.

— OSCAR WILDE

"Time's working against us," Robert said. "I'd like to divide up the tasks among us." He turned to his butler. "Can you inform Turner that I have another job for him? Send him to Maidenhead to fetch Antonia's barrister." He glanced at Antonia. "What's the man's name?"

"Montlake. Devin Montlake. He's familiar with my case. I trust him completely."

Robert continued giving instructions. "Have Turner stop by to pick up my letter when he's ready to leave. This is urgent. He's to bring Mr. Montlake back with him today. As quickly as possible."

"Yes, sir," Landon said, and left the room.

Robert glanced at Antonia. He couldn't stare at her for long. He found the way her men's garb displayed her limbs to be quite distracting. "I'd like you to accompany me to Lord Tidmore's. You can inform him his daughter is well and that Lady Catherine discovered her identity earlier today."

"Why me? I've never met the girl."

"Tidmore has a reputation as being tough as a piece of dried leather, but I think this good news will help soften him up. I'd prefer it come from you."

Frederick stood. He wore a faint smirk that told Robert he'd noticed the way Antonia's clothing affected him. "Daniel and I can create a distraction just before you and Antonia leave." Frederick draped his arm over Daniel's shoulders. "Let's put our heads together and come up with a plan to draw away anyone who might be watching the house."

Daniel thumped his hand against Frederick's back in a rough but friendly gesture. "I think we can manage that. What if we make it appear we're taking something to the Foreign Office? We could carry something about the size of a church register."

Frederick's eyebrows rose. "That should do it." He gave a decisive nod. "Once we mount our horses, we'll go tearing off. We have to create a spectacle so any spies will give chase. We can separate and then rendezvous along Hay's Mews near Berkeley Square. By then, we should have lost them."

"Be careful," Catherine said.

"Aren't I always?" Daniel bent down to kiss her on the cheek.

Catherine made a noncommittal noise and turned her head so their lips met. "As long as you come home to me in one piece, that's all that matters."

"That I can promise," Daniel said. He and Frederick hurried from the room.

Catherine watched her husband leave, a faint smile on her face. When she turned her attention back to Robert, she flushed slightly when she realized he'd been watching her. "I'll return home to ensure that Miss Tidmore remains there until her parents collect her." She rubbed the edge of her thumb against her lower lip. "Perhaps a fencing lesson," she murmured. "That should hold her attention."

"But your husband won't be there to teach her," Antonia pointed out. "He'll be with Frederick."

Catherine went still for a moment and then nodded. "Of course. What was I thinking? I'll have to find some other way to keep her engaged."

✣

WHEN ROBERT CAME DOWNSTAIRS A SHORT TIME LATER, HE found Antonia waiting for him, ready to depart.

"Daniel and Frederick just left," she informed him. "They should be on the stage. You should have seen them. They even managed to drop the box that supposedly contained the church register. As soon as they went tearing down the road, five horsemen gave chase."

Robert shook his head. "That's why Frederick's the one who's a spy, not me. He loves this sort of challenge."

As they donned their coats, the front door chimed. Landon opened it and ushered Lady Harrington into the house.

"What a pleasant surprise," Robert said. "I'm sorry I can't stay, but Miss Winter and I have an engagement."

"Well, fiddlesticks. I'd hoped to visit with you, too." She glanced at Miss Winter, and Robert realized he'd need to introduce them.

"Lady Harrington, I'd like to introduce you to Antonia Winter."

Antonia made a low curtsy.

"You're performing the lead role in *Anne Blake* , aren't you? I haven't seen it yet, but everyone says you're quite talented."

"Thank you, my lady. That's very kind of you."

Josephine dipped her head acknowledgment and then turned

her attention back to Robert. "How is Frederick today—or more specifically, how is his hand?"

"He's doing his best to ignore the pain. I believe he's out of supplies for the poultice."

"That's why I'm here." She lifted the small basket she carried. "I brought more leaves."

"He'll be relieved." He pulled a pocket watch and glanced at it. "He left to run a quick errand, but he should return shortly. I hope you'll forgive us, but we have a pressing matter to deal with."

"By all means."

He turned to Landon. "Can you please show Lady Harrington to the drawing room and ask Frederick to join her there as soon as he returns?"

❧

A FEW MINUTES LATER, ROBERT AND ANTONIA ARRIVED AT Lord Tidmore's house. He could tell she was apprehensive, so he placed his hand on the small of her back as he walked with her to the front door. "Nervous?"

"A bit. What if he refuses to hear my case?"

"Then we'll look for a new solution." He paused before ringing the front bell and turned to face her. A stray strand of her hair fluttered in the breeze, and he tucked it behind her ear. "Tidmore is called a tyrant for good reason. He's a stickler when it comes to justice—something you've been sorely lacking this past year. I'm certain he'll want to hear your case if he's able."

She gave a sharp nod and then twisted the front door bell.

When the door swung open, Robert handed both his and Antonia's calling cards to the butler.

"I'm sorry, but Lord Tidmore isn't accepting callers today. I'll inform him of your visit, and he'll contact you at his earliest convenience."

Robert opened his mouth, but before he could speak, Antonia said, "Can you tell him we have news of his daughter?"

The butler's eyes bulged. "Come in, come in." He closed the door behind them. "Don't move," he commanded, and scurried from the foyer.

"It's too bad I wasn't able to tell Lord Tidmore in person," Antonia said, "but I don't think he'd have seen us otherwise."

A shout of surprise came from the adjoining room, and then Lord Tidmore came storming through a nearby door. Antonia inched closer to Robert, and he put his arm around her waist.

"You have news of my daughter?" Tidmore's words weren't a question. They were a demand. His thick gray hair was mussed as though he'd repeatedly dragged his fingers through it.

"We do," Antonia said. "I want to assure you she's safe. We would have brought her here, but we were afraid she might run away from us."

"I only met her today," Robert added, "but your daughter strikes me as being very strong-willed. Not the type who would willingly entrust herself to a stranger's care."

"I can tell you've met her." Lord Tidmore's shoulders sagged with relief. Then he glanced around at their surroundings. "Let's not stand in the foyer. Come in here." He waved his arm and ushered them into a nearby drawing room.

As they walked into the elegant room, Lord Tidmore glanced down at the calling cards he still clutched in his hand. "Wentworth. I remember you from school. You and that Huntley fellow were always together."

"As a matter of fact, I came across your daughter lurking in the shrubs outside Lord Huntley's home."

"What the devil?" Tidmore's thick eyebrows rose up and disappeared beneath his mop of hair. "What was she doing there?"

"Apparently she'd heard some tale about fencing lessons and

decided to find out if it was true." Robert didn't want to lie to the man, but this was as close to the truth as he was willing to tread.

"That's right. Huntley teaches lessons. I remember hearing something about that. But what made Imogen think she could sneak off that way?"

"That I couldn't say," he replied with all honesty.

Something he said must have sounded strange to Antonia, because she narrowed her eyes as she peered up at him, but she remained silent.

"And you? Miss Winter, is it?" Tidmore focused his intent stare on her.

"I haven't met your daughter, my lord," she said. She spoke hesitantly, as if choosing her words with care. "Lord Wentworth asked me to join him so that I might meet you and offer my assistance to both you and your wife. I assume you'll want to inform her of our news as quickly as possible."

Tidmore turned to his butler, who had remained standing next to the door. "Fetch Mirabelle," he barked. "Have the carriage brought round. We'll leave immediately." He turned to face them, but addressed Robert. "I can't thank you enough. My wife's been sick with worry."

"I understand your urgency, Lord Tidmore. Once you've brought your daughter home, may we have a moment of your time? We need to speak with you regarding the Queen's business. It's a delicate matter—one which requires a unique set of abilities which I know you happen to possess." Tidmore's graying eyebrows dove down toward the bridge of his nose.

"Yes, yes. We can talk about it later. With luck, I'll have my daughter in hand within an hour." He grimaced. "That is, unless she decides to run off before we can get to her."

"Lady Huntley plans to keep her engaged," Antonia said, giving Robert a sidelong glance. "I don't think Imogen will be going anywhere."

A SHORT TIME LATER, ROBERT AND ANTONIA LED THE WAY IN his carriage while Lord and Lady Tidmore followed in theirs.

Robert noticed Antonia glancing at him out of the corner of her eye as though trying to decide something. He had a guess as to what she would say, but he waited. She'd speak when she was ready.

Finally, she shifted to face him. "I'm beginning to suspect there's more to Imogen's presence at the marchioness's home than you've been willing to reveal. And I think it has something to do with Lady Huntley's unusual talent with a blade."

"That's an astute guess." He let out a heavy sigh. "Don't press me further on this. I'd tell you more if I could, but I gave Catherine and Daniel my word."

Antonia narrowed her eyes, but then she nodded. "Everyone's entitled to their secrets as long as they aren't hurting anyone. Catherine's a good person, of that I have no doubt."

Robert stared at his hand where it rested on the cushion between them, barely touching the tip of her gloved hand with his own. She was so close, but he refused to close the distance. He didn't dare. "Good people often keep secrets." His mother had kept Father's secret after she'd read his letter, but by then no good could possibly have come from revealing the truth.

"I prefer the truth, but I suppose that's to be expected, given what's happened to me over the past year."

He watched her staring down at their hands, side by side, and when she slid her fingers over his, he nearly pulled away, but didn't. Instead, he forced himself to relax. She wanted truth from him, and he wasn't able to give it. That knowledge tarnished this moment.

She squeezed his hand gently. "There have been too many lies and deceits in my life. Too many secrets and misdeeds. All the lies that reached through the years to sabotage me were originally told for selfish reasons. My parents broke the law by entering into an illegal marriage. I know they tried to correct their error, but because of their lingering shame, they didn't trust their solicitor enough to make arrangements to provide for us after they died. Their secret stole our birthright from us. My grandfather was driven from his village by the father of the woman he loved, and the truth of his child was kept from him until it was too late." Catherine shook her head. "Those are the lies that hurt. The secrets that should never be kept in the first place."

Robert nodded. The lies that had been forced upon him were of a similar nature. He'd simply been fortunate that they'd never come to light. "I assure you that Catherine's secret is nothing like the ones that hurt you and your sisters. She and Daniel are the only people who would be harmed if it ever came to light, and they're both fully aware of the consequences."

She nodded. "I hope you're right. In fact, if what I suspect is true, I would think the only consequence would be ostracism, and since she's a marchioness, it wouldn't be nearly as severe as what my sisters and I have endured. We live in a progressive age, so perhaps being known as a woman fencer wouldn't be such a terrible thing."

So, she'd guessed Catherine's secret, had she? Clever girl. He had to admire her for not trying to pry the information out of him. She wasn't even watching him to see if she'd guessed correctly. "Things aren't quite so progressive for members of the peerage. We're expected to be bastions against change rather than champions of it. But people like Catherine and Daniel are driven to push the limits of those restrictions. They're already considered unconventional, so if her secret comes out, perhaps it would be viewed as nothing more than an eccentricity."

"I hope so."

If the secret he'd kept for so many years came to light, would he be so easily forgiven? It had been a long time since he'd considered the question in this light. Perhaps it would. After all, many years had passed, and he'd done much to help the injured parties during that time.

But treason was treason. Frederick's reaction to Antonia's theft of the book was proof enough of that. But then again, Frederick had relented, hadn't he? And that was doubly surprising since he had a particular hatred for that crime. Of course, Antonia's situation was a unique one.

It was difficult to choose the right path when one weighed the many factors involved. Right became wrong and white became black. Choosing the best alternative became a fluid decision, one that was altered with each new piece of information. And right now, the information was all in Antonia's favor.

The carriage drew to a halt outside the Huntley home. Robert jumped down, leaping over the step, and offered Antonia his arm as she stepped down. The Tidmore's carriage was pulling to a stop as they approached the front door. He felt something brush against his calf and glanced down to see her skirts enveloping his legs.

He didn't suppress his smile. There was comfort in this sort of closeness and shared companionship.

The judge and his wife joined them a moment later, and they were all quickly ushered inside the foyer.

"Lady Huntley asks that you wait for her in the drawing room," the butler said.

"Then she's here? My daughter?" Lady Tidmore asked.

"Yes, Lady Tidmore. Lady Huntley will bring her to you as soon as I send her word that you've arrived."

"Very good," Lord Tidmore said, and then turned to Robert and Antonia. "Meet me back at my home in an hour," he told them. "We'll have brought our daughter home by then and we can discuss your urgent business."

Robert hesitated, surprised at being dismissed in this way, but then nodded. This was a family moment. He and Antonia would only be in the way.

"I'll see you there. I'd have preferred to give you and your family more time together, but I don't have that luxury. Once you hear what we have to say, you'll understand."

❦

WHEN ROBERT AND ANTONIA ARRIVED AN HOUR LATER, IT WAS already dark outside. They found Lord Tidmore waiting for them in his drawing room.

"Thank you again, Lord Wentworth. Miss Winter," Lord Tidmore said. "We've been searching for Imogen for over a week. I hired a man who specialized in this sort of thing, but he had no success. How could she have traveled so far alone? I must say, I'm thankful she had the sense to go to Lord Huntley's home for help."

"I assume your daughter didn't bolt before Lady Huntley was able to bring her to you," Antonia said.

"We were fortunate there. Imogen had no idea we were in the room until the door had already closed behind her. And then her mother ran to her and began crying with relief. I don't think Imogen realized how worried we were." He shook his head. "I'm not sure what led her to think we didn't care, but that will change."

Lord Tidmore crossed to a sideboard and began clinking a bottle and glasses. A moment later, there came the sound of liquid being poured. "Can I offer you both something to drink? I have some fine sherry," he called over his shoulder.

Antonia nodded, and Robert said, "Yes. Thank you."

Tidmore sloshed more liquid into glasses, handed them to Robert and Antonia, and then dropped into the wing-backed chair to face them.

Lord Tidmore narrowed his eyes. "The niceties are out of the way. It's been a long day, and I'd like to rejoin my family as quickly as possible. You said you came here for a purpose unrelated to my personal problems— and it's urgent. Is that correct?" He cocked an eyebrow.

"I'm here to ask you to help expedite a case that has ties to a matter of intense interest to the queen," Robert said, setting his sherry glass on the end table next to him. "You happen to be uniquely qualified to examine the evidence and make a ruling, and your knowledge of the Russian language and legal system will be integral to your decision-making process."

Tidmore puffed out his lower lip and then nodded to himself. "Due to my daughter's disappearance, I am not currently adjudicating any cases, but I have a number of them waiting for my return. If I agree to hear yours, you'll need to obtain a barrister and be ready to see me tomorrow." He held up his hand as though warding off the objections he was certain would come. "That's the best I can do."

"We've already sent for Mr. Montlake. He's a new barrister and formerly did some work as a solicitor. Do you know him?"

"The name sounds familiar." Lord Tidmore sipped his sherry as he gazed into the distance. "Ah, yes. He was involved in that strange affair at the Mivart Hotel when a jewelry collection was stolen. I believe he helped capture the thief, did he not?"

"Yes, he did," Antonia said.

"He's never been in my courtroom, but the man has to have a first time. If he can be ready by tomorrow morning, I'll hear the case at nine o'clock."

Robert nodded, not bothering to hide his relief. "That will be acceptable. May I outline the pertinent issues for you as they pertain to the queen's interests?"

As Robert spoke, Tidmore opened a desk and extracted some paper and a pen. "Only if you can speak in broad strokes. I realize you aren't a trained barrister, so I won't expect you to behave as such, but please don't try to sway me regarding the case. All you'll accomplish is to irritate me. I'll make my decision based on facts and on the law. Is that understood?"

"Completely. That's all I can ask."

Robert quickly outlined the importance of the book to the queen. He explained the danger Antonia was in as well as her relationship with the czar. "This is why the matter needs to be addressed as quickly and quietly as possible. The contents of that church register are simply too explosive."

"Then why do I need to see it at all? Shouldn't you give it to Her Majesty?"

"The book records the marriage between Miss Winter's parents. Without that, she and her sisters are considered illegitimate."

"Ah. Go no further," Tidmore said, holding up his hand to stem the flow of words. "I'd prefer to have those details presented to me tomorrow in court." He scrawled a few more notes before returning his attention to them. "Thank you for outlining the pertinent facts. I'll expect to see you and Miss Winter tomorrow morning." He rose, indicating that the meeting was over.

40

The general who wins the battle makes many calculations in his temple before the battle is fought. The general who loses makes but few calculations beforehand.

— *SUN TZU*

A ntonia felt triumphant as she stepped into the foyer of Woolsey House.

"Antonia. Good, you're back," Frederick said by way of greeting. "You'll be pleased to learn that Mr. Montlake has already arrived and is in Robert's study preparing for court."

"That's excellent news," Robert said as he closed the door behind them, blocking the cold, swirling wind. "You couldn't be in better hands."

"Did Lord Tidmore agree to hear your case?" Frederik asked.

Antonia smiled broadly. "Yes. Tomorrow morning at nine."

"Then, it's a good thing Mr. Montlake arrived so quickly."

Frederick rubbed at his chin. "Have you thought of anything else we need to do to prepare?"

"I need to send Father Sergey a letter informing him of tomorrow's proceedings. Mr. Montlake will need to call him as a witness."

"I can draft the letter if you like," Frederick said. "That would leave you free to meet with Mr. Montlake. He's been asking for you."

Antonia considered the idea and then nodded. "Thank you." She pressed her finger to her lips and stared at Frederick for a moment. "Perhaps you can help with a bothersome problem. I still need to prove my uncle was the man who stole the book from the Russian Orthodox church. Father Sergey recognized him, but —he's concerned his memory could be faulty. The thief's hand was severely burned that night. You're a clever fellow. Can you think of a way to get my uncle to remove his gloves while he's in court? He wears them all the time and Father Sergey needs to know if he conceals them because they were scarred by the fire."

Frederick cast a contemplative gaze toward the ceiling. "That's an interesting challenge. Gloves, eh?" Then he gave a curt nod. "Rest assured. I'll find a way." He walked away without saying anything more and headed in the direction of the plant conservatory, seemingly hard at work devising a plan.

"My brother is clever. If he says he'll find a way, its as good as done."

"I'm relieved he decided to help me rather than hinder me."

"He'd make a formidable foe." Robert gestured toward the hallway leading to the study. "Mr. Montlake is in the room you and I used last night," Robert said.

A faint heat washed over Antonia at his oblique reference to what had taken place between them less than twenty-four hours ago. So much had changed since then.

When she didn't move right away, Robert placed his hand on the small of her back and gently urged her to move toward the hallway. His touch sent a surge of warmth through her, and that faint heat began to intensify. She moved into the hallway, and then swayed toward him, ever so slightly.

Robert moved closer, his eyes sharp with concern. But when he took in her flushed appearance, he wrapped his other arm around her waist, encircling her and pressing her body against his.

"You aren't feeling faint again, are you?" The corner of his mouth twitched as though he was teasing her.

"Again? When was I faint?"

"That night at the embassy," he said, leaning down so that his cheek brushed against her temple and his breath was warm on the side of her face. "When I first saw you, you were feeling faint."

Antonia swallowed. "But that—that was only a ruse." The heat continued to rise, and she could feel her heartbeat pounding in her ears. She laid her palm against his chest. At first she meant to push him away, but then she slid it up, sliding her hand around his neck to cup it.

Robert's mouth came crashing down on hers. One moment they were still talking, and the next she found herself falling into his kiss.

Antonia let out a tiny whimper of delight. Delight at his touch. Delight at his taste. His feel. Him.

A door opened down the hallway, and a burst of girlish laughter came spilling forth.

Antonia jerked away. She glanced down the hallway and spotted Robert's sister. Fortunately, Emily was glancing back over her shoulder at Stephanie and Evalina and seemed oblivious to what she'd interrupted.

The girl wore a white Grecian-style costume that flowed around her legs as she moved. Antonia's sisters appeared to be similarly clad. Catherine stood behind them, pressing her hand against her lower back. She looked weary.

Robert reacted with aplomb and tucked Antonia's arm through his. He continued escorting her down the hallway as though nothing of note had just transpired. Antonia could only hope that if her sisters noticed her flushed cheeks, they would attribute it to the fact that Antonia had just come in from the cold.

"You're back," Emily said, catching sight of them.

"We've been working on the pantomime all afternoon," Evalina said, twirling around. "Do you like our costumes?" She darted forward to greet them and gave Antonia a quick kiss on the cheek.

"Everything is coming along splendidly," Stephanie added. "Lady Emily—"

"No, you must call me Emily. I insist."

Stephanie bounced on her toes. "*Emily* also insisted that we stay for dinner."

"She *can* be a bit insistent," Evalina added, "but I like that about her. She insists about the most wonderful things."

"She also insists that we sleep here tonight since we won't be able to perform our pantomime until after dinner," Stephanie said, rushing the words out as though she was afraid that her sister might utter them first.

Evalina scowled at her.

"That's another problem solved," Robert murmured. "I assume they'll want to be in court tomorrow morning too."

"Court?" Evalina asked. "Why would we want to go to court?"

"Has something happened? Have you found the church register?" Stephanie asked. She moved closer to Evalina and wrapped her arms around her waist as though afraid to hear the answer.

Antonia hesitated, not wanting to get their hopes up only to dash them again, but tomorrow was just as important to them as it was to her. They needed to know. "Lord Wentworth was able to find a judge who will hear our case again. Tomorrow."

"Tomorrow!" Stephanie squeaked in surprise. "Why didn't you tell us sooner?"

"We only just returned from arranging things. You really don't need to be in court."

"Is that why Mr. Montlake is here?" Evalina asked, looking somewhat mollified. Then she furrowed her brow. "Why do you want to go before another judge? It's not as if this one's likely to make a different decision than the last one did."

"Because Stephanie was right. I *was* able to locate the church register." Evalina's eyes widened.

"That's wonderful news! Now we have the proof we need!"

"And Mr. Montlake will help," Stephanie added. "Everything could change for us tomorrow. Our lives could return to normal."

Antonia opened her mouth, but then closed it again. She wouldn't tell them about the czar—their newly discovered half-uncle—at least not today. Nobody had specifically told her to keep it a secret, but it was obvious that if the information could incite a war, it probably shouldn't be entrusted to her sisters. At least, not until they were a few years older.

"Miss Winter?" Mr. Montlake said, opening the door of the study. "I thought I heard your voice. It's wonderful to see you."

"Thank you for helping us," Antonia replied.

"I'm happy to be of service. I'm well prepared. I already know your situation, and with the church register as evidence, I'm certain we can get a reasonable judge to rule in your favor."

"If you'll excuse us," Catherine said, "we have to finish rehearsing if we want to be ready in time for tonight's performance." The four of them continued down the hallway and passed Frederick, who was heading toward them with the church register clutched firmly under his arm.

They stepped into the study, and Robert closed the door.

"Can you read Russian?" Robert asked Mr. Montlake.

Montlake raised his eyebrows. "Never studied it."

"Then allow me to translate," Frederick said, crossing the room to take a seat at the desk. He flipped to the pertinent page of the leather-bound book, and then began copying the words onto a fresh sheet of paper.

Mr. Montlake waited until Frederick was finished to glance at what he'd written. "What do these X's represent?" He pointed to a spot on the page.

"Those are places where the ink is blurred and unreadable."

"Very frustrating." He frowned and then lifted his gaze to Antonia. "I'm concerned that this won't be enough to convince a judge that the wedding took place before you and your sisters were born." Mr. Montlake took off his eyeglasses and rubbed at his eyes with his thumb and forefinger.

"What?" Robert looked thunderstruck.

Antonia touched his arm in a soothing gesture. "I was afraid of that." She hesitated for a moment. "There's another item that contains the date of their wedding, but I'm afraid it might be difficult to obtain."

"There is?" Montlake asked, sounding hopeful. "What would that be?"

"It's a painting my grandfather gave my parents the day they were married. On the back, he wrote a dedication and mentioned it was a wedding gift. It gives the date of their wedding. Is that enough?"

Montlake's eyes lit up. "That's excellent. On its own, it might not be enough proof. But in combination with this book?" He gave a sharp nod of satisfaction. "It should easily persuade a reasonable judge. But you foresee a problem in obtaining it? Why is that?"

"It's in my uncle's house. He has it hanging on the wall in his drawing room. Do you think we should sneak into his house tonight, steal it, and show it to the judge?"

Montlake frowned at her. "Don't be foolish. The last thing I need is for you to get caught breaking into Walter Winter's house. Since we have to appear in court tomorrow, that would ruin every-thing. No, no. I have a much simpler solution. All we need is for the judge to issue an administrative summons instructing Walter Winter to bring the painting to court tomorrow. We can make him think it has nothing to do with you. Perhaps we can write the summons to suggest that his ownership of the painting is in question."

"You're a clever man, Mr. Montlake," Antonia said.

"I hope I'm clever enough. It would seem your uncle is devious. I'll need to work hard to stay one step ahead of him."

"I think I can help with that," Frederick said. He glanced at Antonia. "I have a plan for getting him to remove those gloves."

41

The human heart has hidden treasures, In secret kept, in silence sealed;
The thoughts, the hopes, the dreams, the pleasures, Whose charms were
broken if revealed.

— *CHARLOTTE BRONTE*

Dinner was a pleasant diversion, as was the girls' pantomime. Frederick and Mr. Montlake excused themselves from attending the entertainment so they could prepare for court.

Once the impromptu performance reached its conclusion, Robert excused himself. He and Antonia found the two men sitting at his desk in his study, poring over the church register.

"How are the burns?" Robert asked as he strolled across the study to stand across from them.

"They hurt," Frederick snapped, casting him an irritated glance. Then he glanced down at the pen he awkwardly clutched in his left hand. "They're a bit better, I suppose. I can manage to hold this in my off-hand." He tossed it on the table and flexed his fingers. "How was the pantomime?"

"Excellent. Diverting. The girls are nearly as talented as their sister." Robert gave his brother an assessing gaze. "Should I prepare the poultice again?"

Frederick shook his head. "All the herbs are gone. Lady Harrington must have finally taken me at my word and decided to stay away." He frowned.

Antonia gave him a sharp glance. "That's odd. She arrived just as we were leaving for Lord Tidmore's house. She had the poultice supplies with her."

"Perhaps she grew tired of waiting for you," Robert said. "I believe that was the gist of her complaint the night of the ball as well."

Frederick reddened and opened his mouth to retort, but Mr. Montlake pushed back his chair rather loudly and rose to his feet. Robert had the sense that the interruption was intentional. "I think the best way I can finish my preparations for tomorrow is to sleep for a few hours," Montlake said.

"Certainly," Frederick said, rising to his feet as well. "I'll direct you to your room. I could do with some rest as well."

The two of them were gone before Robert had a chance to bid them good night.

As soon as they were alone, Antonia strode over to the desk and picked up the church register. Her fingers tightened around it. When he caught her eye, she gave him a nervous smile. "I'm worried about the book."

"What do you mean? Are you worried about those X's?"

"No. Well, yes, I'm worried about that too. But I meant I'm worried about where we should put the book while we sleep tonight. What if the ambassador has his men break into the house? What if they steal it?"

"We could hide it," he suggested.

"That's what I thought too." She clutched it tightly against her chest with both hands. "Where?"

He glanced around the room. "What about right here on the bookshelf?"

"That's no good. That's where my uncle hid it, and you know how that ended up."

Robert nodded, but he continued to stare at the bookcase. A moment later, he stepped closer to examine it. "If I remember correctly..."

"What?"

Robert pushed aside some books he'd placed on the shelf only a couple of months ago as he searched for—yes—there it was. A small wooden latch. He pushed on it, but it didn't move.

He leaned over to look at it more carefully. Yes, this was the spot. He stepped closer to the shelf and pushed harder this time, using his body weight to provide leverage. Finally, the latch moved with a grinding sound.

"What's that?" Antonia asked.

"It's where we'll keep the book." The bookcase sat slightly askew. Robert grabbed its frame and pulled. "Pick up that lamp."

He peered into the inky opening. As Antonia moved closer, the light she held drove away the blackness.

"What's this?"

"A secret passageway. I've scarcely thought about it in years. It leads up to one of the bedrooms." He glanced down at her. "Yours."

Her eyebrows jumped. "Mine? I'd have thought a secret staircase would have led to your room."

He grinned at that. "Another family secret. I'll tell you about this one. My great-grandfather was an insomniac. He often chose to sleep alone so he wouldn't disturb my great-grandmother. According to family lore, when he built this house, he had a staircase hidden inside the wall so he could come down to his study at night without waking anyone."

"A secret passageway seems excessive."

Robert shrugged. "He was a bit of a romantic as well, from what I've heard, or perhaps they said he was an eccentric."

"Are you suggesting all romantics are eccentrics?" She cocked an eyebrow at him.

"Perhaps not *all*. Either way, he'd always wanted a secret passageway in his house, so he built one."

"The latch seemed stiff when you tried to open the door."

"We haven't used this space in years. Emily was fascinated by it. She accidentally locked herself inside it one day when she was quite small. My parents blocked off both ends so it couldn't happen again. After my father died, Mother went on a frenzy of closing down rooms and blocking off areas. I think it was her way of taking control of her life. I haven't thought about the staircase in years. Mother locked the study as well, and I only recently started using it again."

The area behind the bookcase was dark and narrow. It had been built between the walls next to the fireplace, so the space was warm.

"This should do nicely," she said, placing the book on a narrow shelf.

Robert looked past her and noticed some items stashed in the hidden space. He took a few steps closer and spotted a soft-sided traveling bag.

"What is it?" Antonia asked.

"I'm not sure. It looks like luggage. Perhaps it belonged to my father. No one's been in here since he died."

Excitement mounted as he stared down at it. What if the contents provided an explanation for his father's actions that last year of his life? That thought surprised him. Had he really been holding on to a childish fantasy that his father had been innocent? They'd had a letter in his own hand admitting what he'd done.

Suddenly, he wished he hadn't opened that door. Whatever was in this bag couldn't be good.

Despite his growing sense of dread, Robert dropped to one knee and tried to open the case. The metal clasp didn't want to move after fifteen years of disuse. Robert dug his fingers under the edge of the latch and forced it open.

He leaned forward to look inside, and in the light of Antonia's lamp he could see the mounds of crisp bank notes piled inside. He dropped his other knee to the ground, shocked, and shoved his hand deeper in the bag. It was completely filled with banknotes.

Not proof of his father's innocence.

Proof of his guilt.

Antonia let out a soft gasp. "Is that what I think it is?"

"If you think it's a bag full of money, then yes." Anger clipped his voice, but he couldn't soften his tone.

He tried to latch the bag shut, but he must have broken the clasp. Instead, he shoved it to one side as he continued his search. It toppled over, spilling bills onto the floor of the small chamber.

He ignored them. Behind it he found a similar bag, but when he forced its latch he found men's personal items. His father's.

Robert sat fully on the floor as the meaning of this sank in.

It would appear that his father had packed both bags with the intention of slinking away. What had made him abandon the plan and commit suicide instead?

Robert shook his head in shock and bemusement. That long-held childish dream of proving his father innocent had been dashed, quite thoroughly.

"What does this all mean?" Antonia stepped closer, leaning down to look at the spilled bills. "Did someone hide it here?"

"I assume my father did—shortly before he died." This explained why they were never able to find any of the money. It was here all along.

She reached into the pile of bank notes and fumbled around for something. She plucked out something small and heavy. "What's this?" she asked, turning as she held out a square box.

Robert's chest tightened. As soon as he saw it, he knew what it had to contain, and he didn't want to open it. He knew it had to be his own version of Pandora's Box, full of all the evils in the world. Or in this case, all the evils that could destroy his family.

"Put it back," he said, snatching the box from her hands. "It was my father's."

"Is it important?"

Robert swallowed. "I—I think it contains the evidence that proves my father—" He couldn't bring himself to continue.

"What?" In the flickering lamplight, he could see her concern.

He shook his head sharply and shoved the box back in with the pile of money, feeling like a coward. "I can't deal with this right now. It's waited here for fifteen years. Another two days won't make any difference." Was that the truth, or was he instead afraid to reveal his secrets the way Antonia had?

"Are you sure?"

He tensed, hating himself. "I'm certain."

He was relieved she didn't continue to push the issue. He needed time to think. He should tell Frederick. He'd know what to do.

He pushed himself back, suddenly wanting to distance himself from the evidence of his father's shame. From the evidence of his treason.

He needed to leave this room. He reached out and found a long wooden post and used it to pull himself up.

Unfortunately, what he though was a post turned out to be a lever that moved under his weight. He stumbled, barely managing to right himself so he didn't fall over. The paneled wall of the study slammed shut under the force of his weight on the lever.

"Blast!"

"What happened?" Antonia asked. "Why did the door shut?"

"It was my fault. I accidentally pulled on a lever."

"Can you open it?"

"Move the lamp closer," he said, shuffling over to the door. "I need to find the mechanism."

"Don't you simply push the lever in the opposite direction?"

"There's a catch I need to release first. Once I find it, all I need to do is push on the door."

Antonia joined him, holding up the lamp so he could see, and he quickly located the latch. It was small, and over the years it had become stiff with disuse. That was probably why he'd had so much trouble opening it from the other side. Try as he might, he couldn't get it to release. Perhaps if the latch had been bigger he would have had better luck, but as it was he could only get his thumb on it.

"The mechanism on the other side of the door is much larger, so it was easier to open," he muttered. "I can't get this to budge."

"You said this leads upstairs to my bedroom. Perhaps we can use the door up there."

"The door that's blocked by your bed?" Robert let out a heavy sigh as he stepped back. "Let's try. I'll lead the way."

She nodded and passed him the lamp.

He approached the staircase and held the lamp high. Antonia followed him up the tall, narrow steps. There was a small landing at the top. Robert hung the lamp on a small peg and began tracing his hands around the edges of the door. He quickly located the latch, and it immediately released. He pushed his shoulder into the door, shoving both it and the bed until there was enough room to get through the opening.

He snatched up the lamp and ushered Antonia into her bedroom. As she moved past him in the narrow space, her entire body brushed against his.

The feel of her jolted through him. He wanted nothing more than to reach out and press her against him. To forget what they'd just discovered. To wipe away the sense of inadequacy—the shame.

He followed her through the opening. They stood behind the

headboard, and he set the lamp on the table against the wall next to where her bed should be.

He should leave.

Logic told him to stay away from her, but his good sense was failing him miserably.

He reached for her hand. He couldn't resist touching her.

At the brush of his fingertips, Antonia turned to face him. She twined her fingers in his and moved closer to him as she stared up into his eyes.

"Oh, my darling Robert." And then she slipped her hand behind his neck, pulled him down, and kissed him.

$\maltese$ 42 $\maltese$

Now a soft kiss Aye, by that kiss, I vow an endless bliss.

— JOHN KEATS

Antonia knew this was insanity, but she couldn't seem to stop herself. Ever since she'd kissed Robert in the hallway, it was all she'd been able to think about . Every time she glanced at him, she found herself staring at his mouth. At the gentle curve of his lips.

Even if the judge ruled in her favor tomorrow, she and Robert could never be together. Not the way she wanted them to be. Their worlds were too far apart.

She was an actress. He was an earl.

If Lord Tidmore *did* rule in her favor, this might be her last night under Robert's roof.

What about today, though? Should she spend her life waiting for everything to be perfect? That would never happen. Life was messy and imperfect. There would always be an excuse not to take a chance. She couldn't let moments like this one pass her by.

His look of deeply felt pain finally pushed her over the edge. She didn't know his secrets, but she could tell that this one cut him deeply. The anguish in his beautiful eyes pierced her like a knife.

So she kissed him.

She kissed him with all her pent-up frustration and desire. She demanded that he kiss her back. She insisted that he respond. That he react to her.

And he did.

Robert wrapped his arms around her waist as he kicked the hidden door closed with his heel. He lifted her into his arms without breaking their kiss and moved though the semi-darkness around the headboard and toward the mattress. They tumbled onto it as they shared hungry, desperate kisses.

The lamplight flickered, partially blocked by the headboard, and Robert's eyes were like pools of darkness surrounded by rings of pale-blue light.

"If I don't leave now, I won't be able to stop," he said gruffly. "Not this time."

"I don't want you to. Don't leave. Don't stop."

She slid her hands under his coat, pushing it over his broad shoulders. He needed no urging, and an instant later he pulled his shirt over his head. He loomed above her on the bed, bare-chested. A soft curling ribbon of hair wended its way down his chest and disappeared beneath his trousers. Antonia couldn't resist touching it. It was as soft as it looked.

Robert let out a gasp of air, and his abdomen tensed. He grabbed her exploring hand and pulled her to a sitting position. He quickly undid the fastenings of her bodice and skirt and then pulled her to her feet to divest her of them, leaving her standing in her underthings. He loosened her corset strings and then undid the metal fastenings that held it closed. She'd never been undressed so quickly and efficiently before, and in a trice she stood before him wearing only her chemise.

He kicked off his shoes and trousers so that he was naked, and he pulled her against him. "I've been thinking of you like this all day," he murmured. "Soft and willing and in my arms. I've never wanted anyone like this. I don't—"

"Don't say more. I want you now. Tonight. Nothing more." She slid her palms up his back and curled them over his shoulders, pulling him down to her. Kissing him.

He gathered handfuls of her chemise, pulled it up and over her head, and tossed it to one side before crushing her against him. The heat of his skin against hers was overwhelming. He was both velvety soft and firm, and the soft hair of his chest tickled the tips of her breasts.

He snapped back the coverlet on the bed and then pulled her into his arms and tumbled into it with her. She was on top of him at first, but then he rolled with her so that he was above her, pressing her down into the mattress with his weight.

Antonia reveled in the sheer delight of being tossed about so easily by him. He leaned on one arm and gazed down at her. The soft, orange lamplight left one side of his face in shadows, but she could easily make out his roguish grin. He touched her collarbone and then slowly slid his hand down, down until he cupped the weight of her breast. When he brushed the tip with his thumb, she let out a gasp and arched her back slightly. He turned to the other breast, lowering his head to kiss it. A moment later he was suckling and nibbling at it, leaving her gasping in surprise and quaking with desire.

She abandoned herself to his tender passion. He lifted his head and began nibbling at her neck, then closed his teeth on the small lobe of her ear. A shudder of excitement coursed through her.

"Do you like that?"

"Yes. It's—I never imagined—I—I can hardly think clearly."

He suckled the lobe of her ear as he slid his leg between hers. He traced the rim of her ear with his tongue, and she couldn't think about anything except the sensations that he awoke within her.

His hand cupped her breast again, and then traveled down her stomach. When he touched the short, curly tangle between her legs, she gasped. He kissed her, his tongue sliding against hers. She moaned into him.

He cupped his hand between her legs. One of his fingers delved between her folds. She gasped in surprise at the intimacy of his touch, but he didn't stop. He continued exploring her body, and she reveled in each discovery he made. She shifted her legs to allow him better access.

He adjusted his hand, and a moment later his finger moved inside her. She arched her back, aching with desire to have him there. To have him between her legs.

He moved his hand, sliding his thumb up to a small, hard nub that seemed to have no other purpose than to be touched by him. She arched her back again, pushing into the sensation.

Robert let out a low chuckle. "Like that, do you?"

"Mmm." She wanted more of him. She grabbed him by the back of his neck and pulled him down, kissing him as she wrapped her legs around his waist, pulling him close. She loved having him inside her this way, but she knew there was more. Much more.

"Are you certain?" Robert asked.

"I've never been more certain about anything," she managed to say.

"It will hurt this first time. Your opening is small because of your maidenhead, and it will tear, but only this one time. If you want me to stop, you need to tell me now."

"I only want you to stop talking."

He pulled his hand away from between her legs and shifted her weight. A moment later he slid down her body, leaving a trail of kisses in his wake. "I want this to be perfect for you. I want you to want it so much you can't imagine stopping."

He pressed a kiss to her damp curls and she let out a whimper. As his mouth covered her soft inner folds, her eyes rolled back. His tongue touched and swirled around the hard nub as his fingers slid in and out of her.

A force began to build within her. An urgent need that consumed her. All that existed was this moment and this man. Nothing else.

An explosion of delight tore through her, and she tried to muffle her cry of release. She turned her head into the pillow to stifle it.

Robert shifted his weight and wrapped her legs around his waist, then settled his hips between them. She felt something much larger pressing against her opening.

His mouth lowered to hers and he kissed her, thoroughly and completely, until all thoughts disappeared from her mind. A moment later, he pushed into her and she felt the sharp, hot tearing of her maidenhead, just as he'd predicted. She froze and swallowed a cry of pain. Robert stopped moving, and the pain receded to a mild ache. A moment later she shifted against him, testing to see if movement would cause the pain to come roaring back. It didn't.

"Should I stop?" he asked.

"No." She shifted again, and Robert slowly began to move inside her. His hand slid between them and he gently teased the sensitive nub. Soon she was feeling that gathering of sensation again. She arched her back instinctively, and her belly slid against his. A sheen of perspiration slickened both their bodies.

She gasped and pressed her nails into his shoulders. Then she pulled him closer. Her heart beat harder and harder, and she could see the quick flutter of his pulse in his throat.

He thrust deeper into her slick embrace, and a moment later she began to shudder as spasms caused her to clench around him.

He pushed in a long, gentle slide, moving faster and faster, plunging deep into her body. Fast, rhythmic slaps of flesh against flesh caused the bed to shake. His body shuddered with his violent release, and then he collapsed on the mattress next to her, rolling her with him.

For a moment, they didn't move. They stayed pressed against each other. Her heart continued to pound, easing ever so slowly. Robert's breath was loud as well. She laid her palm flat on his chest and felt his heart thud. It wasn't as fast as hers, but it beat hard, as though it might burst from his chest.

He pulled her closer, kissing the top of her head. He ran gentle fingers up and down her spine, causing her to tremble against him. She shifted her leg, resting it across his thighs, reveling in the simple intimacy of the act.

She traced her fingers down the dark, straight, soft hair of his chest, smoothing and stroking it into place. He hugged her against him and then stopped her fingers with his hand. "That tickles."

"I didn't know you were ticklish." She grinned at him. "That makes you vulnerable to me." She blew on his neck and he turned to kiss her, which turned out to be an efficient way to stop her.

"There's a lot you don't know about me," he said, and then planted a second kiss on her forehead. "We haven't known each other long enough—"

"Things happened quickly between us." She laced her fingers in between his. As she gazed at them, she realized their intertwined hands represented both their unity and their isolation.

"I've heard that dangerous situations can forge emotional bonds quickly," he said, murmuring into her hair. "I never believed it before, but now—"

"Now that you've experienced it?"

He lifted their entwined hands up higher, staring at them in the low lantern light. "I'm a convert," he said as he pulled her hand to his chest, just over his heart. "You and I have seen each other in the worst of circumstances. We've seen how the other reacts in times of stress. I think a person's true nature shows in those moments."

"You're a noble man, Robert. You would have made a wonderful knight. I can easily imagine you slaying dragons and saving damsels."

He stiffened. "Me?" He shook his head. "I think you're wrong. I've gone through life avoiding entanglements. Dragons? Damsels? Never. It isn't in me."

She recalled the way she'd feigned being lightheaded the night they'd first met. He'd helped her, even when he'd put his mission in danger, and later that same night he'd rescued her from those men in the alley. Even when she'd tried to send him away, he'd come to the theater to make sure she'd be safe. If he hadn't, the Russians would have kidnapped her, of that she was certain. At every turn, he'd watched over her and taken care of her again and again. He'd even opened his home to her. "I don't think you see yourself clearly. You've saved me many times in the past few days."

He brushed his thumb over the outside of her hand in a gentle caress. "I suppose you bring it out in me. I'm not like that with others."

"I haven't seen you around many other people, so I don't have much of a comparison, but you certainly seem protective of Frederick."

"He's my younger brother. I don't have much of an alternative."

"Admit it. There's more to you than you like to pretend. I think you've been hiding who you are for so long you've begun to fool even yourself."

"No. It's you. It's this situation." He disentangled his fingers from hers. "If you saw me on a normal day instead of whatever this is we've been sharing, you'd see the real me. As soon as things go back to normal, you'll see me as I truly am. I don't think you'll like me as much."

She clutched at his hand before he could pull it away. "Let's not talk about the future. Not even about tomorrow. I don't know what will happen, and I'd prefer to spend these moments in a blissful bubble. Let's not spoil it."

"I understand, but..." He let out a heavy sigh. "There's my brother. My sister. The servants. Your sisters—"

"You're afraid we'll be discovered."

"We have a house full of people who might find us in here."

"Can't you stop thinking, just for a while?"

Robert's stomach trembled with his suppressed laughter. "Apparently not. I don't think I'm constitutionally able to." He sat up and reached for his shirt at the foot of her bed.

Their interlude was over. The bubble had burst.

Antonia rolled off the bed, immediately missing the warmth of his body. As she tugged her chemise over her head, he dragged on his trousers and tucked in his shirt. "Since the door leading back into the study is jammed, I'll have to use your bedroom door. The sooner I slip away, the better."

She nodded as he sat down on the edge of the bed directly in front of her and tugged on his boots. As she watched him hurry to leave, something tightened in her chest. It must have shown on her face, because when he looked at her, his expression became tender.

He took her hand and pulled her to him so she stood between his legs. As he wrapped his arms around her waist and gazed up at her with those gorgeous, soulful eyes, her heart melted. "I wish I could stay," he said. "I can't tell you how sorry I am I have to leave you. I'd love to sleep here with you wrapped in my arms."

She gazed down at him, his face soft and vulnerable in the dim light. "*Are you sure that we are awake? It seems to me that yet we sleep, we dream*," she murmured.

He smiled in recognition. "Shakespeare?"

"*Midsummer Night's Dream*."

He pressed a kiss on her breastbone, and she couldn't resist smoothing his tousled hair with her fingers. If she wasn't careful, she'd fall in love with this man, and then where would she be? She already knew. Foolish and alone and dreaming of a life she could never have.

He gazed up at her, his eyes full of longing. "I want to be able to stay with you. To claim you. Maybe we can—"

She cut him off by stepping away. "No talk about the future. I won't think about it right now. We have tonight." She grabbed both his hands and pulled him to his feet. "Go."

43

*He that gives good advice, builds with one hand; he that gives good
counsel and example, builds with both; but he that gives good admonition
and bad example, builds with one hand and pulls down with the other.*

— FRANCIS BACON

Robert found his brother in the breakfast room. "We
need to talk. I made a disturbing discovery last night."
Robert dragged his hand through his hair.

Frederick stilled his movements, focusing entirely on Robert.
"Come to my study."

Without a word, Frederick tossed his napkin on the table and
followed Robert down the hallway.

This early, the house was still, but Robert took no chances.
Once inside the room, he locked the door. He met his brother's
curious gaze and said, "It's better if I show you."

Frederick's expression grew more intent.

Robert crossed to the bookcase with Frederick on his heels. He deftly manipulated the release. The door sprang open.

"The staircase?"

Robert gestured toward the lamp on the table. "Bring that."

Once inside, Robert pulled a small can from his pocket and dripped some machine oil onto the corroded latch. He didn't want to risk being trapped in here again.

"Last night, I realized this was the perfect place to hide the church register." Robert gestured toward the two bags. "I was right. In all the years since Father's death, we never found these."

Frederick moved closer. "The missing money?"

Robert nodded. "This changes everything for us. I can compensate everyone he swindled without delay. Don't worry. They won't know where the money came from. Since starting down this path a few years ago, I've grown adept at convincing people of their own good fortune."

Frederick let out a heavy sigh. "That only solves the smaller part of our problem. With the evidence regarding the treason still missing, our family will never be safe. The Queen will never stop searching for her proof. Even now it could be catastrophic if it fell into the wrong hands."

Robert couldn't hide the smile of satisfaction that slid over his face. "In that case, you'll be pleased to learn I found this as well." Robert picked up the small box and handed it to Frederick. "I'm giving it to you. You're better suited to deal with it than I am. I'm confident you'll examine all the risks and choose the wisest path."

Frederick opened the box and peered inside. "You found it," he said, his voice almost a whisper.

"You decide what to do with it. I'll support whatever choice you make."

Frederick's grip tightened on the box, then he handed it back to Robert. "I need to speak with someone about this and get his advice. Keep this here for the time being. I'll seek him out after we leave court today. He'll be able to help me look at this clearly and determine the best course of action."

Robert took the box, staring at it. "Do you believe in fate? Destiny?"

Frederick's eyebrows dove down as he furrowed his brow. "I believe people determine their own destinies. Fate is an excuse weak men use to explain away their shortcomings."

Robert shook his head. "I used to agree with you, but from the moment I first noticed Antonia the night of the ball, even before we spoke, I sensed fate brought her to me. I brushed it aside, but after she stole the book, I attributed that odd sensation to the theft. Now—what if this all happened for a reason? What if she came into my life to finally compel me to confront my past? She's been the driving force behind everything that's happened over the past few days. She made me care—made me become involved in something real. And now, if not for the fact that she wanted to hide that book, I never would have opened the door to the staircase and found this box."

Frederick shook his head sharply. "Coincidence. You embraced the changes in your life because you were ready to move on, not because of fate."

Robert stared at him. "You've always said you don't believe in coincidence. You can't have it both ways."

Frederick opened his mouth, and then closed it. "You're a bad influence. Fate. Coincidence. Bah. Next you'll be talking about love." He turned and stalked from the chamber, leaving Robert alone with his thoughts.

❧ 44 ❧

At his best, man is the noblest of all animals; separated from law and justice he is the worst.

— ARISTOTLE

Daylight awoke Antonia early the following morning and she stretched languorously, only to freeze at the twinge of pain between her legs. The sensation was akin to being badly chafed—but she'd never before experienced the sensation in that particular part of her anatomy. She shifted around in bed, testing the extent of the pain, and determined it was nothing that would bother her overmuch throughout the day. As it was, the sensation served to prove that last night truly had happened. It wasn't simply a dream. It had been real.

She smiled to herself as she rose from her bed, and the smile remained as she quickly bathed and dressed. She glanced at herself in the looking-glass, trying to see if she looked different. The same face stared back at her. She looked as she always had.

That was strange. Such a life-altering experience should have marked her in some way.

She hurried down the hallway to check on her sisters. The moment she knocked on their bedroom door, Stephanie yanked it open and dragged her into the room.

They were already dressing, and judging by the dresses on their beds, they planned to attend court. "I see you didn't change your minds about coming to court today. I'd hoped you had."

"This doesn't only concern you," Evalina pointed out. "This is our future too."

Stephanie gave a yank to tighten Evalina's corset strings. "You can't simply go about making decisions regarding our lives without consulting us."

"What if someone sees you?" Antonia protested. "What if your names are printed in one of those scandal sheets? You could lose your home at Miss Hermitage's school if the other parents complain."

"We'll hide our faces and we won't give out our names. Besides, if the judge rules in our favor, we'll never have to go back to Miss Hermitage's again."

"But Lord Tidmore plans to close the court when he hears the case," Antonia insisted, hoping to bolster her stand. "He's not allowing visitors."

"We aren't *visitors* ," Evalina said as she turned and began yanking at Stephanie's corset strings. "We're plaintiffs"—yank—"or whatever we're called"—yank. "Since this is about *our* claim on *our* inheritance, then we most certainly are *not* mere visitors."

She had a point, though Antonia hated to admit it. "You might want to stop tugging on those corset strings. Stephanie looks like she can't breathe."

Evalina's eyes went wide and she began loosening her sister's lacings. "Sorry, Steph," she murmured.

"S'no problem," Stephanie said in a strained voice as she gasped for air.

"Honestly, you'll both be bored," Antonia said, unwilling to give up without one last try, but since even she didn't believe her own words, her voice didn't have any conviction behind it.

"We'll be *fine* ," Evalina said in one of those tones that suggested Antonia was talking nonsense.

"What could be more interesting than hearing a judge decide our future?" Stephanie added, now that she could breathe again.

Antonia shook her head in defeat.

Robert didn't appear surprised when all three sisters came downstairs together. He locked gazes with Antonia. She read volumes in those sky-blue eyes, but apparently no one else did. She glanced away, afraid that the tender smile teasing his lips would betray them.

"You and your sisters and Miss Galloway can take my carriage," Robert said. "Frederick and I will follow on horseback. I'm also having six footmen accompany us as guards. I don't know if the Russians have caught wind of today's court proceedings, but if they have, the extra men should dissuade them from trying to take the church register by force." \Antonia glanced at the cluster of tall footmen standing near the door. They all wore Robert's livery, and their grim faces made them appear stern and competent. "They'd frighten me," she murmured.

Robert must have heard her, because he caught her eye and smiled reassuringly. "I retrieved this for you this morning." He handed her the church register.

Antonia's reticule was large enough to allow her to slip the book into it with ease. The unaccustomed weight dragged at her wrist. Surely anyone observing her would know it was there, wouldn't they?

She wanted to clutch it tightly to her chest, but instead she forced herself to let it dangle as though it didn't contain the key to her future.

"Circle around her," Robert said, waving his footmen closer. "Don't let anyone come near."

The footmen surged forward, closing ranks around Antonia until all she could see were men's backs, arms, and shoulders.

As they left the house, the footmen remained bunched around Antonia, keeping her at the center of their cluster.

Antonia's sisters preceded her into the carriage, and the footmen continued to surround her until she was tucked inside with Evalina and Stephanie.

"Are you comfortable?" Robert asked through the door of the carriage.

"I'll feel much better once this book is no longer my responsibility."

He nodded. "It won't be long now."

Antonia felt edgy as the carriage pulled away. She peered out the window, her gaze darting from one potential threat to the next.

Twenty minutes later, the carriage arrived outside the courtroom and Antonia prepared to run the gauntlet again in order to reach the courthouse doors. She wouldn't feel safe until she'd handed that book over to the judge.

As soon as she exited the carriage, the pack of footmen gathered around her. Once she stepped into the courtroom, they finally backed away enough for her to view her surroundings. The wood-paneled courtroom had few people in it, and no onlookers sat in the benches.

It took a moment for her to recognize Mr. Montlake. In his white wig and black robes, he looked almost identical to every other court official in the room, but when he smiled at her he immediately put her at ease.

The rows of seats which had been filled with onlookers the last time she'd been in court were now empty. Last year her public humiliation had been just that. Public. Her exoneration would be carried out in private.

Please, let it be her exoneration. Because honestly, whether or not this took place in public didn't really matter, as long as the judge decided in her favor.

What if Tidmore the Tyrant ruled against her? That's what Frederick had called the man, wasn't it? Or had it been Robert? Either way, the nickname sounded bad. What if he decided that she and her sisters were illegitimate? What recourse would she have?

None. This was her last chance.

She needed to stay calm.

As her gaze swept the room, she noticed Uncle Walter, and she made the mistake of looking into his furious eyes. Eyes that were so similar to her own copper-colored ones, only brighter—more intense.

"Is this your doing, missy?" he hissed, his plump lips shiny with spittle. "I was woken from a sound sleep before the sun was even up. Do you know how it makes a man feel to be woken by policemen pounding on his door? Not charitable, I can tell you that much. Not charitable indeed." He narrowed his too-familiar eyes at her. Why had she never before noticed the strange, intense glow they held? Perhaps it was because she'd never before made him this angry. "I should have known you had something to do with this. You and those illegitimate sisters of yours. The three of you should be ashamed to show your faces in public, let alone to harass the one other person who was so gravely wronged by that man you insist on calling your father."

"I'm sorry to hear you were inconvenienced, Uncle Walter," Stephanie said.

"Don't call me that." His look of scorn could have melted iron. "I'm no uncle of yours. That's been established in court."

Antonia stepped between Walter and Stephanie. "Don't speak to my sister, Mr. Winter . Not ever. If you have something to say to anyone in my family, you can say it to me."

"Nothing would make me happier. In fact, I'm done with this

conversation. I'll let my lawyer do the talking." He turned away in a huff and returned to the other side of the courtroom.

Robert moved to stand next to Antonia, and he shot a menacing look in Walter Winter's direction. "That was your uncle?"

"Yes and no. Apparently, he doesn't want us to refer to him as such," Antonia replied.

"No great loss."

"Exactly what I was thinking."

"All rise," a man intoned from across the room.

A bewigged and bespectacled Lord Tidmore entered the courtroom, and everyone fell silent. The glower he wore made Antonia's stomach clench. Tidmore the Tyrant indeed.

"I'm here for one reason alone," Lord Tidmore stated in a forceful tone, "and that's because this case is of interest to Her Majesty, Queen Victoria. I plan to reach a decision as quickly as possible. I will tolerate no delaying tactics."

"I must protest, Your Honor," Walter Winter's barrister said. "My client was dragged from his bed and brought here without being given pertinent details regarding this case. We have no idea why we're here." Antonia had to give the man credit for his audacity. She'd never have had the temerity to interrupt the judge after what he'd said.

"If you'll be silent, that should become apparent rather quickly. If you can't, I'll have you gagged."

Walter's lawyer closed his mouth, and his Adam's apple bobbed up and down. Perhaps he wasn't as dauntless as his speech suggested.

"The first issue we must address today is one of property ownership," Lord Tidmore continued. "Miss Winter has made a claim against Squire Winter. She states that her grandfather's art was left to his daughter, and that it should, in turn, have been passed on to the three daughters, Antonia, Evalina, and Stephanie Winter. Is that correct?"

"It is, Your Honor," Mr. Montlake said.

"I must object, Lord Tidmore. This issue was addressed, and the previous judge ruled that—"

"Gagged. I mean it. Did I give you permission to speak?" barked Lord Tidmore. "No? I thought not." He glanced at a man standing at the side of the room. "Bailiff, bring in the painting that was seized from Mr. Winter's home this morning."

Two men wearing white gloves brought in a large canvas-draped painting and set it on an easel at the front of the room. Once it was securely in place, they removed the cover to reveal the artwork.

Antonia gasped as her gaze snapped toward the central figure. It was her mother, radiant with happiness, just as Antonia always remembered her. A band tightened around her chest, making it difficult to breathe. She missed her parents so much it hurt.

"Squire Winter, please examine the painting one more time. Is this your property, and if so, has it been damaged or altered in any way?"

Walter bustled forward to peer at it. As he reached out a gloved hand to touch the frame, Mr. Montlake interrupted him.

"I'm sorry, Squire Winter, but if you'd like to touch the painting while it is in the court's possession, I need you to put on cotton gloves. I want to ensure that the gilt frame isn't damaged by any trace oils your leather gloves might have absorbed."

Walter looked as though he'd like to argue the point, but then shrugged. "That isn't necessary. I don't need to touch the painting."

"Examine it now, please. I need your confirmation that it is, indeed, your painting," the judge instructed.

The squire glanced at his lawyer, who gave a cautious nod. Walter then approached the painting and examined the canvas and frame. "Yes. It's mine." He returned to his seat.

"Miss Winter, is this the painting you claim as your own?" Lord Tidmore asked.

"Yes, Your Honor. The central figure is my mother."

Her uncle's face tightened. It was obvious that he hadn't known.

Walter's lawyer glanced at Antonia and then whispered something in his ear. Walter pressed his lips together and gave a sharp shake to his head. Whatever the lawyer had said, Walter didn't like it.

The lawyer cleared his throat. "Although Squire Winter was unaware of the identity of the central figure, he is unwilling to relinquish ownership of the painting. Since he was deprived of his rightful claim to his inheritance for many years while his brother wasted it on the illegitimate offspring of his bigamous relationship, Squire Winter feels entitled to reclaim that lost income in any way he can."

Mr. Montlake glanced at Antonia, but she didn't meet his gaze. She'd heard these claims from her uncle before. None of this man's insults could shock her anymore.

However, Mr. Montlake wasn't as willing to let the comment stand. "Surely the value of Vladamir Nevsky's art far outweighs anything the former Squire Winter could have spent on raising his daughters."

"This court does not recognize them as his daughters," Lord Tidmore interrupted, "so refrain from referring to them as such."

A flush crept up from beneath the collar of Mr. Montlake's starched white shirt. "Yes, Your Honor."

"And you," the judge barked, turning his attention to Walter Winter's barrister. "What's your name? You never introduced yourself."

Walter's lawyer had been smirking at Mr. Montlake, but the question caught him off guard. "I apologize, Your Honor. I'm Mr. Parish. Leonard Parish, of Parish and Gromley."

"Thank you, Mr. Parish. Since you just claimed that the former squire was involved in a bigamous relationship with Miss Winter's mother, how can you claim her inheritance as belonging to your client? By your own testimony, you hold that their marriage was not legal."

"The day before their deaths, the former Squire Winter took his mistress, Miss Nevsky, to Gretna Green and married her in a hasty ceremony. The proof of the marriage has already been given to the court. As soon as she legally married Squire Winter, all of her property automatically became his. That's the law."

"And they made no specific arrangements for Mrs. Winter's three daughters?" the judge asked.

"None," Parish replied. "Squire Winter's will left everything to his daughters, but by law, these three girls are not his legal daughters. I know they use the surname of Winter, but Squire Walter Winter, in a show of great kindness, did not insist they stop using the name. Since they have used it all their lives, he believed it would be too difficult for them to use the surname Nevsky."

Of course, he had no way to force them to, either. But Mr. Parish didn't bother to mention that fact.

"Mr. Montlake, do you have any proof that the marriage in Gretna Green did not take place?"

"No Your Honor, we do not. Our argument today is based on another, earlier marriage ceremony."

"That's a ridiculous claim. The first marriage was found to be illegal since Squire Winter was already married to another woman at the time." Parish threw his hand into the air. "How many times do we have to keep going in circles?"

The judge glowered at him. "Hush, Mr. Parish. It isn't your turn to speak. Now, I understand that although another judge already ruled on this case, he left open the possibility of overturning his decision if proof was brought forth regarding a marriage that purportedly took place in Russia. Is that correct?"

"Yes, Your Honor," Mr. Montlake said.

"Again, I must protest, Your Honor," Mr. Parish said. "The last decision was quite definitive. There was no question in the judge's mind that—"

"Stop. Just stop," Judge Tidmore interrupted. "Your client was not the only person who didn't get enough sleep last night. I arranged to have a number of people's slumbers interrupted. That last judge you mentioned? I woke him as well. And everything you just said directly contradicts what he told me. Please, stop wasting my time, or I'll gag you and your client will have no one to speak for him. Is that understood?"

During the judge's entire diatribe, Leonard Parish's face went paler and paler. Now he barely managed to squeak out a "Yes, Your Honor."

"Frederick Woolsy claims to have a record which will prove that another marriage, a legal marriage, did, indeed, take place. Mr. Woolsy?"

"I apologize, Your Honor," Frederick replied, "but I cannot allow this item to leave my possession, by order of the Queen."

"Yes, yes, I'm well aware of the restrictions you placed on the item," the judge said with a careless wave of his hand. "But the entire point of today's session is for me to examine the book, is it not?"

Antonia watched Walter Winter and noticed that at the mention of the book, he became still. Then he turned and glared at her.

"Yes, Your Honor." Frederick crossed the room with the book and handed it to the judge. "If you look at the pages marked with the red ribbon, you'll be able to read the pertinent information."

"I must protest, Your Honor. How can I refute the information in that book if I cannot be permitted to see it as well?"

"By all means, Mr. Parish, please join us. You can inspect it right alongside me."

Mr. Parish scampered across the room to peer over the judge's shoulder. After looking at the page for a moment, he stood up straight. "How am I expected to read that, Your Honor? It's in Russian or Cyrillic or whatever it's called."

Walter's face went beet red. "This is quite unreasonable," he shouted. "How can I protect my inheritance if my lawyer cannot read the information being presented?"

"Please silence Mr. Winter, otherwise I'll have him gagged." Lord Tidmore didn't even bother to look up as he made the pronouncement.

Walter's mouth snapped shut. But he still looked furious.

Lord Tidmore glanced from Frederick to Mr. Parish and back again. "I have a suggestion. Let's have Mr. Woolsy write down his translation of the pertinent information, while I write one as well. If they match, then you can trust that we performed the task correctly. Will that do?"

The judge left Mr. Parish with little choice. He could either agree to accept the translation, or object and impugn the judge's abilities. Of course, if the translations didn't match, the case would go no further. But Antonia had no doubts. They would match.

Mr. Parish nodded. Frederick pulled a folded sheet of paper from his coat pocket. "I already translated it." He handed the paper to one of the court clerks.

"Perfect. Just give me a moment." It only took a few minutes for the judge to write the translation on a sheet of paper. Once he was done, he passed it to the clerk as well.

The room fell silent. Antonia glanced at the man who denied their kinship. His forehead was beaded with sweat despite the chill in the courtroom. He pulled out a handkerchief and mopped his face before shoving it back into his pocket.

"Are the translations the same?" Judge Tidmore asked his clerk.

The man opened the sheet of paper and read first one and then the other. "They're virtually identical," the man finally said.

"Virtually? How do they differ?"

"Um, Your Honor, one translation uses a squiggled line to indicate that there is more information on the page that isn't translated, and the other uses dots."

"Dots?"

"Yes sir. Dots. Like, in a row down the page."

"Mr. Parish, would you concede that dots and squiggly lines are suitably similar?"

The poor man jerked his head up and down while Walter Winter glared at him.

"Then please, read out the pertinent translation of the contents of the book."

"Weddings. Squiggly line. August 3, one-eight-three-X. Anya Nevsky and Marcus Winter. Squiggly line."

"For the year, you said 'one-eight-three-X,' did you not?" Mr. Parish asked. "Why did you mention an X?"

"Because that's what's written. On both translations. An X."

"The page was damaged," Lord Tidmore said, "and each entry's last digit was obscured. None of the weddings recorded on that page can be verified. It would appear that their wedding did take place in Russia, and that it occurred sometime between 1830 and 1839."

"But the ending digit of the year provides crucial information," Parish said, sounding elated. "The late Squire Winter's first wife died in early 1832 and Miss Antonia Winter was born in 1833. The youngest child, Miss Stephanie Winter, was born in 1838. If the wedding in Russia took place either before 1832 or after 1838, all three children are still illegitimate."

Mr. Montlake took a step forward. "If the wedding took place at any time after the death of Squire Winter's first wife, some if not all of the girls would be considered legitimate."

"The legal system does not use guesswork when rendering a decision," Mr. Parish said. "Without a precise year, it's impossible to know how this information affects the disposition of the estate."

"We have a quandary here," Lord Tidmore agreed. "Mr. Parish is correct in his assessment. Although it is clear that a wedding took place, without a definite year associated with this record, I can't make a ruling."

"Your Honor," Mr. Montlake said, "I have a witness I'd like to bring before the court. This man not only attended the wedding ceremony, he performed it."

The judge's eyebrows rose high enough to disappear under the edge of his white wig, which had the effect of making him appear extraordinarily surprised. "By all means, bring him in."

One of the court officials stepped into the hallway and returned a few moments later escorting Father Sergey. His dark clerical robes swallowed his thin frame. A long white beard reached halfway down his chest, and a gold cross peeked out from beneath it. His round black hat perched upon his head, making him look like an inverted exclamation point. The poor man looked exhausted, and his face was nearly as pale as his beard. Antonia's heart went out to him. He must be in his mid-eighties, and today, every year seemed to weigh heavily upon him.

Father Sergey scanned the room, but when his gaze locked on Antonia's, he paused and stared at her as if trying to convey a silent question. She knew what he wanted from her—confirmation that she'd seen the burn. But she hadn't. She shifted her shoulders noncommittally, letting him know she still didn't know.

The lack of confirmation hit him hard, but he didn't look defeated. He looked angry. The priest faltered slightly as he gritted his teeth. The last vestiges of color drained from his face as he halted and turned to face Walter Winter. Disgust flashed in his eyes. Then his baleful gaze seemed to blaze with anger and he threw off the assisting arm of his escort, lifted his chin, and walked the remainder of the way into the courtroom alone.

Antonia glanced at her uncle—or rather, at Walter Winter, since he'd denied their relationship so vehemently. He seemed taken aback. In fact, the man looked genuinely terrified. He began tugging frantically at Mr. Parish's sleeve. The barrister leaned closer to his client to hear what the squire had to say.

"Thank you for being here, Father Sergey," Montlake said in low tones as the elderly man came to a halt next to him.

"Your witness is a priest?" the judge asked, breaking some of the growing tension in the courtroom.

Mr. Parish straightened and shot Father Sergey an irritated look.

"Yes, my lord," Montlake replied. "He officiated at the late Squire Winter's wedding and can attest to the date of the ceremony."

Antonia glanced over at her uncle and his lawyer. The two men were whispering furiously, and they kept glancing at Father Sergey. Mr. Parish finally moved his hand in a quelling gesture to silence his client. Based on the way Walter kept glancing at the door, Antonia wondered if he might try to bolt.

The judge surveyed the elderly priest from head to toe, and Antonia followed his gaze. Father Sergey didn't look well. She'd noticed he'd seemed frail when they'd first met a couple of weeks ago, but he had a keen intelligence and a clever mind. Now as she watched him, she noticed a tremor. The shock of being in the presence of his wife's murderer seemed to have taken a greater toll than she'd anticipated.

Lord Tidmore pinned the priest with a sharp gaze. "Can you tell me what year this is?"

Father Sergey pulled his gaze away from Walter Winter to glare at the judge. "What kind of question is that?" he demanded in a thick Russian accent. "Are you saying I'm—I'm—" he glanced around the courtroom as if looking for help. "What is word for *ne kompetenten?*"

"Incompetent," Frederick offered.

"*Da.*" Father Sergey nodded. "Are you thinking I am incompetent?"

"I need to make that determination before I allow you to speak in my court," Lord Tidmore replied. "Please answer the question."

Father Sergey pressed his lips together like a recalcitrant child, but then answered. "The current year is 1854."

Lord Tidmore nodded. "And I believe you're here to give testimony regarding a wedding you performed. Is that correct?"

"*Da* . Anya Nevsky came back to village so her father could be at ceremony. It meant much to him."

"And in what year did the wedding take place?"

"1832."

"How can you be so certain?"

"Do you think I marry local girl to Englishman every day? Of course I remember. It was momentous event."

"I don't doubt that you remember the event," Lord Tidmore said. "It's your recollection of the precise year that concerns me. Do you have any evidence to support your claim?"

"My church register. You have it in front of you. What more proof do you need?"

"The book's been damaged," Lord Tidmore said, holding the church register up so that Father Sergey could see it. "The edges of the pages are stained, and the last digit of the year was destroyed." He set the book to one side. "Establishing the date when the wedding took place is essential. Are you quite certain about the year?"

Father Sergey shot Walter Winter a scathing look. "If book is damaged, I can tell you who is culprit."

"I must protest, Your Honor," Mr. Parish interrupted. "How the book was damaged is not relevant to our current discussion. What most concerns me is Father Sergey's obvious friendship with Miss Winter. Of course he'll support her claim."

"Yes, Mr. Parish," the judge replied. "I am aware that the witness could be biased. But Father Sergey is, after all, a priest. We can offer quite a bit more faith in the veracity of his testimony."

Mr. Parish glanced at his nervous client, frowned, and then scrubbed his hand down his face. "What if his memory is faulty? I suggest that you ask him about another event that took place during the same year. Can he remember something else from 1832?"

"Now, *that* is an excellent idea." The judge looked surprised to hear such a thing come from Mr. Parish and gave him an approving nod before facing the priest. "We turn to you then, Father. Can you mention some other event recorded in your register that year?"

Father Sergey frowned. "I remember event. It sticks in my memory. But—" he paused as he seemed to think back, "there was child born to different family not long after wedding—but which one?" He slid his hand down his white beard. "If you check page where I recorded births, you should find boy listed. Vanechka Brechkovsky. He was born same summer as wedding."

The judge flipped through the leather-bound book until he found the page he was looking for. "Here it is. Hmm. No. It appears that Vanechka Brechkovsky was born in 1831."

"Ah. I make mistake. I remember now. It was Grigori Filischkin who was born after wedding, not Vanechka Brechkovsky."

"Or were you wrong about the year?" The judge peered at him.

Father Sergey's mouth tightened. "It was 1832. I know this for fact." "

Quite a lot depends on the exact year. Is it possible you've made a mistake?"

"*Nyet,*" he said, glaring at Walter Winter. "No mistake. I remember date. It sticks in mind, like granite carving."

Father Sergey looked so very pale. A strong breeze could knock him off his feet. As she watched, she noticed him lift a shaking hand to grab the nearby railing for support.

"Is Father Sergey permitted to sit?" Antonia asked.

Lord Tidmore glared at her for speaking in court, but then he turned his gaze to Father Sergey. His eyes narrowed as he peered at the elderly man. "I think that would be wise. In fact," he said, glancing at the young man who'd escorted Father Sergey into the room, "you need to bring him a chair as quickly as possible."

The young man rushed to drag a chair across the room. When Antonia glanced back at Father Sergey, she saw he was leaning precariously to one side as he braced himself on the nearby railing. He wobbled slightly, but before she could react, Robert stepped forward and wrapped his arm around the elderly man's waist. The clerk arrived with the chair, and Robert helped Father Sergey lower himself into it.

Mr. Parish took a step forward. "This might sound insensitive, but it's quite obvious that Father Sergey is incapable of—"

"If you don't wish to sound insensitive," Mr. Montlake interrupted, "I suggest you stop talking."

Antonia knelt next to Father Sergey to peer into his face. He was much too pale. She placed her hand on his paper-thin cheek and was surprised to find it cooler than she expected. "Would you like some water?"

He nodded. "Am thirsty."

She glanced up at Robert, and he turned to the nearby table and sloshed water into a cup. After he handed it to her, she held it up to Father Sergey's lips. He wrapped his hand around hers and took a small sip, then another.

Was a bit of color seeping back into is face? "Are you feeling better?" Antonia asked.

Father Sergey waved away her question. "I do not know what happened. I am not normally so weak. Maybe I am tired from lack of sleep."

Antonia glared at Lord Tidmore. How could he have been so thoughtless as to wake an octogenarian priest in the middle of the night?

He returned her glare with a level one of his own, and after a moment Antonia had to drop her gaze. How could she place the blame on Lord Tidmore's shoulders when they were assembled here for her benefit?

The judge's stern expression softened as he again focused on Father Sergey. "Perhaps you should rest. We're done with your testimony for now. I'll call you back if we need you again. You can rest in a room down the hallway. My clerk will escort you."

Antonia leaned closer and spoke so only Father Sergey could hear her. "I promise, we'll see justice done. We have a plan, and your testimony has been an important part of it." Father Sergey's head wobbled slightly, and it took a moment for Antonia to realize he was nodding.

The young escort hurried forward, and his vigor made Father Sergey seem even older in comparison. The muscular arm the younger man offered appeared twice the size of Father Sergey's.

After staring at the proffered arm for a moment, Father Sergey wrapped his through it. "*Spasibo*," he said, thanking the man. He leaned heavily on the clerk as they made their way to the door.

The entire courtroom remained silent as they watched. Father Sergey's shoulders were slumped in a defeated posture. What would it be like to face your enemy so late in life and then to be forced from the field of battle not by him, but by your own infirmity?

Walter Winter would pay for what he'd done. And pay publicly.

Once the door closed, Mr. Parish wasted no time in continuing his argument. "Your Honor, since Father Sergey is no longer in the room, I'd like to point out that his testimony was faulty and inconsistent. I don't think he can be relied upon regarding the date of the wedding."

"I'm afraid I must agree with you." Lord Tidmore inhaled deeply and let out a sigh. He surveyed the room and then locked gazes with Antonia.

"It appears we need to provide additional evidence," Mr. Montlake said.

"I must object," Mr. Parish said. "The court shouldn't be

expected to allow you to submit an unsubstantiated item as your 'evidence.' Given its poor condition, the church register was highly suspect. Since Lord Tidmore has already stated he must come to a decision by the end of today's session, I see no need to waste the court's time with additional delays."

"Is justice to be rushed?" Mr. Montlake stepped forward, pushing past Mr. Parish as he addressed Lord Tidmore. "Are these women expected to graciously and silently set aside their claim simply because Mr. Parish wants to hasten the court's decision before all the facts have been considered?"

"There's no need to be melodramatic, Mr. Montlake," Lord Tidmore said, frowning at him. "Rest assured that the court will consider all of the evidence before making a decision."

Mr. Parish harrumphed, but then seemed to think better of it and tried to pretend that he'd been clearing his throat.

Montlake shot Antonia a satisfied smile. "Thank you, Your Honor. I'd like to assure everyone that I do not intend to bring in any additional evidence at the moment. Everything we need is already in this room."

$\mathbf{\$}$ 45 $\mathbf{\$}$

Laws should be interpreted in a liberal sense so that their intention may be preserved.

— *MARCUS TULLIUS CICERO*

Antonia leaned forward in anticipation as her heart pounded in her throat.

"Could two gentlemen offer me some assistance?" The spring in Mr. Montlake's step betrayed his eagerness as he crossed the courtroom toward the painting.

Robert and Frederick stepped forward, and at Mr. Montlake's gesture, they moved to stand on either side of the painting.

"Please be so kind as to put on these white cotton gloves," Mr. Montlake said. "As I mentioned to Mr. Winter, the trace oils on your leather gloves can damage the gilt frame."

Robert and Frederick both tugged off their kid gloves and tucked them into the pockets of their frock coats before donning the white ones.

Once they turned to face Mr. Montlake, he nodded his approval. "I'd like you to turn the painting around so everyone can view the back."

Robert and Frederick lifted the heavy piece of framed artwork from the easel and stepped forward until they had cleared the stand.

"Be careful," Walter Winter admonished.

In what looked like a precisely choreographed dance, the brothers rotated places so that the back of the painting faced the room. They gently placed it back on the easel and stepped back.

"That's perfect," Mr. Montlake said. "Thank you, gentlemen."

The ivory muslin covering the back of the painting was marred only by a small, six-inch-long horizontal tear at the very top. Other than that, it looked perfect.

Just as Antonia remembered.

Robert's brow furrowed, and he shot a sharp glance toward Antonia.

Why? Oh, of course. He'd never before seen the back of the painting. She should have warned him about the covering. He must have expected to see the dedication to her parents as soon as he turned it over.

She gave him a very slight nod, hoping that would be enough to reassure him.

Apparently it was, because his forehead smoothed and he gave the slightest of nods in reply.

He trusted her.

"Squire Winter, I notice a mark or a tear on the back covering of the painting. Has that always been there?" Lord Tidmore asked.

Mr. Winter nodded. "I believe so. I noticed it when we took it down from the wall this morning."

"And do paintings normally have this sort of backing? I don't recall ever seeing something like this before."

"I wouldn't know, my lord," Walter Winter said.

"If I may, my lord?" Antonia said.

He turned his attention to her. "Yes, Miss Winter? Do you have something to add?"

"When I was about ten years old, I recall my father tacking that piece of fabric on the back of the painting. He didn't explain why, but he seemed secretive about it. At the time, I suspected that he might be hiding something in the space between the fabric and the back of the canvas."

Judge Tidwell's face brightened with interest. "Could whatever was there have been removed through that slit at the top?"

Antonia shrugged. "I'm not even certain that anything ever was hidden there. It's simply that he seemed secretive when I walked into his study without knocking."

Walter watched her intently as she spoke, his eyes bright with interest. Was he hoping to find something valuable hidden in there? He glanced at the tear in the muslin. "Perhaps we should investigate. After all, the fabric was added after the fact and has no value on its own."

"The court agrees, but before you proceed, can you examine the covering carefully? Does it appear to have been tampered with?"

Walter Winter, Mr. Parrish, and Mr. Montlake all moved closer to inspect the back of the painting. After a few moments, the three men conferred. Mr. Parrish then turned to face Lord Tidmore. "We've examined the fabric and the tacks holding it in place. We cannot find any sign of tampering. The tacks all appear to be identical and are uniformly tarnished with age."

"Then you are satisfied it hasn't been removed since it was added by the late Squire Winter?"

"Yes, my lord. We are."

"In that case, your client may remove the covering."

Walter licked his lips as he approached the easel. He reached up and began tugging at the slit, trying to widen it.

The painting wobbled on the easel, but both Robert and Frederick quickly grabbed the frame to steady it. Walter hardly seemed aware of their assistance, so intent was he on the widening hole in the fabric. The small tacks popped off the edge of the fabric, stuttering to the wood floor in a clattering spray of metal.

Antonia held her breath as she tried to catch sight of the written dedication on the back. Had she glimpsed the edge of it? That wispy bit of dark-brown paint?

Walter gave a stronger tug, tearing away a large swath of the muslin in one jerk.

Intent on his goal, Walter remained completely unaware of the moment when everyone else's attention became fixed on the words written on the back of the painting rather than on him. Something else caught his attention. His hand darted forward to snatch the small item he had revealed.

He extracted a sheaf of papers, but before he could examine them, Mr. Montlake extracted them from his grasp.

"That's mine," Walter said, shooting the judge a furious glance.

"Yes, Squire Winter," the judge said. "We are all in agreement that anything found hidden in the painting is yours. But you seem to be under the misconception that you should be able to examine it before I can. Allow me to disabuse you of that notion. This is my courtroom."

Walter reddened, but he didn't protest as Mr. Montlake carried the sheaf of papers to the judge.

Lord Tidmore glanced through the papers, pursing his lips. Then he shook his head and glanced up at Antonia. "It would appear your father had a romantic nature. These appear to be letters he and your mother exchanged. If Squire Winter has no objection, I believe they should rightfully go to you and your sisters."

"I do object. They're mine, as is everything else in that house."

The judge's lips narrowed, but he passed the letters back to the clerk, who then carried them back to Walter.

As he took possession of the letters, he shot Antonia a look of pure malice.

When would Walter notice what had been revealed on the back of the painting? The tattered bits of muslin dangled below the bottom of the gilt frame, like remnants of a torn dress. But Walter Winter was too busy gloating to bother to look at it.

Lord Tidmore glanced at the back of the painting and then widened his eyes in surprise. "Squire Winter, you seem to have uncovered more than we expected when you removed that piece of muslin."

Walter Winter turned to follow the judge's gaze. Antonia had already read the words. They were now burned into her mind. She watched as her uncle began to read them and relished the look of shock and dismay that flashed across his face.

Because it read: *"To my daughter, Anya Nevsky, in celebration of her wedding to Marcus Winter on July 7, 1832. May love always nourish and sustain you. Your loving father, Vladamir Nevsky."*

"It appears that we've found your proof," Lord Tidmore said to Antonia.

"I don't understand," Uncle Walter blurted. "How is this proof? You can't possibly believe this scrawl is proof."

"Of course I can. You've already stated that this painting has been in your possession until this morning and that it hasn't been altered."

"She did it," Uncle Walter said, turning to point an accusing finger at Antonia. "I don't know how, but she did. She added that dedication. I'm certain of it."

"But how, Mr. Winter? And when? You examined the covering and determined it hadn't been tampered with." The judge shook his head. "Are you now suggesting that Miss Winter added the dedication a decade ago, before she even knew her legitimacy was in question?"

Her uncle's expression turned petulant. "It had to have been last week. One of my servants let her into the house. She stole that church register while she was there. She could have altered the painting as well."

The judge leaned forward, peering at Walter intently. "Excuse me, Mr. Winter, but are you telling me that Miss Winter stole this"—he held the book up—"from your home? That's a very serious accusation."

Walter nodded so vigorously that the skin on his neck wobbled. "Yes. The cook let her in. That Antonia is a conniving one, she is."

"And how is it, *Mr.* Winter, that Father Sergey's church register was in your possession?"

Walter went still. Antonia could swear that he stopped breathing as he realized what he'd just revealed.

"Perhaps we should ask Father Sergey to rejoin us. I believe he mentioned Mr. Winter would know why the book was damaged. I'd like to hear more."

At the judge's gesture, the helpful young clerk left the room and returned moments later with Father Sergey. The elderly man looked much improved. Some color was back in his cheeks, and his step seemed more confident as he rejoined them.

"Father Sergey," the judge said, "can you tell the court what you know about how this book came to be in the possession of Mr. Winter?"

"Book was stolen from church." His thickly accented voice boomed in the courtroom, and Antonia imagined him speaking before his congregation, holding their attention with his intense force of will. "Man who stole book also killed my wife. My Magda." He paused as the intense pain of her loss flickered over his lined face. "Man set fire to church, beat my poor Magda sense-less, and left her to die."

Other than the small gasp of horror from Evalina, the court-room was silent.

Still.

Lord Tidmore frowned deeply and then glanced meaningfully at the young clerk who immediately ducked out the door.

"Doctor from nearby village helped man with bad burn on hand and arm," Father Sergey continued. "When soldiers questioned doctor, he told them about this man. Said he carried book that seemed—what is word?" He mumbled something in Russian.

"Precious," Lord Tidmore translated for him.

"Yes. *Precious*. That was word. Doctor said book seemed precious to this man. It had cross on cover, like this book. He would not let anyone touch it, even when doctor bandaged his hand. But this man, he disappeared during the night. Soldiers never found him."

"How do you know who stole it?" Mr. Montlake asked. "Did you ever see the man?"

"Yes. Before fire, man came to me. He wanted me to destroy book, but I said no. Man tried to give me money," he said, indignant. "Still, I said no. It was long ago and man had thick beard, but I will always remember his eyes." He raised both hands, touching the sides of his own eyes with his first two fingers. "Unusual eyes the color of cognac." He turned to look at Walter and pointed at him, his arm strong and straight. "Your eyes. It was you. I would know you anywhere. You are man who stole book, burned church, and murdered my Magda. You are man who ruined my life."

With a look of panic in his distinctive cognac-colored eyes, Walter sprang for the aisle in an attempt to run toward the door. Antonia was so surprised she froze, but Robert didn't suffer from the same reaction. He immediately began to move.

He rushed after Walter and grabbed his arm, yanking him to a halt. The courtroom doors flew open, and the young clerk who'd slipped away moments ago now pushed into the room flanked by two burly-looking guards. They bore down on Walter, quickly subduing him.

"Have him stand with Mr. Parish," Lord Tidmore said.

The three large men herded Uncle Walter back to his place next to his lawyer.

"Running, Mr. Winter, strikes me as an admission of guilt," the judge said, glowering at him.

Mr. Winter trembled, shaking his head from side to side, but he didn't utter a word.

"Check hand," Father Sergey said. "Man who set fire has burn on hand and up to elbow. Bad burn."

At the judge's nod, the young clerk took Walter by the arm. He tried to pull away, but the clerk ignored him and pushed up Walter's sleeve, revealing the shiny, puckered skin. It was smooth and lumpy, like melted wax. Walter tried to yank free from the younger man's grasp but couldn't.

Lord Tidmore looked thunderous. "This is Chancery Court, not Criminal Court, and therefore we cannot try you here for your crimes. I can, however, hold you in custody until that time when you can be made accountable."

Antonia's knees went weak, and she clutched at Robert's arm for support. The judge continued to speak, stating that he'd seen adequate proof of her parents' marriage and declaring the three daughters as their legitimate heirs.

She reveled in her uncle's dumbfounded expression.

They'd done it.

They'd actually won.

❦ 46 ❦

Make haste! The tide of Fortune soon ebbs.

— *SILIUS ITALICUS*

Robert wanted to shout in triumph as Lord Tidmore ruled in Antonia's favor. Her glowing, jubilant smile warmed his soul.

He'd known she'd win, and she had. She and her sisters could finally go home. A feeling of rightness with the world swept over him. Their plans were coming to fruition.

At least, the first step had.

He wanted nothing more than to take her into his arms, but he couldn't. He could only stand by her side as she and her sisters basked in their triumph.

Frederick took Robert by the arm. With reluctance, he allowed himself to be pulled him to one side.

"Collect the book," Frederick murmured. "Keep it safe. My

meeting should take a couple of hours, and by then I'll know the best course to follow regarding the—other situation."

"Shouldn't the book take precedence?"

Frederick looked grim. "I can't be in two places at once. The man I must confide in is leaving London today, and if I don't speak to him now, I'll have to wait a fortnight. I don't want the other matter to linger." He appeared to think for a moment, and then moved closer. "Deliver the book to Queen Victoria, without delay. I wouldn't want her to suspect we postponed doing so any longer than absolutely necessary."

Robert's unease began pricking at him, but Frederick was right. They'd delayed too long already. He needed to give her the book and be done with it. It would be a relief to be rid of it.

Frederick swept him with an assessing glance. He seemed to like what he saw because he gave a sharp nod, turned, and hurried out the door.

A few moments later, Robert joined Mr. Montlake and the three sisters in an empty room down the hall from the courtroom.

Robert moved to stand next to Antonia and placed his hand on her waist. He might have been in close proximity to her over the past few hours, but there'd been few opportunities to touch her.

He wanted her close.

Strike that. He wanted her in his bed.

She seemed content to stand next to him. In fact, now she leaned into him slightly. Robert wanted nothing more than to pull her into his arms and give her a kiss that would curl her toes. But he couldn't. Not here. Not now.

Mr. Montlake sorted through some court documents and seemed to notice the restlessness of everyone in the room. "You can sit in here while your carriage is brought around."

"Sit?" Stephanie retorted. "How could I possibly sit? I'm much too excited." She grinned as she began pacing the room. She appeared to vibrate with elation. "You did it," she told Mr. Mont-lake as she whirled to face him. "I can hardly believe it."

"I know," Evalina added. Even she couldn't keep her normally stoic expression serene. "I dreamed of this for so long, it hardly seems real. I do hope—"

"But wait," Stephanie interrupted. Her eyes widened as she grabbed hold of Antonia's upper arm, dragging her away from Robert. "This means we can return to our home in Maidenhead immediately, doesn't it? Could we go there today?"

Antonia blinked in bemusement. "I suppose so. Mr. Montlake, can we?"

He nodded. "I don't see why not. The house is yours, after all. Just as it should have been all along. You might want to stay here in London one more day and make plans. Some of the other prop-erty might still be in question, since your uncle should have inher-ited his share when your grandfather died, but the house was solely your father's. Everything your mother inherited from your grandfather is yours as well."

"We're wealthy again?" Evalina asked. "No more living at the school?"

"No more hiding in shame?" Stephanie added.

"I wish we could undo everything that happened to you over the past year," Mr. Montlake said. "It's a travesty that your lives unraveled based on your uncle's lies. He was clever."

"Not clever enough," Stephanie said.

"If not for the painting's dedication—" Mr. Montlake shook his head. "But that's behind you now. I think your sister is right. Take a day to prepare for your homecoming. Tomorrow you can return to Maidenhead in triumph. Your uncle will be the one forced to hang his head in shame from this moment on."

"Until he's hanged for murder," Robert added, glancing at Antonia to watch her reaction. She didn't seem surprised by his comment. Apparently she'd already reached the same conclusion.

"Did he really kill Father Sergey's wife?" Evalina asked, sounding both frightened and fascinated.

"It certainly appears that way," Antonia said.

"He always intimidated me," Evalina said. "Those eyes—so filled with anger." She gave a shudder.

"Let's not think of him," Stephanie said. "Let's think of our future and of Maidenhead."

The girls began making plans to return home, so Robert pulled Antonia to one side to speak with her. "I need to retrieve the book from Lord Tidmore," he said. "It's imperative that I deliver it to the Queen without delay."

Antonia nodded. "I'll join you. I want to thank him for expediting our case."

They made their way through the courthouse to a dark-paneled waiting area outside the judge's chambers. A servant carried their message to Lord Tidmore. They barely had time to take their seats before the judge swept into the room and they rose to their feet again.

Lord Tidmore no longer wore the white wig or blackrobes of his office. He looked more human in a frock coat, and his intimidating aura had all but disappeared. "Miss Winter," he said, smiling at her. "I'm so glad the evidence supported your claim. A grave injustice was done to you and your sisters. I only hope my decision will help mitigate the damage."

"Thank you. I never imagined things would be resolved so quickly."

"Although many of the Chancery Court's cases linger for years, yours was a relatively straightforward one. With the substantial evidence you provided to prove your parents' marriage was legal along with the clear instructions of his last will, my decision was a simple one. It isn't often that I uncover the identity of a murderer in my courtroom. This is a case I'll remember for years to come." He took Antonia's hand. "Congratulations on regaining both your name and your inheritance, but you need to be aware that your uncle might still try to claim he should have inherited a portion of your grandfather's estate. I'm referring to your father's father. That is an altogether different matter and outside of today's ruling."

"I don't know if it will ever come to that," Antonia replied. "It's likely my uncle will be too busy defending himself against a murder charge."

He frowned. "We have yet to see how this ends. I only hope nothing bad comes from revealing that book's secrets. And on that note, I have something to give you." He reached into a voluminous pocket of his frock coat and plucked out the leather-bound volume.

"I hope you recognize how dangerous this book is," Lord Tidmore said, handing it to Antonia. "It may have solved your problems, Miss Winter, but it brought your uncle low. If I'm not mistaken, it contains secrets even more potent than the ones already revealed." His gaze darted toward Robert. "I quake at the thought of the trouble it would cause if it fell into the wrong hands."

Robert slid a protective arm around Antonia and moved closer to her. He didn't know how he'd do it, but he'd keep her safe. "You've read it?" Robert asked, raising his eyebrows. Lord

Tidmore sucked in his breath and held it for a moment. "I believe it would be wise to deny all knowledge of that book's contents."

"Agreed," Robert said.

"I only hope no one assumes I've read the entire thing." He looked grim. "I wish you both the best. I suggest you divest yourself of that dangerous item as quickly as possible." He gave them a slight nod and then excused himself to return to his chambers.

Antonia tightened her grip on the volume, staring down at the cross on the cover. "This book is quite the mischief maker," she muttered. With a sigh, she opened her reticule and slipped the book inside it.

Lord Tidmore's warnings resonated. Robert glanced around them, searching for any potential threat. Tidmore was right. They wouldn't be safe until they'd rid themselves of the church register. He came to a quick decision.

"Let's leave immediately," Robert said, taking her by the elbow and hurrying her toward the main entrance of the courthouse.

"What about my sisters and Mr. Montlake?"

"They can take my carriage while we hire a cab. If we leave quickly, no one will be able to follow us. The sooner this is out of our hands, the better. We'll take it directly to Queen Victoria."

"The Queen?" Antonia repeated, stumbling. Robert steadied her. "Don't you mean you'll deliver it to someone at the palace?"

"Her Majesty doesn't want any intermediaries involved. The book is too precious. Entrusting it to anyone else would be extraordinarily foolish."

Robert paused at a desk and quickly scribbled out a note explaining their sudden departure and then handed it to one of the footmen at the entrance. "Please deliver this to Mr. Montlake," he told the young man as he handed him the folded paper. "You'll find him in the room next to Lord Tidmore's courtroom." The footman nodded and hurried off to complete his task.

The first carriage available for hire happened to be a clarence. With its closed interior, it would be more discreet than an open hansom. Robert hurried Antonia inside before anyone else could claim it.

It wasn't until Robert closed the door behind them and they started moving toward the palace that she finally spoke again. "I'll wait in the carriage while you deliver the book."

He grinned in response. He couldn't resist kissing the corner of her mouth. "Is my intrepid young thespian afraid of the Queen?"

Antonia blushed at his kiss, even as she huffed her irritation. "Do be sensible. You can't introduce someone like me to Queen Victoria. I'm an actress. A nobody. And she's the monarch of the

United Kingdom of Great Britain and Ireland. She's the most powerful person in the world."

"You underestimate yourself. You're the daughter of a squire, the granddaughter of Vladamir Nevsky, and an amazing woman in your own right. Don't forget, you're also the niece of the Czar of Russia. That's no small thing."

Antonia paled and then pulled her lower lip between her teeth. "That's the real problem. That's why this book is so dangerous." She tugged at the strings of her reticule and then extracted the church register. She frowned as she handed it to him. "Can't you deliver this to the Queen without me?"

He wrapped his arm around her, pulling her close and pressing a kiss to the top of her head. As he took the book, all his lingering good humor faded. He fell silent, letting the volume fall open in his hands. Either by design or frequent use, the pages which caused the most consternation were the ones to which the book always opened of its own accord.

Antonia burrowed against him, trusting him. Trusting that he'd help her.

He wanted to be deserving of her faith. "I want to protect you, but how can I?" His words were muffled because his lips were still pressed against her hair. "As long as this book is in the world, it poses a threat."

He closed his eyes, hoping to envision a solution, but all he saw was darkness. There was no clear path forward. Not as long as the book could reveal Antonia's relationship to the czar. He opened his eyes and shook his head as he stared down at the odious volume. "Perhaps I should simply destroy it," he said, tightening his grip on the cover. "I can't think of another way to keep you safe."

"No. Please don't." Antonia jerked back and clutched at his hand, causing him to ease his grip on the leather-bound book. "That would be treason. I can't let you betray England to protect me. We need to find another way." Robert sighed.

"I can't think of one."

She took a deep breath and then shook her head in frustration. "Perhaps if we examine the book we'll find something. A solution."

"If that were possible, Frederick would already have found it."

"Let's try. Can you tell me what it says?"

Robert removed his arm from her shoulders as he glanced down at the open book. He smoothed his hand over the pages. Although he could still recall a smattering of Russian, translating it would normally have been beyond his abilities. Fortunately, Frederick had explained the translation to him, and Robert remembered most of it. Robert dragged his finger down the left side of the page. "This is where Father Sergey recorded your uncle's birth along with his mother's death," he said, pointing to a spot halfway down the page. "And this is where he mentions the arrival of the czar's entourage, including Czaritsa Maria and their infant son," he said, pointing to the bottom of the page. "Maybe he decided to record their arrival because so many of them died while in the village."

He dragged his finger along the last line, squinting down at scribblings of ink. "Here is the infant's name. Nikolai Pavlovich, third son of Czar Paul," he muttered, sliding his finger to the top of the next page, "and here's where Father Sergey recorded the date of his death. A number of other deaths are listed here as well. The illness that struck must have been a terrible one."

"What a tragedy. Grandfather's entire village must have been affected. Everyone must have lost someone close to them." Antonia leaned closer as she peered down at the page, and he caught the fresh scent of her soap and saw the flash of pale skin at the back of her neck below her upswept hair. "Where does he mention my uncle's adoption?"

"Here." Robert flipped the page. "The entry is slightly cryptic. Frederick had to explain it to me, otherwise I never would have understood what I was reading. Father Sergey writes that the motherless child was adopted by the childless mother. He doesn't list their names, but it's obvious to whom he's referring. Especially since Czaritsa Maria was often referred to as the childless mother."

"Because Catherine the Great took each of her children from her? Poor Maria. I feel sorry for her. How could her mother-in-law have been so heartless?"

"Stop that carriage!" a man shouted. Robert felt their carriage slowing, followed by an angry shout from their coachman. The carriage lurched as the horses surged forward, but then the carriage slowed again.

Something was very wrong.

He leaned forward, peering out the window. More horses clattered up, and people on the street began shouting in protest to the disruption.

Robert closed the book, bookmarking it with his finger as he leaned closer to the window to assess the situation.

A group of horsemen surrounded them. Robert recognized many of the Russian riders. Their eyes were hard and determined. Today they weren't pretending to be footmen—they were soldiers —trained and deadly.

They must want the book. Did they plan to kidnap Antonia as well? They couldn't be that reckless.

They forced the carriage driver to pull to a stop. A moment later, someone yanked open the door closest to Antonia.

A pale-skinned, black-haired man jumped onto the step and stood silhouetted in the doorway. His broad shoulders blocked most of the sunlight, but Robert immediately recognized Davydov—one of the Russians who'd hunted them beneath the theater.

Davydov's gaze darted around the carriage until it fixed on the reticule Antonia clutched. He lunged for it, and Antonia immediately let go.

The Russian hesitated, seemingly thrown off by her willingness to let him take her bag. He suddenly lunged forward again, surprising Robert by seizing Antonia's forearm and dragging her from the carriage. Robert made a grab for her, but she slipped away.

Robert stumbled onto the street, the book still clutched in his hand. Davydov shoved Antonia toward his cohorts. They twisted her arms behind her back as Davydov whirled to face Robert.

Davydov stood between Robert and Antonia, his black hair disheveled from the tussle. He kept his gaze fixed on Robert, and then he spied the book Robert held—his prize.

He threw Antonia's reticule to the ground where it landed with a splash in a grimy puddle of melting snow.

A crowd gathered around them. Apparently no one wanted to interfere. Some of the men grinned at one another. It was as though they were all watching a juggling show or a street performance. These weren't gentlemen. They were laborers and shopkeepers. Workmen and stevedores. Men who were curious about the goings-on of the gentry, but would avoid getting involved.

"Hand over the book," Davydov demanded. "If you do, my men will release her."

"You're bluffing." Robert narrowed his eyes. "You won't hurt Miss Winter. She's too important to the ambassador. The czar would have your heads if anything happened to her. Let her go." Robert wasn't certain his words were true, but nevertheless he imbued them with confidence and scorn.

"That does not mean we will give her to *you*." Davydov turned and jerked his chin toward of one of the men holding Antonia and he began to drag her away.

Antonia struggled. "No. You can't do this. I'm a British citizen."

Some of the men in the crowd began to shift their feet, and one of them yelled something indistinguishable.

"*Bystro*," Davydov shouted, urging the soldier to hurry.

"Wot's that jabber?" a man yelled in an angry tone. "Them

blokes is Russian. We don't want no foreigners comin' 'ere an' stealing our women off the streets."

The irate crowd surged forward, swarming around the soldiers. Davydov glanced back, but he'd already been cut off from his men. Antonia's small form disappeared in the chaos.

Robert barely noticed Davydov turn to face him. Where was Antonia? He couldn't see her. She'd been swallowed up by a sea of brawling men.

Then he caught a flash of a shiny bit of silver down low, near the cobblestone street. He spotted Antonia leaning over and plucking a small item from her boot. It glinted in the winter sunlight. Her knife? It had to be.

Only one man still held Antonia. The others were defending themselves from angry Londoners. Fists thudded into flesh and men grunted in pain. The remaining soldier holding Antonia tried to yank her upright as he pulled her out of the throng and toward Davydov. She stumbled forward, and as she pulled away she jabbed at the soldier's hand with her blade. It sank into his flesh, and her captor let out a loud yelp.

Antonia broke free, sidestepping the man as she darted toward Robert.

"I want that book!" Davydov yelled. "It belongs to the Russian government."

"It belongs to Father Sergey." Robert risked a glance at Antonia. Her gaze was calm and steady, and he fumbled as he enfolded her small hand in his.

"No," Davydov said in a tone that offered no compromise. "It belongs to Czar Nicholas and to Russia."

Antonia lurched toward the carriage, pulling her hand free. Was she reaching inside? She spun back, brandishing his cane. She presented the handle to him. He gave her a sharp grin as he grabbed hold of it and withdrew the blade.

The Russian who'd been holding Antonia abruptly barreled toward Robert, his gaze fixed on the church register. But then the man's eyes widened as he caught sight of the épée. Even so, he didn't attempt to change course as he hurled himself toward his goal—the book.

Robert lifted the tip of the blade to point at the man's chest, but the Russian didn't swerve as he continued his charge.

The slender tip of the blade slipped between the soldier's ribs, and at least two inches of the steel disappeared within his flesh before Robert felt its edge catch on something—a rib perhaps. The man came to an abrupt halt.

The Russian's eyes widened as he stared down at the circle of red blossoming on the left side of his white shirt. The blade pulled free as he dropped to his knees and collapsed face-first into the dirty London street.

Stunned, Robert took a step back, then another. He didn't think he'd killed the man, but the wound was a serious one. He'd probably punctured his lung.

Davydov let out a roar of anger and dove forward. Before Robert could react, Davydov knocked him to the ground. He slammed his fist into the side of Robert's head and yanked the book from his hands.

"No!" Robert yelled. He quickly climbed to his feet.

Antonia tugged on his arm, trying to pull him to his feet. "Let it go. We need to leave," she pleaded. "Hurry." She began pulling him toward the still-open door of the carriage.

It was only then that Robert realized the mob had been driven away and Davydov's soldiers were now staring at their fallen comrade.

They looked momentarily stunned, but for how long?

As Robert climbed into the carriage, he glanced over his shoulder to see the soldiers' attention shift to him. Davydov waved the book he'd recovered, but then he became aware of the soldier lying on the ground, his blood pooling around his body. Davydov's face contorted with rage. He and the others began lurching toward the carriage, stiff at first, and then faster. Faster. Their eyes were filled with fury and retribution.

"Go!" Robert shouted to the driver. The vehicle lurched forward, throwing the unlatched door wide open. As Robert stretched his arm outside the carriage to grab the flapping door and close it, the nearest man giving chase lunged forward and barely missed grabbing hold of the door handle. Through the window of the carriage, Robert locked gazes with the man.

Davydov.

He'd made an enemy.

⁂ 47 ⁂

— CHARLES DUDLEY WARNER

Antonia gripped the edge of the seat as the carriage rocked to a halt in front of Robert's house. Numbness spread through her. She still couldn't quite assimilate the fact that they'd lost the book after everything Robert had done to help her. It seemed absurd.

Absurd but true.

Robert held his silver-headed cane in a fierce grip as he exited the carriage. He reached up to help Antonia. As soon as her feet were on the ground, he turned and flung open the door of his home, the knob slipping from his grasp so that the door bounced forcefully against the wall. Antonia quietly closed it and then hurried to follow him down the hallway.

Robert stormed past Landon, who appeared nonplussed by

the display, and then burst into the study. Antonia followed him into the room, but Landon paused at the doorway as though not quite certain if he should enter.

Antonia helped him with his choice by removing her hat and holding it out for him to take. He swallowed and then stepped forward, taking the hat and then assisting her with her coat.

Robert tossed his cane on the desk with a clatter and began shedding his outer garments with jerky movements. He shoved them toward Landon and then nodded a dismissal. Landon immediately scurried from the room.

Antonia surveyed the room. Little had changed since she'd last been there. Was that chess set a new addition? Perhaps not. The game appeared to be in progress—or perhaps abandoned.

A statue, or rather a bust of Apollo, seemed to stare at her in a smug and superior fashion from its perch on a pedestal across the room. Apollo's cool gaze seemed to arrogantly dismiss the folly of mere mortals, so she stuck her tongue out at him in a fit of pique. She didn't need some ancient statue glaring down its nose at her all night. Perhaps she should turn it on its pedestal to face the corner.

Robert moved stiffly across the room and then turned to retrace his steps. Judging by the rug, it happened frequently. He dragged his fingers through his dark hair, leaving it in disarray. She wanted to reach out and soothe him, but it wasn't the right time. He needed to burn off some of his anger, like a top spinning and careening off the walls until it spun itself down and toppled over.

How had the afternoon altered so dramatically? The judgment had finally gone her way in court today, but then their luck had deserted them. As if transmuted by an alchemist's spell gone awry, the golden day had turned into a dull, leaden one. The moment she'd begun to relax and believe that life might work out for someone like her, everything had upended. Again.

It was as though every bit of her bad luck from the past year had rolled itself into a sticky ball before seeking a new target. Unfortunately, the closest, most convenient one had been Robert.

This was all her fault. If not for the way she'd complicated his life, none of this would have happened. She rubbed her hands up and down her arms, trying to warm herself.

Her actions must have caught Robert's attention, because he stopped to stare at her. An instant later, he stepped closer and covered her hands with his. He was warm. So warm.

"You're freezing." He moved past her toward a chest and plucked a wool blanket from its depths.

She recognized the soft-brown blanket with the reddish-yellow flecks of color. Ocher, she thought, naming the color. Her half-naked body had been wrapped in its soft folds when Robert had carried her to her bed, and she'd developed a strong attachment to it. It had been missing from her room the next day, and she'd wondered where it had gone. One of the servants must have put it back where it belonged. Apparently, Antonia had disturbed the normal order of things.

Robert moved closer and reached around her to drape her in its woolen warmth. She might be disruptive, but Robert seemed to cherish her despite the complications she brought with her.

As the soft, richly-colored blanket enfolded her, a sense of rightness enveloped her. She belonged here with this man. He completed her. It was as though they were a matched set that had been separated long ago and had finally been reunited. He filled a spot in her soul that had remained empty for far too long.

Robert gathered the front of the blanket under her chin and she took hold of it so it wouldn't fall from her shoulders. He gently pulled free a strand of loose hair caught between her collar and the blanket, his fingers tracing along the sensitive skin under her ear. He brushed the hair away from her forehead and then leaned down to place a kiss there. His soft, warm lips lingered on her skin and he inhaled deeply, as though drawing her in and savoring her.

She leaned toward him, her body responding to him of its own accord. Her arms were pinned inside the blanket, but she managed to free one and slide her hand to his waist. As she touched his jacket, he stepped back, breaking contact with her.

Their gazes locked. "I should have anticipated they'd do something like that." He stopped and rubbed his hand down his face. "What if they'd harmed you?"

"I'm perfectly fine, as are you. The attack wasn't your doing, it was theirs. I'd never have imagined they'd have the audacity to attack us on a public street in London. And in broad daylight? It's nearly beyond belief. We must have been followed."

"Of course we were followed."

She stiffened at the irritation in his tone. But then she realized he was angry with himself, not her.

He began pacing again. "I shouldn't have let my intentions be so obvious. I'm sure they knew I was taking the book to the Queen."

"You couldn't have known they'd be so bold. So desperate."

"I should have. Frederick certainly would have predicted it. He trusted me, and I let him down again." Robert's voice was thick with self-reproach. "He always thinks seven steps ahead of everyone else." He glanced at the chess set with its pieces arranged in mid-game. He froze and then crossed the room, staring down at the chess board.

"Castling was what was called for, not charging into danger like an angry bull."

The image of the Russian soldier charging toward Robert's raised épée flashed though her mind. She shuddered at the vision and shook her head, pushing it away. "Castling?"

His gaze slid across her without stopping. "It's a chess move. You have your king swap places with the castle—rook—whatever you choose to call it. You can only do it if they haven't yet been moved."

"Are you saying you think the book should have traded places with something else?"

"Exactly. I should have used subterfuge. At the very least, I should have created a distraction. Remember how Frederick and Daniel made the watchers follow them yesterday? I should have known they hadn't given up."

"Surely you don't see yourself and your brother as a pair of Cassandras who can foretell the future," she chided.

His gaze finally fixed upon her rather than sliding over her. A faint smile pulled at the corner of his mouth. "Perhaps that would explain it. Perhaps I was cursed by the god Apollo." He glanced at the bust on the pedestal, and Antonia followed his gaze.

"I thought we'd planned for every contingency." He strode to his desk and stared down at the map of London spread on the gleaming wood surface. The map they'd used when planning the route they'd take to court this morning. Four ornate brass weights sat pressing down on the curling corners of the large sheet. Robert braced his rigid arms on the desk and glared at the criss-crossing squiggles and lines representing London. His fingers tightened until his knuckles turned white against his tanned skin. "Obviously we missed some things."

Antonia watched him silently as she took Apollo's cold marble head between her hands and turned him to face the wall. She glanced at Robert, but he was unaware of what she'd done. It was obvious he was angry with himself. Angry that he had failed his brother. His queen. His country.

Robert lashed out suddenly, ripping the map from his desk and sending the brass paperweights tumbling. The heavy bits of metal flew in arcs as he crushed the map into a ball. One piece flew in a particularly large arc and landed all the way across the room on top of the chess board. It clattered its way across the squares, knocking about the chessmen and sending them flying.

Antonia was speechless for a moment, but then she simply began collecting the brass paperweights from the rug.

"I'm sorry," Robert said. "I'll do that."

"We can both do it. Perhaps you can put the chessmen back on the board."

Robert began collecting the black and white pieces as Antonia placed the small weights in a neat row along the edge of his desk. She held the last trapezoidal bit of brass in her hand and slid her thumb back and forth over its smooth side. As she watched Robert, she realized he was putting the chessmen back exactly where they'd been positioned mid-game. At least, she thought they were on the same squares. She only remembered where the queen and the rook had been standing. She couldn't swear to the positions of the rest of the pieces. But the rook's position—that was something she knew with certainty.

"We still have time," she blurted out. "We can get it back."

Robert paused as his hand moved to place a pawn on the table, and he tightened his fist around the piece. "They'll have taken it to the Russian embassy. Of that I have no doubt. We won't be able to get past the front door. If they're prudent, they'll lock every entrance to prevent anyone from entering or exiting the building."

He unclenched his hand and set the pawn on the table, placing it to join the neat row along the side of the board among the other captured pieces no longer in play.

Antonia watched the chessboard as it continued to sprout pieces in its former arrangement. There was nothing like a bit of recklessness to throw things into disarray. Her eyes widened. "Perhaps we need to think about the problem from a different angle. If we can't go through the front door, then we need to enter the embassy another way."

Robert turned to face her. "The servants' entrance?"

"No. Something even more unexpected."

"What are you suggesting?"

Antonia licked her lips. Her idea was a bold one. Perhaps too bold. But still, they were desperate. They'd need to be bold in order to succeed. She forged ahead. "When I made my plans to steal the book from the embassy, I examined several alternatives. It wasn't until I learned about the winter solstice celebration that I decided to simply walk out the door with it. There is another way."

Robert took a step closer to her, and the tip of his shoe sent a chess piece skittering toward her feet. Antonia reached down and scooped it up, taking the brief moment to collect her thoughts. When she stood back up and met his gaze, she saw a hesitant gleam of hope in his keen blue eyes.

"The roof," she said, clenching the chess piece in her fist. "It's possible to access the roof from the next building."

Robert's gaze shifted slightly to her right and lost focus. After a moment he nodded. "You're right. The buildings are close. They might even touch."

She rubbed her thumb across the crown of the chess piece she held. The white queen. "It would be a simple matter to enter one of the upper windows and steal the book."

Robert lifted his brows. "Simple? I don't think I'd describe it that way."

"It would require nothing more than a sturdy rope and some nerve."

Robert shook his head. "It also requires two strong hands. That eliminates Frederick. Those burns are far from being healed."

"You don't need Frederick," she said, holding the queen out to him. "You have me."

"What?" He seemed stunned and took the piece from her hand with hardly a glance.

"Why not?"

"You'd climb down the side of a building with your skirts billowing in the breeze?" A quick grin flashed across his face. "You'll have to let me climb down first."

"Don't be silly. I'll wear trousers, of course."

"Of course," Robert said, but then his grin slipped and turned into something different. "But you don't mean—you can't possibly —do you plan to climb down a rope? You can't possibly have the strength..."

"I don't think you understand the life of an actress. I've acquired a number of unusual skills in the past year." She leaned over, brushed her skirts aside, and deftly pulled her knife from the ankle of her boot. "Have you forgotten this?"

Robert took a step back. "I had—until you used it on that man." He scratched the back of his head as he turned to face the chessboard. "You're an unusual woman, Antonia Winter." He stared down at the piece in his hand and then placed it carefully in position. "Unique."

Antonia's chest tightened until she couldn't breathe. Had she revealed too much? Was she too unusual? "Is that good?"

"It's who you are. The toast of the London stage."

"That can change in an instant. Just a year ago, I was the sparkling debutante from Maidenhead. Then everything changed." She looked at him levelly. "I changed."

"And within the past year you've learned to wield a knife and climb a rope?"

She let out a sigh. "In my last show I played the role of a fairy. I lost count of the number of times I climbed the scaffolding behind the set so I could perch in a tree with the other fairies. They assigned me the highest spot because I was so good at scampering up the bars. The quickest way back to the floor of the stage was via the rope I placed there for just that reason. I became quite proficient."

He stared at her a moment, his expression deadpan. "You continue to astonish me," he finally said. "Don't you understand what you're risking? How can you blithely offer to risk your life climbing across the roof of the embassy? It's insanity."

"It isn't insanity. I've already done the research and I know I'm perfectly capable of crossing that roof and climbing down to a window." Not that she wanted to, but she would. For him.

"This is too much. I won't let you."

"Then I'll go to Frederick. I'm sure he'll support my plan."

Robert's shoulders sagged. He turned away from her and let out a heavy sigh. "He certainly will, but then again, he's not the one risking everything." Robert shook his head in resignation. "Fine. Do it. You already know I'll be there to save you. Isn't that what I'm best at?"

Something in his tone sent a feeling of dread through her. Some note of finality. It was as though he'd closed a door. One that left her firmly on the other side.

Had she revealed too much? Pushed him too far outside his conventional life? But what choice did she have? How could she live with herself if she didn't do everything in her power to help him recover the book? He'd sacrificed his honor and the trust of both his brother and his queen in order to help her. She couldn't simply abandon him.

Not even if it meant losing him.

❧ 48 ❧

Opportunity makes a thief.

— *FRANCIS BACON*

As Robert stepped through the door and onto the roof, the frigid winter wind tugged at his hat. He pulled it more snugly in place and in doing so managed to dislodge the coiled length of rope looped over his shoulder. As he shrugged it back in place, a gust caught the board clamped under his arm, causing it to wobble. The wind was making everything more challenging than he'd anticipated. He adjusted the angle of the long, flat piece of lumber and glanced back at his footman standing next to the door.

"You're overloaded. Let me carry the rope," Antonia said.

Robert hesitated, but when the wind gusted again, he relented. He shrugged the coiled length from his shoulder and handed it to her.

Antonia took it, apparently unconcerned by its hefty weight.

She didn't fumble with it at all. Instead she simply slid it up her arm and onto her shoulder with the ease of someone who'd performed the same action many times in the past. She'd managed to surprise him yet again.

He hated that she was here. Hated that he couldn't do this without her—without putting her in harm's way. Why did she have to be so stubborn? Try as he might, he'd been unable to turn her from this course. It didn't help that he hadn't been able to come up with a better plan. She was right. There was a good chance this would work.

Either that, or they'd both end up dead—or as prisoners hidden away somewhere in Russia.

"Give us an hour," Robert said, peering at the footman, Turner. "If we aren't back by then, leave your rope here and head back downstairs. Frederick will be waiting for you in the carriage."

"Yes, my lord." Turner dropped the second rope he was carrying so that it settled near the edge of the rooftop.

If they were caught and the Russians discovered they'd gained access to the embassy via the building next door, he didn't want the owner implicated. The man had already put himself at risk by allowing Robert access to his roof. A carefully placed rope dangling to the street below would divert suspicion away from the owner. Robert only hoped no one would question the man too closely. He was a nervous one. They'd been fortunate Frederick had been able to convince him to help.

Robert was thankful they hadn't had to scale the side of the building. That would have been a treacherous undertaking. He had to admit, despite Antonia's confidence in her rope-climbing abilities, he doubted she could make a three-story ascent.

"Shall I wait here on the roof, m'lord?" the footman asked.

"It's too cold for that. Wait just inside the door. Start watching for us in about twenty minutes. If all goes well, we'll be back by then."

Turner gave a respectful bow and then stepped back inside the doorway.

Without a word, Antonia struck off across the roof toward the adjoining building and Robert turned to follow her, hunching his shoulders against the frigid gusts.

He wasn't sure which would be worse, having her trailing along behind him and out of sight, or in front of him so she'd be the first to face any perils. Since they were unlikely to encounter anyone on the roof, having her in the lead seemed the lesser of two evils. At least this way he could observe her in men's garb.

Robert was struck once again at how remarkably unremarkable Antonia appeared when dressed as a man. It was unsettling. It was unlikely he would have given her a second glance if he'd passed her on the street. Considering the relaxed and unselfconscious way she moved, she must be comfortable and at ease. The clothes provided her a level of invisibility that she could never have when dressed as a woman, one she clearly appreciated. He'd already noticed that when she went about in her normal attire, people tended to watch her every movement.

Antonia paused at the edge of the building and glanced down. The gap between this building and the embassy was about three feet wide. If the weather had been good he might have simply jumped across, but the icy surfaces and the wind made that option too dangerous. He slid the plank out from under his arm as he made ready to set it down, but the wind teased at it, trying to pluck it from his grasp. This was a devilishly cold night.

Robert wrestled the plank under control and laid the front edge of it on the decorative stone balustrade that edged the roof. He balanced it there as he pushed it forward until the other end was braced on the balustrade of the next building. The ornamental parapet was smooth and level, and the two buildings were almost exactly the same height.

He glanced at Antonia, taking in her excitement and her tension. Was this how she appeared just before she walked on stage? He could almost believe that if he reached out and touched her, he'd feel a jolt of electricity as sparks of her excitement shot into the cold winter sky like bolts of lightning.

"I'll hold the plank in place while you cross," he said. "Then you'll need to do the same for me. I don't trust the wind. Hand me the rope."

She passed the coiled length to him, and he tossed it across the gap to the adjoining roof.

He nodded at Antonia, and she responded with a broad grin. The unexpectedness of that smile swept through him, banishing his unease. He'd hated the tension that had grown between them all afternoon. This was the way he wanted to be with her. Relaxed.

She placed her hand on his shoulder for balance as she stepped up onto the stone railing, and he did, indeed, feel that jolt he'd anticipated at her touch. Pleasure struck him to his bones.

He gazed up at her, perched before him on the plank with her arms slightly extended, like a figurehead mounted on the prow on a ship. She radiated excitement as she took a deep breath and then quickly darted across the gap.

As she landed on the roof, she must have hit a patch of ice because her foot slid to one side. Her legs spread wide, but then her foot bumped against the coiled rope and stopped. She quickly righted herself.

She turned back to face him and grabbed hold of the plank, her grin still plastered on her face. "The wind is stronger between the buildings," she called. "Be careful."

Robert's heart pounded in his throat at her near fall, and he had to force himself to relax. She wasn't injured. She hadn't plummeted between the buildings. She was safe.

He stepped up onto the balustrade. As he inched his foot onto the plank, it felt solid. He inhaled. The wisest course would be to follow Antonia's example and do this quickly. He hunkered down slightly and put his hands out for balance. Halfway across the gap, the breeze from below caught his overcoat and caused it to billow up. The frigid cold swept up to his chest. As soon as he reached the far side of the plank, the wind could no longer tease at him, and his coat drifted back in place.

He was careful not to repeat Antonia's misstep as he dropped to the roof. He paused and surveyed the flat rooftop. "I see patches of ice everywhere. It's no wonder you slipped." He moved closer to Antonia, blocking her from the wind. The tip of her nose was pink, and he couldn't resist planting a quick kiss on it.

She widened her eyes in surprise.

"I've never kissed a man before," he said, lifting up the collar of her coat so that it blocked the wind. He tugged slightly at the points of the collar so they met just under her chin.

"You still haven't."

"True. But I have to admit, I like seeing you in men's clothing." He kissed her nose again before forcing himself to turn away. He reached down and pulled the plank toward them. He didn't want to risk having it fall between the buildings. It was an essential part of their escape route. He carefully stowed the length of wood along the balustrade where the wind couldn't catch it.

"I'll take the lead," he said as he picked up the coiled rope and slid it onto his shoulder. "Watch your step."

Robert headed directly for the second chimney. He and Antonia had pored over the drawings of the embassy with Frederick, and they had decided that anchoring the rope to it would be their best plan.

He stopped next to the brick chimney and could feel the heat radiating from it. He undid the coil and wrapped it around the chimney.

There was a heavy metal hook at the end of the rope which he used to secure it in place. If they managed to escape with the book, he planned to retrieve the rope so that no one would guess how they'd managed to gain entry.

He glanced at Antonia. "Once I have the window open, I'll give the rope a shake so you'll know it's safe to follow me."

She gave a quick, decisive nod. As he moved closer to the edge, Antonia pulled him short by grabbing his hand. He turned to face her.

"Be careful," she said, entwining her fingers in his.

He pulled her closer, placing her hand behind him and wrapping her arm around his waist. He slid his gloved finger down her cheek, wishing he could feel her skin. This time when he leaned down, he didn't kiss her nose. Instead he captured her lips. They were soft and cold, but they quickly warmed under his. As he deepened the kiss, his hat brim bumped against hers, knocking it askew. He pulled away and grabbed at it so the wind wouldn't catch it.

Antonia smacked her hand to the top of the hat and pressed it down over her ears. "Go," she said with grin. "I like kissing you, but there are better venues than the roof of the Russian embassy."

He flashed her a broad smile and gave the top of her hat a firm pat. "I have the perfect one in mind. It includes a warm fire, some glasses of whiskey, and a blanket."

"The light-brown blanket with flecks of ocher in it?"

"The very one."

"I approve. That's a superior venue in every way."

"Tonight then," he said, his voice rough with emotion. "I'll keep an image of you there in my mind."

"Is that a promise?" she asked, her tone teasing.

"If you tell me you'll still be wearing those trousers, I'll promise you anything." He leaned in for one last lingering kiss.

One perfect kiss.

It took all his willpower to break away from her and turn to face the edge of the roof. He didn't dare glance at her as he flung one leg over the edge of the railing, grabbed hold of the rope, and began lowering himself down.

Robert came to the quick realization that he didn't enjoy dangling off the side of a building. He kept his feet braced against the wall as he slowly moved down it. When his foot brushed the top of the lintel above the window, he cautiously put some weight on it. He carefully lowered himself to the window ledge below.

It was only about six inches deep, barely wide enough to stand on. He held tightly to the rope as he fished a long, slim knife from his boot. He carefully wedged the fine blade beneath the window sash just below the catch and then used the tip to unlock it. He raised the window and then slipped inside.

The guest room was dark, and he quickly confirmed that it was also empty. A vacant bed sat against the wall to his right, and directly in front of him, a rectangular seam of light leaked in around the bedroom door.

He turned back to the window and shook the rope roughly. He kept his hand on it, and a moment later he felt it vibrate as Antonia began climbing down.

As soon as he glimpsed her knees, he slid one thickly gloved hand behind her thighs and helped guide her feet to the ledge. Her legs were firm beneath his hand, and her trousers clung to them, revealing every curve of muscle. As he helped her inside, he took pleasure at the sheer intimacy of touching her, even so briefly. A wave of desire filled him, and he wanted nothing more than to pull her against him so he could feel her entire body pressed to his.

Instead, he let her go.

She seemed unaware of her effect on him as she turned to slide the window closed. "I don't want a gust of wind alert someone to our presence," she whispered.

He crossed the room and paused to listen at the door.

He heard nothing. The corridor was silent.

He turned the knob, only to discover that the door was locked.

As he reached for his set of lock picks, Antonia laid her hand on his arm, stopping him. "This will be faster," she said softly.

Despite the thick gloves he wore, he could still feel her slide something into his hand. His fingers were so clumsy from the cold and the thick leather gloves that he nearly dropped the small object. Fortunately, he caught it.

A key.

"As I recall, you aren't particularly quick when it comes to picking locks in the dark."

Robert grinned. "That's quite clever of you."

"You're lucky it was still hidden in the pocket of my petticoat the night the Russians found me at the theater, otherwise we'd have to rely on your nefarious skills."

He let out a soft chuckle as he inserted the key in the lock and turned it. It worked perfectly.

"Well done. If you don't mind, I'll hold onto this for now." He dropped the key into his pocket rather than risk passing it back to her in the dark.

He opened the door only an inch and peered outside.

The corridor was empty.

He and Antonia stepped into the hallway and came face-to-face with a painting of Czar Nicholas on the opposite wall.

Antonia paused to peer at his image. "I think I can see traces of my grandfather in him," she whispered. "It's in the eyes and the tilt of the mouth."

Robert stared at the man. His eyes were quite different from Antonia's. His were a deep brown, while Antonia's eyes had that remarkable copper hue to them. But their mouths were undeniably similar. This painting was from the czar's youth, and the mustache he now preferred wasn't in evidence.

Antonia turned away from the painting. "Is the office this way?" She pointed to their left.

Robert nodded and began leading the way toward the door to the ambassador's suite of rooms. Antonia followed him, and when he stopped to listen at the door, she waited silently next to him.

When he didn't hear any voices, he gave Antonia a nod and reached for the doorknob. He wrapped his hand around the porcelain and—

"You! Stop!"

Robert whirled around as the sound of feet came pounding down the corridor toward them. Three burly-looking footmen were upon them so quickly that Robert barely had time to step in front of Antonia to shield her from them.

He came face-to-face with the man in the lead and frozet.

Davydov.

Of course. It had to be Davydov.

Another man sidestepped Robert and grabbed him from behind, wrapping his arm around Robert's neck in a choke hold that cut off his air. Davydov grabbed him by the arm, while the third man grabbed Antonia in a choke hold identical to the one disabling Robert.

"We have been waiting for you," Davydov hissed in his ear. "The ambassador believed you would try to steal the book. I did not think you would be so reckless."

Davydov yanked Robert closer to the door and then rapped smartly on it.

"Enter," came a man's voice.

Davydov pushed his way through the entrance, dragging Robert with him.

Robert could barely breathe with Davydov's arm clamped around his throat, so he tried to swing to one side and inhale some sweet air. He caught a glimpse of Antonia before Davydov shoved him forward again. They weren't treating her as roughly. Probably because she wasn't struggling. Robert forced himself to submit, and after a moment, the pressure on his throat eased a little.

When he finally surveyed the room, he found Ambassador Revnik sitting in a wing-backed chair facing the fireplace, looking entirely at ease.

There, on the small round table between the two chairs, sat the church register.

But what surprised Robert the most was the other person in the room sitting in the chair opposite Revnik.

Lord Percival. The same man who had started the fire that had burned Frederick.

Lord Percival's demeanor wasn't as calm as the ambassador's. In fact, the man looked horrified to see Robert.

Cold fury settled in Robert's chest. This man—this bumbling fool—had this traitor been nestling in the bosom of society all this time?

"Consorting with the enemy, Lord Percival?" Robert asked. "I must admit. You had me completely fooled. I never suspected you."

This was Lord Percival? This enormous man was the one whose antics set in motion the events the night of the Koliada Ball?

"What?" Lord Percival roared as he rose to his feet. "How dare you!" His trimmed beard tapered to a point, and as his face reddened with anger, Antonia decided he looked very much like an angry Lucifer.

She would have shrunk away from him if she could have, but the arm around her neck held her in place, so she could only let out a yelp of terror. Her captor tightened his arm around her throat, making it difficult for her to breathe. She pulled at his forearm, trying to loosen it. Was he trying to silence her, or merely use her as a shield to protect himself from Lord Percival's fury?

Ambassador Revnik's gaze fixed on her, his dark eyes boring into hers. She saw a flicker of confusion in them. A hint of recognition that faltered as his gaze swept over her men's attire. Then his jaw dropped as the full realization of her identity hit him.

"Are you mad?" Revnik barked at the footman with his arm around her throat. "The czar ordered that Miss Winter not be harmed! He was most explicit. Unhand her immediately. If you ever touch her again I'll have you sent to the Crimean Peninsula!"

The terrified guard let go of Antonia so quickly that she stumbled forward and had to brace her hand against Robert's arm so she wouldn't fall.

The guards holding Robert released him as well, backing away as though she and Robert were plague-ridden.

Robert recovered quickly and looped a protective arm around her waist, pulling her close to his side.

Revnik waved his hand in a dismissive gesture toward the guards. The one man, Davydov, looked as though he wanted to argue but then thought better of it. The three men filed out of the room and closed the door behind them.

Lord Percival's anger quickly fled, and he now seemed thoroughly confused. He glanced around the room as though looking for someone. "Who is 'Miss Winter'? And who is that young man?" he asked, gesturing toward Antonia. "Why does he have the czar's protection?"

Revnik cleared his throat and then smoothed his horseshoe-shaped beard with his thumb and forefinger. "May I present Miss Antonia Winter. Not only is she an actress of great renown, but she's also the—" he stopped himself and cleared his throat again. "She's also the granddaughter of the illustrious Russian artist Vladamir Nevsky."

"Nevsky?" Lord Percival moved closer to Antonia. "And you say he's a woman—I mean, she's a woman?" He squinted at her and then pulled a pair of spectacles from his coat pocket and settled them in place. "Ah! I see. Yes." He took a step back.

"Rather confusing, I must say. I prefer women to dress as—well—as women. But I suppose an actress is quite capable of employing her craft in such a manner. After all, the granddaughter of the incomparable Vladamir Nevsky must be permitted to do as she pleases. It would seem that even the czar agrees." He grinned.

Robert stared at him in stony silence.

Lord Percival cleared his throat. "I must say, Miss Winter, I am an ardent enthusiast when it comes to your grandfather's work. I especially love his Kozinski period."

"You aren't alone," she replied. As she gathered her thoughts to make a coherent reply, the surreal nature of the conversation wasn't lost on her. "He poured much of himself into that series, and his strong emotions come through on the canvas." Her ears rang with an odd vibration, and her voice sounded strangely hollow and distant. She glanced at Revnik, but he seemed to be genuinely enjoying himself. "However, I must admit I prefer his later work. His composition and use of texture were brilliant."

"True, true," Lord Percival said. "But the depth of passion revealed in his earlier work was—"

"Are you going to continue nattering on about Vladamir Nevsky's art, or can we address your treasonous acts?" Robert gave Lord Percival a look of scorn. "I happen to find the latter a much more pressing issue."

Lord Percival looked at Robert as though he'd forgotten about him. "Why do you keep using that word? What can I possibly have done that could be considered treasonous?" He glanced from Robert to Antonia and frowned. "Do you mind telling me how you've come to be here? I've been locked inside this embassy for the past four hours and I'm certain I've already spoken with every other British citizen who has also been trapped here. You, sir, were most decidedly not among them." He jutted his chin forward, indicating Robert's coat. "Judging by your heavy winter attire, I'd wager you entered this building only moments ago." He stroked the tip of his pointed beard. "Since the Ambassador would have already informed me if I could leave, I can only assume that you either had special permission to enter, or you broke into the embassy." He smirked. "My guess is that it's the *latter.* " He emphasized the last word, mimicking Robert's use of it.

"Of course I broke in. Revnik left me with no other choice. The man is both audacious and rash—a bad combination. His men attacked my carriage here in London just hours ago and stole that from me." He gestured toward the book. Lord

Percival cast the church register a doubtful gaze. Antonia couldn't blame him. The innocuous-looking object sat on an embroidered silk runner draped over the table. Its tattered cover looked incongruous in the sumptuous room, yet it was close at hand, situated between the two chairs facing the fire, appearing like nothing more than a well-thumbed reference book. Nothing about it would make anyone presume it had any significant value. Let alone that men would go to such extreme lengths to possess it.

"There's obviously been some misunderstanding—" Revnik began, but Antonia cut him off.

"I can assure you that Lord Wentworth is speaking the truth," she said. "The British government wants that book. In fact, it would appear that many governments want it."

Robert leveled his gaze on Lord Percival. "If that book remains in the ambassador's possession, I'm quite certain the Queen will see its theft today as an act of war."

"*War?*" Lord Percival repeated. "Is that why we've been locked in here? Is the Queen on the verge of making a declaration of war against Russia?" His eyes darted back and forth between Robert to the ambassador until they finally fixed upon Ambassador Revnik. A look of fear crept over his face, and he began to slowly back away.

Revnik raised his hand in a soothing gesture, but Lord Percival flinched at the motion. "Please, sir," Revnik said, taking a step closer to Lord Percival. "Do not alarm yourself. I can explain everything."

"Don't believe a word he utters," Robert said. "The man lies. Frequently."

Lord Percival edged backward toward the fireplace, his eyes widening in alarm. He reached blindly for the poker and managed to wrap his hand around it, snatching it up and raising it into the air as a weapon. But the hearth was slightly raised above the floorboards of the room, and when his heel bumped against it, he stumbled.

Lord Percival reached out to steady himself against the mantel. His aim was off and he teetered backward. In a panic, he thrust his arm against the wall and pushed himself away from the fireplace.

He raised the slim poker to balance himself as he stepped forward. His toe caught on the edge of the rug, causing him to stumble yet again.

He fell forward. His poker slammed downward and smashed into the round table. It toppled forward, causing the book and the two glasses of whiskey to come arcing toward him.

The church register seemed to sprout wings as it flew through the air, speeding directly toward the fireplace. It landed with a smack in the center of the flames, sending up a shower of sparks.

Antonia shrieked in alarm as the pages began to darken from the heat. She darted forward, ducked around Lord Percival's flailing form, grabbed the poker from where he'd dropped it on the floor, and crawled to the fireplace.

She flipped the book out of the fire and onto the rug amid a flurry of burning embers, its leather cover smoldering. Some of the embers flew onto the silk table runner drenched with spilled whiskey, and others landed on the cushion of one of the wing-backed chairs.

Antonia stomped on the book with her heavy boots to put out the flames, but it continued to smolder.

To her horror, the table runner and the upholstered chair caught fire. Ambassador Revnik rushed over and began beating at the weak flames with the flat of his hand.

Antonia tugged at the muffler wound around her neck. When she finally yanked it free, she dropped to her knees and carefully wrapped the scorched book in the length of wool, smothering the last of the glowing orange embers that edged the pages.

"Fire!" the ambassador shouted as more of the greedy embers burst into flames. Small blazes began cropping up throughout the room. "Fire!"

The three guards came running back into the room. They barely noticed Antonia as they attacked the flames. Antonia scooped up the muffler with its precious contents and scurried out of their way.

She gave the men a wide berth. Everyone was focused on dealing with the catastrophe. Even Lord Percival had managed to stumble to his feet.

As she watched, he threw open a window. A frigid gust of wind swirled into the room, fanning the flames and causing them to burn higher.

Antonia grabbed Robert's sleeve. At his glance, she tilted her head toward the unguarded door. He followed her gaze and then nodded. She took her chance and darted through it with Robert close on her heels.

They tore down the hallway and she threw open the door across from Czar Nicholas's portrait. Robert shoved it closed and then used the key to lock it.

How would she climb the rope carrying the book? She glanced down at the muffler-wrapped package and then remembered the technique Robert had used when he'd stolen it. He'd tucked it down his trousers. She quickly crammed the bundle under the front of her waistband and then refastened her coat buttons. It felt snug and secure against her belly. She should be able to climb the rope without fear of losing it.

Just as Robert pulled open the window sash, Antonia heard the doorknob rattle. They both froze, afraid to make a sound. Muffled voices said something unintelligible, and then heavy feet hurried off.

"You first," Robert whispered. "I'll close the window behind us."

Antonia gave a jerky nod. Climbing back up that rope would be much more difficult. It was time to live up to her boast about her rope-climbing abilities. She could do it, she knew she could, but the three-story drop below made her nervous.

She took a deep, shaky breath and then flung one leg through the window opening.

Robert put a hand on her upper arm and she stopped moving. She gave him a questioning glance.

He leaned over so they were face-to-face, eye-to-eye and then kissed her. Hard.

"Don't you look down, Antonia Winter," he said fiercely. "You'll be fine. I have faith in you. Remember, I'll be right below you on that rope. If you fall, I'll catch you." He grinned. "I won't have any other choice. Not to put undue pressure on you."

She felt the blood drain from her face as she imagined her body hurtling toward him and knocking him from the rope. They'd both go tumbling down to the paving stones below. The image was stomach-churning.

And Robert was grinning.

"Gallows humor. Bah," she said, giving his chest an irritated shove, intending to push him away. But he only swayed ever so slightly. Perhaps if she fell, he really could catch her. He seemed so large and solid that it was hard to imagine that anything she did could impact him.

Until she met his eyes. His teasing grin had disappeared and had been replaced by an expression of unbearable tenderness and vulnerability.

And it was all for her.

Why had he granted her this power over him? She was nothing. Just the disgraced daughter of a squire. Even now, with her inheritance restored once again, it was inconceivable that he'd even consider linking his life to hers. She'd offer a dreadfully disadvantageous match. After all, she'd supported herself as an actress this past year. That alone should be enough to eliminate her from consideration as anything other than an earl's mistress. It was inconceivable that they could truly be together, not as husband and wife. Yet here she was, conceiving of it. But no. He was out of her reach. Even if the events of the past year hadn't transpired, the simple daughter of a squire could never dare to dream of marrying an earl.

But he looked at her now with those clear, blue eyes, so vulnerable with worry, so intense, so filled with tenderness, that she found she could barely draw a breath.

He stroked her cheek. "Stop looking so doubtful. You're the best thing that's ever happened to me, Antonia." He planted a kiss on the top of her head. "Now go. We don't have much time."

Dazed, she turned away and ducked through the window as she took the rope in both hands. She took a deep breath, wrapped her legs around the rope, and began pulling herself up.

It was easier than she'd feared.

When she reached the top, she scrambled to loop her arm over the railing. She managed to grab hold of it and pulled herself over the edge, slamming her elbow hard against the balustrade in the process. Once she was standing on the roof, she realized she'd been so dazed by Robert's kiss that she'd forgotten to worry about falling.

Robert stood next to her just a moment later. "Well done," he said, grinning.

He deftly gathered up the rope. They crossed the roof to where he'd stashed the plank and he paused to toss the loosely coiled rope across the gap between the buildings. The toss was slightly short, and the rope landed on top of the ledge. The wind buffeted it, and for a moment Antonia was certain it would fall to the alleyway below, but then a hard gust seemed to work in their favor, and the tottering coils stabilized. Robert set the plank across the gap.

"Do exactly what you did before, and you'll be fine."

She darted across the gap and then held the board for Robert. Once they were both on the other roof, he retrieved the board.

"I nearly forgot," Robert said. "I'm supposed to drop these between the building so Frederick can collect them." He tossed them over the side and then hurried toward their exit route. Ahead, a small figure broke away from the shadows—the young footman who was assisting them. He gave them a jaunty wave and then immediately began retrieving the rope they'd left dangling down the side of the building.

They entered the dim stairwell from the rooftop door and dashed down to the ground floor, where a butler waited for them. With practiced indifference, he opened the door and let them out, as though helping spies escape from the Russian embassy happened on a daily basis. Antonia had to admire his aplomb.

Just as they stepped out the front door, Robert's carriage pulled to a stop before them. She spotted the plank they'd tossed off the building already tied to the roof of the carriage.

Frederick pushed open the door from within and beckoned them inside as young Turner untied his horse from the rear of the carriage.

Frederick stared at them both. After a moment of silence, he said, "Well? Do you have it?"

Antonia reached inside her coat and pulled out the wrapped bundle. She handed it to Frederick. "Revnik's men captured us. If not for Lord Percival, we wouldn't have escaped. There was a fire and—well—"

"A fire? Again?" Frederick looked stunned. "Was Lord Percival in his cups?"

"It wasn't that." Robert said. He briefly explained Lord Percival's unintentional bit of arson. When he mentioned the book's flight into the fireplace, Frederick looked aghast.

"The book was damaged," Antonia said. "I'm not sure how badly. I haven't had a chance to examine it yet. I grabbed it in the confusion and we escaped while they were trying to put out the fire."

Frederick stared down at the wool-wrapped bundle in his hands with horror. He quickly tore off the wrapping. The smoky odor was pungent inside the confines of the carriage. Frederick turned the book over, but the light was too dim to assess the damage.

"Turn up the lamp," he told Robert, who reached over to adjust the wick on the kerosene lamp mounted next to the carriage door. As the interior brightened, Antonia kept her gaze fixed on the book.

The leather was scorched. Frederick opened it carefully, but even so, flakes of blacked paper broke away and drifted to the floor.

Carefully, Frederick turned to the crucial passage in the book. No one breathed as he examined it.

Finally Frederick shook his head. "It's gone. There's nothing left to reveal Czar Nicholas's secret. The book is worthless." He closed the church register and clutched it in his hands as he dropped his head in defeat.

"That means the Queen won't be able to use it to force the czar to withdraw his troops," Antonia whispered.

"That's right," Frederick replied softly. "And that means war is inevitable."

❄ *50* ❄

The confession of evil works is the first beginning of good works.

— *SAINT AUGUSTINE*

R obert wanted to believe Frederick. He wanted to believe Antonia was safe—but until he examined that book—until he held it in his own hands—he simply couldn't allow himself to relax.

He removed his thick gloves and extended one hand to his brother, silently requesting the church register.

With a sigh, Frederick passed it to him. The cover felt rough against his skin—grimy with soot and badly scorched. Robert shifted on the carriage seat to hold up to the lamp. The edges of the pages were singed, yes, but the small volume seemed intact.

He let the book fall open, and as always, it turned directly to its most dangerous pages.

Pages which were now entirely black.

Relief crashed through Robert as he stared at the ruined

paper. No legible writing remained on the uniformly black surface.

The text must have fallen open in precisely this same manner in the fireplace. Had this been its destiny all along? Had its eagerness to reveal its secrets been its downfall? Robert shook his head at his own flight of fancy. That was absurd, of course. A book had no destiny.

Still, he rather liked the thought. It held a certain symmetry for him. A certain grand design.

He solemnly shook his head as he handed back the book. "The relevant pages were completely destroyed."

Frederick tossed the book on the seat next to him and turned toward the window, staring pensively into the darkness.

Antonia shifted her body so she faced Frederick's profile. "What if—"

He only turned his head partway to glance at her. "If?"

"What I mean to say is, the Russians don't know the book was destroyed. What if Queen Victoria bluffs?"

"It isn't as though there's another alternative." Frederick's gaze became unfocused as he considered the idea. "That might actually work," he murmured, and then turned back to stare into the night.

Robert lowered the lamp's flame. Antonia's profile reflected the light, and her pale skin seemed to glow. Her hat was gone, probably lost at some point during the struggle in the embassy. The wig concealing her hair canted to one side, her neat features incongruous with the disorderly mop of hair atop her head. He couldn't suppress a delighted grin.

She was safe, she was beautiful, and nothing would keep him from her. Not the Queen, not the czar—nothing.

The carriage halted in front of Woolsy House and Frederick fled its confines without another word. Robert followed him out into the gusting wind and turned to assist Antonia. She stumbled, and he caught her about the waist, catching her in midair and depositing her next to him.

"You keep saving me," she said, and then yawned. She widened her eyes and belatedly covered her mouth.

"Long night," he said, letting her go, "and you didn't get much sleep last night." He grinned when she blushed. He ought to be exhausted as well, but he simply wasn't. He was energized. He was giddy. He was euphoric. All because of this diminutive woman and the daring theft she'd orchestrated.

His grin grew wider. Life was good. A night like this should be savored and appreciated. The air was crisp and clear, and the stars above were shining only for them. Antonia was by his side, and the church register no longer represented a threat. Everything was wonderful.

She linked her arm through his and turned toward the front door. Her casual touch felt so right. So perfectly ordinary and appropriate. He wanted the pleasure of this sort of careless caress from her forever.

Turner hurried ahead and pushed open the door for them. Robert placed his hand over Antonia's as he escorted her inside.

"You can retire for the evening, Turner. You've earned your bed, and then some," Robert said.

The footman murmured a thank-you and hurried away.

Frederick made his way up the staircase and then paused, his back stiff. He barely turned as he spoke. "Please excuse me. I need to prepare my report. I'll deliver it to Queen Victoria first thing in the morning. The loss of the book complicates matters for me." He glanced at Antonia. "I'll pass on your suggestion. It's a good one." As he turned away from them, he let out a deep sigh and continued trudging up the stairs. Robert's heart ached for him. Frederick hated to fail.

Antonia paused, staring tiredly at the staircase. Robert could tell she was trying to decide if she should go up as well.

"Join me in the study," he said, tightening his arm to tuck hers more firmly against his side. "There's something I need to tell you. Something long past due."

She hesitated.

"I also want to keep the promise I made to you on the roof of the embassy."

She stared at him blankly for a moment, and her cheeks turned slightly pink. "I recall some mention of a blanket."

"Light-brown with flecks of ocher," he said, his voice rough. He cleared his throat.

"It would be highly improper," she said, glancing down at her attire, "but after all of the other improper things I've done tonight, why stop now?"

He closed the gap between them. She tossed him an impish grin and let him escort her into his study.

Everything was as they'd left it. Well, almost. For some reason, the bust of Apollo was facing the wall. Had one of the servants moved it? He frowned but then turned away, dismissing it as he turned his attention to Antonia.

"I oiled the latch on the door leading to the passageway," he said.

"Did you now?" She removed her coat and draped it over her arm as she sauntered across the room. It seemed strange to want to stare at someone dressed in trousers, but as long as that person was Antonia, he didn't care what she wore. In fact, in a perfect world, she'd wear nothing at all.

That thought surprised him. Had it been inspired by the gentle sway of her hips as they moved from side to side in that undeniably feminine way? They certainly provided ample inspiration. Her movements had been moderate and subdued earlier tonight. Hips that swayed like these could never be mistaken for those of a man. Not ever.

He tried to brush aside his memory of her naked body in the lamplight last night, but now that he'd called it forth, the vision firmly planted itself in his mind.

As she turned to face him again, she held up the coat and raised one eyebrow. "Where should I put this?"

"Here will do," he said, taking the garment from her and draping it on the back of one of the chairs. He shed his coat as well.

He turned back and found her staring down at the church register. She must have picked it up in the carriage. As he stepped closer, he spotted a reddish abrasion along the side of her neck.

"Let me look at you," he said. He took the church register from her and placed it on his desk. She offered no protest. "Does it hurt?" he asked, tilting her chin up to examine the mark. "Did he injure you anywhere else?" His gaze raked over her.

She touched his hand gently, soothing him. "No, I'm fine," she said. "I don't think the guard intended any real harm. At least, not after he realized who I was. It was convenient to have the czar's protection at that particular moment."

He dropped his hand to his side as he glanced down at the half-burned register. "And once we hand this over to the Queen, you'll be safe from everyone else as well." He noticed as her muscles tensed. He'd become attuned to her every movement, her every mood.

"How can you be so certain?"

Robert paused. He wanted to give her an honest answer, not simply to placate her. "I suppose there are no guarantees," he finally said as he reached out and pulled the lopsided wig from her head. "Since the book provided the only evidence of the czar's adoption, I see no reason why you'd continue to be a target. Without proof you're his relative, you're of no tactical value."

He tossed the wig onto his desk and picked up the church register. He let it fall open as it always did. "It's all gone."

She plucked hairpins from her tresses as she bent down to examine it, and she set them in a tidy pile on the desk. She swept her hair to one side, leaving the arc of her pale neck exposed. She appeared achingly beautiful in her intensity. She gently touched a blackened page and tried to turn it, but the brittle paper crumbled at the slight pressure. She yanked her hand away and brushed the soot onto her trousers. She grabbed her cascade of hair and held it in her fist to keep it out of her way as she leaned even closer to the book.

As she stared down at the blackened pages, a change swept over her. Her tension vanished as quickly as shadows in a burst of bright light. "I'm safe. I didn't want to let myself believe it until now—until I had a chance to see it for myself." She closed the book. "It's completely destroyed. No one could possibly use this to prove I'm related to Czar Nicholas. I'm simply Antonia Winter once again—daughter of Squire Winter and granddaughter of Vladamir Nevsky."

The daughter of a squire—Lord Tidmore's ruling. That seemed like weeks ago, not scant hours. Antonia's world had shifted on its axis once again and returned to its original trajectory. "Thank god the judge ruled in your favor."

She glanced toward him as her smile faded. She straightened her spine to meet his gaze as she let her hair fall loosely again. "What about you? What of Queen Victoria? Won't she be angry with you and your brother?"

"Only if we can't convince her otherwise."

Suddenly he wanted nothing more than to touch his lips to hers and feel her smile slide across them again. He wouldn't stop there. He'd move on to nuzzle the spot just below her ear, then he'd trail his kisses down her neck, pausing to soothe that angry red mark. He could push her collar open, exposing her throat and exploring the intriguing hollow at its base.

He swallowed. Undressing her from her men's attire would prove to be a fascinating endeavor.

He slid his hand around her nape, cupping it as he gently caressed her cheek with his thumb. "If I could do it all over again, I'd make the same decision. Hopefully, Frederick and I can convince Queen Victoria we were in the right."

Their eyes locked as he bent his head, and she shifted closer to him. As their lips touched, she closed her eyes. The soft kisses he'd intended to give her weren't enough. This woman—this amazing, vibrant woman—she did things to his mind and senses that drove him toward a precipice. Once he allowed himself to fall over that brink, he knew he'd sink into her. Into Antonia.

She surrounded him and filled him, becoming everything to him. Every thought, every breath, every taste—touch—heartbeat was only for Antonia. He was imbued with her. Saturated with her essence.

He trailed a line of fiery kisses across her skin, starting at the spot just below her ear and ending at the top of her shirt collar. He tugged at the silk neckcloth, unused to removing the long-familiar garment from this angle, but his fingers were deft and sure. A moment later he tossed the length of fabric to the floor and began trailing kisses down her naked throat. The ivory skin hidden beneath the brilliant white of her dress shirt was perfection. Soft and warm—it beckoned his explorations.

He pulled her with him as he moved back until he came up against his desk. He lowered his weight onto the edge and felt a hard object pressing into his backside. He glanced over his shoulder to push it away and saw the church register.

He froze.

Its precise location reminded him of a smaller, slimmer item that had rested in that spot twelve years ago. This small book and that long-ago letter from his father had much in common. Both contained dangerous secrets and disturbing revelations.

Antonia had shared everything with him when they'd walked through the park near her boardinghouse. All her secrets. All her shames. But he'd never been able to return the same level of faith and trust. He still held his secrets close.

Antonia deserved to know about the ghosts that haunted him. He desperately wanted to ask her a question, offer a proposal, but he couldn't. Not now. Not yet. Not as long as he kept his past hidden from her. How could he base their relationship on a false beginning? If he wanted a future with her, then she needed to know the risk involved. It was the right thing to do.

The honorable thing.

Robert took a deep breath and stilled his movements, relaxing his hands and letting them fall to his sides.

"Is something wrong?" Antonia asked, taking a step back from him.

"I have something I need to tell you."

She brushed her hair away from her face and then pressed her fingertips to her lips. She kept her gaze fixed on the corner of the desk as she worked to compose herself.

He drove both hands into his hair to stop himself from dragging her back into his arms. All he wanted to do was kiss away that look of hurt and confusion. To pull her closer and repair their broken connection.

She glanced at him, and when she took in his turmoil, her expression softened. "What is it?" she asked. "What do you want to tell me?"

"It's a long story. It has to do with what we discovered in the passageway last night. Wait here a moment. I need to get something."

Robert moved to the bookcase that hid the entrance to the passageway and deftly twisted the release, opening the door wide. It only took him a moment to locate the small box. He stepped back into the study and closed the door behind him.

"Now I'm ready," he said as he reached for her hand. "Come. Sit with me." He noticed the wool blanket on a nearby table and snatched it up as they moved toward the sofa.

He set the small box down on an end table. The room was cool, so he tucked the blanket around them both. Antonia lifted his arm up and draped it over her shoulders. She tucked up against him, fitting perfectly in the hollow next to his heart.

Robert inhaled deeply, and then began. "You entrusted your

secrets to me, and I'm humbled by your faith. I'm ashamed to say I haven't been as open with you."

"I deserve no compliment for revealing my secrets," she scoffed, tilting her head back to gaze into his eyes. "I would have kept them if I could, but after weighing my options I realized I had little choice in the matter. One does what one must."

"I left you no other alternative."

She opened her mouth to reply, but he touched his finger to her lips to forestall her. She raised her eyebrows at him in irritation.

"I know you want to help, but I need to get through this. Please. Just let me speak."

She nodded. "No more interruptions. I promise."

He gathered his thoughts. "When I was twelve, I learned my father had committed an act of treason. He informed me of this in a letter he left for me. I found it in there on the desk in front of his body." He gestured toward his desk. "I was the first person to enter the room after I heard the gunshot." He swallowed. "It was suicide."

Antonia's eyes widened.

He took a deep, steadying breath. "The letter next to his body was addressed to me. In it, he confessed his crimes, said he couldn't live with the shame any longer, and asked me to help Mother."

Antonia watched him. He could tell she wanted to offer words of comfort, but she was true to her promise and didn't interrupt.

He had to force himself to continue. "A second letter was found with his body. It was addressed to a woman—not my mother—but my mother read it anyway before handing it over to the other woman. In it, he told the woman he couldn't live without her."

Antonia shook her head in confusion.

"Which story was the truth and which was the lie? Is that what you're wondering?"

She nodded, but didn't speak.

"The story about the other woman was the lie. He hoped it would protect us from his crimes."

Antonia seemed to murmur his name, but her voice was as soft as a breath, and he couldn't be certain she'd even made a sound. He wanted to pull her closer and bury his face in her hair, but instead, he splayed his fingers and raised his hand before them both, examining it as a way to gauge his self-control. Would it shake or remain steady?

"His letter to me insisted that Mother and I protect the family from his misdeeds by promoting the alternate story he'd concocted. The second letter he wrote was to a widow known for her many lovers. In it, he claimed to have become obsessed with her. He accused her of spurning his affections and banning him from ever seeing her again." A single tremor ran through his hand. "Mother and I were obliged to conceal his crimes with a despicable lie. I don't know if I would have been able to do it if she hadn't begged me to. Father provided ample evidence to support the false story. The widow's footmen ejected him from a dinner party the night before his suicide. Apparently he'd tried to force his way in to see her during a dinner party and created quite the scene." He clenched his hand into a fist—steady and solid.

"Father intended the rumor as both protection and retribution. In truth, the widow in question had been blackmailing him after discovering his secret. He paid her for a while, but she'd become greedy. He'd gone to her house that night because she'd threatened to expose his secrets to the House of Lords the following afternoon. Father's death and the subsequent rumor of their relationship effectively prevented her from revealing the truth. In the eyes of London, we'd become her innocent victims.

"As the days passed, we concealed Father's treasonous act. We did what we could to make amends to the people he'd harmed with his scheme, but we couldn't repair all the damage. It was too far-reaching. Ever since then, I've been tormented by the fear that his secret would come out and the world would shun my family. After all, at what point does his secret become my secret? I share in his guilt."

Antonia took his hand and slid her fingers inside his fist, easing it open. Then she took his hand in both of hers, holding it gently but firmly. At her touch— her forgiving, tender touch— some of his tension eased.

Robert sighed. "I made sacrifices, but not to the extent my mother did. She and Father had been lauded as one of the few true love-matches of their time, so the fiction he'd invented proved to be a humiliating one. The lies she had to nurture were almost as bad as the truth. And Frederick?" Robert let out a huff of air and shook his head. "His guilt drove him to dedicate his life to serving the Queen as one of her spies. This way, he can both ease his feelings of shame and burnish the family's tarnished honor." He gave Antonia a half-hearted smile. "He's been trying to convince me to join him in that world for a long time, but I was able to resist until that night at the embassy. After this experience, I can promise I'll never be tempted to do it again."

"I'm glad you helped him. If you hadn't, we never would have met."

Robert's throat tightened. He hadn't considered that possibility. What if he'd made a different decision? What if Frederick hadn't been burned? A sudden thought struck him. What if Lord Percival hadn't been drunk at the ball? Bloody hell. Did that mean he owed Lord Percival a debt of gratitude? He closed his eyes for a moment to contemplate the complex bit of logic, but the idea was too irritating to focus on for long. He opened his eyes to discover Antonia gazing at him, her brows furrowed together.

"What did your father actually do? What was his crime?"

Robert let out a deep sigh and shook his head. "Treachery, deceit, larceny—take your pick. He was guilty of them all—and many more. He used his position in the House of Lords to lure people into investing every penny they owned in a proposed railway project. Some people even borrowed money to invest. He owned part of the new railroad that was selling shares. The scheme worked well for him, but he wanted even more. He ended up devising a plan to make himself even richer. He manipulated the process so an entirely different route and railroad would be chosen. He sold off all the shares in his own company and invested everything in the competing one, taking it over. He made an obscene amount of money, and some of his closest friends lost everything, but his most egregious crime, the crime which would have ruined him, was treason. In his blind drive to convince people to invest in his company, he forged the Great Seal of the Realm."

"Was he mad? Forging the monarch's seal is high treason! Queen Victoria would have been incensed."

"She was, but she never had any proof he was the one to blame."

He reached out and picked up the small box sitting on the end table.

"Look inside," he said, handing it to her.

She accepted it cautiously. She hesitated a moment before opening it. When she saw the engraved disk, she let out a gasp of shock. "Is this what I think it is?"

"I'm afraid so. It's the forged copy of Queen Victoria's Great Seal. It's been hidden right there all along, behind that bookcase."

"What are you going to do with it?"

"I'm not sure. I told Frederick about it this morning. He plans to take it to the Queen."

"Why would your father be so foolish as to forge the Great Seal?"

Robert raised his hands in submission. "I've never been able to make sense of his thought process. Mother says he changed that last year of his life—became a different person. I never saw it. When he was with me, he continued to be the same measured and controlled man he'd always been. Father was a demanding taskmaster. He was fond of saying that people would live up to expectations, but they'd live down to them as well. Perhaps that mindset explains why he thought he could get away with forging the seal—he simply convinced himself he'd never be caught."

"But he was."

"Only by his blackmailer, but she never revealed the truth after he implicated her in his suicide. She probably realized no one would believe her without proof."

"I'm sorry, Robert. I can't imagine how difficult this must have been for you."

"Losing my father was terrible, but when I learned how many of our friends had been financially devastated because of his scheming, it was like losing him all over again. The man I'd believed him to be died as well. I became furious with him. I didn't know how to help the people he'd swindled at the time, but I promised myself I'd do everything in my power to return every farthing he stole. It's working, and so far I've been able to keep them from learning I'm behind their good fortune."

"They don't know you've been helping them? How?"

"Bit by bit," he said. "A favor here, a windfall there. So far, they've all chalked it up to good luck and wise investments." He paused. "Your father was one of the men Father swindled."

Comprehension swept over her face. "That's why you were at our house five years ago. You were returning the money."

"I'm sorry. I—" But wait—how did she know he'd been to her house?

"I saw you that day, you know. I slipped downstairs to watch you. I knew who you were the night of the embassy ball."

He must have looked stunned, because she grinned at him. "You and I recognized each other that night, but for entirely different reasons."

He kissed the top of her head. "At least I was able to return the money your father lost before he died."

"How did you do it? Come up with all that money, I mean. Didn't we discover all of it hidden in the passageway last night?"

"Lord Huntley was generous enough to advise me regarding a number of investments, and I've made enormous headway. Now that we've discovered the missing money, I'll be able to give back the rest of it immediately."

Antonia looked impressed. "Even I've heard of Lord Huntley's Midas touch." She thought for a moment. "It's good you were able to help the people your father swindled. It must have been an all-consuming task."

"When Mother asked me to keep this secret, my only condition was that we pay everyone back. She agreed, but with a single condition of her own. Any aid I provided needed to remain anonymous. She didn't want to remind them of my father's misdeeds."

"Living that lie, day in and day out—it must have been terrible for her."

"Terrible doesn't begin to describe it." He brushed a strand of hair away from Antonia's cheek. "People can be spiteful. They might not have realized my father intentionally swindled them, but nonetheless they lost money based on his recommendations. Since he wasn't around to face their anger, they'd occasionally unleash their ire on Mother. She endured their barbed comments with grace, but they still stung. She tried to conceal her pain, but I saw it. Frederick did as well. Children see more than their parents realize." Robert tucked the blanket up under Antonia's chin and gave her a sad smile. "She found it galling, but I suppose that's why Father chose that particular bit of subterfuge. If everyone believed Mother was mortified because Father committed suicide over another woman, they'd never suspect she was only supporting the fiction in order to hide something even more humiliating."

"That's terrible. How could he have been so cruel to her?"

"I've given up trying to understand the man. My best guess is that he thought the lie he invented would be easier for her to endure than the truth."

"Did your mother believe the same thing?"

"I assume so, since she perpetuated the lie."

"Perhaps knowing that she was protecting her children made the sacrifice worthwhile."

"You might be right," he said, and then thought about it more carefully. "In fact, I believe you are. She would have done anything for us. I asked her once how she managed to bear their scorn, and she said, 'People can only hurt you with their words if you grant them the power. I choose not to. Nothing they say matters because I'm doing this to protect my children.'"

"Your mother sounds like a strong woman."

"I wish the two of you had met. She would have liked you."

Antonia reddened. "An actress?"

"A woman who protected her sisters. You did everything you could to provide them with a home and recover their birthright. Mother would have been impressed. You both were willing to do whatever it took to shield the people you loved."

Antonia's eyes filled with tears, and one spilled down her face. "I did what I had to do."

He cupped her cheek and brushed the tear away with his thumb. "You never turned your back on them. Never saw them as a burden."

She took his hand in hers and then looked down at it. She wiped her tear from his thumb. "It struck me that you and I have another thing in common. We both faced the consequences of our parents' poor decisions. If my mother and father hadn't willingly entered into a bigamous marriage, Uncle Walter never would have tried to prove my sisters and I were illegitimate..."

"...And if my father hadn't tried to swindle people and commit treason, my family never would have been obliged to conceal his crime with more lies."

"In fact, my newly discovered half-uncle happens to be in the same situation. If his father hadn't lied to his mother about the loss of her infant, a kind gesture I might add, albeit ill-advised, Nicholas never would have been named Czar of Russia. After all, he has two living older brothers. Surely one of them could become czar." She shifted to face him again. "I'm certain if we search through our family trees, we'd discover a multitude of secrets hidden among the branches. In my opinion, as long as revealing those secrets does no great good in this world, they should remain private."

He gazed into her eyes as he interlaced his fingers with hers. "You're safe now. The book is of no use to anyone."

"Everything's changed."

"For you, but I still have that Sword of Damocles hanging by a thread over my head. If someone reveals my father's treason, my entire family could be denounced and our property seized."

"That danger has always been there for you, hasn't it?"

"It always will be. His blackmailer died a year ago, but I don't know if the truth died with her. That's why I wanted you to know. At any moment, that slender thread could snap and the sword could impale me."

Her eyes clouded with confusion. " That's why? What's why? I don't understand what you mean."

"I want you to be fully aware of the risk associated with becoming a part of my life. It was necessary for you to understand so you can answer my next question."

She tensed and closed her eyes. She appeared to be bracing herself for something she both did and didn't want to hear. "What might that be?" she asked in a voice barely louder than a whisper.

"Will you marry me?"

Her hands clenched, squeezing his fingers. She sat bolt upright as she swiveled to face him. She stared at him with an intensity that seemed to transform her face with a luminous glow. "What did you say?"

"Will you marry me?"

"You'd marry an actress?"

"I don't care if you're an actress, a lady, or a scullery maid. It's you I want, not the position you hold in this world."

"But no one will receive me."

"Then we won't receive them either. Our true friends will support us, and as for the others, most of them will come around if we give them long enough. In a year's time, almost every door in London will be open to us. If you prefer, we could live somewhere else. What if we divide our time between London and Maidenhead?"

She cocked one brow and the corner of her mouth twitched. "You know people in Maidenhead?"

"There's you," he said, holding up a finger as he began enumerating people on one hand. "Your sisters, your governess, although I think she ought to count for two since she's worth her weight in gemstones after everything she's done for your sisters..."

"She might disapprove of you counting her on two fingers."

"One then," he said, folding the digit back down again.

"And my barrister."

"Mr. Montlake," Robert said, grinning as he held up his last finger once again. "He has a lovely young wife. The Lady Cecilia."

"I haven't met her. Besides, I've run out of fingers on that hand," he said. "I think we've made an excellent start. Does that mean we've reached a decision? You'll marry me and we'll divide our time between Maidenhead and London?"

"We barely know one another."

"I'll argue with you there. We may have met only a few days ago, but in that short time we've come to know each other very well. We've been forced to push past each other's facades. You know me better than anyone else. You've seen who I really am, and I believe I've come to know you as well. This experience has tested us. We've learned we can trust and depend upon one another. I can think of no stronger foundation for a marriage."

Rather than pleasing her, his words seemed to have had the reverse effect.

"What's wrong?"

She shook her head and tightened her hold on the blanket. He closed his eyes.

He was a complete idiot. Of course he knew what was wrong.

"There's one more reason. Perhaps the most important one." He scrubbed his hand across his face. "I've never done this before and I think I'm blundering."

"Done what before?"

"Proposed marriage. You're the only woman I've ever asked, and I'm doing everything wrong."

Suddenly he lurched forward and fell to one knee in front of her. "Perhaps the tried and true method is the best." He took hold of her hand and gazed up into her eyes. "Antonia Winter, you've freed my spirit and changed me forever. I love you and can't imagine a life without you in it. Will you marry me?"

Marriage is the highest state of friendship. If happy, it lessens our cares by dividing them, at the same time that it doubles our pleasures by mutual participation.

— *SAMUEL RICHARDSON*

Antonia couldn't speak. Her ears seemed to buzz. He loved her. He honestly loved her.

A slow grin spread across her face, but then it turned sly.

"Finally, a declaration of your love. I was wondering about that." Antonia tapped her chin. "I must admit, that was an excellent marriage proposal. On bended knee even. How could a girl possibly refuse?" When he gazed at her like this, his ice-blue eyes made her heart melt.

"I hope you don't intend to try," he said. The way he cocked one eyebrow made her heart skip a beat.

She simply grinned at him. "I'm savoring the moment.

Stretching out the suspense. It's one of those things an actress learns to do."

"Is this the sort of treatment I should expect from you over the next fifty or so years? Or do you plan to use up all of those fifty years making me wait for an answer? I don't know if I'll be able to endure the suspense." He placed his hand on her knee, and she jumped at his touch as the heat of his palm seared through the fabric of her trousers.

He shot her a crafty grin.

Oh, but he'd pay for that. She turned up her nose in a show of indifference. "I suppose you think I should put you out of your misery and give you a definitive answer." She glanced down at her left hand and examined a fingernail.

"A wedding band would look attractive there, don't you think?" He began rubbing small circles on the inner side of her knee with his thumb.

"I suppose so." Her voice squeaked ever so slightly. She cleared her throat. "What kind?"

"A copper-hued topaz to match your eyes," he said without hesitating. His thumb stopped moving. "In a brilliant cut and encircled with diamonds. That was the first thing I noticed about you. Your eyes." Just when she thought he'd given up on teasing her, his thumb resumed its steady movement, and a pleasant heat began to build within her.

"You like my eyes?" She batted them at him playfully and he leaned closer.

"Most certainly. I love staring into them."

He skated his hand around to the outside of her leg and slid his fingers into the crevasse behind her knee. Even through her trousers, it was an undeniably sensitive spot, and she jumped at his touch, letting out a faint gasp. Lord, but that man could be insistent. "I noticed you staring at me when we first came into the study," she said, her voice breathless, "but it wasn't my eyes you seemed fascinated with."

"No?" His pale-blue eyes grew darker with hunger.

"No. It was an entirely different portion of my anatomy. Quite a bit lower."

"Hmm." He pushed her knees apart and moved forward. He stared at her mouth as he skimmed his hand farther up the outside of her thigh. "That might be true," he said, squeezing her hip as he moved his lips closer to hers, "but then again, it might not. Since I'm not your fiancé, it would be improper for me to comment on anything other than your eyes." He leaned in, and she reflexively moved forward to meet him, but he suddenly pulled back. "Quite improper."

She narrowed her eyes at him. "That wasn't nice."

"No, it wasn't." He skimmed his hand along her hip and paused where her men's shirt was tucked into her waistband. He gave it a sharp tug, pulling it free.

Her heart thudded in her chest. The last of her resistance crumbled. "Perhaps—perhaps you've earned an answer." She licked her lips. "You're distracting me. What was the question again?"

"Will..."

Tug.

"You..."

Tug.

"Marry..."

Tug.

"Me?"

He tugged the last bit of her shirt free of her trousers and slid his hand beneath it, just grazing her bare skin.

"I—"

His hand slid up toward her breast, but when she stopped speaking, he stopped moving. "You—what?" he asked. "At this moment, I must insist on an answer."

"I—I will."

"Marry me?"

"Yes."

"In three weeks?"

"Yes. Anything. Tomorrow if you like."

He chuckled. "At last. I thought you'd make me wait for at least another week before you'd give me your answer. You might have some tricks for building suspense, but it appears you're susceptible to my tricks as well."

What on earth was he going on about? Didn't he know she needed to be kissed?

He slid his arm around her waist as he moved onto the sofa next to her and pulled her close. A moment later their lips were together and her arms flew around him, holding him tight as she melted into his body.

SHE MUST HAVE DOZED OFF, BECAUSE SHE SUDDENLY AWOKE. Robert had pulled the soft blanket over them both, and he held her nestled against his chest.

Either he'd already been awake or her movement had woken him as well, because he planted a kiss on top of her head.

"I do too," she said, wrapping her arms around him and hugging him fiercely.

"You do?"

"Yes." His chest hair beneath her cheek was smooth and fine. She pulled back to examine it more closely. The dark hair tapered down below the blanket, and she stroked it.

"What is it that you do?"

She turned her head to face him. "I love you. I neglected to mention that earlier."

He closed his eyes for a moment and then a smile slowly spread across his face. It grew wider and wider until it seemed filled with so much joy she thought it might strike her blind.

CHAPTER 52 - THREE MONTHS LATER

All's well that ends well.

— WILLIAM SHAKESPEARE

April, 1854

Robert swept his wife into his arms and onto Lord Huntley's dance floor where they joined the other dancers in a waltz.

"Everyone's staring at us," Antonia whispered.

"They're all hoping to catch a glimpse of the notorious Countess of Wentworth," he murmured, recognizing her spike of fear and hoping to tease her out of it. "That's why the Huntleys' ball is so well attended tonight. Some of our onlookers will be dining out on this story for months."

"That's exactly what I'm afraid of," she said testily. "I can't believe I let you talk me into this."

"Let them look. Think of the excitement you'll bring to their dreary, closed-off lives."

"You aren't helping matters any. How will I manage to win them over?"

"Those aren't the ones you'll win over," he said in a more serious tone. "They're the ones who will never accept you, so why bother? Why worry about pleasing them?" His gaze locked with hers as he tried to communicate his love for her. He wanted to lend her his confidence. He wanted her to shine brightly and blind the onlookers.

She met his gaze, and he felt the shift as her confidence began to grow.

"You need to smile," he added. "If they're going to watch us anyway, we might as well irritate them. Let them know we don't care a whit about them."

Her face brightened with delight. "Are you saying you plan to flout the staid members of society?"

"Most certainly. Since they're watching us so closely, I plan to do something quite scandalous."

He felt her tense in his arms. "Do tell me you're teasing," she said, her tone pleading. "When you get that glint in your eye, I'm never quite certain."

He gave her a devilish grin. "Here it comes." He loosened the arm around her waist, lifted his other arm, and pushed her into a twirl on the dance floor. It was a move they'd performed during their wedding trip to Italy, but never before in London.

He pulled her back into his arms and continued twirling her around the room in the waltz, ignoring her stern look.

"Robert. I'm appalled," she said, the obvious laughter in her voice belying her severe expression. "You might have gotten away with spinning me around on the ballroom floor while we were in Italy, but the British frown on such extravagant behavior."

"You loved it. I can tell. In a moment, you'll burst out laughing."

She finally grinned at him, her deeply felt delight shining in her eyes. A moment later, they twirled past a furious-looking matron who glowered at them in disapproval.

Antonia noticed the woman as well, and her laughter fled. "You're a bad influence. When did you decide to start flouting every convention known to society?"

Robert pulled her closer and planted a quick kiss on her cheek.

Antonia flushed with pleasure. "Have you always been this way? I had no idea you were such an exhibitionist."

He grinned back at her. "You bring out the devil in me."

"Everything worked out well for your brother." She glanced around the room. "I'm hesitant to mention anything about him in a public venue. Suffice it to say, he seems happy with the changes in his life."

"At least he finally isn't asking for my help any longer. I don't know if it's because I made such a mess of things with the book, or if he's simply happier with his new—" he glanced around as well—" associate . Either way, it's a relief not to be at his beck and call."

As the waltz ended, Robert escorted Antonia to Lady Huntley's side.

Catherine lifted her arms in welcome. "I haven't had a chance to talk with you since your wedding," she said, taking Antonia's hands in hers. "You're both looking marvelous. Marriage must agree with you."

"Most certainly," Robert said. "I'm finding domestic life to be quite enjoyable."

Catherine smoothed her hand over her belly. "I feel the same way. I never would have believed I would have taken to it so readily. Perhaps it's because I found my perfect match."

Robert glanced at Antonia. Their gazes locked for a moment, and a contented warmth enveloped him. "That must be it."

"Did you enjoy Italy?" Catherine asked.

"It was marvelous." Antonia focused her attention on

Catherine even as she shifted closer to Robert. "We're planning to return next summer and take my sisters. They'll adore visiting the museums and the Roman ruins."

Robert found Antonia's hand and entwined her fingers in his. He found himself needing to touch her constantly. He hated having her far from his side. Fortunately, she seemed to have developed the same sort of attachment. They were quickly becoming one of those tedious couples who were obviously in love.

"Is there any news concerning your uncle?" Catherine asked.

"Squire Winter still refuses to acknowledge us," Antonia said, "but that's for the best. He's currently in jail awaiting trial."

Catherine tutted. "Oh, my. I hadn't realized things had progressed so far. I'm glad to know the wheels of justice can move quickly."

"He *did* admit in court he had possession of the church register," Antonia said. "With Father Sergey positively identifying him, he's almost certain to be convicted of murder."

"How are your sisters adjusting to all of the changes?"

"With astonishing aplomb." Antonia's smile was bright and open. "I wasn't certain if their friends in Maidenhead would accept them back into their circle, but it seems my fears were unfounded. They've been welcomed like soldiers returning from the war. The other girls seem quite impressed by their year-long adventure in London. Even their parents are being surprisingly welcoming. I think the fact that they lived at Miss Hermitage's school helped."

"That must be a relief."

Robert noticed a woman approaching Catherine with a smile of greeting on her face, but when she met Robert's eye, she came to a stumbling halt. She glanced at Antonia, and with a flush of embarrassment, she turned on her heel and hurried away.

Antonia stiffened. Robert rubbed his thumb over her knuckles, hoping to soothe her.

With a look of resignation, Catherine watched the other woman flee. "It will take some time for people to adjust," she said, giving Antonia a sympathetic look. "Don't let it bother you too much. Another scandal will come along soon enough to divert them. There's always a scandal brewing."

"But I was on stage. That's hard for people to forget."

"And some never will." Catherine lifted an open palm as though tossing those people aside like chaff. "But others—well, times are changing. You'll be surprised." She glanced after the departing woman. "In a year, you won't be facing that sort of response."

Antonia nodded slowly. "Seeing her reaction convinces me we've made the right decision to keep my sisters in Maidenhead for now. I'd hate for them to come face-to-face with that sort of scorn. It's my hope that if Evalina chooses to enter London society in two years, they'll accept her."

A few moments later, Robert and Antonia left Catherine's side, and another guest quickly took their place.

Robert gestured toward one of the open doors letting in a late-spring breeze scented with lilacs and freshly turned earth. "Would you care for a walk under the stars?"

"Nothing would please me more," Antonia said, wrapping her arm around his.

As they stepped through the doorway, Robert spied a row of torches lighting the entrance to the garden, and he could see more in the distance. The sight was an enticing one, and it made him think of exploring dark garden alcoves with Antonia.

Before he could suggest it, Monsieur LeCompte strolled over to join them. He greeted them both and then turned his attention to Antonia.

"*Ça va?*" he asked—How are you?

"*Bien,*" she replied—I'm well .

LeCompte gave her an evaluating gaze. "The last time I saw

you, you were dressed as a man. May I say, I much prefer your current attire. Your silver gown is stunning."

"Thank you. Robert has a particular fondness for it."

"Thank you for your letter informing me of the book's eventual disposition," LeCompte told Antonia. "I'm relieved it was of use to you. I also admit I'm pleased England has finally joined France in our war against Russia."

"Was that your preferred outcome?" Robert asked, his curiosity piqued.

"It was among my optimal ones, yes. Having our adversary withdraw from Crimea would have been a perfect outcome, but it was a highly unlikely one."

Robert nodded. "I came to the same conclusion. I doubt anyone would have believed the book's secrets. They were too incendiary."

Considering that the book had gone up in flames, Antonia's mouth twitched at Robert's pun. She glanced down the garden path, and LeCompte's face softened as he took in her wistful gaze. He shuffled his feet, turning toward the doorway leading back inside. "I do hope you'll excuse me. I have a great deal of gossip to uncover, and since you've been traveling, I doubt you have any to offer me. Newlyweds tend to be singularly unaware of anything beyond themselves."

Antonia grinned and Robert nodded at him.

LeCompte shook his head at them. "*Lord, what fools these mortals be*," he said as he turned away.

Antonia chuckled as she turned toward the pathway and tugged on Robert's arm. "I didn't know LeCompte could quote Shakespeare." Her eyes filled with a flirtatiousness he'd learned meant wonderful things were in store for him. "Come," she said. "The night is calling."

"Do you plan to take advantage of me, Lady Wentworth?" he asked, following her lead. Inside the ballroom, Robert heard a clock begin to chime the hour.

One, two, three—

"At every possible opportunity." She held him by the hand as she walked backward, down the torch-lit path. "*I know a bank where the wild thyme blows, Where oxlips and the nodding violet grows, Quite over-canopied with luscious woodbine, With sweet musk-roses and with eglantine.*"

Four, five, six—

"Is this what's in store for me?" Robert asked, following her eagerly. "To have you woo me with lines from Shakespeare?"

Seven, eight, nine—

"Does it please you?" she asked, pulling harder and moving faster.

"Most definitely."

Ten, eleven, twelve. She turned away, let go of his hand, and darted down the flickering path. "I know exactly the spot," she said over her shoulder.

Robert let out a delighted laugh and began chasing his wife. "*The iron tongue of midnight hath told twelve; Lovers, to bed; 'tis almost fairy time.*"

Antonia let out a squeal of delight. "A husband who quotes Shakespeare? Be still my heart!"

A moment later she whirled to face him and snatched up his hand again to pull him down a side path into a darkened arbor where she dropped down onto the soft, spring grass.

"*Lovers, to bed,*" she whispered to him as he lay down next to her, "'*tis almost fairy time.*"

He stripped off his coat and placed it on the grass to cushion her head, and then propped himself up on one arm as he stared into her eyes.

"My own silver fairy queen," he murmured, and then took her mouth with his own.

The End

ALSO BY

Historical romances
By Sheridan Jeane
Gambling On a Scoundrel

Secrets and Seduction series:

It Takes a Spy...
Lady Catherine's Secret
Once Upon a Spy
My Lady, My Spy
Along Came a Spy

Also available:
Lady Cecilia Is Cordially Disinvited for Christmas
(only available via Sheridan's VIP club)

View the full Secrets and Seduction series and leave a review

Duke By Dawn (Novella, part of the anthology *Dukes All Night Long*)

The Shadow of the Black Rose - a Victorian-era Romantic Suspense trilogy
Whispers and Spies
The Spy In Disguise
Protect the Prince

❧

Contemporary Romances
By Sheri Tyler
The Way to a Woman's Heart series - the **Coming Home** trilogy
Slow Simmer
Here's the Scoop
From Bitter to Sweet

The Way to a Woman's Heart series - the **Destination Wedding** trilogy
One Cup of Chemistry

Say Cheese!
Kebabs and Kisses

ACKNOWLEDGMENTS

My thanks go out to my wonderful and supportive family.
You've been with me through everything and
have accepted many nights of pizza and Chinese food when my
writing took over.
You're the best!

I want to thank my critique partners in the Sunshine Critique
Group: Wendy, Mary, Miranda (aka Mary Jane), Chris Anna, and
Vicki. Your constant hard work and your high standards in writing
have helped me hone my skills. Thanks as well to my good friend
Kristi Avalon for all her invaluable advice and late-night
brainstorming sessions, and to Sheila Larkin for making those
monthly commutes from Pittsburgh to Cleveland with me, for
her wacky ideas that always seem to inspire me, and for being my
cheerleader.

The wonderful writers I've met through the Romance Writers of
America (RWA) have been a supportive and welcoming group.
I've been fortunate to be the recipient of invaluable advice and
guidance from established authors and chapter-mates such as
Madeline Hunter, Erin McCarthy, Kristine Mason, Gwyn Cready,
Jamie Dentin, Casey Clipper, Miranda Liasson, Becky Lower, AE
Jones and Christy McKee. (When I start listing them, I worry I'll
leave someone out... if I did, I apologize!)

Finally, I want to thank my parents, Joe and Winnie Ferguson. I
couldn't have done any of this without you.

I miss you, Mom.

Sheridan Jeane is an award winning author of historical romance novels. She grew up in Huber Heights, a suburb of Dayton, Ohio, and now lives just outside of Pittsburgh.

When not reading or writing romances, Sheridan can be found learning how to salsa dance, falling downhill on skis, or taking part on a local fundraiser to support kids in need in southwestern Pennsylvania. Sheridan has always been an avid reader and a dedicated writer. She earned a bachelor's degree in computer science with a minor in English.

I'm thrilled to have the opportunity to share my stories with you. Please visit me at SheridanJeane.com. and drop me a line at sheridan@sheridanjeane.com! I'd love to be your new friend!